GODS OF THE WELL OF SOULS

By Jack L. Chalker
Published by Ballantine Books:

AND THE DEVIL WILL DRAG YOU UNDER
DANCE BAND ON THE TITANIC
DANCERS IN THE AFTERGLOW
A JUNGLE OF STARS
THE WEB OF THE CHOSEN

THE SAGA OF THE WELL WORLD
Volume 1: *Midnight at the Well of Souls*
Volume 2: *Exiles at the Well of Souls*
Volume 3: *Quest for the Well of Souls*
Volume 4: *The Return of Nathan Brazil*
Volume 5: *Twilight at the Well of Souls: The Legacy of Nathan Brazil*

THE FOUR LORDS OF THE DIAMOND
Book One: *Lilith: A Snake in the Grass*
Book Two: *Cerberus: A Wolf in the Fold*
Book Three: *Charon: A Dragon at the Gate*
Book Four: *Medusa: A Tiger by the Tail*

THE DANCING GODS
Book One: *The River of the Dancing Gods*
Book Two: *Demons of the Dancing Gods*
Book Three: *Vengeance of the Dancing Gods*
Book Four: *Songs of the Dancing Gods*

THE RINGS OF THE MASTER
Book One: *Lords of the Middle Dark*
Book Two: *Pirates of the Thunder*
Book Three: *Warriors of the Storm*
Book Four: *Masks of the Martyrs*

THE WATCHERS AT THE WELL
Book One: *Echoes of the Well of Souls*
Book Two: *Shadow of the Well of Souls*
Book Three: *Gods of the Well of Souls*

GODS OF THE WELL OF SOULS

A WELL WORLD NOVEL

JACK L. CHALKER

A DEL REY® BOOK
BALLANTINE BOOKS · NEW YORK

A Del Rey® Book
Published by Ballantine Books

Copyright © 1994 by Jack L. Chalker

Library of Congress Catalog Card Number: 94-94358

ISBN: 0-345-36203-9

Cover design by Dave Stevenson
Cover art by Peter Youll

Manufactured in the United States of America

First Edition: October 1994

10   9   8   7   6   5   4   3   2   1

This one's expressly for
David Whitley Chalker and Steven Lloyd Chalker—
To the future, wherever it leads!

A FEW WORDS
FROM THE AUTHOR

This is the third and final book in the new Well World project, *The Watchers at the Well*, which began with *Echoes of the Well of Souls* and continued in *Shadow of the Well of Souls*. It completes the massive novel.

If you've just come across this and haven't read the other two, you should immediately look for them where you found this copy. Any reputable, responsible, intelligently run bookstore should have the previous two so that anyone happening on the third one by chance doesn't have to hunt for them just to read the entire work. If they don't, tell them what they aren't and find a better bookstore!

There are also five original Well World books. You don't need them in order to read *Watchers*, but it would be a good idea to start at the beginning. The first was *Midnight at the Well of Souls*, followed by (in order) *Exiles of the Well of Souls, Quest for the Well of Souls, The Return of Nathan Brazil*, and *Twilight at the Well of Souls*. All are still available from Del Rey Books, and don't let any book dealer tell you differently!

The Well saga now spans sixteen years, although with a twelve-year break. Will there be any more? None are intended, but I didn't intend to write this one, either, and I'm quite pleased with it.

Those of you who have been waiting, I've planted some good action, added a lot of nasty plot twists (but you were ahead of me on those already, right?), and tied up all the loose ends in nice, neat knots. You may not like all the things I do (I am expecting some adverse reaction to the very last one), but they are, I assure you, carefully and logically thought out. And if, along the way of entertaining you, I've raised a few points and made you think a little, well, that's fine, too.

And now (drum roll, curtain up) here's the way it works out . . .

JACK L. CHALKER
Uniontown, Maryland
August 1993

THE WELL WORLD
Section of Southern Hemisphere*

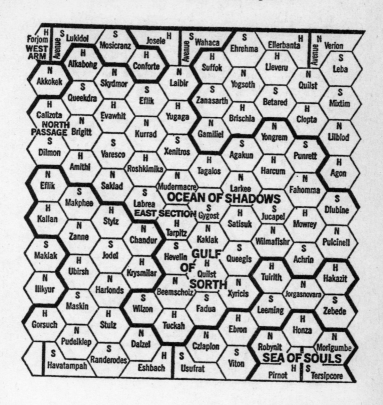

H—Highly Technological
S—Semitechnological
N—Nontechnological

*continued on overleaf

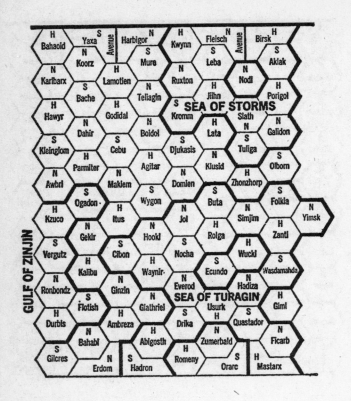

THE WELL WORLD
Section of Southern Hemisphere
(continued)

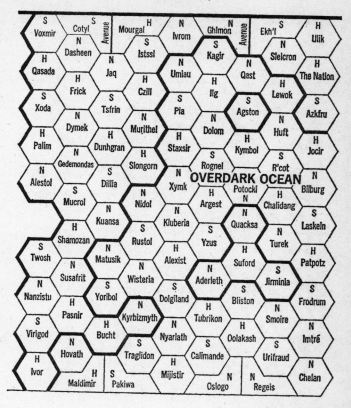

H—Highly Technological
S—Semitechnological
N—Nontechnological

GODS OF THE WELL OF SOULS

BETWEEN GALAXIES,
HEADING TOWARD ANDROMEDA

The Kraang had been wondering much the same thing. The limitations placed on it still prevented it from direct contact with beings on the Well World unless, thanks to the happy accident that allowed it net access, someone was in the transitional stage, totally energy within the net in midtransmission. Otherwise it was strictly read only, and that was proving less amusing now than frustrating.

Monitoring the lives and thoughts of these beings had reawakened in the Kraang a feeling it had thought long dead, a taste of what it was to be *alive* again. It wanted that now more than anything; the lust for it was cracking its heretofore absolute self-control, bringing back longings that it had believed it had long outgrown.

The Well perceived no threat to itself or its master program; it only desired that what it considered an anomaly—the relinking, however tenuous, of the Kraang to the net—be rectified. A simple matter, really, for anyone capable of plugging into the net; not even seconds to find, comprehend, and repair, cutting the Kraang off once more from the system. Brazil was the threat—he'd been there many times, been changed into the master form, and would hardly even think twice about it. He'd do whatever the damned Well said and be done with it, and he would understand the threat sufficiently to be impervious to the Kraang's entreaties and offers. There was nothing Brazil really wanted except, perhaps, oblivion, and the Kraang wasn't so certain that the captain would really take it if it were offered in any event. Brazil was so damned . . . *responsible*. Duty above all.

No, if the Kraang were to effect a return, it would be Mavra Chang. Human, inexperienced, self-involved, and unencumbered by any sense of duty or mission. Mavra Chang would listen before she acted and believe what she wanted to believe. She was certainly tough, no pushover, but she was far too—*human*—to blindly obey the dictates of an ancient race she neither knew nor understood. According to the data, she'd been close to being a goddess before, going from world to world, taking many forms, playing both explorer and missionary to the misbegotten.

The Kraang could deal very comfortably with an activist.

Brazil was at the moment romping in mindless joy with that silly girl on that speck of land in the ocean, but the Well would never leave him there. If Mavra Chang's progress to the Well had been stopped, then Brazil would again get the nomination and be forced to accept. The longer there was no movement or probability of movement by Chang, who was by far closer to the Well gate than Brazil, the more likely the Well would be forced to make the switch. The others would never find her, and it would be all the worse if they somehow did track down Campos but never recognized Chang in her current form.

Campos was the key. Such a *limited* mind! Not stupid, not by the likes of the races there, but sadly warped. Campos was so enjoying her revenge and was comfortable enough in an environment not all that different from the one back on the home planet that had bred and shaped her, that she was in danger of losing sight of the ultimate game. The Kraang had not counted on her adjusting, though, and that was the real problem. Since Campos had been a male from a background that had little value for women, the Kraang had been certain that she would be driven to the Well to reclaim her manhood.

It wasn't happening.

If Campos had gotten hold of Mavra Chang earlier, it would have, but the Well had its own ways of subtly adjusting a subject to a form. The brain chemistry, the hormonal balances, and being completely immersed in a new culture eventually took hold. A transformation that seemed horrible when first discovered began to seem normal; prior life and existence were distanced in the mind as it adjusted, becoming more and more remote. If one were to go mad from the process, it tended to happen rather quickly; otherwise that barrier the mind erected became progressively insubstantial until it either shattered, as in the case of Lori and Julian, or, as in Campos's case, just slowly evaporated to nothingness.

Without even realizing it, or perhaps admitting it to herself, Juan Campos no longer thought it odd, or even wrong, to be female, let alone a Cloptan female. She had managed in a relatively short time to gain a fair amount of power and influence, in part because she was attractive to male Cloptans who already had that power and influence, and she was actually enjoying it. Experience counted. The Well might have played a joke on Campos by making her female, but it also had dropped her into a totally familiar milieu. Being the tough girlfriend of a drug lord wasn't much different from being the son of one, and the knowledge and ruthlessness actually made her a valuable asset to the organization. After that first month she hadn't even experienced much of the fear and insecurity that being a woman in such a society inevitably produced; everybody dangerous knew how suicidal it would be to mess with the boss's girl and how vicious that girl could be if she perceived one as a threat.

Not that Campos didn't want to get at all the power the Well represented; it was just that she was smart enough to know that before she let Mavra Chang near the Well, her control had to be ironclad. And until Juan Campos figured out how to do that or was forced by circumstance to gamble, she'd keep things pretty much the way they were.

It was frustrating to the Kraang. If only Campos would go through a Zone Gate. *Then* some contact, some influence, could be attempted. But Campos wanted no part of those Gates if she could avoid them. She remained where she could ensure protection.

Somehow there just *had* to be a way to kick Campos in the ass. There just *had* to be!

But until and unless it found a way to make contact, the Kraang knew it had to depend on forces beyond its control. The psychotic former Julian Beard—now turned into a complaisant wife for that female astronomer turned male swordsman who was now gelded and trapped as a courier for the Cloptan drug ring—was showing some promise, after all. Aided by the Dillians, who were somewhat in the pay of the Zone Council, she might well disrupt things sufficiently to cause a major move. When one no longer cared if one lived or died unless one attained one's objective, it made for a spicy and dangerous time for all those in one's way. The threat there was the Dillians. If they *did* come upon Mavra Chang by some miracle, helpless though she was, would the Dillians' first loyalty be to their former Earth comrades or to their new leaders and lives? Unknown to any of them, forces were moving in on the region and the situation was getting very, very dicey as the council and the various hexes weighed their own options. If they captured Chang, no matter what her form, while the surprisingly resourceful Gus liberated Brazil, everything could go wrong. Of course, there was always the colonel . . .

Possibilities! Far too many! This was getting much more difficult than the Kraang had originally thought. And there were far too many ways for things to go wrong . . .

BUCKGRUD,
CAPITAL OF CLOPTA

Lately, it was always pretty much the same dream.

A dense, living forest filled with strange, twisting plants shimmered in a nearly constant but gentle breeze. Not familiar in any waking sense, yet familiar somehow to her in her dream. Comforting, safe, secure.

She would awaken into this living darkness in the Nesting Place, along with many others of her kind, and then proceed out from the hollow tree and onto the forest floor. Most of the night would be spent in the hunt, sometimes searching out and sometimes lying in wait as still as one of the bushes that were all around, waiting for prey to venture forth. Tiny animals, large insects, it didn't matter, so long as it was alive and small enough to be swallowed whole. There was always plenty of prey, for they bred all the time, or so it seemed, but much needed to be eaten to satisfy, and it was a task that consumed much of the night. There was no particular fear on her own part, though; there were no natural enemies in this forest for such as they, and the Big Ones who lived among the treetops ate no flesh and seemed appreciative of the service she and her kind did in keeping the crawling things in check so that they could not become so numerous as to threaten survival. She knew each by the scent and by the sounds it made.

The scent from a small mound nearby told her that there were delicacies inside; she moved to it, and her powerful claws dug into it, and she bent down so that her long, sticky tongue could go inside and sift through and find and draw the little insects into her beak . . .

It was near dusk when Mavra Chang awoke. She slept more than she was awake now, it was true, but that was blessed relief in more than one way. It not only meant escape from the sadism and torments of Juan Campos, when, of course, the Cloptan was awake and not busy with other things, it also was relief from the strange and unpleasant sensations that seemed unending.

There were feverish flushes, dizziness, unexpected pains of varying degrees in various places, and, above all else, a nearly universal itch that was driving her crazier than Campos ever could.

At first she thought that the sadistic surgeons employed by the drug cartel had been butchers as well, but over the passing weeks she had come to realize that it wasn't that, either. Something—strange—was happening to her, something even someone with her vast life and long experience in what evil could do had never undergone before. Still, that life allowed her to understand to a degree *what* was happening, if not exactly why.

She had been surgically altered, mutilated, disguised, but that was only the start of it. She had become other creatures before, but always the way the Well did it: quickly, without pain or sensation. She was becoming another creature again for the first time since she had last been on this world, but by a different method, and slowly by the standards of the Well but with astonishing speed by any other means.

She knew that now for several reasons, not the least of which was that what the surgeons had removed, such as her arms, had not even begun to grow back. She recalled that sensation well. Her body was changing. Grafted feathers were being replaced by real ones just as colorful and even more dense. Her center of gravity had moved down, and her midsection had thickened, while her head seemed to be enlarged and set flush on the shoulders, but with a neck that could pivot the head amazingly far. All this had been at the cost of an already shortened height; she was now a bit under a meter tall, but somehow she knew she would grow no shorter.

Her backbone had become increasingly limber, to the point where she could bend backward and almost touch the floor with the top of her head while still standing or lean forward so effortlessly and with such good balance that she could touch the floor with her beak.

From that vantage point she could see that her stubby, mutilated legs were rapidly changing into huge, thick drumsticks; the rather stupid feet they had fashioned for her now were solid, enlarged, and black and were gaining almost the prehensility of long, thick fingers, with sharp needlelike nails developing at the tips. Even the large, curved beak they had fashioned over her mouth was no longer the crude but effective graft; her tongue, now thin and greatly elongated, told her that beyond the beak was the gullet. Bright light blinded her, and even normal daylight was pale, washed out, and difficult to see in, yet the darkness glowed with sharpness and detail. Through the beak, countless strange odors came to her, each somehow separate even when mixed, and it was a bit of a game to try and identify and classify them. It was something to do.

The same went for sounds, although she could understand nothing of speech. She could understand only Campos, and then only when Campos directed something specifically at her; only Campos's translator could accept the eerie clicks and moans, some from deep in Mavra's chest, that passed for her speech. *That* little gift of a dedicated translator remained, but she was glad of it somehow in spite of her hatred of Campos. She knew that the sounds she could make were really bird sounds, animal sounds, not any sort of intelligible language to any race.

The animal urges disturbed her more. She could no longer physically tolerate any vegetable matter. Campos had been feeding her raw, bloody meat strips, it being a bit too civilized in the city to go pick up a carton of worms or grubs, even if Campos would have entertained the idea of live creepy crawlies in her nice apartment. Although Cloptans resembled giant humanoid ducks, they were omnivores and even had tiny rows of teeth inside those remarkably elastic, oversized bills of theirs.

Campos had hardly failed to notice the metamorphosis; it was happening at a rate that could not be seen by the naked eye but fast enough that something new would be evident between the time she left in early evening and the time she returned to sleep.

Now she came in the door and turned on the light, washing out Mavra's vision. The door slammed, and the Cloptan kicked off her shoes and threw a purse on the chair.

Campos looked over at the corner where Mavra stood, held there by a strong chain fastened to an anklet and to a welded-on socket in the wall, allowing perhaps a meter's movement one way or the other.

"Ah, my pet! And how are *you* this evening?"

"Food, master! Please! Food! Birdy begs you!" The worst part was, she no longer even felt humiliated by begging. It said something about Campos's mind-set, though, that she had insisted on being called "master," not "mistress."

"In a minute, my sweet. I need to freshen up and get a drink. It is going to be a long evening, I fear."

"Please, master! Feed Birdy!"

"Shut up! No more, you miserable little shit or I *might* just forget to feed you at all!"

It was not a threat to be taken lightly. The craving for food after sunset was overwhelming, more even than the craving for the exotic Well World drug that Mavra's made-over body no longer needed or even noticed. Mavra had not, however, volunteered that fact.

Campos went into the bathroom, and after an agonizing wait there was the sound of a toilet flush and then water running. Finally the Cloptan emerged, now naked.

Although it was nothing unusual now, the first sight Mavra had had of Campos naked had been something of an odd feeling. The shape was very human to a point, but even the breasts were covered with countless tiny white feathers except at the very tips. The shoulders were unnaturally squared off, it seemed, the arms and thinly webbed hands oversized for the body. The neck was quite long and thin to be supporting that oversized head. Below the waist it became more birdlike, with a definite rounding, almost turnip-shaped, with the turnip top angled back and slightly up, becoming short but large tail feathers. The legs extended straight down, a golden yellow color, and ended in two wide, thickly webbed feet that could still be consciously rolled up and fit into shoes.

She shared the huge apartment with two Cloptan females who were apparently attached to other drug cartel kingpins, but they stayed away from the big bird's area and Campos rarely referred to them or appeared to interact much with them. They ignored their roommate's "pet" and gave it a wide berth and seemed otherwise to be fairly typical of their type.

There had been more than a few naked males in as well. If they were representative of the race, they tended to be larger, chunkier, with almost wrestler builds, bent a bit forward on the hips in a slightly more birdlike fashion but without much in the way of tail feathers at all. Male genitalia weren't visible at all; they were apparently hidden by a thick clump of feathers growing forward between the widely spaced legs, which explained why they all seemed to be bowlegged.

Campos went to the cold storage compartment and took out a box of something, then popped it in a fast defroster that might have been operated by microwaves or some other means.

"Ah! I should tell you that I got word today from those nice doctors who made you so very pretty for me," the Cloptan said as the defroster whirred in the background. "They said you were genetically reprogrammed using the *actual* genetic code of a *real* bird in a hex very, very far away. I forget the name, but what does it matter? They said not to worry, that you would still be able to think and remember but that you'd also have all of the bird's instincts. They even said that by three months or so you would be so physically like this bird that you would even be *fertile*!" She laughed. "Just think! The zoo here doesn't have any of your birdie kind, but you're on their wish list, and the other girls here still seem a bit frightened of you and keep trying to talk me into getting rid of you."

Mavra said nothing. Anything she could say would only cause trouble.

"Just think of it!" Campos went on, enjoying herself. "The nice zoo people say that if they had you, they could secure at least the loan of a male of the species. That might be quite the answer here. I won't have to worry about your care or suffer your presence here, but you'll be secure and in a happy little nest I can visit any time. That would be *very* amusing, seeing you sitting there hatching eggs, knowing that all your children would be birdbrains. Would you like that?"

"Whatever master wishes Birdy will do," Mavra responded as if by rote, eyes on the defroster.

"You bet your sparkly feathered ass you will!"

It was far from hopeless, but how the hell she would get this stupid asshole to head for the Well was something Mavra Chang was far from figuring out yet. The zoo wasn't a very appetizing new destination, but maybe it would provide some way out. Zoos didn't usually plan on animals being as smart as humans.

Somehow, some way, she had to get to the Well. She was building up too long a list of people to get even with to fail.

SUBAR,
A CITY IN NORTHERN AGON

It was a region of thick forests and rolling hills, with mild days and chilly nights; if it hadn't smelled something like an overcooked egg, it might have been very pleasant.

Agon was a high-tech hex with just about everything one could expect of modern life. Private cars were banned; there just wasn't enough room to tolerate them or anywhere to dump the old ones. Still, public transport of just about every kind was available for a very low fee, along with taxis and buses that seemed to glide on air working not only every city and town but every rail and road crossing as well.

The Agonese were a strange lot, looking to Anne Marie like something out of a children's fairy tale. In fact, they resembled nothing so much as squat turtles without shells, but with very tough greenish-gray hides that might have been at home on elephants or rhinos back on Earth. But unlike those animals they were bipeds, walking on two short, thick trunks of legs that terminated in wildly oversized feet out of the age of dinosaurs. The omnipresent if unpleasant odor was nothing less than their collective body odors, to which they of course were oblivious.

"We are strangers very far even from our native Well World homes," Anne Marie noted as they approached a medium-sized city, the first they'd seen since making their way south from Liliblod. "We have no choice. We must contact the authorities and ask for help."

Tony, reluctantly along on this new quest and not liking it a bit, sighed. "You are correct, of course. But it makes me uneasy to do so. Such an operation could not go on in this kind of setting and with this technology without some connivance from high local officials. We are far from the places where the foul stuff is grown and into where it is distributed. This close to the business end, the government official who comes to help us might well be in the pay of those we seek. I would feel more at ease if we could contact our own government. They, after all, sent us on this great expedition in the first place. If we vanish outside their knowledge and contact, then we vanish forever."

Anne Marie nodded. "Agreed. But there *must* be a way of getting a message to our people in—what is that place called?—Zone? Where the embassies are. They have telephones, radios, probably much more, here. I think our best course is not to mention any more than we have to at the outset about why we're here and simply ask as stranded travelers to call our embassy. That would be a reasonable and natural request, wouldn't it?"

Tony nodded. "We have to do it that way, but something makes me uneasy about it. I still do not feel very clean about our role in this so far, even though we had nothing to do with the current problem. And I was born and raised in a very different society than you. I feel, unfortunately, far more at home with the governments here than I ever did with the British government I very much prefer."

There were a great many stares as the two large, blond, twin centauresses came into the city, one with an equally exotic if very different creature on her broad equine back. Alowi, the former Julian Beard, had said virtually nothing and seemed almost disinterested in the city or its inhabitants or anything else. Without a translator, she was merely along for the ride in most of the alien environments. That, both Tony and Marie agreed, would be a top priority. The Erdomese would get a translator or give up any thoughts of tracking down her kidnapped husband. There was no alternative. This was certainly a hex with the technical abilities to install one, although it would take more money than any of them had.

In fact, money was going to be the first problem if they remained here in the north. They hadn't been allowed to take much more than basic packs and provisions when they'd been forced off the ship off the coast of Liliblod, and Mavra had been the dispenser of funds for the group.

They didn't need much to just survive; although all three preferred nicely prepared and cooked dishes, their constitutions were such that they could survive on grasses and leaves if need be. As for clothing, the Dillians in particular could gallop forty or fifty kilometers a day without even sweating hard, and they at least had been allowed to keep their coats for use in colder climates. Still, they were well aware that they were very far away from anything or anyone familiar, and while they could use the Well Gate in any capital city, it would take them only to their home hexes, not to anywhere they wanted to be.

"Not much hope of finding any work around here, either," Tony noted. "Everything that we could do is automated. If the council won't stake us, we're through."

"Yes, I keep worrying that they will thank us for our service and tell us to go home, that they are sending the professionals in," Anne Marie responded. "Still, their professionals haven't been any good up to now, have they?"

Aside from a small Liliblodian consulate, there was nothing in the way of government offices in this fairly remote city, or much need for it, when cheap, fast magnetic trains could take anyone to the centrally located capital in under an hour and a half. While that also implied that the local cops could have somebody who had some authority there in a matter of hours, it didn't prove to be that easy. In fact, it almost seemed as if nobody were interested in doing anything for them except telling them how to get home and suggesting that they do so at the earliest opportunity.

Unable to get any information on anything else, let alone help, they held a conference to decide just what to do.

"You should both go home through the big gate," Alowi told them. "It will take you home, I know, in very quick time, as they say."

"But dear! What will *you* do?" Anne Marie asked, worried.

"I will do what I must. I will *never* return to Erdom. Never. With no husband or family, I have no wants or needs. So far I have been able to eat the grasses, leaves, berries, fruits, and such that grow in these lands. I cannot starve. My body seems most adaptable. I have become accustomed to the chill nights here to the point where the coat is now uncomfortable, so I need no clothing. I will search as I can; if I find him, that is fine, and if I do not, nothing is lost."

"But you cannot even *speak* to people! You have no translator!" Tony pointed out.

"You do, and I do not see that it has helped you much. In truth, I do not expect to find him. I expect to wander this world, or as much of it as can be wandered through, taking little from it and seeing what is seeable. Sooner or later I will find a place for myself or I will die. Either way, it is the most I can expect."

"But you're talking about living like an *animal*!" Anne Marie exclaimed. "You are better than that! Not to mention the fact that by your own admission you are defenseless against the horrid beings that are a part of this world. It is a death sentence either way."

"I will never go back to Erdom," she repeated, "but I will die an Erdomese. Those are facts. I choose my own course. It is more than any Erdomese woman has been able to do before."

Anne Marie sighed. "Then we shall simply have to contact our embassy in Zone and tell them the situation and location.

Then we will find some part of this land that has some decent pasture and a few trees and wait them out."

"Or wait until they throw us out," Tony noted.

"Then we will leave, but only far enough to find some hospitality elsewhere," Anne Marie proclaimed. "I positively *refuse* to abandon this poor child to the wolves!"

Tony sighed. "Don't overdramatize, Anne Marie. There are no wolves in a place like this except perhaps the foul creatures who run the place. But we must also be practical. If we remain, we need to find some sort of work, and this is a high-tech hex surrounded by others that are not."

"But the closest ones are water!"

"True, but what of that? If a ship cannot come in to high-tech, then there is at least some point where it must be handled by the old means. Compared to one of our men we are not very strong, but the closest of our men is probably half a world away. In *these* parts we are probably quite strong, and even if we cannot lift what is required, we can certainly *pull* great weights."

"And Alowi?"

Tony shrugged. "She can cook. And supervise if need be. If we must remain in this godforsaken country, let's try and make the best of it."

This time it was Anne Marie who was doubtful. "But for how long?"

Tony shrugged. "Until one or more of us goes crazy or gets fed up or something breaks. It is better than *this*. Who knows? The council might at least extend us some seed money. It was they, after all, who got us into this."

"Oh, Tony! You're such a dear! You're making me feel guilty about dragging you along on this!"

"I have never been dragged," Tony responded. "I followed of my own free will, and I stay for the same reason. And when all hope is gone, *then* I will go home the same way!"

Anne Marie squeezed Tony's hand and then kissed her. "Of *course* you will, dear!"

• • •

If there had been no hope, they would have headed home long before this, but the problem was, as Anne Marie put it, they had been placed on hold but no one had hung up on them. Anne Marie noted that in spite of many areas where the Well World seemed futuristic to the point of being magical, the lack of any way to fly or even send signals any great distance between the worldlets led to everything more or less moving at, at best, a nineteenth-century pace. Nobody was ever in a hurry here, it seemed, unless it was to do evil, and so long as they were no threat, even evil seemed willing to leave them alone.

The council, still divided over exactly what course to take and thus taking very little, or so it seemed, asked them in fact to stay on "in the Agon region." They advanced the Dillians some credit and even found the pair a job of sorts, although not quite what they had in mind. Hexes in the region produced a variety of products that were of great interest to Dillia, but it had never been practical to manage much trade with nations so far away without some sort of permanent trade office coordinating things locally. Dillia was half a world distant—almost five thousand kilometers away over a vast stretch of water going west from the Ocean of Shadows and across the entire Overdark. Deals could be made in Zone in the traditional way, but without somebody on site, there was no way to guarantee quality, compare prices and deals, and put everything together. Dillians had never been the sort to relish staying long periods of time in remote and alien lands, and so they'd pretty much had to accept the traditional "take it or leave it" deals from their nearer neighbors. Merely the threat of competition could only help, and here were two who *wanted* to remain, at least for a significant period of time.

Dillia itself was something of a hotbed of semitech innovation, conservation plans and concepts, and agricultural management, particularly forestry, and had much to trade in areas most nations largely ignored. In exchange, it needed steam vessels, particularly for internal lakes and rivers, and other heavy industrial items either impossible or impractical to make at home. Dillians also had a taste for things that could not be grown locally, including many tropical and subtropical products, coffee, tea, cocoa, and tobacco. The Dillian government was more than happy to set Tony and Anne Marie up as a trade office and see what they could do.

Neither of them was under any illusions that this was a permanent job or that the opportunity wasn't created because, for reasons of its own, the Zone Council saw some value in keeping them in the region at that time, but as it served everyone's purposes, there were no objections.

Alowi was not so fortunate. She was nothing to Dillia, of course, and even less to Erdom, who clearly was disinterested even in whether or not one more female came back at all. Nor did the council as a whole see any use for her. So she became basically the Dillians' housekeeper, keeping their new home clean, cooking the meals, and doing other chores, all of which was made much easier by being in a high-tech hex where things not only worked smoothly, they seemed in some ways futuristic compared to Earth.

Because she had no translator, Alowi spent the time studying and learning Agonese, a language that sounded bizarre but that, she soon discovered, followed a pattern not too different from some Earth tongues. It was soon clear that Julian Beard was not dead inside her brain but merely dormant; it was in fact Beard's knowledge of Japanese that gave her the clue to understanding Agonese. Not that they resembled each other in obvious ways, but the structure wasn't all that different.

The trade mission had some initial frustration but then some startling successes. Tony was adept at business, and Anne Marie seemed able to spot a con or a sucker deal almost instantly and knew just when to give in on a negotiation. The initial commissions weren't huge, but they no longer had to worry about going broke.

They used some of the first money to buy Alowi a translator. She made no objections this time, spending much of her time doing a great deal of studying, using the Agonese computer libraries. Their written language was actually pretty basic; for a high-tech society, it appeared that they were surprisingly illiterate and used voice and picture technology for all their information sources. Her greatest frustration lay in her inability to really use her hands; the oversized split hooves proved unable to push even a few small buttons on a console, but she managed by gripping a wooden stick and using that instead.

There was an ancient language of commerce on the Well World that had evolved to cover just about every conceivable situation. It was a written language only—translators filled the gap for spoken tongues—and it had arisen from a pictorgraphic alphabet so ancient, nobody now knew its origins. It was extremely complex—it had to be to cover so many tiny worldlets and so many varying races—but it was used on virtually all interspecies documents and everything from contracts to treaties. If one could learn it, there was nothing really closed to that person. To Tony, its sheer complexity made Mandarin Chinese, with its mere thirty thousand or so characters, seem like child's play, and he barely tried before giving up. Anne Marie didn't try at all, noting that the English had never had to learn other people's languages and she did not intend to start. Alowi, however, managed to read many basic texts at the end of only three months.

It had been learning Agonese that had been the key. With both Agonese and Erdoma to go by, she was able to isolate and assemble key concepts from the two totally different languages and see how the trade language accommodated the concepts of both. It still wasn't easy, but it seemed, well, *obvious* to her, and it had already become merely a matter of memorizing vocabulary.

Tony in particular was impressed. While still back on Earth she'd considered herself something of a linguist, which was useful for an international airline pilot. In addition to her native Portuguese and essential English for aviation, she knew Spanish, French, and German well enough to converse and read a newspaper. *This*, however—*this* was Sanskrit as written by a mad chicken that had gone amok in an ink factory.

"You can really read this?"

Alowi shrugged modestly. "Enough. What I do not know, I can usually interpolate. I think that if I were writing books or treaties, I would need several more years, and about a third that applies to specific races and hexes that I cannot imagine would require some context for me to understand, such as going there and talking with them. But yes, I can make do in it. I will never *write* it, though. With these hands I can stir, chop, pick up, do quite a number of things, but only those things which can be done with broad motion and much toleration for error. To make these fine marks with pen or brush, where slight deviations change whole meanings—no. Even doing block English letters is crude, much like a child just beginning to learn them."

"Then why go through all this?"

"Because the one thing that works as well as before, perhaps better, is my brain. It is odd—I seem to be able to concentrate as I never could before, to grasp and memorize things easily that before would have been much more difficult. I have always been a good learner, but I do not know why it is suddenly much easier. What is not so easy is chemistry."

"What?"

"This body was built for sensation. It *demands* things, and the cravings can become overpowering at times. I have compensated with creativity and with some unconventional use of objects I have picked up in stores here, but it is not the same as the real thing, and the only place I can get what I truly need would also almost certainly give me a lobotomy. Erdomese just are not *built* to be loners. I know that now. I have been kidding myself all along. So I cannot go back, but if I do not go back, I will go mad."

Tony sighed. "So what are you going to do? We're here

mainly because of you and because we hope to find out what the hell happened to the others, but time is dragging on and on. The council is only certain that nobody has yet entered the Well. There are certain places at the equatorial barrier, called Avenues, where anyone who knows how—and only two people on this world do—can get in, and those are all carefully monitored. It is almost as if one of those hex gates opened and swallowed the two of them."

Alowi nodded. "I know. I truthfully have expected to hear the worst, but I never expected to go this long and hear *nothing*. That makes it all the harder." She paused a moment. "Do you remember the clinic here that had some doctors of other races as well as Agonese? Where I got the translator?"

"Yes, it mostly serves the ships' crews and passengers and other travelers passing through. There are stories that the doctors are here because they cannot go home, that they are wanted for some sort of criminal activities. Certainly they can't support all this high-tech equipment off what they're paid to fix broken legs and such every once in a while. I did not like the feel of the place when we took you there. Why?"

"The locals tell tall stories about them. About how they do terrible experiments and create horrors, but they are protected because they leave the Agonese alone. It is also said they are of use sometimes to the government and perhaps to criminal gangs. I do not like them one bit, but I have been thinking of going to them. Only faint hope that perhaps my Lori could be found has stopped me."

"Why? Are you sick?"

"As I said, I have—problems. They are the only ones with a data base on all the races, including mine, within who knows how far. Their practice here is certainly honest and above board or they would have been forced to move elsewhere. I have been thinking of going to them and asking if there was something they could do to help me control this or damp it down. When you find yourself not merely sweeping with a broom but making love to it, it is time something was done. I have no money, and they are unlikely to be cheap. I am ashamed that I must ask you if you will cover my bill if I go there."

"Well, yes, of course—if you're sure. But I don't like it, and I know Anne Marie won't, either. If even part of their reputation is true, you could wind up far worse off than you started."

"I'm aware of that, but this will not be some hapless captive coming into their clutches. You will know that I am going there, and it will be all up front. It is not likely that they could stand to create a monster in public, let alone have a distinctive patient vanish, and I will know the options and be able to choose which or whether to do anything at all."

"Very well, then, dear, go to them. I fear as much for your mind and soul as for your body, though. I have already seen you undergo so many personality changes, I am not sure who exactly I am talking to sometimes, if you will pardon my saying so."

Alowi smiled. "I understand. In fact, I understand a lot more about myself than I did. The truth is, I think those all *were* different people, or different parts of me, all mixed up inside. It has taken me a long time, and many shocks, to put any of it together. Julian Beard is essentially dead. I have all of his knowledge, but I have no direct memories or feelings of *being* him. It is more like—well, viewing a very long motion picture of somebody's life. It is very odd. I know every detail, but not as if I had actually *done* it. Rather, it is as if I had been standing there, ghostly, watching it all being done. I can think about how to do things with soft, five-fingered hands, but I cannot really imagine having such a hand. When I look in a mirror, what is reflected there is *me*. And the odd thing is, I like what I see. Nothing else—*computes*, you might say. I hate the Erdomese government, church, and system, and I cannot say that I wish I had been born with the freedom a man has there, but I am who and what I am, and I am comfortable with that. I just wish *they* would be. So, for better or worse, I am Alowi and I am too damned smart to go home."

"I—I *suppose* I understand. At least as much as I could without being you. Certainly I have undergone something much milder myself. I know how to fly a 747, but the knowledge seems academic now, not personal, even though it was what I loved more than anything else. Somewhere, near the end of that last long voyage that left us here, I just suddenly woke up one day and felt absolutely comfortable and normal, not just as a Dillian but as a woman and a woman with a twin sister. And it did not even disturb me—I didn't fight it at all. When I finally admitted this to Anne Marie back in Liliblod, I found that she felt the same. Since then I haven't even *dreamed* of the past, although I have had a few nightmares involving being on a ship at night. Yes, perhaps I *can* understand, to a degree at least."

"You have changed more dramatically than that, starting from when we set out, but it has become a *real* change since we have been here."

"Huh? In what ways?"

"No matter how identical you looked, it was always easy to tell you apart. Anne Marie was more of a motherly type, and she had many affectations that came out in how she spoke and even moved. You moved very differently, with a bolder, prouder manner, a tough, more masculine way of speaking, that sort of thing. If you bumped yourself, you would curse; Anne Marie would say, 'Oh dear!' or something equally quaint. As we went along, I began to notice that the two of you were growing more and more alike. You lost a degree of that masculinity, began to move in more feminine ways, while Anne Marie seemed to pick up that part you lost, becoming tougher and more confident. You have added more feminine words, and she has dropped some of her more obvious old-fashioned quaintness. You now pay attention to jewelry, cosmetics, hair, that sort of thing, even though you are hardly doing it for her or for some man. You are doing it for yourself, and it is exactly why *she* does it. And then there are the half conversations."

Tony was fascinated by this. "The what?"

"I am sure that neither of you is aware of it, but when you talk to each other, what must seem like whole complicated dialogues are really often sets of unconnected half sentences, words, and such, and often you will finish one another's sentences."

"I—I never *realized*—"

"I did not think you did. Physically you are absolutely identical, I think more so than any natural identical twins could be. Together, over time, while I have sorted myself out, you two have been doing the same, only less dramatically, more slowly and subtly. You are not really Tony anymore, nor is she Anne Marie. You are someone different, an average of the two. Only the difference in your *knowledge* bases keeps you from being almost one individual in two bodies. That alone will keep you slightly different, which is, I suspect, all to the good. Everyone should have a *little* something to make them different. But that *is* the extent of it."

Tony thought about it, not sure if she was pleased with the idea but seeing the ultimate point, which was the same one Alowi had made about herself: they were who and what they were. One either accepted that and learned to live with it or one killed oneself. Period.

The Well World worked some of the magic; the rest had to be supplied from inside, from the mind and soul.

"Make your appointment," Tony told the Erdomese. "But make no rash or irreversible decisions."

Doctor Drinh was an Agonese, and after all this time in the province, learning the language and the culture, Alowi *still* couldn't tell one from another without a uniform or badge of rank. He specialized in treating aliens but was a diagnostician and planner. Others, some so alien that they made Erdomese and Agonese look like relatives, did the actual work.

Drinh put the Erdomese profile on the computer, then took samples of blood from Alowi for comparison, then ran them through a myriad of automated tests and looked over the results.

"Well, I *can* say that your feelings will not get much worse than they are, but they won't get any better, either. It must make for early marriages and active honeymoons, at least." He paused. "Sorry if the attempt at humor was offensive."

"No, no," she assured him. "It is absolutely correct. Child marriage is the norm in Erdom."

"Yes, but you see, in this sort of thing the tension builds up, releasing an overdose of all sorts of brain chemicals, and it stays pretty well 'on,' as it were. You seem extremely intelligent and self-controlled, but I would be remiss if I didn't tell you that if a male of your race, *any* male, came within your eyesight, you would become, pardon, a whimpering, begging fool. It is inevitable with these sorts of readings."

"I know that. It is why I am here. The odds of me meeting a man of my race while I am over here are pretty slim, but as you say, I am smart enough to know that I cannot go home and remain so."

"Just so, just so," Drinh muttered. "We don't have much on culture here except those sort of taboo listings so that we don't do anything to someone that would cause social or mental damage or the like, but I *did* note that the society is labeled 'patriarchal.' So what would you like me to do, assuming it is doable?"

Alowi sighed. "I—I need it to be damped down. Some way to put it under control so I can live with it."

"Well, the most obvious way if you never intend to have children or have any sexual relations with another of your kind would be to remove the sexual organs. It is a radical and permanent solution, but it would cause the hormones and psychochemicals to shut off eventually, and with it all sexual desire."

It was a more radical solution than she wanted, but she

couldn't quite dismiss it out of hand. "It is something to think about if all else fails, but I would rather not. It would change me in other ways, too, would it not?"

"Well, I couldn't know, although I can put in for research notes via Zone and find out. Logic and experience with other races suggest that there would be complications, yes. With someone of your type, basically mammalian, the breasts would sag and be encumbrances, you'd probably get extremely fat, there might be some long-term problems with bone integrity and the like, and your energy levels would tend to be down, at the very least."

"I like myself as I am. I think I would rather try going for the one problem rather than something that radical."

He shrugged. "Well, there are drugs that might work, but they would have to be specially formulated for your species—we wouldn't exactly be expected to stock Erdomese materials—or brought from Erdom via Zone, and either would be expensive and require that they be taken regularly over *decades*, judging from your apparent physical age. If you are wealthy, well connected, and will be in one spot, like this city, it would work. Otherwise. . . . And if you came off them, particularly suddenly and dramatically, your system might go wild. There would be a danger of losing all control, of becoming little more than an animal in heat, and how long this would go on until you came back to present levels is impossible to say."

Alowi was feeling less and less like she had any way out.

"There is a third way," the doctor went on, thinking. "Radical and somewhat costly up front, although possibly not, depending on how much work is actually involved."

"Yes?"

"Before going further, I must tell you that it is not approved medicine. Strictly experimental, although we have had tremendous successes with it and few failures. I am quite certain that it would work in your case. It has come out of our own research work here."

"Go on."

"The process is complex, but basically it is rewriting your genetic code, rather rapidly. Do you understand what that means?"

She was shocked at the idea that they had such abilities, but she nodded. "Yes, I do, at least in its implications. Can you really do it?"

Drinh sat back. "We can do more than you ever dreamed with it. We take only a few cells, and we alter the code. Then the mathematics of the coding is fed into tiny semiorganic devices, machines if you will, but on a scale so small, they could be seen with only the finest microscopes. They replicate themselves with astonishing speed, enter every cell in your body, and rewrite the code. Then they die and are passed out in the normal way or allow themselves to be consumed by the body's defenses. The process is quite rapid. The cells quite literally become other cells. Major changes can cause a great deal of temporary discomfort and disorientation, but relatively minor ones such as we are talking about might well not be noticed, or no more than catching a minor virus at the worst."

"You can really *do* this?"

"We do it regularly. Of course, there are limits. I could not, for example, turn you from being an Erdomese into one of my own race. At some point you would be neither one nor the other, and the stress would kill you. But if you merely wanted to *look* like an Agonite, *that* I could do. Of course, we are talking far less than that here."

She couldn't believe what she was hearing. "Look like an Agonite? The process is *that* comprehensive?"

"Oh, yes." He seemed somewhat uncomfortable all of a sudden, though, as if he'd already said more than he had intended.

She had a sudden thought. "You could not turn me into a man, could you? An Erdomese man?"

"Alas, no," the doctor sighed, and seemed to relax a bit.

"The reverse, yes, because in your race and many others the male contains only half the genetic makeup; the other half is female, coming from the mother. But you have two sets of female genes, so there is nothing there to edit. If you were male, I could remove the male chromosomes, duplicate the female ones, alter them somewhat, and recombine them so you would turn into a perfect, fully functioning female. But the other way—well, one must have *something* to work with, and your race is even more peculiar than most bisexual races in that you have no male hormones or male psychochemicals at all. Disappointed?"

"No, not really," she answered, realizing that what she was saying was true. "But what *could* you do to me?"

"Oh, a lot of things. The possibilities are vast. To address the immediate problem, it would be a matter of finding the triggers and dampening them down. The work is complex because it is subtle, exacting, and challenging. It must be done just right. If we got it wrong, we might not catch the problem; or it could throw you off and create violent mood swings, intermittent pain, or even psychotic episodes. If we had an Erdomese clientele, it might be rather simple, but as we do not, it would be a matter of trial and possibly error. In fact, let me put the data into the computer and see what the risks might be."

He turned in his chair to a console, and although it had full audio input capabilities in Agonese, he used a complex keyboard instead.

All the better to keep trade secrets and control the conversation, she realized.

In less than a minute a string of Agonese text came up on the screen, much of it punctuated with graphic images of things that were beyond her comprehension. Also, the screen was angled sufficiently to keep her from reading more than bits and pieces without being obvious.

Finally he turned back to her. "There are two possibilities that seem just about equal. Now, understand, I do not mean two different things we might attempt. Rather, there are two equally possible outcomes to the attempt as postulated. There is absolutely no way to be positive short of, well, experimentation. We have no case histories to tell which way it will go."

She couldn't imagine where he was heading. "Yes?"

"Well, there is about a three percent chance of serious complications. I tell you that up front, but that is actually a very small percentage in this kind of process. There is no risk-free solution. Beyond those unknowables, there is a better than forty-nine percent chance that it will decouple your mind from your desires."

"I beg your pardon. What does that *mean*, exactly?"

"Basically, you would be fully capable of performing as a woman, but you would lack all desire to do so, even in the face of stimulus-response. You would simply be incapable of arousal. There is a medical term for this, but I do not know how it would translate. It is physiological frigidity."

She nodded. "I understand the idea. I would be turned off of sex, as it were." She thought about it. "Is it—reversible?"

"I would not recommend attempting a reversal. Changing the changed is always a hundred times more dangerous, because we would have even less to go on and the risk of things going terribly wrong would be major. Of course, you could always take injections or oral hormones to artificially restore it to some degree or another, but it would be temporary and administered by a clinic like this one, which could determine and synthesize what was needed."

"I see." It was in many ways an attractive possibility. "But Doctor, I can add. You have left almost forty-eight percent unaccounted for."

"Um, yes, I was coming to that. The problem is, the same regions of the brain and the same chemical balances serve more than one function, and without prior research we can be only so delicate. The nearly equal chance would be to achieve not a neutral balance but opposition. You would have no arousal or desire to copulate with males, but you would find yourself attracted to and potentially aroused by other females. You would not suffer the borderline psychochemically induced nymphomania that is at the heart of your problem, but you would be vulnerable, as with most sexual creatures, to stimulus-response."

"You mean I would react like a man."

"No, not precisely. In the sense of stimulus-response to females, yes, but you would not think of yourself as male or have male responses and desires. In some races a small percentage of people are born this way. It *would* solve your problem, because you would be unlikely in any event to encounter females outside of Erdom, but not as completely as neutralization, and of course drug and hormone therapy to restore normalcy would be *very* unlikely."

She considered it. Bizarre—that the worst-case scenario would be to wind up viewing women close to the way Julian Beard was brought up seeing them. But Beard had always been fully capable of giving up almost anything, even sex, for very long periods, and certainly, if it couldn't be Lori, she would rather not ever be tempted, even accidentally, by one of those native men.

"How—how soon would I see a difference?" she asked him.

He shrugged. "Impossible to say for sure. Still, only automatic and stimulus-response chemical actions in your brain would be affected, so the change would be quite rapid. The practical effect might be noticed in days, perhaps hours, although total and permanent change might take a few weeks. We are dealing here only with a very small reprogramming of an even smaller area. But the permanence of the process is important to remember; if you wish to have anything else done, it is best to have it done all at once."

"Anything else?" She could see his gaze. "Oh, the hands. I thought about that after what you said, but . . . Well, you said it would take away my desire. Would it do more? Would it make me antichild, for example, or incapable of loving someone or having other normal emotions?"

"Again, you'd need an Erdomese physician to fully answer that. It is not like this has been done before, let alone repeatedly, with someone of your race. There are bound to be some ancillary changes we can't foresee, but not drastic ones. I doubt if you will become some sort of emotionless, cold individual or anything like that. It might even work the other way. You might find that your emotions in other areas are stronger. There is often that sort of compensation. But would you love your child if you had one? Of course you would."

"Then I cannot have the hands done. If you check your data base, you will see that these are essential for one of my kind to have a normal childbirth. I want as few options closed as possible. I just want relief."

"Then you shall have it," Doctor Drinh assured her. "We have your residence here. I will get our computers to work on this and see what is what, then call with price and such. I really do think this might well be the best thing for you, considering your circumstances."

Alowi left, and the doctor immediately went into the back of the clinic and walked briskly into the laboratory portion of the building, where a huge, sluglike creature was working at a machine using countless wormlike tendrils.

"You heard and followed, Nuoak?" Drinh asked the other.

"I did. The problem she seeks relief for is real."

"I know, I know, but I haven't felt fully comfortable since they moved here. I almost told her there was no help, but I think that would have been worse than the truth in arousing suspicion."

"Your professional pride and bragging got the best of you, and you know it. She is *exceptionally* bright and knowledgeable and as an offworlder has the education and possibly the cultural background to eventually put two and two together, particularly with the added detail you gave her. I don't like it."

"But what can we do? We can hardly dispose of her. The Dillians are her comrades and titular employees of their state. They have council contacts that make them too dangerous to involve. But if we play normal, she will almost certainly put the facts together and start snooping in earnest. *Then* what?" He thought a moment. "I suppose we could slow down her data processing speed and limit her retention. Do it slowly, and she wouldn't even be aware of it or even care if she did notice. If the Dillians noticed and wouldn't accept it as some natural mental problem, we could always claim it as an unfortunate side effect."

"Too obvious," Nuoak responded. "The data that we got from the security police suggest she learned Agonian in only a few months and is well on her way to reading Standard. No, looking over the data, a more interesting suggestion comes to mind."

"Yes? You have an idea?"

"I do not believe that she is a direct threat to us. The chemistry here is fascinating. She is almost totally nonaggressive, quite literally incapable of defending herself against any significant threat. It must have taken every bit of her willpower to just come here on her own. She might well suspect the truth to a very great degree, but she would be incapable of acting upon it."

"She had the guts to come in here and be pretty cool about it."

"That is less a function of biology than force of will over biology, resulting from the fact that before Well processing she was male and, to some degree, by her mind battling against her body. The urges inside her must be excruciating. But no, we must accept that she will suspect, or already does, and perhaps even tell her friends about her suspicions. The fact is, though, that they can do nothing at all about it. They remain here only as her friends and protectors and possibly out of a bit of fear of actually returning to Dillia and taking up normal lives there. It must be quite a difficult thing to actually bring yourself to do. Still, they must be unhappy here, and bored and frustrated. They would leave if they saw a way, I feel certain. They are held by the one pressure this Erdomese girl can bring to bear; a version of passive aggression. 'If you leave, I'll stay here and die.' Remove *that* and you remove the problems, all of them."

"I am listening."

"The odds you quoted were correct, but surely you noticed that we can tip the scales on one of them. We have the orientation model from the male Erdomese in the computer now. If we use that as our model, it would also be possible to introduce a tapeworm of sorts. It would search through her catalog of memories while she slept looking for the specific pattern of her memories of her husband and their time together, and allow her mind to restructure those events."

"A tapeworm is the most dangerous thing you can do in a sentient creature," Drinh noted nervously. "We might as well change *all* her memories for the mess it would be likely to cause! Best to just kidnap her and be done with it if *that* is your solution!"

"You misunderstand. The limited nature of this program is so subtle, she probably will not even be aware of it. At worst, she will either blame it on the results of the reorientation and accept it as a minor side effect or take it as an inner revelation of something that's been there all along. It won't matter. It will not change her relationship with the Dillians one bit, and it will produce a logical result. She will not only have little motivation other than friendship to want to find this husband of hers, she will have an even greater motivation for fearing finding him as she remembers him. As this plays out, we can find someone, perhaps connected to the Great University at Czill or some lesser institution, with the potential to offer her some sort of position. She would be among many species and would not stand out as particularly alien, and her knowledge of Standard would allow her to do academic research. I believe her offworld profession was some sort of geologist, at least judging from those secret police reports. A passive, productive, rewarding job in a protected setting. You see?"

"I see. It is a good plan."

"Only you do not agree?"

"I agree because I have no choice," Drinh replied, "and nothing better to offer. But you are a logical scientist from a race that does not have the sexual context both her race and mine share. People do not always react logically in this sort of situation. Nor do I think the Dillians stayed for her alone. Not this long. There is something to be said for comradeship and for the sense of personal violation, of insult, when it is broken up the way their group's was. I don't even think the two lost people are at the heart of it, not anymore. Some people simply have a strong urge to see justice, and I think that may be in play here."

"There is no such thing as justice if you have a good enough attorney," Nuoak commented.

"There you go being *logical* again!"

The call came in only a day later. The clinic could perform the procedure at any time, given a few hours' warning to actually synthesize and program the tiny microgadgets. They were confident, it was a simple procedure, and the price they quoted was considerably less than the translator had cost. *Considerably* less.

"Well, I don't like it," Anne Marie said flatly. "It isn't *natural*. And what's to keep them from fouling your brain chemistry all over to hell and gone? Why, suppose they *can* do all they say! Why, after that stuff's inside you, you won't be able to *stop* it! You could wind up being turned into a cow or something worse!"

Alowi shook her head. "I do not think he would do that. He might if I were some captured guinea pig, but not to paying patients who come in the front door. I got the impression that they were a *lot* more experienced with this than they want to admit. And they have probably won friends by doing big favors—fixing congenital defects, perhaps regrowing limbs, maybe even the reverse of what I am thinking of."

"But what if, somehow, sometime, we or somebody finds and liberates Lori? How's *he* going to feel with a permanently frigid wife?"

"I—I thought about that, but I can no longer let that enter into my plans. If I am to be the first totally free Erdomese woman in history, then I have to go all the way with it. If he is found, then I will still be me, and if he wants more, well, Erdomese are polygamists. Actually, I have had more dark thoughts about Lori since consulting with Drinh."

"Huh? What do you mean?" Tony asked her.

"Well, everybody says that the clinic works with criminal gangs, and we know who is most likely to have that kind of clout and protection. Suppose there is a really good reason why nobody has seen a trace of Lori or Mavra. Suppose they were two of the clinic's guinea pigs for its ambitious experiments. He said he could actually make me look Agonese. What could he make either of *them* into?"

"Oh, *my*!" Tony exclaimed, sounding *exactly* like Anne Marie.

"But that makes putting yourself in their hands even *worse*!" Anne Marie protested. "If they *did* do something to Lori, something monstrous, then they almost certainly know who you are. Suppose they think you're *really* there to spy on them! That you're on to them! They could do something to you and then, when it was noticed, say, 'Oops! Sorry! We made a big mistake! But it *was* experimental and we didn't know *everything* about Erdomese women and you were warned of the dangers.' What could we do? Nothing!"

"I thought of that, but I do not think they are the kind to panic, and I really believe they will be extra careful *not* to do anything wrong simply to keep us at a dead end. Besides, if I do not do *something*, I am going to go crazy. If they are the ones who stole the life I was content to lead, then they owe me a life of independence at least."

"I have a bad feeling about this," both centauresses said in unison, another thing they did more and more often. "But if you are determined, we will not stand in your way."

"Thank you."

"If they do anything other than what they promised . . ." said one.

". . . Then we will be on them like a ton of lead," the other finished.

They set up an appointment with Doctor Drinh.

Alowi sat there on the stool as before, in the outer office, feeling nervous but determined.

Drinh was the competent physician now, taking final samples, giving her a thorough checkout, and running the resulting data through his medical computers. Finally he said, "All seems in good order. All that remains is to ask once again if you really wish to go through with this, because once done, it is done."

She nodded. *Sorry, Lori, but I just can't stand this otherwise.* "I would not have returned if I had not already decided. Let me get it over with."

Doctor Drinh walked to the back of the office and opened a compartment, removing a clear rectangular container in which there was some equally clear liquid. He took out an Agonian syringe, which resembled a small flashlight with two nubs, put it against the container, and pushed a button on the syringe. Almost instantly the fluid was gone, drawn into the syringe. He then walked over to where Alowi sat and stood by her. "This is it," he told her. "Say no now or it is done."

She swallowed hard. "Do it."

She felt the two nubs of the syringe against her right rump, then a sudden tingling sensation much like a minor electric shock, and then nothing.

The doctor put away the syringe and replaced the container. She sat there a moment, wondering what was next.

"You may go now," he told her, sounding satisfied.

She felt surprise. "That is it? That is all there is?"

"That's it. Period. You might feel some dizziness or disorientation off and on, and you might run a slight fever, so take it very easy for a few days. There might also be some confusing or bizarre dreams and thoughts for a bit, but that should last only a day or two. You should certainly notice a lessening in your tension by tomorrow at the latest. Also, I would walk back rather than ride if you feel up to it. It will help distribute the serum in your system."

She got up. "I hope it works," she told him.

"I hope it works, too," he responded with a sincere smile.

Lori, too, could not help but notice that Juan Campos's well-planned and fiendish revenge was not as complete as it had been intended to be. Overloaded with the mind-numbing drug, sent through a training course over and over and over again until all action was automatic, he had been beyond even caring what had happened. Weeks of Pavlovian training and then the real thing, trips back and forth by night without the slightest deviation along back trails laced with an over-powering scent unique to him, all seemed to be one continuous blur, without a sense of time, place, or event.

How long this had gone on, he could not know, but slowly, ever so slowly, he began to come out of the stupor. Rational thought returned with the same slowness, in fits and starts. He was unable to distinguish what was real from what was dream, but eventually he came to understand that for some reason that drug no longer affected him, that its power was fading with increasing quickness.

There was some sense of denial about that fact. He didn't *want* to come out of it, didn't *want* to think and perhaps face the pain and monotony of this life, but his own inner strength denied him the oblivion he needed.

What did it matter that he was no longer addicted except to

add to the torture? If they found out, they might not trust him anymore, and that would mean his finish.

But that, too, was an odd thought. Wouldn't death be preferable to a life of *this*?

The answer, though, was no.

That left escape, even though he was a four-footed freak far from any home or help, forever cut off from rational communication with the outside world. Even if that weird new translator didn't encode everything in and out, it would probably be useless. His mouth felt funny; it wasn't malleable as it always had been. Even the limited communication he'd had with the handlers who had special translators to make themselves understood was now one-way. The only sound he seemed capable of anymore was from very deep inside and sounded more like a bray and meant nothing. His handlers, usually none too bright underlings, had found that amusing.

Still, it had been a shock to find out that indeed he had changed so radically and that after all this time of staring down at the ground, his neck was somehow now long enough and flexible enough to allow him to look straight ahead. In fact, it became increasingly flexible as time wore on.

They had fused his hands to form hoofs and, after castration, had filled him with female hormones that had produced grotesque travesties of Erdomese breasts. Yet now the breasts seemed to have shrunk away while the legs and hooves seemed to have solidified and changed. Through the fragmented and confused mental haze he was in, he realized at some point that he was very, very different from what Campos had intended or how he'd started out under the hands of those maniacal butchers.

His vision was weak, distorted, and without color, but it had tremendous contrast abilities. It was hard to imagine that there were this many scales of gray. Vision was short-range but sharp straight on, but there was little if any peripheral vision to speak of. To see something to the side, he had to move his head rather than his eyes. It took some getting used to once he started to try to use his vision again for more than spotting things to step over. Anything outside a two- to seven-meter range was a gray blur. This was true day or night, although night was more comfortable. Bright light, even reflected, blinded him for a minute or more after he turned to avoid it. Hearing and smell were much more trustworthy than sight.

I've become some kind of a horse, he realized after a while. Not any horse he knew, but close enough. The forelegs were true forelegs, the front hooves true hooves, and the joints angled like a horse's joints. Everything was proportional, comfortable, balanced. His nose and mouth had elongated and combined into an equine head, and somehow he'd grown a long bushy tail. His ears felt funny, too, but he couldn't tell why. The one thing he still had as before was the horn.

A unicorn, he thought at last, the old vision coming from deep in the past. But a unicorn with no interest in virgins; most definitely a gelding.

How did it happen, and how long had it taken? No way to know, but it was likely that those butcher bastards had access to technology far in advance of mere mutilation, perhaps some kind of rapid genetic manipulation.

Still, how rapid was "rapid"? Not only were the days under the drug's influence a blur, but even when his mind had returned, his sense of time had not. When he was hungry, which seemed to be most of the time, he ate large quantities of grass and bushes and whatever else looked green and tempting. He wondered how much he weighed. He didn't seem all that much bigger, certainly not true horse size. Probably the size of a Shetland pony, but perfectly proportioned.

The thought of the virgins made him aware of just what had been removed. He remembered Alowi fondly but could not even recall what kind of sexual attraction she'd had. It was more than the loss of ability or desire; he seemed to have totally lost even the memories of the feelings that sexuality had brought, human or Erdomese, male or female. He knew the lack of it should have bothered him, but it didn't; instead, it only bothered him that there was now a hole somewhere inside him where something once valued and prized had been, something now utterly excised. It was in many ways the same as the loss of any sense of time and, oddly, no more disturbing or important to him.

There was a certain satisfaction in that. To deny him sexuality had been the heart of Campos's revenge. That he neither missed it nor gave it any more thought after this was another slap in the bastard's face.

He had become a unique animal but a consistent one. It was stupid and meaningless to dwell on anything he lacked, particularly something that was now no more than a set of definitions for how a species reproduced itself. If he could get a better handle on what it had once meant or felt like, perhaps he would think it a tragedy, but for now it seemed somehow—*liberating*. When one was without sex, one had no stereotyping, no fears or expectations based on a factor that did not apply to one, and when one was one of a kind, as lonely as that might become, there were neither expectations nor fears from peers. It was gone, every last bit of it, and being gone, it took with it all sense of deprivation or loss. It was irrelevant. "Relevant" was learning everything there was to learn about what he now was and how he interacted with everything else.

The scent he followed, whose slightest trace he could pick out of hundreds of others, he soon realized was the scent of his own excrement. It interested rather than revolted him to discover that he had virtually no bladder or bowel control. It came out when it was ready and had to, but only when he was in motion, never when he was still or asleep. Once discovered, that fact, too, was simply discarded and not thought of again because it didn't matter. That was how he was, period.

Each trip through the dim forests of Liliblod found him growing more and more comfortable with this new form and thinking about things that were important rather than dwelling on his twin pasts, both of which seemed to have decreasing relevance or even interest to him. Instead, he concentrated on developing his superior sense of hearing, which could pick out the song of a distant bird or a chorus of sonorous insects with ease, and in determining and cataloging what each sound meant. Similarly, classifying every scent, every odor, analyzing not only the ground and trees but the very breezes, provided vital information once he'd matched scent to source. Since there was a mind behind that classification system and nothing else to do but walk, smell and sound proved to be more precise than sight had ever been.

He knew he'd have to become an expert at this, since the same line of thought told him that he would have no choice but to escape as soon as he felt it was safe to do so. Not that he had any illusions about the rest of his life even if he *did* get away. He would neither understand nor be understood by anyone else, he had no hands or tentacles with which to write, and he didn't know how to read any native languages. He'd be an animal, period, able to perhaps study and explore for the sake of knowledge but not to interact. It wasn't what he would really want, but it was absolutely preferable to staying where he was. *Death* was better than that and more moral, but somehow he didn't want to die. Not now. Not yet.

The fact remained, though, that he was carrying a drug that allowed evil people to poison other people, to steal their very minds and souls, and he simply could not continue to be a part of that. He felt bad about what he'd already carried for them, but to continue to serve them once he felt confident enough to get away was unthinkable. And, too, his careful studies of Liliblod had revealed something of the nature and nastiness of its inhabitants, and he knew that when someone got a whim or when he was older or perhaps got sick or hurt, those who now worked him would not hesitate to feed him to those damned tree-dwelling monstrosities.

He'd seen them clearly only once, although he knew their

sounds and scents and knew that they were always there, high up above, a thought that also made escape seem attractive. Accompanied by one of his handlers, he had carried in a huge load of what smelled like monstrous chocolate bars. Part of the payoff, he understood, for the creatures keeping the back trails used by the couriers open to the drug runners and no one else. And down they'd come, from the very tops of the trees, where their vast ropelike webs created almost a roof over the hex. Huge spiderlike creatures the size of a ten-year-old child, with eight hairy legs that ended in small but malleable pincers and bright, shiny brown bodies topped by demonic heads with gaping mouths and hateful, bright red eyes. He and the handler left as quickly as possible, since chocolate had been known to send the Liliblodians into a frenzy of uncontrollable and often violent behavior. All female, the handler had told him. The tiny, mindless, wormlike males crawled literally into the wombs and were sealed inside, their outer skins dissolved by special juices releasing the sperm, and the remainder provided the food for the brood until they were ready to be hatched.

It was not a nice thought that so many of them, perhaps tens of thousands, were clustered up there and could drop down at any moment if the bargain suddenly seemed not to their liking. That was why they used "mules" like Lori for most of the work.

No, there would have to be an escape, and if this trail went only from Agon to Clopta, then his escape would have to happen at one of the ends of the route. He was pretty sure that there was no real escape in Liliblod.

He wished he knew what had become of the others. Although he felt no physical attraction, poor Alowi, or Julian, was still as close a friend as he had here, and without him she was in a real mess. She would never go home, but she might well kill herself, and that was the most worrisome thing of all. The Dillians were probably well out of it—he'd never really understood why they were *in* it in the first place, except that they'd once been human and were at least still a bit human, as were the others. Still, they had potential lives back in their home hex and no stake in this affair.

And then there was Mavra Chang. If they had done *this* to *him*, what had they done to her? Or was that a long-term concern? Didn't Mavra claim that she could not be killed, that anything injured or lost would regrow, that no damage was permanent to her? Sooner or later, no matter what monster they'd made of her, they'd have to take her to that Well, whatever it was. They'd have to risk it, whoever "they" might be, because the other fellow might get there ahead of her if they didn't. *Then* she would be in real trouble, but then, whoever had Chang and hadn't at least made the attempt would probably be in worse shape.

Well, there was little chance he'd ever find out how any of them had made out. It was enough to try to figure out how and where to escape.

Agon would be better geographically; it hadn't seemed overly developed for a high-technology hex, and there was a lot of rough country in the north, and it was connected, if he remembered correctly, to other hexes for vast distances. The trouble was, he wasn't ever technically in Agon; the cleverly concealed entrance to the headquarters was in Liliblod even though the whole underground complex was under Agon's soil. It wouldn't be much of a run to bypass it, but there were so many guards and so much in the way of defenses that it was a sure route to capture and disaster.

That left Clopta, which seemed almost paved over from the moment one reached the border, as overdeveloped as Agon seemed just right. But the warehouse there where the trail ended was well within the border and was in the middle of what appeared to be an industrial district. Most of the time a handler was right there, waiting, but every once in a while they missed him, and he would have to make his way several blocks along dark back alleys between warehouses and factories to the rendezvous. If they did it again, he would go. He felt as ready as he would ever be, and the alternatives seemed increasingly bleak. They wouldn't expect it; they thought he still needed that drug.

He was always surprised when he reached the border, even though he could smell a bit of Clopta as he grew near. With no time sense and no more drug craving, he never seemed to know how long he'd been on the trail or just how far along it he might be. It was daylight by the time he reached it this time, and that meant he would have to stop and wait. There were clear instructions that under no circumstances was he to enter Clopta in daylight or while there was any traffic in the immediate area.

The hex boundary remained the most dramatic feature of the Well World, even now. It appeared to his altered eyes as a thin but infinite piece of semitransparent gauze at which the endless Liliblodian forest stopped with amazing suddenness, replaced by a brightly lit but sterile-looking mass of metallic buildings. It was hard to look at them too long; sunlight would catch some window or piece of polished metal, and he would be suddenly blinded. Muffled sounds of much activity came through the barrier: sounds of machinery operating, men yelling, vehicles going this way and that, huge doors sliding open or closed—all the sounds of a manufacturing district, although what they made there he did not know.

They had built right up to the boundary, too. Space was at a premium in lands with rigidly fixed borders, and they used it well. Most likely this had always been an industrial district; it was possible that the whole border with Liliblod was this way and that all heavy industry was concentrated in a strip. If *he* had these kind of neighbors, that was what *he* would do. He certainly *hoped* that it was so. It might mean that the rest of the hex was a lot more livable and perhaps had trees and forests into which he could disappear. If no one met him, it would make sense to go right, then left, keeping to the alleyways but off the trail. That would take him into the hex and away from any sort of activity.

The trail had only ten or so meters in the open before it

went into a thin alley between two tall, smelly structures. It *did* have to cross a few broader streets, some with loading docks on either side and a set of rails going down the center—he had to watch his step in order not to get a hoof caught in the gap. But the trail mainly kept to the back alleys and side streets until it reached the one warehouse where things went on after dark that were probably unknown to those who worked in the area during the day.

He hadn't seen Campos, there or anywhere else, since the first couple of runs right at the beginning. Apparently she was satisfied enough by her first visits and didn't need to see much more. It didn't matter, anyway. *Some* things of an emotional nature had not been excised, and one of those, now that the drug had no more hold, might well cause him to impale a certain person on his horn no matter what the cost to himself and any future he might have, no matter how bleak. *That* might well be worth it.

I'll bet Mavra spends at least a little bit each day regretting she didn't listen to us and kill the little turd or at least leave him to the mercies of the People.

He ate and slept most of the day, waking up occasionally but not for long and mostly to eat some more. It seemed like no time before the shadows fell and night came upon the Well World.

He went close to the boundary but didn't yet cross. He wanted all the sounds to vanish into the distance first.

Maybe this is it, he thought anxiously. *Maybe nobody will show this time.*

But somebody did. No Cloptan except someone expecting him would *ever* go through that barrier in this direction, not unless it was on one of the main roads. The spider bitches would just love a little duck.

He recognized the little man by his scent. The Cloptan was a decent sort as handlers went, not too bright and very loyal but not cruel to the mules, either. He looked like some bastard relative of Gladstone Gander, except that he wore pants.

"Ah, it's you, is it?" the man, whose name was Banam,

commented, although it sounded like nothing but deep melodic rumblings to Lori. "Well, you can come along now. It's a holiday here tomorrow and everybody's taken off early, anyway. I'll just get my pushcart and follow you in as usual."

Lori was used to people speaking to him when he couldn't understand a word. In a way, he was even more cut off than a *real* horse, since even real horses could pick up a few common sounds or terms. It was the worst part of it all, an utter loneliness that came from having no way to truly communicate with anyone except, of course, the absent Campos.

There was a pronounced difference in air pressure when he penetrated the boundary and also a marked rise in humidity. He couldn't tell much about the temperature, though, except that Banam wore only a light jacket, so it probably wasn't very cold. That was another thing Lori seemed to have lost; he wasn't very aware of, or very sensitive to, temperatures of any sort. Early on, Clopta had been cold enough for him to see people's breaths, but he'd barely felt a thing.

His hooves clattered against the paved street, echoing off the close-in walls. He'd been a bit annoyed that they hadn't shoed him, since there was always the danger of a split hoof, but now he was glad of it. There wouldn't be any blacksmiths able to provide the service if he cut out.

"Your design's been a big hit with the bosses, I hear," Banam commented chattily, never knowing if he could be understood or not and really not caring all that much either way. "I watched you change over the past coupla months from a real mess into a pretty slick-lookin' animal. Heard 'em say they're gonna do it to anybody who can stand the operation or whatever it is. Ain't for everybody, of course. They'd need black magic to make *me* into somethin' like *you*, I think." He chuckled at the thought. "Only thing different'll be that horn. No horns on the others. Makes some of 'em kinda nervous, y' know. Dunno why."

The old fellow just kept chattering as they came up to the warehouse and the end of the trail. Then Banam walked to the front and pushed a series of numbers on the security lock. There was a sudden rumble, and the door slid up, allowing them to enter.

It was pitch dark inside, as always, but when the door came back down and settled with a crash, the lights came back on automatically. No sense in shining a beacon to the world that something was going on here.

They had a sort of stall for him in the back, reached through a maze of shelves, boxes, and palettes and well hidden from view even when the day shift was in. There were a couple of bales of hay there, a tub with water in it, and some thick straw on the floor. That was pretty much all he required.

Banam unhooked the cinch and let the packs drop before he went into the stall area. He fumbled inside, removed a greasy-looking cube, and put it over on top of the hay. "There's your big reward, fella. Enjoy. I gotta get help and get this up to the boss."

It was the drug, of course, and now it smelled and tasted as bad as it looked and did nothing for or to him, but he had to keep eating it just to make sure that they didn't suspect.

The one thing that seemed certain was that it would be another round trip before he could escape. Or was it? Had he been thinking the wrong way, perhaps? They almost always accompanied him back to the border but no farther. If he hugged the border and walked down quite a ways, he might well be able to escape on the way *back*. It made more sense than the other way, and the thought excited him.

If he escaped just after leaving *here*, then they wouldn't expect him at the other end for quite a while. They might even write him off as having been injured and thus made a banquet of by the Liliblodian locals. Now, *that* seemed to make real sense!

He tried hard to remember the maps. Clopta, Liliblod, and Agon were all on the coast. That meant Liliblod would be the border along this segment of the hex, going—what?—probably northeast. Southwest would mean the ocean, and that was no good, and north would most likely take him through the heart of Clopta, not a good option. In a high-tech hex it would be impossible to remain hidden forever. If he only knew how far along the border they were! It might well be *shorter* going north if they were near the point where three borders came together. Best not to take that much of a chance, though. Stick close to the border, check every once in a while, and go when it no longer smelled of spiders.

After that it would be time to stop running and start exploring until he came up against something with an appetite as bad as a Liliblodian that he couldn't outrun or impale.

No. Wait a moment. There *was* a potential destination, wasn't there? The same one they'd had since the start. That place, that break between the hexes at the equator where those who knew how might be able to enter the inside of this strange planet. If anyone got there and could get inside, he wanted to be there. It was the longest shot in the universe, but it was all he had.

If he could just survive, get up there, get to that entrance-way, and wait, no matter how long it took . . .

It wasn't much, but it was better than nothing. It was somewhere to go and something to do, and it was at least a sliver, no matter how microscopic, of hope.

If not this trip, then the next. The first time they gave him an opening, he had to have the guts to take it. To get away, to get free, that was the first objective. Then, once safe, use the sun as a guide and head north all the way to the barrier, which he assumed was much like the barrier that formed the southern boundary of Erdom. Then west, toward where the sun rose on this backward-turning world. West until there was a door.

If not this trip, then the next. Or the next. Whenever it was possible. As hopeless as it all was, it was the only thing he had.

AGON

Alowi had walked home from the clinic feeling nervous and uncertain about what she had done. Nearing the place where she and the Dillians were staying, essentially a huge tent struck on some deserted landfill north of the city, she began to feel light-headed, and by the time she was inside, she had the start of a serious headache. Dizzy and sick, with a throbbing head, she lay down on the pillows in the rear area of the tent and pretty much passed out.

More concerned and suspicious of everything were the Dillians, who found her out cold and decided that there was no purpose to rousing her. Some of this was to be expected from a radical injection, but as Doctor Drinh had feared, they were also quite suspicious at what Alowi had told them about the capabilities of the process. While Tony took care of some business at the port, Anne Marie put in a call to the capital.

While embassy operations on the Well World were best handled within Zone, most hexes had small offices whose function was to pass messages to and from Zone via Well Gate couriers. Reciprocity gave any race the right to use the service of any hex at all, and under diplomatic seal. It wasn't beyond being compromised, but it was effective, and any hex found compromising the system would of course lose its own rights and privacy.

Anne Marie had no intention of giving an oral report but used a recording cube of the type standardized by Zone and put it under a password that was known on the other end only to the Dillian ambassador. She dispatched the cube via messenger service on the next train to the capital, where someone alerted by her call would pick it up and stick it in the next courier pouch. She had no idea who would ultimately hear the report and no real hope that those bureaucrats could decide on whether they had to go to the bathroom, let alone anything important, but it was worth trying.

In the message she had simply summarized Alowi's experience to date and related the claims of Drinh and his reputation and voiced her suspicions with hope that all this would be relayed to the inner council committee that was in charge of the "immortals problem," as they so euphemistically put it.

At least the committee had proved honest and reliable. While it had been next to impossible to sit on the rumor that the ancient and legendary Nathan Brazil might be back, the fact that Mavra Chang might be an immortal equal to Brazil had been suppressed to a remarkable degree. The most that seemed to have leaked was that Chang was wanted because she had known Brazil and *might* prove useful in motivating the mysterious man to make a deal. Brazil, however, remained the real target for all the factions out there nervous about either his possible powers or his potential; Chang's cover story had been increasingly reinforced to the point where no one outside the council took her as more than a minor player, of no great advantage unless one had Brazil and perhaps not even then.

Now, with the readily recognizable Brazil missing for so long and the Avenues well covered, even the mild hue and cry of earlier times had faded. Most believed him a fable and the missing man simply a man, no more or less, a man who had caused stupid panic and rumors and who was now probably dead. The council was doing a nice job of covering up, but it had neither of its own objects in sight, let alone in hand. Brazil had vanished and was possibly at least neutralized as far as could be surmised from current information, and Chang had been abducted by the drug cartel and was undoubtedly a prisoner or worse by now. The fact that the drug lords had done nothing with her, though, indicated that they didn't know who and what they had, and it was feared that any attempt to find her might just tip them off to a key to potentially vast powers.

It was for this reason that they had allowed nothing to be done, since that was what they preferred as a normal course of action, anyway. Now, though, the report from Anne Marie caused a great deal of concern. If the drug lords had worked their usual tricks on Mavra Chang, she could literally look like just about *anything*; if she really was Brazil's equal, then she could not be killed and thus eventually had the potential to get free—or, worse, break under the strain and try to make her own deal with the drug lords out of desperation. If Mavra Chang no longer bore any resemblance to Mavra Chang, then the guards at the Avenues had nothing at all to go on, and they could hardly be obtrusive about barring all and sundry from those equatorial entrances without tipping the game to everyone.

If there was a chance of locating Mavra Chang, the committee knew, then it had to be taken. But patiently and with sufficient safeguards, no matter how ruthless, to keep the true value and nature of the quarry from those who might use her.

Once they decided that they *had* to move, they wanted to move yesterday, but it had to be done *right*. Still, it seemed to them that their long lag time had finally run out.

"The Dillians in Agon will almost certainly move on this if we do not," one councillor argued. "This cannot be left to amateurs. If they move, they will certainly fall into the hands of the cartel, who will be merciless in finding out why they were willing to make such a risky move. If the cartel even suspects Chang's true value, all could be lost."

"True," another agreed, "but neither can we leave them out, unless we want them disposed of."

The Dillian ambassador objected. "That is out of the question! Only if the future of the Well World and our authority were clearly at risk would we permit that! Besides, if Chang now looks nothing like she did, they may well be the only ones who could establish that a suspected being *is* Mavra Chang. Remember, *two* were taken, and we have no way of telling if we capture one just which one we have. We agree, however, that this is no job for amateurs alone. Who do we have in the region?"

"The Agonese authorities are compromised," another pointed out. "That leaves only that immigrant Leeming and the renegade Dahir in the area, both trying to find Brazil. The Leeming has proved reliable and has some feel for this sort of work—"

"But he lost Brazil!" the first councillor pointed out. "He enjoys the work but clearly isn't all that competent at it!"

"And we are, I suppose?" the Dillian retorted. "We've managed to lose *both* of the immortals while we engaged in endless debate and delay. Still, I agree that a native, one of us who is beyond reproach, must be in charge. Preferably someone who knows the area and has familiarity with the drug cartel. Any candidates?"

The problem was fed to the Zone computers, and after a process of elimination, one name, and only one, stood out.

"Now the only trick is to prepare a cover story for going after Chang," the Dillian ambassador said, nodding. "That and convincing the Agonese government to give him full authority in this matter without their corrupt elements tipping off the cartel."

"That," said another, "will be far easier than what we are asking *this* fellow to do!"

Anne Marie, however, had finally galvanized the council into action. The long wait was about to end.

• • •

For their part, the Dillians, knowing nothing of this, waited to see what the disreputable clinic might have done to poor Alowi.

The answer, at least from their point of view, seemed to be nothing more than what had been claimed. Alowi seemed more content with herself and more confident and no longer seemed troubled by runaway inner drives.

No one, of course, was more nervous about this than Alowi herself. Becoming a guinea pig possibly at the hands of one's enemy was an act of desperation but reasoned action nonetheless.

At first she simply felt, well, *normal*, and for a while that was enough. Those inner urges, those bouts of losing control, of nearly sick cravings, seemed to vanish while leaving little in their place. This was not, of course, normal to an Erdomese, but it seemed normal in almost any other context. She felt, well, much like Tony and Anne Marie seemed to feel, or Mavra. She was simply herself, but in complete control, not *needing* anything just to remain sane. Free.

Free to study, free to learn, free of any thought of returning to Erdom.

Yet when she looked at herself in the mirror, she liked what she saw. If anything, she liked it more than she had, felt more comfortable about the person who stared back at her. Although those urges and emotions had at times been overwhelming and omnipresent for what had seemed forever, it now was difficult, even impossible, to remember what that had felt like. She felt every bit a female, no less than before; certainly she didn't feel sexless or frigid or an "it." And yet, well, those things she'd gathered around or made or picked up in the markets that were so obviously *phallic* now seemed pretty silly. She wasn't quite sure just what sort of change other than allowing her independence the doctors had wrought, but if this was the extent of it, well, it was something she could surely live with and might have died without.

Tony came back from the city with what she hoped was an

answer to Anne Marie's report of only a few days before. Anne Marie, at least, was excited. "This is the first time they *ever* sent a reply to one of our reports! And so *quickly*, too! Perhaps they've found something out! Play it!"

Tony removed the cube and pressed her thumb firmly on the one side that had an inlaid red surface. The cube took a few cells of skin, compared them with the genetic code it carried, seemed satisfied, then said in a voice that came through as a soft and pleasant woman's voice, "Please do not play the rest of this inside your home. Take it to an open area well away from any others, particularly natives, and repeat the process. The cube contains a small zonal scrambling device that will cover an area about three meters square, so be close to it. The message will play only once, erasing itself as it plays, so pay close attention. When done, burn the cube in any open fire. The message will now pause until you take these precautions, and you will not hear this preamble again."

"My goodness!" Anne Marie exclaimed. "Sounds rather *serious*, doesn't it?"

"It certainly sounds as if *something*, at least, is going to happen," Tony agreed. "Let's take the precautions and go down to the jetty and see what they have to say." She paused a moment and had a puzzled look. "I wonder why that many precautions. Surely they do not think that even this tent is bugged—could they? I mean, who would bug *us*?"

"Someone who is certainly near death from boredom," Anne Marie responded. "Still, let's do this cloak and dagger business by the rules, dear."

They all left the tent and went down perhaps two hundred meters to the jetty, where the gentle ocean water, softened by far-off undersea reefs, lapped against the sides. It was a nice, bright day, warmer than usual and with a gentle wind. There was nobody else around close enough to observe them. The three gathered close, and Tony took out the cube and pressed again on the red area.

"This is Ambassador Aliva speaking for the Special Committee," said the female voice in Dillian, which the two centauresses understood directly and made an extra authenticity check possible as well. "We have evaluated our report on this clinic and its specialists, which coincides with intelligence from other sources, and we believe that you have stumbled on the key to the disappearances and also to why action is now mandated. As a result, we have arranged for an Agonite whose character is beyond question and who has both knowledge and authority in combating this criminal syndicate to assume command of a special unit that will follow up this lead.

"His name is Janwah Kurdon, and he is an officer in the Agonese Secret Police. Please do not be put off by this; Kurdon has been in something like an exile since mounting a campaign against the syndicate and being blocked by corrupt higher-ups. We have arranged for his restoration of rank and position, and it is understood that any Agonite official who gets in the way of the special unit will be placed under suspicion by the Zone Council of aiding and abetting interhex criminal activities. It is very likely that they will do their best to stay out of your way to avoid even the slightest hint of corruption, but it is inevitable that they will use their own people to try to anticipate your actions and report them to the criminal gang. Agon itself has become too industrialized to be self-sufficient in food; it is also clearly understood that anything less than government cooperation could mean a blockade and embargo. We have already notified the government of this and have heard the protests, but we have the votes here on our side."

"Goodness!" Anne Marie said. "They can certainly knock heads if they decide they want to!"

"You may, if you wish, become part of this special unit, but understand that the personal danger is very great, that this cartel is totally ruthless, and that while we can act against officials and the nation if need be, we cannot protect you individually. Also, you must accept Agent Kurdon's complete authority and act only under his orders. Otherwise, you will have to leave the country and return home or go elsewhere. You may also not travel to Liliblod or Clopta without being under the unit's authority; the former does not consider what the gang does a criminal act and operates under a different and not altogether scrutable logic, while the latter is at least as corrupt as the government of Agon and far less competent. As we cannot protect you and as you must suspect Kurdon is less than excited about being saddled with those he considers both aliens and amateurs, nothing will reflect on you if you choose not to continue, and you will be informed of any results. However, if you *do* accept the terms, complete what business you might have yet to do and meet the special unit in Subar, the northern city where you first made contact with us, in precisely four days. Go to the Central Prefecture there and simply ask for Agent Kurdon. He will then brief you on what will be happening next."

"One more thing," the message concluded. "Do not return to that clinic or contact the staff there again even if something is scheduled or they call and ask to see any of you. Make any excuse, but do not go. Operations are already under way as regards them that you might only jeopardize or, worse, alert the staff about. For the record, the cover story is that we believe genetic reengineering is being employed to possibly replace or enslave existing officials or whole populations and we are going after the proof of that. Under *no* circumstances is anyone, least of all the gang, to suspect that we are after more than that. We have also planted information that your two missing comrades have vital information for the council and that if they are located, in *any* form, and the reengineering stopped, we will not act further against the organization. We can only hope that this will buy them their lives, or at least enough time to locate them.

"May the blessings of all the gods be with you in this endeavor. This message is at an end. Please burn this cube and do not attempt a replay. The message in it is already gone, but another attempt will produce nasty consequences. Farewell."

"I'm not sure I liked the last of that," Tony commented. "It really sounded like a rather formal kiss-off. Like she never really expected to hear from us again."

"Well, we will just have to surprise her, won't we, dear?" Anne Marie responded, then looked over at Alowi. "Well! Why so glum? This is what you wanted, isn't it?"

Alowi nodded, but slowly and hesitantly. This *was* what she'd wanted all along, of course. So why did she feel so little like following up on it?

Lori, after all, had saved her life at the start of all this and for a very long time had been her only friend.

"I am glad something is happening, of course," she answered lamely, "but, well, I am just concerned. Concerned about what we might find, where this is all leading. I will be all right."

But it was more than that. After the Dillians began their preparations to shut down their trade operation, leaving her to begin the packing-up process, she tried to put her finger on it. She really did know at least a part of her problem, and it was tough trying to get around that. Lori wasn't just a friend, he was her *husband*, and the last thing she wanted right now was a husband, now or ever again. Memories of long conversations, the sharing of intimacy down to her very soul with him, now seemed distant and colored with an unpleasant veneer that seemed somehow impossible to remove.

She certainly wanted Lori liberated, but their relationship couldn't be like it had been even if by some miracle he was unchanged or could be restored to his previous form. *Particularly* not in that case . . . A whole litany of things that had attracted her and turned her on to him in the past now seemed in retrospect to be the opposite. Even his personality, mannerisms, the way he interacted with her and with others seemed distant, alien at best, and in some ways downright repugnant to her.

Finding him a malformed invalid seemed at least less threatening to her, and she felt awful for thinking that thought. Even so, she felt no duty toward him, no real attraction at all.

She had been happiest right here, with Tony and Anne Marie, free to explore her own potential without any feelings of repression or any demands she didn't like. Tony and Anne Marie had remained for her sake, and she loved them for it, and while she knew deep down that this arrangement could never be permanent, she didn't want it to end.

One had to have been on both sides of the sexual boundary to know just how defining the roles were, how they shaped and misshaped people. Seen from Alowi's perspective, she hated, despised Julian Beard. He'd been swaggering, loutish, and self-centered to a fault, committed to his own goals but seeing no commitment toward others—it was no wonder he couldn't stay married to anybody. Yet she saw the essence of all that was wrong in him in just about every male she'd met or could think of, regardless of race. It was almost as if every quality she valued seemed lacking in every male yet present in the vast majority of females. Lori—Lori by the end had been no more a former woman than Alowi had been a former man. Instead he'd become more and more like . . . Julian Beard.

Here, during this period, she'd also discovered something else. She liked herself now. First she had struggled to expunge all that was Julian from inside her, then she'd become someone else, a creature with no ego or sense of self-worth unless it was defined by what she could do for Lori. That creature, too, was gone, and for the first time she was an individual again with the qualities and capabilities she desired. She didn't want to be anyone else. Here the heavy weights placed upon her by her past and by the Well World and Erdomese culture and biology had been lifted, revealing a real person. Now it seemed as if some of that weight was being forced back upon her, and there was nobody else who could understand her problem.

It had to be done, of course, but it seemed as if freeing Lori was the worst thing that could happen to her.

● ● ●

If everyone elsewhere noted that the Dillians were genetic twins, it was harder for them to tell one Agonite from another. That meant that the creature who showed up at the police station in Subar where they'd been instructed to check in looked very much like all the other natives, except that he wore a yellow sleeveless shirt and a pair of baggy denimlike trousers. It was clear from the reaction of the police in the station, though, that he was far more important than he looked.

"My name is Chief Inspector Janwah Kurdon," the newcomer told them, "of internal security."

"We are—" Anne Marie started, but the newcomer waved her off.

"I know who you are. I know who all three of you are and how you came to be here. What I *don't* know is why you are here in Agon or still anywhere in this region. After all this time, I'd think that you would have grown weary and be on your way home by now."

Anne Marie gestured toward a sullen Alowi. "She has lost her husband. In her culture that is about as close to being killed as you can get. Her honor demands that she find him or, for her, life would not be worth living. Since she's alone and friendless and because we don't like being pushed around and, yes, betrayed ourselves, we've remained with her."

Alowi said nothing. She didn't want to disillusion the Dillians or make them feel as if they'd wasted their time for nothing, and frankly, she'd taken an instant dislike to this chunky little reptile.

The secret policeman sighed. "So what did you think you could do?"

"Us? Probably not much. Not without a great deal of help, anyway. On the other hand, we must do *something*. Even if we fail, we *can't* simply let this go. Surely you understand that."

"I understand that you were stuck in a strange country with

no resources and you actually thought you could find and take on one of the most powerful criminal organizations in the history of the Well World," Kurdon replied. "Amateurs," he sighed. "You realize, I hope, that these people will kill at the drop of a leaf and that they can do things far worse than death."

"We more or less assumed that, yes," Tony put in. "We are not unfamiliar with such groups. They exist on our original native world as well."

Kurdon glanced around. "Come. We will walk a bit together. It is a nice afternoon for the highlands."

They walked from the police station, one of the few buildings that was large enough for the Dillians to comfortably enter, and out into the street, following the inspector. For a while he said little except to comment on the nice weather and give a little inconsequential local history, but eventually they reached a large public park. Some locals were there playing various games or sitting around, but much of the area was empty in the predinner hour and the inspector was able to find a large area without trees or nearby people.

"I prefer to discuss other things in settings like this," he told them. "Of course, we can still be spied upon, but it is much more difficult to do so without being obvious. Subar is a nice peaceful city, but it is also one of our most corrupt." He reached into his pocket and brought out a small conical device that seemed to have no features except a red tip, which he pushed. "This will keep anyone from overhearing us by electronic means. Not totally foolproof but more than adequate here, as I know from experience."

"I take it that we are in the midst of our enemies," Tony said nervously.

"You are in their hometown, as it were, at least the home-grown sort. They live here, work here, do many good and charitable works, and launder their cut of the illegal money through the banks here, which are among the richest and most successful in the nation. They used to be very good at what they do, but in recent months they have become even more efficient and creative. We believe that it is because another of your origin species has affiliated with them. Do you know the name of Campos?"

Both Dillians nodded in unison. "Mavra Chang spoke of him. A vicious man, she said. Is *that* what this is about?"

"Man? Interesting . . ." The security man thought for a moment. "As to the other—yes, I believe that it is exactly what all this is about. In fact, it explains much that was puzzling, particularly why *both* of your friends were kidnapped. Chang we could understand—there are reasons I believe you might be aware of why such an organization might like to get hold of her, although it seems they don't know just who or what they've got or they'd have done something with her by now. It was the Erdomese that puzzled us. Now it becomes much clearer. Not politics, not power in the sense that we'd originally thought. Revenge. Pure revenge. How typical of that type. Reassuring in a way, too."

"How's that?"

"We have no particular drug problem here. Can you guess why that might be?"

Tony saw his point at once. "Because they are protected here. The government and the cartel have an agreement."

Kurdon nodded. "Exactly. It is not official and is never mentioned, but it exists. Not everyone is involved, of course, but they have clever ways of getting around just about anything. Once, a year or so ago, I came very close to breaking some of the big shots involved in it. Their laboratories and most of their operation are run out of a vast headquarters complex not very far from here, along the border with Liliblod. I had everything ready to go and spread out for my superiors to approve. We would have gone in with an army team and cleaned them out. Instead, I found my plans and papers confiscated, my informants met quick and untimely deaths or simply vanished, and I was made division chief of the coastal watch unit in the southeastern city of Magoor. No-

body said I'd done a poor job or that I wasn't right; technically the new job was a promotion in pay and authority—but
a shift away from all my previous investigations and contacts.
I wasn't stupid, and I knew the choice was to accept or follow my informants. I am still a young man."

"Our message indicated as much," Anne Marie told him.
"But I must say it doesn't sound very encouraging."

"On the contrary. A few days ago I was called to the capital and told to stand by. Much of my original paperwork
mysteriously reappeared. Then, yesterday, I was promoted to
chief inspector, given a great deal of power and authority,
briefed on your situation, and told to form a special unit and
proceed here. Some very important government ministers
whose honor has not been for sale have been involved in the
watch for these two alleged immortals that the council at
Zone has been most concerned about. They lost not one but
both of them. Then word comes that two creatures were taken
off a courier boat by agents of the cartel just off the northwest coast, and the remainder of the party fits the description
of three members traveling with the Chang woman. The three
of you are rather difficult to mistake in this region. Everyone
from the ministers to the council was initially panicked that
Chang had fallen into the hands of the best organized criminal organization on the Well World. Then, for months—
nothing. The only logical conclusion was that the ones who
had Chang had no idea who or what they had and for some
reason hadn't even bothered to interrogate them in the manner that they have of extracting your closest secrets. Why?
The bottom line was that they felt any search or heavy pressure would simply alert the still-ignorant criminals of the
value of their captive. Now we know why. A revenge kidnapping probably arranged directly by Campos without any of
the higher-ups even being aware of it."

"But surely someone would know!" Tony exclaimed. "Or
at least notice!"

"Not necessarily. You have no idea of the range and scope

of their operations. It probably seemed quite routine for the people at the headquarters, and it is not healthy to ask questions. Now, I ask you: If you were Campos, bent on revenge and now having the means, and you had seen or heard of what services these so-called physicians could and probably routinely perform for the gang, what would *you* do? Campos was once of the same race as your birth race. You tell me."

"Turn them into monsters. Unrecognizable, tortured, probably addicted," Tony said flatly.

"Why not just torture them to death? Wouldn't that satisfy?"

"I do not know this Campos, but I know his type," Tony told the agent. "He would not want to just kill them, even painfully. If he had the means, he'd want to see them in a continual torture, to spread his sadistic revenge out over a very long time. They could be killed any time, but until then . . . no. He would want to *enjoy* it."

"I thought as much," Kurdon said, nodding. "It is not common here, thank heavens, but it does occur. That is another reason why Campos got away with it so far. It is *not* a common attitude in Agon or Clopta; both races are far more pragmatic. They torture for information, kill when someone is in the way or no longer useful, but this sort of prolonged torture for personal gratification isn't something they would think of doing. Risky and wasteful. We have found that your doctor friends were mostly using such creatures for experimentation and eventually doing away with them but that they did some pragmatic work as well, primarily in converting creatures into couriers. I wondered why *two* women were targeted, since clearly only one was of interest to them if they suspected her true nature, and now you have told me that what I suspected is true. It is something I did *not* bother to suggest to those who are suddenly my friends."

"Couriers?" Tony repeated. "Why turn people into couriers? Couldn't anybody do that?"

"Not this type. They are designed—reengineered as couriers, dedicated to that specific task, while being physically limited from doing much else. Essentially pack animals smart enough to be autonomous yet limited enough that they had nowhere else to go and nothing else they could do."

"You know what they've been doing, then!" Anne Marie said excitedly.

"We do now. Thanks to you, we were able to wage a clandestine operation in their clinic and tap into their computer banks. Very difficult to break their codes, but Zone has capabilities beyond anything else on the Well World. We found the entire genetic codes of many individuals from a number of races in there, but we found only one male Erdomese and one female Glathrielian in the memory banks. It would take a very long time, however, to match up precisely the original and the changed structure and get a true picture of just what they became. The work is extremely advanced and, I must say, extremely frightening. Frightening enough that this alone has outweighed any loyalty to, and even much of the fear of, the organization in Agon by high officials. This explains my free hand."

"What do you propose to do?" Anne Marie asked him.

"I have a clear directive. This Chang is to be found, arrested, and brought to Zone no matter what her shape or form or condition. I may use whatever resources I require to get this done, step on any toes, go through any barriers. When I suggested that this might require going straight through the cartel's headquarters, they did not even flinch. To not do it ourselves would at this point almost certainly mean it being done in spite of us, with Agon the object of an invading army of other races. There is already a council military man in the south setting up this possibility. I find myself, therefore, with a very strong hand. Our objectives are not quite the same. If we can recover both, well and good, but it should be understood that Chang is my objective."

"Our first objective is to recover Lori for this poor dear's sake. We've been through a lot together already," Anne Marie told him. "As for Mavra, well, I don't see any other choice for us or for her. She is quite a capable individual, and if she must deal with the council, so be it."

"Agreed. Most pragmatic and satisfactory, actually. You should be aware, though, that they are both unlikely to be anything like you remember them, and it is entirely unclear whether anything can be done for them."

Anne Marie sighed and looked at Alowi, who seemed still curiously ambivalent about all this, then turned back to Kurdon.

"Somehow I do not think that will stop Mavra Chang," she told the agent. "Not if half her own stories are true. But . . ." She decided not to finish now. There was no sense in panicking Alowi, at least not yet.

"When do you move?" Tony asked Kurdon.

"In a few days. I want more information from the local agents here before I begin. I do not underestimate this bunch."

"What about going directly for Campos?" Tony asked him. "I cannot imagine such a type not having the objects of revenge close by so he could lord it over them."

"Campos is a Cloptan. Out of my jurisdiction. If we turn in a report linking Campos and the kidnapping, it will be out of our hands immediately. Besides, there are dangers to the direct approach. The quarry could go underground in its own home territory or even be killed in such an attempt, in which case we might never find those we really seek. Or our objectives could be destroyed in a final act of vengeance before we can reach them. Remember, too, that they could be literally *anywhere*, just as long as Campos can get to them. No, when I move on Cloptans on Cloptan soil, I want it to be *my* party, fast and unexpected, but with the full authority of the council. At the moment I have no idea where Campos even *is*, except somewhere in the port city of Buckgrud, a high-tech metropolis with a population of more than a million. Think of this as well: Can you *honestly* tell one Agonese from another aside from size, weight, and clothing? Honestly, now."

"Uh, um, not without great difficulty, I admit," Anne Marie managed.

"So how do you expect to directly penetrate a criminal organization and pick out the one correct Cloptan from the masses? You see? In the end we will require Cloptan help, but that will have to be very carefully done. I don't believe that they are even as honest as we are, and that is not going very far. I would prefer we deal with the Cloptans *after* we strike here. Trust me on this. This is my territory and my profession. It will be difficult enough having to somewhat involve Liliblod. Nobody can really deal with them, and they will not like this at all."

"It seemed a nice, quiet peaceful place when we went through," Anne Marie noted. "Yet we keep getting horrid warnings about it."

"Yes. By the terms of their agreements, the roads are kept absolutely safe for travel. They are not without their own odd vices, and so some commerce is permitted as a concession to their own needs. But they are not—*rational*—in the sense that we are here. They have a rather egocentric view of the universe and are quite unpredictable beyond certain bounds. The organization pays them well for protection in a sort of currency that they could not legally acquire, and they will not like to see that cut off."

"Another corrupt government?" Tony sighed.

"You misunderstand. The Liliblodians believe that all other races were put here as their prey. By—consuming—others or, more accurately, the fluids of others, they believe they gather in inferior souls and all the strengths of the prey. The cartel pays them in two ways. It provides live prey for them of the type they love—alien flesh, as it were—and the one other substance which is their own drug weakness."

"Disgusting," Anne Marie commented. "Eating live beings for *pleasure* . . ."

"Yes, it is almost as bad as their own drug of choice. You cannot imagine anything more bizarre than seeing a mass of Liliblodians literally rolling in a chocolate stupor . . ."

DLUBINE

The master computer that was the heart of the entire planet called the Well World was just a machine; its powers were far too vast to have ever trusted making it self-aware in the sense that it could act outside its makers' predetermined instructions. And while it was true that machines had infinite patience, they could also have very little if something required was not getting done. Now, as the Kraang continued its assaults and made tiny slivers of inroads into the system, it calculated that the time to solve this problem was no longer inconsequential. In that sense the Well could be said to have become impatient with the progress of events, and when the Well wanted something, it tended to be less than subtle about it.

To summon the two Watchers to see to repairs, it had sent huge meteors crashing into the planet where the Watchers were living. Extricating Mavra Chang so that she had any reasonable chance of success appeared to be very difficult and would require a great deal of subtlety and patience. Going after Nathan Brazil, on the other hand, would not. The fact that Brazil had willingly taken himself out of worldly care was to the Well entirely irrelevant.

Nathan Brazil had been on the Well World for over eleven

months, having come in with Tony and Anne Marie. It had been almost seven months since Theresa "Terry" Perez had come through on her own, following Mavra, Lori, Gus, and Juan Campos by a mere hour or so and quickly coming under the influence of the bizarre Glathrielian Way that the race that shared common ancestry with Terry's had followed. Prepared by the Glathrielians, she had attached herself to Brazil within only a week, and they had been inseparable since. For four months they had been deliberately held up, stalled, far from the goal of the Well Avenue, and then for two weeks they had broken free and escaped across the sea, been reunited with Gus, and then lost him again as they crashed on an undersea reef in a storm.

But on their tiny tropical volcanic island in the middle of a fairy-tale sea, Nathan Brazil and Terry had no concept of the passage of time or any cares or thoughts beyond sheer childish fun. The tropical rain forest on the windward side of the island provided enough wild fruits and vegetables to feed them, and the frequent but brief storms always provided a supply of fresh water. Brazil had opened himself to the Glathrielian Way but not to the elders' master plan of co-opting him as he entered the Well. There he had remained, happy and carefree, unaware of that nonhuman part of him, that deep alien nature that had thwarted the elders' control.

The tropical sun had browned him almost as dark as Terry's natural color, and his hair and beard were long and unkempt, giving him almost a wild man's appearance. His bare feet were hard and callused, toughened from months of volcanic rock and soil; the day-to-day life of climbing for treetop delicacies and over the craggy rocks had bulked out his muscles.

Terry had not been as active of late, for she'd developed a large, hard belly and some considerable fat and felt unbalanced and odd, but she accepted it as the way things were. Part of the Glathrielian Way was acceptance of whatever was and dealing with it as best one could.

This proved difficult suddenly, though, when they were awakened one morning just at dawn by a series of severe tremors. The ground shook, and trees swayed, and rocks fell from the high mountain. This went on for a day or more, and suddenly a huge piece of the mountain about halfway up the side seemed to collapse, opening a gaping wound from which belched forth steam and black ash. Then beginning what seemed a wondrous light show, a volcanic fountain played against the sky. But the earthquakes continued in increasing frequency and intensity, and from the masses of grainy rock laid down by the fountain there came puffs and plumes of smoke and ash that set part of the forest on fire.

They made their way around to the beach on the opposite side of the mountain from the eruption, having to stop or risk falling down with each tremor. Something inside them knew that they had to leave this place, and quickly.

But leave for where? And how? There was nothing on all sides but the water.

There were other islands, of course, some of which could be seen across the expanse of sea, but they were not as close as they appeared. None would be a problem to reach with a boat or a raft, but they had nothing but themselves. An inner sense of urgency told them that there was little time to consider any alternatives. Reluctantly, they entered the water and made their way out past the reefs, Brazil using his strength to support Terry and keep her afloat.

They made it to perhaps a kilometer from the beach and found themselves suddenly carried along on a warm current, able to pretty much just float and let the water do the work, which was more than welcome. The current carried them at a steady pace away from the erupting island and toward the calmer ones beyond.

Then a sudden, tremendous explosion hit them like something solid, deafening them both, and they could see the onrushing wall of water from where the island, now a vast and dark mushroom-shaped cloud, had been, a huge tidal wave coming straight for them. It was taller than the tallest trees and with a roar that sounded like thousands of caged beasts roaring at once, and they stopped swimming and watched it come, knowing it was death.

When it struck, their world became all water and whirling forces and then oblivion.

The Well had issued its wake-up call to Nathan Brazil.

The island exploding, the rushing wall of water, then ... What?

She awoke as if from some strange dream, much of which had been very nice yet only dimly remembered, like some great childhood treat now far in the past and unrecoverable.

But watch that last step, she thought. *It's a dilly.*

She sat up painfully, groaning and stretching. She felt as if she'd been beaten to a pulp by some gigantic fist, but just as everything seemed bruised, nothing seemed broken.

The beach was warm and wet. It was made of yellow sand, the kind built up from the discards of coral reefs over thousands upon thousands of years, but it was soft and somewhat comfortable.

She shook her head, trying to clear it, trying to think. She remembered a tremendous bang and a big wave but nothing afterward.

And nothing before.

It was as if she'd just suddenly come into existence here on this beach. A big bang and here she was.

It was quite dark, but out in the water she could see a million lights underneath the gentle waves, burning with a multitude of colors and shapes and patterns that she knew couldn't be anything from nature, although she didn't know how she knew. And on the water, too, in the distance, things seemed to float, lights up upon the water rather than deep below it.

Boats, she understood at once, although again she had no idea where this information was coming from.

I've lost my memory, she realized. *Something, some accident or shipwreck or something like that caused me to lose my memory.* She had no idea who, or where, or even what she was.

She ran her hands over her body in the dark. It was a woman's body. It wasn't that this was wrong so much as basic information about herself that she had had no sense of before. Somehow, she hadn't seen herself as a woman, and there was a sense of wrongness about it somewhere deep inside her.

She knew so many things! There were all sorts of facts and behaviors and other pieces of information swirling around in her head, yet about herself she had no information at all. No past, no memories of actually being anywhere, doing anything, interacting with anything or anybody at all. *I am a woman* became the first, and so far only, definition of herself as an individual.

It seemed to her that there had been Another somewhere, somebody very important. A girl . . . Another girl? That didn't seem right. But who and what?

She cast about with her mind, never even considering speech, but there was no response from the immediate area. She was alone on the beach, without memory, without anything at all, in a place she couldn't remember for reasons that were a total mystery.

Perhaps . . . Perhaps out there, among the floating lights? She cast a mental net and caught far more than she expected. Thoughts . . . *Lots* of thoughts from what seemed to be lots of different creatures. Their words, their very sounds would mean nothing to her—she knew that—but thoughts were assembled from stored information into holographic concepts before they were translated as sounds, and *those* she could pick up if she concentrated.

The power came naturally to her, although something inside said that it was a new thing, something she hadn't done before, yet something she *had* done before. That didn't make sense. Nothing really did.

It seemed somehow indecent to peek into their thoughts, to

see who was tired, who was bored, and who was thinking of killing the captain. Indecent but kind of fun, too. Some thoughts, though, were a lot harder to figure out than others; some of those creatures out there weren't even close to her form, and their thinking wasn't much closer, either.

She cast about for others of her own kind but found none. Wherever she was, she was more than merely unique in her own psyche; she was one of a kind.

No, that wasn't true. There were others. Something told her that. Men, women, children . . . But not here.

In the general casting about, though, she found spots where in fact not only words but complete sentences came through to her as if spoken in her native tongue—whatever that was. But it took some mental fine-tuning until she could fully understand those thoughts, kind of like tuning a radio.

Tuning a radio? Where had *that* come from? God! She sure knew a lot for somebody who couldn't remember anything except what was discovered by direct examination.

Maybe *they* knew. Maybe they were looking for her. If so, she'd better find out if it was in her best interest to want to be found.

"*. . . Still getting reports from the Dlubinians that there is a great deal of damage and loss of life below . . .*"

Those underwater lights. There were *people* of some kind who lived down there! If that explosion that seemed to start her existence wasn't just some metaphysical memory, then . . . Oh, God!

"*. . . No previous indication of volcanic activity in the area in any recent period, and it's monitored as closely as you can in a semitech hex . . .*"

Some of that made sense, some of it didn't. A volcano—*that* would account for the explosion and the big rush of water that had followed. If she were anywhere in that area, she would have been hit with tremendous shock. That had to be it. But it didn't explain anything else.

She listened for quite some time, gathering details of what

had happened but clearing up her own personal mystery not one bit. Had she been on a boat, or on an island, or what? Not alone, surely. Not out here in this strange and alien place. But if not alone, then with who? How? And why?

The aches and pains made it impossible to just sit there. She began massaging the stiffness and found herself somehow mentally surveying her physical condition. Bruises, twists, all that, but nothing serious. As each region was surveyed, she dampened down the pain there and went on. Only one area stymied her, the area around her abdomen. It seemed odd, at once detached and yet not detached, but certainly *different*. Well, it wasn't anything she could figure out now. She was aware that she was using, almost matter-of-factly, powers that were extremely unusual, powers that even she hadn't realized were there. But she thought nothing about using them.

She felt a strong urge to pee and then find something to eat and drink, if she didn't have to wander too far in the darkness. She certainly hoped that there was some sort of food and water on the island; otherwise a lot of choices would be made for her right off.

Her body felt clumsy, unfamiliar, and it took some getting used to before she felt confident enough to really try much. She wished it were light; there was nothing but darkness beyond the beach and no way of telling what might be waiting for her there.

Almost at once, unbidden by any conscious thought, the darkness was replaced by endless colors, all soft pastels with occasional flashes of brightness, and without a lot of difficulty she began to make out which were trees, which bushes or flowers. She intuitively understood that other colors represented living things great and small. It seemed magical, a counterpoint to the great lights beneath the waves in back of her, but after a while she realized it didn't help. This new form of vision didn't show rocks or fallen dead timber or other hazards. Best to stay out of the jungle until she knew it better and was more comfortable with the way her body moved.

Instead of going inland, she walked along the beach, not quite sure what, if anything, she was looking for, but the terrain was at least manageable by the light of the spectacularly bright starry sky. Here and there were great rocks—perhaps spewed by volcanoes, perhaps eaten away by the sea—and all sorts of wood and shells and coral washed up and deposited on the sandy shore. Walking closer, she thought she heard something, a gurgling sound, almost drowned out by the sound of nearby breakers. In a couple of minutes she found it—a tiny spring coming out of the rocks and jungle, cutting its way through the sand, and flowing into the great sea beyond. She got down on her knees, cupped her hands, and brought some to her lips. It was fresh! At least she would not die of thirst! It was lukewarm, but she splashed some on her face to wash away the last of the cobwebs that seemed to be lurking in her mind.

She drank her fill and got up unsteadily and went on down the beach, feeling a little better. After a few minutes more the beach ended, tapering to a stop around a fair-sized cove. There was a large rectangular box where the last of the sand vanished, clearly there to be accessible by land or sea, and she went to it. It was the first artificial thing she could remember ever seeing. For a moment she hesitated to get close to it, let alone touch it. When everything was an unknown, then everything was a potential threat, if not directly then because of her own ignorance of the world around her. It was such an odd feeling to have a lot of facts in her head but not be able to relate them to anything until she had some logical reason to do so.

She realized on at least one level that this was the next step in defining herself. She'd exercised caution and stayed out of the forest not out of fear but for very practical reasons. She *was* afraid of this box, though, just as she was afraid of the boats out there and the creatures on them. Now she had to decide if she was going to let that fear rule her and hide out from everything or if she had the guts to explore and discover new things. That really wasn't a choice; she did not like being alone and without any memories in a place she had no knowledge of.

Cautiously, she approached the box until she stood right next to it, examining it as much as she could in the starlight. It seemed featureless, colored some kind of bright yellow except for a bunch of marks in a dark shade etched into the front of it. Those marks made sense to somebody—what was it? Writing. Yes, writing. But they might as well have been just marks to her.

She reached out hesitantly and touched it, then immediately pulled away as if it were some burning hot fire. Nothing happened. Emboldened, she ran her hands over it and around it and found in the top a series of indentations with small marks inside each one. Touching one didn't seem to do anything, so she ran her finger along each in turn.

There was a sudden, terrifying *woosh!* from the box that so startled her, she fell over backward, then scrambled away on hands and knees, staring.

The box lid rose up as if being opened by a giant hand until it was a bit more than straight up; pulses of light began emanating from it, aimed toward the sea. As suddenly as it started, the flashing stopped and the light burned steadily. After perhaps a quarter of an hour of staring, waiting for some horror to climb out, she finally felt bold enough to go back carefully and see what she'd done. Curiosity was outweighing fear; if that light or whatever it was kept going, somebody would see it and come anyway, so she might as well check it out before they did.

The box was a bit more than a meter high and deep and perhaps two meters long. Conscious for the first time that she wasn't very tall, she stood on tiptoe and peered in.

It was full of more boxes.

Big boxes, little boxes, square boxes, long thin boxes— boxes and boxes. She wondered if she could pull herself up and stand inside and whether it was a good idea to do so. That lid might well come back down . . .

The inside of the lid itself was a long, very shiny surface with a bar of bright glittering lights along the top and both sides. The light was irritating, but that shiny surface inside was very, very tempting. Angled just enough that it showed no reflection of her head at ground level, it would certainly do so if she were at or near its height.

She looked back out at where the beacon was shining and scanned the area. Lots of thoughts out there, as before, but no signs that anybody had yet seen, let alone was coming toward, this new beacon. Not yet.

She *had* to risk it. She just *had* to. She tried various ways of pulling herself up and into the box, but while she'd get close, she just couldn't seem to manage it. After a few minutes of frustration she remembered the driftwood nearby and went and carried some thick loglike pieces over to the box and stacked them one at a time. She was winded after a while, but she managed to build herself enough of an unsteady pile to get high enough to pull herself the rest of the way into the box.

Standing on the smaller boxes in the center of the big one, she could see herself from the thighs up in the smooth mirror of the lid's interior surface.

Staring back at her was the unfamiliar face of a very young woman, perhaps no more than midteens, with big brown eyes and finely wrought, attractive features, the hair thick and black and curly, making a frame around her face. The face did show definite chubbiness, although it did not detract from her overall pleasing looks. The weight also showed in large fatty breasts and in a fat ass and thighs, and there was a fair bulge of a tummy centered on the navel that didn't seem as natural-looking as the rest of her and was clearly the cause for her feeling ungainly when she walked. She stared and stared at the image in total fascination as it was illuminated by the beacon lights around the lid.

It was the face and body of a complete stranger.

And yet it was *her* face, *her* body without a doubt.

Who are you, girl? she wondered. *And how long will it be before I am no longer surprised to see you staring back at me?*

Reluctantly she tore herself away from the image and concentrated on the boxes. Most used the same system—one put a finger in some indentations one at a time in a line, and it hissed and opened. Clearly the seals weren't designed as locks but rather to keep them from being opened and unsealed by accident, waiting until somebody needed them.

Some of the stuff inside the boxes was weird, some of it was bizarre, and some of it was downright disgusting. However, one box contained what smelled like cake, and in fact, it *tasted* like plain yellow cake; another held hard biscuits, and yet another had something that looked like a miniature loaf of baked bread but turned out to have the taste and consistency of soda crackers. There was also, in one larger container over in the corner, a deep box that contained a liquid—one of the terms flying around in the back of her head leapt out at her: "beer." After the cakes and biscuits and crackers, she drank a fair amount of it.

When she finished, she was feeling a little light-headed and had to pee again, and she realized she had to get out. Piling up boxes got her to the top, but turning around and getting down to the logs and from there to the sand proved challenging.

She slipped and fell back, landing on her rear in the sand, but she wasn't hurt and the whole thing seemed somehow very funny. She tried to get up, but her body responded even more awkwardly than usual, and she finally was forced to crawl on hands and knees. She finally made it perhaps twenty or thirty meters away, back onto the beach but up near the rocks and the start of the jungle. It was all she could manage, and she picked a spot that seemed comfortable. She sank onto the sand and lay there, awake for quite a while but not thinking of anything at all except a vision reflected in a mirror by a glittering of light, of a face and body that said, *You don't know me, but I'm you.*

And, for a little while, until sleep took her, it didn't make any difference.

It had been a typical Dlubine night; clear one minute, fast-moving thunderstorms the next. In between the brief bursts of rain, fog and mist lay in patches all over the open sea, some natural, some the result of activity below the waves, lay where the people of the hex lived. For most of the evening visibility to the west had been obscured by fog, but now it was lifting, dissipating as the first signs of false dawn came upon the ocean. A lookout on the patrol corvette *Swiftwind Thunderer* spotted a flashing light through the thin mist and called it out to the watch. It was soon verified by other look-outs, and the watch officer located it on the chart. Then it was time to notify the captain.

"Sir! Emergency beacon activated on Atoll J6433!"

Captain Haash, a Macphee, stirred from his sleep and opened his blowpipe, cursing semitech hexes and their limitations. "Probably nothing—those things malfunction all the time on their own, and when there are earthquakes and eruptions . . . Still, might be survivors from a ship that got swamped. What's the weather like?"

"Squall moving in, sir. Looks to be one of those short but nasty types."

"Hmph! How soon?"

"Ten, fifteen minutes, no more."

"Too short to make a run in and send in a shore party safely. How long to sunrise?"

"About forty minutes, sir."

"Well, we'll wait until full light and, when the storm clears, take her over and investigate. No use in getting banged up or beached. I'll be on the bridge by then. Make to other ships that we'll handle the beacon so they don't have to bother."

"Very well."

The storm hit within minutes with the usual ferocity of small storms in the hex, but it was no volcanic eruption or tidal wave, and the crew was used to this kind of weather by now.

While riding it out was routine, sleeping through it wasn't much of an option, and it wasn't long before the captain was pulling himself up through the bridge hatch. It wasn't easy to catch his mood at this moment, but then, it never was—unless one was another Macphee. His huge eyes always looked as if they were about to rip somebody apart, and beaked creatures always tended to have less physical expression, even those which didn't also look like a large squid covered from enormous head to halfway down his tentacles with thick brown hair.

"What's that banging I hear?" the captain demanded.

"Not sure, sir," the mate responded. "We think it might be debris and such from the explosion in the water striking the hull. We can put somebody over to check if you like." All the cutters had several air-breathing water species aboard for any such eventuality.

"Absolutely not! I'll not have anybody brained by a tree checking to see if we're being struck by a tree! That hull is tough; it'll take a few dings."

It was one of the reasons his crew would go almost anywhere with and for the old man. He was as tough as they came in a fight, but he cared about every member of his crew. He'd willingly risk all their lives for good reason, but never for nothing. It was a bargain he had with them, he liked to tell other captains. The Macphee might have resembled squids, but they were not aquatic creatures and the thick hair was not particularly coated. If he fell overboard and could find nothing to hold on to, that waterlogged fur would cause him to sink like a stone. That meant that he had to always sail with a crew that would be anxious to throw him a line just in case . . .

In a little over a half hour the storm was over, and the captain immediately ordered the crew to check the condition of the ship and see what, if anything, was still in the water near them. Two Effiks, large green and yellow banded insectoids whose legs could stick to just about anything, went over the side and down it, walking around the hull as easily as if they were walking on the deck. The one on the port side suddenly gave a yell. "Here it is! *Big* sucker of a tree; looks almost like it got launched straight up, it's in such good shape! Hey! Wait a minute! There's something stuck in it! An animal, perhaps. Hey! Everybody here!"

There was a general rush to the port side, and two otterlike Akkokeks slid off into the still-choppy seas and approached the big tree cautiously from both sides. Seeing what might have been a leg or some other appendage sticking out of the still-green fronds near the former treetop, they turned upright in the water, bouncing like corks, and hands carefully peeled away the greenery to get a look at the whole creature.

"Never saw anything like *that* before!" one exclaimed. "What the heck *is* that, anyway?"

"Looks like a sentient race," the other remarked. "Bipedal, hands with opposing thumbs . . . Definitely a male. My! That's so *exposed!* Let's see . . ." It carefully began poking and probing and was suddenly startled to see the jaw open, then close. "*Woof!* Reflex action, or . . . Hey! This thing might still be alive!"

"Lower a stretcher on floats and send it out with Doc!" the captain ordered. "Don't touch it until Doc gets there! If it's been stuck in a damned tree since the explosion, it's probably beat up all to hell. Don't want to do anything that'll kill it now, not after it came through all *that!*"

It took some time to get the float to the far end of the tree and for the bewildered medic, who had a lot of practice on dozens of races but knew nothing about this one, to supervise extricating the body from the tree and moving it as gently as possible onto the flotation device.

"Take it easy!" Doc cautioned. The doctor, a birdlike Mosicranz, had little strength in the long, spindly arms beneath her white wings and had to supervise without directly manipulating the body. Once on board and in the clinic, she might be able to do a bit more, since those same fragile limbs possessed an incredible delicacy in control, although she would have preferred to be in a high-tech hex where all the medical equipment that would easily answer her questions would work.

"How should we lay it out, Doc?" one of the Akkokeks asked her.

"How should *I* know? I'm going by deduction here. Flat on the back, I should think, face up. Keep the legs together and the arms against the body. Damn! Whatever he is, he sure looks like he's been through the dominion of evil! Yes, that's good. Fine. Make sure the arms don't drop off or out and let's get him aboard as quickly as possible. I can see some respiration, although I look at the rest of him and I can't understand why. I don't have to know anything at all about his species to know that there's no rational reason in the world why he isn't deader than a stone!"

It took about ten minutes to get the new find aboard and below and another ten or fifteen minutes before the doctor came back up to the bridge.

"There's very little I can do except lay him out and hope for the best," she told the captain. "Anything I do may finish him—if he doesn't die beforehand anyway. There's been some loss of blood from all those gashes and tears, impossible to tell how much, and probably some broken bones, although I can't say without a full scan, which I can't do here. The gash in his head is particularly deep and nasty, and there's some swelling in the skull. If we're going to try and save him, we have to get him into a high-tech facility, and fast. There is no such thing as fast enough."

The captain thought a moment. "We could make Mowry in less than an hour and a half. That would activate your onboard equipment."

"Yes, but it might not be nearly enough. I need *data*. What good is a full scan and examination if I don't know how much blood and fluid he needs or its composition? In order to fix him, I have to know his definition of 'normal.' That means a land hospital."

The captain thought a moment. "All right. The fact that we have a survivor who is of no race known in the region is worth a risk. If we get up full steam, I can get us into Deslak in . . ." The mean-looking eyes went to the mate.

"About three hours, sir," the mate responded.

"That be good enough?"

The doctor sighed. "It will have to do. He's likely to die before we get there, but the gods only know how he managed to live this long. Maybe his will to live is so strong, he'll make it."

"Very well. Notify the company we are rushing an injured survivor to Agon and will be off station for eight hours," the captain said to the bridge staff. "Order the engine room to get up full steam and proceed to Deslak at flank speed as soon as practical."

"Aye, sir. Um—sir? What about the distress signal?"

The captain froze for a second. "Oh, yes. Totally forgot about that. Let me think . . . All right, head for them now. Do as quick a shore recon and pickup as you can. If nobody's there, don't hunt for them, but if there *is* another survivor there, they might even know who or what this fellow below is and what he was doing out here. At the very least, they'd have to be taken in somewhere, anyway."

"Captain, I really think we ought to head for Deslak straight away," the doctor protested.

The captain gave a clicking sound that was more or less the equivalent of a sigh. "Doctor, I appreciate your concern, but he probably won't survive to get there anyway, and if he does, he does. He's held out this long. Another half hour to perhaps save somebody else probably isn't going to make a whole lot of difference."

• • •

On the beach, the girl had woken with the coming of dawn. With the morning light, she had lost some of her fear and was beginning to wonder what to do next.

It was strange how clearly she could think and see things yet know so little about herself or much else. There were a lot of terms that meant nothing, a lot of concepts that seemed more confusing than clear, and absolutely nothing at all to anchor her own self upon. She did know that as far as she could tell from the thoughts she could intercept, she seemed to be the only one of her kind.

The storm itself took her by surprise; she didn't run from it but rather was fascinated by it. All that energy, all that sound and fury and noise and light, and all that rain.

The rain in particular fascinated her. Not that it fell in such great quantities but that it seemed unable to quite touch her. It was like she had some kind of second invisible skin that was keeping her and even her hair dry. She could feel it as a series of constant pulses against her skin, but it didn't penetrate. With a little effort she could see it, a thin and transparent layer of energy that gave off a vague lavender glow. She reached out her hands and cupped them, and the glow receded to the wrists, allowing the torrent to strike and quickly overfill her hands. The force of the rain and its weight startled her, and the glow quickly shot back around the hands once more.

They couldn't do that, those creatures out there. None of them could. She didn't know that as much as sense it through the mind's eyes of the unlucky sailors who had to be on deck awash in wind and rain and crashing waves. It wasn't merely that they didn't want to have it; they simply didn't. That was clear.

So whoever and whatever she was, she had powers they did not. She was not, however, so naive as to think that those powers would give her more than a slight advantage over the rest in some situations. They could hurt her, even kill her, if they wanted to do so.

That knowledge brought things right back to the start once

again. What was she to do? Run into the forest here, hope that there was enough to eat and live on, and remain here alone, one of a kind? That didn't seem very appealing. But what would those creatures out there do if they found her? Would they take her to more of her own kind, or would they put her in a cage or, perhaps, eat her? It was impossible to get a handle on that because they really didn't know she was here and didn't seem to have any concept of her kind in their heads.

It was lack of knowledge of the world out there that was so disturbing. Surely she must have a past. Those terms which kept popping up in her mind now and then had to come from someplace. And yet, hard as she tried, there just was nothing there. The only thing she knew for sure was that she was here and that somewhere out there there was another, one of her kind yet not like her. She knew this not from memory, though, but because there was some kind of link between them, something she felt. She tried reaching out through that link, but what she got back was unintelligible, confusing, like a thick fog.

Yet, reaching out, there *were* a few such sensations she could decipher. Water . . . wetness, and something sharp and misshapen. Then something—some *things*—grabbing, moving the other out of the water, up onto one of the boats . . .

There was suddenly no choice on the course of action she had to take. One way or the other she had to get on that boat. The other was the only link to any existence beyond what she now knew, the only other one of her own kind. For her own safety she could rely only on instinct and on the strange powers that came unbidden. Basic logic just wouldn't work here; she didn't know the rules. Best to go with feelings until she knew enough to make decisions on her own.

They were coming for her now; the very boat on which the other had been taken was approaching, apparently drawn by the lights she'd triggered. She left her hiding place and went down toward the big box to meet them.

AGON,
SOUTH COAST

The colonel oozed into his temporary headquarters on the patrol dock and formed an eyestalk to better focus on his surroundings. It looked quite empty.

"Come! Come! Gus! I know you are here!" he said rather casually. When there was no immediate response, his irritation was clear in his tone. "What would you like me to do? Send off a report to Dahir that they should come and pick you up?"

"If you were gonna do that, you'da done it by now," responded a deep growl of a voice behind the Leeming.

"Ah! What a talent! If I only had such as you back home in São Paulo! There would have been no secret closed to us!"

"I was in the news business," Gus reminded him. "Maybe it's *you* who wouldn't have had no secrets. All the stuff you did in them cells and damp basement rooms woulda been on the evening news. Now the only joy I have left in life is making you as paranoid as you probably made half of São Paulo."

"Ah, my friend! How many times do I have to remind you that my country was a democracy?"

"Not in your version of the good old days," Gus responded. He didn't like the colonel very much, and he knew the colonel didn't much care for him, either, but at the moment they needed each other. "Any news? We've been wallowin' here for too long now."

"There was a major volcanic eruption on one of the islands a couple of days ago."

"So? I understand that's pretty old stuff."

"Maybe. But it was in the very area we searched so long and so hard, my friend. On the very island where you were convinced they had to have been."

Gus was suddenly concerned. "*That* one? You think maybe they . . . ?"

"Who knows? If they are, it is the end of this part of the problem since this Brazil person would obviously not be an immortal and would certainly not be the man with the keys to the Well, now, would he? But if he is, and many people do believe he is, then, my friend, either he was not there or he would escape, no?"

"But Terry—the girl! *She's* no immortal!"

"That is true, and I understand your concern. She was a friend. Perhaps she lives, perhaps not. What would you do if you found her? Found her separated from the captain, I mean? I have heard of some odd couples in my time, but *this* is a bit much, I think."

"It's not like that! It wasn't sexual. It was different than that."

"Indeed? And which planet are you from? I know where *I* was born and where I am now. Or perhaps you are a throwback to the days of romance and chivalry, to Platonic love and honor and duty and all that? Or were you honorably married and religiously faithful? Or perhaps it was *she* who was married?"

"No, she wasn't married, and neither was I."

"I can see why not! You might as well be a monk. Or did you perhaps not find women sexually attractive?"

"I wasn't gay, if that's what you mean, and I wasn't no monk, neither. If you want to know, I didn't want to make it with her because I thought it would spoil things. She was the closest thing I had to a best friend. We had what they call mutual respect, and she sure as hell had guts. Maybe I'm wrong. Maybe we were *both* married. Not to other people but to the job, to the life-style. There wasn't nothin' neither of us wanted to do with our lives than what we was doin'. Both of us. If either of us had been willin' to stop, I guess it mighta worked, but we was two of a kind, you might say. I guess you could say we shared the same lover, if you want to make it like that. No use beatin' this horse anymore. If you don't get it now, I could never make you understand it."

"To each his own," the colonel responded. "I think perhaps that things are not so different here as they seem. Only back on Earth we all looked pretty much the same, so we thought of ourselves as one when really, our cultures and natures were as alien as, well, a Dahir and a Leeming. And perhaps, too, we change less here than we think we do, eh?" The colonel sighed. "Well, that is neither here nor there. The question is, What do we do next? Do we go back out and see if we can find anything in the aftermath of this, or do we wait and see what gets picked up?"

"I'm for going back out," Gus replied without hesitation. "If either or both survived, then things got really stirred up, didn't they? It might have spooked 'em—and remember, they got the knack like me. If they don't want to be seen, you can't see 'em. *You* can't, but *I* can." And that was precisely why the colonel needed Gus. For his part, though, Gus did not underestimate the colonel, who had managed to accumulate a whole hell of a lot of authority and rank, which implied trust, in a very short time on the Well World. That kind of man was dangerous in and of himself, but even more so when it was not at all clear to whom the man gave his loyalty.

The colonel considered Gus's response, then said, "I think perhaps you are right, my friend. If I'd had a boat at my disposal, we would have left at the first reports, but they have a veritable armada out there, from patrol boats to scientific teams, and that left them thin in other areas. There's one due in for refueling and reprovisioning this afternoon, though. I think when it sails, you and I should be on it."

The colonel's question had bothered Gus more than he let on. What *was* he going to do if he found Terry? What sort of future did he have in mind, particularly considering the state she'd been in when he'd found her? Her only hope was the captain, and while he seemed like a decent enough guy, he didn't seem to be all there in a number of ways. In a sense, *his* only real hope was the captain, too, since he sure couldn't go back to Dahir and didn't see much of a future anywhere else. In point of fact, until things had stalled, this business had been the most fun he'd had since he had arrived in this strange place.

They'd probably let Terry go. She wasn't much good to anybody, but she wasn't very good company as it was, either. But Brazil—that was a different story. At best, they'd lock him up and try to get enough guts to trust him on any deal he might make, or they'd march him into that whatever it was up north with guns pointing at his head. Not a good condition for granting favors, although Brazil always seemed confident that if he got in there, he could handle anything.

Still, old Gus wasn't one of the folks likely to be invited to the party, and Brazil would have a lot more on his mind than his brief acquaintance and shipmate.

Damn! he thought. *Kinda like* The Wizard of Oz, *only you got to steal the wizard and carry him off, too.* Yeah, and when they'd gotten to the wizard, he'd proved to be a fake, anyway. Wouldn't *that* take the cake! All this crap and you get Brazil inside and he's just another con man. Hell, the captain had even described *himself* as a con artist! Seemed damned proud of it, although where had it gotten him up to now?

As always, he'd have to just wing it. At least those two somehow had learned the same knack for not being noticed that was built into the Dahir; they might be pretty damned hard to keep locked up. *That* was something of an advantage, although, as the colonel said, it wouldn't take forever to get somebody else here, somebody native, who could see through the trick.

"Ship off the port bow!" the lookout cried. "Coming land-ward and at full speed! Looks like one of ours!"

"Make to approaching craft by signal lantern as soon as she's in range," the ship's captain instructed. "Ask them for identification and the reason for coming in. They might have some problems. Nobody was due in for another thirty hours."

The semaphore lantern was soon clicking away, and after an interval during which time the approaching craft had covered a good deal of distance toward them, the signalman read out the reply.

"Corvette *Swiftwind Thunderer*, carries two survivors, unknown species, one in critical condition."

The colonel snapped to. "It's *them*! I *know* it is them! Captain, tell them to approach and lay to next to us. My companion and I are going to board that ship and ride it back in."

"Might not be who you're looking for," the officer pointed out.

"It is. I will chance it anyway. Just give the order before they get so close that they pass us." He paused a moment, then called, "Gus? You hear?"

"I heard. Might as well see what they caught."

The two corvettes were nearly identical, and when alongside they secured to one another with grappling hooks and lines, close enough that a metallic plank could be laid between them.

Watching the colonel move fast when he wanted to was an education. While he normally seemed to just ooze across the floor or deck, his great translucent blob now seemed to shrink, and then an object the size of a basketball extruded and fairly shot across the gangway. The rest of the body followed as if the whole were a rubber band that had been stretched and now was released. It was a bit harder for Gus, but his feet gave him a good grip on all but the smoothest surfaces, and he was able to leap the last meter or two.

"I'm here," he told the colonel, who signaled for the two ships to disconnect.

Captain Haash oozed down from the wheelhouse himself as soon as they were again under way. "What the blazes is all this about? And who are you?" he demanded to know.

"I am Colonel Lunderman of the Royal Leeming Forces, currently assigned to South Zone Council duty. My orders and authority are at the patrol base at Deslak, if you have any doubts.

Haash thought a moment. "Well, I doubt if you'd be on old Shibahld's ship unless you were who you said. Still, can't say as I can figure out if you're comin' or goin'."

"Neither, Captain. I was headed out for another search for certain creatures wanted by the council. I am looking for two Glathrielians, and you have two unknowns from the right region. Am I correct?"

"Glathrielians? Never heard of 'em. So *that's* what they are!"

"Perhaps. If we can just see them? That is the only way to make sure."

"Sure. No problem. 'We,' you say? More'n one of you in that blob?"

"He is referring to me, Captain," Gus put in.

Haash proved that a Macphee could move even faster than a Leeming—and up a bulkhead, too. Then the huge head peered back over, and two enormous but very human-looking eyes peered down. "Don't *do* that to somebody like me! Don't *ever* do that again! I'm likely to take your head off!"

Gus decided that it was the better part of discretion not to point out that the captain's reaction had been not to fight but to flee. After all, it *was* his ship. "Sorry. Can't help it. A defense mechanism that's just built in. I couldn't turn if off if I tried. You haven't noticed this sort of thing with either of your survivors?" Gus was beginning to worry that they'd just blown it on a wild-goose chase.

"No! And from the looks of things it's gonna be touch and go if one of 'em don't disappear into the grave."

The colonel felt impatient. "May we just see them, Captain?"

"Infirmary below. At least the one that's wracked up is there. The other one roams all over the place but generally stays out of the way. Anybody can point you the way."

As they went below, led by a crewman, Gus wasn't at all sure that he wanted it to be they. If it was Terry who was down there, near death . . .

It was pretty clear, though, in the small infirmary that they hadn't wasted any time at all and that Gus's fears had not been realized, either.

Hooked up to a forced breathing apparatus and submerged in a fluid tank that at least insulated the injured man from the effects of the sea was clearly a battered, bruised, and cut Nathan Brazil.

"Jeez! He looks *awful!*" Gus noted, examining the man through the plastic casing. "What the hell did they *do* to him?"

The colonel, too, stared at the man floating in the tank. "He's survived many weeks, probably with very little, on a tropical atoll," he noted. "I doubt if he had a comb, razor, or medical kit. However, note the scars."

"I'm trying not to," Gus responded.

"Be observant! The scar tissue is brown but of roughly the same uniform age, shade, and thickness. The bruises and black and blue areas also look to be rather similar. This says that most of what we see happened in a relatively short period of time. I think that Captain Brazil might very well have been on that island when it exploded and was somehow blown away with the debris. Strange . . . He seems, well, so much *smaller*, more frail-looking than I remembered him. I suppose, like many small men, his personality and energy are in inverse proportion to his real size and strength."

A Mosicranz, looking something like an anemic and sickly angel to Gus, although with a more birdlike head, came into the room. "I am the doctor," she told them. "I understand you know who and what this is."

"He is a Glathrielian," the colonel told her. "Not likely to be an extensive entry in your medical books, I fear. They are generally a very closed and primitive society and do not travel. This man was an exception to the rule."

"I can believe the primitive part," the doctor responded. "The female seems to be totally ignorant of the simplest things, almost like a little child."

"She is not so badly hurt?" Gus asked anxiously. Predictably, the doctor started but recovered quickly. Clearly she'd seen that trick before.

"She's not hurt at all. She apparently made it to a nearby island with a lifesaving chest and beacon and apparently triggered it by accident. That's the only reason we knew she was there and picked her up. She seems very concerned about the male—they were mated, perhaps?"

"In a way," Lunderman acknowledged. "Although I don't think it was necessarily mutual. This man is quite sophisticated about things, while the girl seems about as primitive as you can get."

"You knew them before, then?"

"Yes, indeed. We both did," the colonel told her. "My companion goes back even further with the girl."

"Is that so? Well, I'm afraid that might not count for much anymore," the doctor told them.

"Why? Something happen?" Gus asked. "You said she wasn't hurt!"

"Not *physically*, no. But we Mosicranz are very good healers, sir, with our own set of inborn attributes. I am mildly telepathic. Only surface thoughts, no deep probes, but sufficient to read and respond. She, too, has this ability—to what depth I can't say, although it appears to be very similar to mine. When I say she is like a child, I mean that literally. She has no memories at all before waking up on that island.

None. She doesn't know who she is, where she is, what she is, or how she got there. She is here only because she has a permanent connection of some sort to the male and sensed that even on the island. It is impossible to say where they were when the eruption took place, but I would think it was quite close. They became separated in the water. She made it to the island; he did not, struggling in the channel until he found a large tree floating there and managed to wrap himself in it. That is all deduction but is probably correct. He was so badly injured that it's incredible he managed as much as he did. As for the female, there is no clear evidence of head trauma, so I can only suspect that the memory loss was due to either shock or internal concussion when the thing blew— literally a shaking of the brain inside the skull. I should like to examine her more thoroughly when we get to a high-tech port to see if there is any brain damage or internal hemor- rhaging that I can't now detect."

"Huh? You mean she might really be hurt, after all?" Gus asked her.

"Perhaps. I would have kept her here, but I had no knowl- edge of what she was, so sedation was out of the question. What dosage? Which drug? You see? And she's not one to be kept lying down without forcible restraint."

"Where is she now?" Gus asked her.

"Somewhere aft and almost certainly topside. She doesn't like to be inside for long. But don't expect too much from her. If she is capable of vocalized speech, I haven't been able to get anything out of her."

"She is, but she may have forgotten how," the Dahir re- plied. "Still, I'll see what I can do. Maybe later you can act as a bridge for us and I'll see if I can stir up anything in her memories."

"That might be a very big help," the doctor agreed.

Gus went out to find Terry, leaving the colonel with the doctor.

"So, Doctor, what is your best guess, and I realize that it is only that, on *this* one?" he asked her.

"Frankly, I can't understand how he's still alive. Just looking at the external injuries, I can well imagine what is inside. If he lasts long enough, I hope to be able to do as much for him as possible, but frankly, unless he can somehow heal himself of mortal wounds, I would be shocked if he lasts more than a matter of days."

The colonel thought for a moment, then said, "Perhaps he may surprise you, Doctor. In any event, if you wish to stick with him, I certainly have no objections, but even in the terrible shape he is in, I will insist that from this moment there be a guard posted here or just outside and that he not be moved or treated anywhere without a guard being present."

"That man is not going anywhere!" the doctor pronounced confidently. "Period!"

"If he were on fire and we were watching him burn, I would not trust 'that man,' " the colonel told her. "You and your ship are going to be a little bit famous, I think, Doctor. You see, that man is Captain Nathan Brazil."

There was a long pause, and then the doctor asked, "Who?"

"Nathan Brazil. There's been an all wants and warrants out on him since he stole a sailing ship and vanished many weeks ago."

"I don't pay attention to that. I have enough trouble keeping up with the medical biology of the nine different races represented on this crew alone, let alone others I might have to patch up, regardless of tech level. It keeps me busy."

The colonel was still a bit incredulous. "You have *never* heard the name before?"

The doctor gave a mild shrug. "Well, seems to me that there's a name that sounds something like that in ancient mythology, but I'm afraid I didn't pay much attention to myths and legends."

A pseudopod oozed out and gestured toward the man in the tank. "Well, there lies a genuine mythological legend, Doctor. Nathan Brazil, the immortal who alone remains to work the great Well World machine."

"You're joking, of course."

"Perhaps. Perhaps not. Let's just say that there is ample evidence that such a person exists. Enough to satisfy the Zone Council that he exists, anyway. And this man, who came through the Well Gate from another world far from here, not from ancestral Glathriel, knew an awful lot about the Well World for one from a civilization still not really even into space."

The doctor stared at the man in the tank. "An ancient god? *That* one? *Here?*"

"Wiser heads than we believe it. Certainly it will be a moot point if he dies, won't it? But if he doesn't ... If he in fact makes a full and complete recovery ... What then?"

"You kind of expect your ancient mythological deities to be, well, a bit larger, more imposing, to say the least."

The colonel chuckled. "Only if they *want* to be noticed, Doctor. Not when you want to sneak in."

She hadn't entirely lost her fear, but she was much more relaxed now, convinced at least that she'd done the right thing by coming to the other, hurt though he clearly was. Everything on the boat was so interesting, so new. She understood that the crew members got a lot of amusement at her ignorance. Of course they were sometimes not so amused, like when she'd just taken a piss on the deck, but she didn't mind. A lot of it was too confusing to worry about, anyway. What did it matter if some had clothes and some didn't? What did it matter how one ate, or slept, or whatever?

And they kept going around and working all these things on the boat that didn't make a lot of sense. Some of them even did things that seemed silly on the face of it, like washing the deck when they were on an ocean—when it got rough, the waves washed it anyway. That was why she didn't understand why they got upset when she peed on it. Either they or the waves washed it anyway, and it seemed like she had to pee a lot.

They also had a lot of gadgets and gizmos that made no sense to her. They'd sometimes try to show her the simplest things, at least to them, and she'd try, too, really try, but she just couldn't figure out how to work them. She *had* finally managed to figure out how to open doors, but then they got mad when she kept practicing on every door on the boat. Doors seemed stupid, anyway. All they did was block her way from one place to another. If they didn't have doors, they wouldn't have to bother opening them all the time, she reasoned.

She couldn't figure out why the boat didn't sink, either. One threw something in the water, it sank. Why didn't this big, heavy, ugly thing sink? It didn't make any sense. Well, she didn't worry much about things she couldn't figure out.

From observing and listening to the surface thoughts of the crew, she'd gotten the idea that there were smart people who understood or could figure out most anything, there were others who understood some things, and finally there were dumb people who just couldn't figure out things. Some of the crew members whom others in the crew considered stupid didn't seem so stupid to her, but they also didn't seem to be sad or upset that they might be stupid. All of them thought she was pretty stupid, even the ones the others thought were stupid, too, so maybe she was. She'd asked the nice doctor about that, and the doctor, who everybody said was the smartest one on the boat, had told her that people who tried their best and didn't worry about what they knew or didn't know were happiest, and that seemed like good advice. She'd just try her best and learn what she could and not worry about the rest.

And then there was the other downstairs. It didn't look at all like her, but it looked more like her than anybody else on board. The doctor said he was badly hurt, something that she hadn't needed to be told. The doctor also said that while he might wake up and get better, he probably wouldn't. It was funny, but that news hadn't really affected her. There was just something inside that said that he'd be sick a long, long time but wouldn't die. That just meant that it would be a real long time before he woke up and could tell her about herself, if in fact he could and didn't have the same problem remembering things. She might stick around until he got well, but she knew it would be very long, and what could somebody like her do just staying around? Of course, she didn't have anything else to do or anywhere else to go.

She'd watched unobtrusively when the two boats had pulled up next to one another. It was kind of neat how they could do that. They probably had to be really smart to do something like that without crashing. The two new people who'd come aboard had gone below, and she hadn't found out much about them yet, but maybe she would. She didn't really like the big blob thing; she couldn't say why. The other one almost seemed like, well, like somebody like her, but that was silly.

Gus found her on the afterdeck, just sitting there and seemingly oblivious to the world. Her hair was a tangled mess, but otherwise she seemed unmarked and remarkably the same.

"Terry?" he said gently to her. "You understand me? If you do, nod your head up and down."

Terry. He acted as if he knew her, but the name was unfamiliar. Well, she didn't have one, so maybe that was as good as any. She nodded and felt his glow of joy at actually communicating with her.

"Do you know who I am?"

She looked blankly at the colorful dragonlike creature. Know him? Should she?

"It's Gus, Terry. Gus. Do you remember me? Remember me at all? Even like this? Shake your head up and down for yes, back and forth for no, like this." He demonstrated as best he could.

She thought it looked funny but shook her head no.

"Well, I remember you," he told her, and in his head she could see a lot of images, memories, right at the surface, where she could look at them. Memories of her wearing stupid clothes and working all sorts of strange stuff and in a whole lot of places she'd never seen before. It was like being a character in a story. It was fascinating but bore no relationship to reality at all. The only thing it said to her was, *I was smart once.* That was good to know. Maybe she could get smart again someday. The doctor had almost said as much, although without a lot of conviction that it would happen.

The visions of her doing incomprehensible things in settings totally unfamiliar soon bored her, but something else was interesting, too. It was the creature's vision of himself at these places; he seemed to be of the same kind as she and the other down below. A tall, thin man with a very pale skin and yellowish hair. It confused her. For some reason this person thought of himself as that other one as well as what he was now. He couldn't be both, could he? It was all too mixed up. Like the rest, it was just something she wasn't smart enough to figure out, she guessed.

Still, she had an unmistakable feeling that the creature was important. He wasn't trying to fool her or anything like that; in fact, he seemed to be totally open to her. He *had* known her before she had lost her memory, and he definitely had genuine affection for her from that period. The trouble was, she wasn't that person anymore, even if she wanted to be. It was as if that person were gone, dead, and somebody new had set up shop in the old body, somebody not nearly as smart. She certainly would trust this Gus, but could Gus ever see her as who she was now and not as who she might have been in some past life?

There was little more that either of them could say to one another beyond what had been done. For Gus's part, he began to understand that Terry had changed again, from the mysterious girl of great power to this very childlike creature who didn't even remember the *second* incarnation. This wasn't going to be easy, but at least now he had a little bit of purpose to his life. She sure needed *somebody* right now, and he was the only one she had.

• • •

Glathrielians were in the medical references at all only because of the work of some Ambrezan physicians and anthropologists, but the information was about as complete on the physiological side as it was for most other races and certainly more than adequate. In high-tech Agon, with a diagnostic computer set up and armed with all those data, it was relatively easy to do a thorough checkup on both patients.

"By all rights Brazil should be dead," the doctor told them. "In fact, after going through these data, I'm almost inclined to believe your stories about the mythological god. Virtually every rib is either cracked or broken. One punctured the right lung and caused massive internal bleeding. Several of his organs are in horrible shape, too, and he has lesions in the brain in areas that might well control motor development. As far as I can see, he's been going on sheer will to live. The aggregate of these injuries is enough to kill just about anything carbon-based, but in all cases there is something like a one in a million chance that it might not be fatal. I swear that instant death versus horrible injury was a matter of microns one way or another in a few instances. A surgical team has been on the case since he was brought in, and they're now working on him."

"What you are saying is that he will survive," the colonel noted.

"What I am saying is that he should not have survived and that there are very poor odds that he will survive this massive level of surgery. Synthesizing that quantity of blood alone was a monstrous job, and I have no doubt they will use all of it. If he *does* survive, well, there is no way to know what areas of the brain are affected, but there will almost certainly be some serious problems. In addition, there is major damage to the spinal cord which is *perhaps* reparable over a very long time, when he can stand the additional work, and assuming that it is similar to other spinal cord injuries in the races that have similar torsos. Then again, that is never an exact science. The odds are great that he's going to remain in a coma, which will make him your ward and no longer our problem. If he *does* come out, then he will probably be unable to move much of anything below the neck. They tell me that they can do nothing on the spinal cord injury at this time. They have to do the other repairs first, and it is best if he cannot move anything down there, even involuntarily. The problem is, the longer the spinal cord is left untreated, the less likely it is to respond to treatment. I believe that at best, you will have a being who is totally bedridden and will never be able to move anything beyond his head again. That's the best estimate."

The colonel thought it over. "Oddly enough, if that were true, it might be a very convenient result. He could be questioned but would hardly be a threat. On the other hand, we have information that leads us to believe that he is capable of regeneration, perhaps total, over a long period of time. If he is the man of the legends, then that is what will happen, but it is still a result that my superiors will not find too terrible. It buys time, a lot of it, and no matter what, leaves him in our official custody."

The doctor shrugged. "Suit yourself. Sounds grotesque to me, but considering that he *is* still alive after all that, I begin to think that I can believe anything about him. What I *cannot* believe is that he is going to get up and walk out of here, or even crawl out of here, in the next year or two, if ever."

"A year might be most satisfactory if one remaining complication can be resolved," the Leeming told her. "Unfortunate that he might remain comatose, though. If we cannot resolve our problem, we might have to deal with him much quicker."

"You never can tell for sure, but I wouldn't bet on any conversations," the doctor told him. "Whatever your complication is, you better resolve it."

"What about the girl?" Gus asked her. "Did you run all the tests on her, too?"

"We did. She's in remarkably good physical shape, all

things considered. *Mentally* I'm not so sure. From what we were able to get from the Ambrezans through Zone, we have a theory but only a theory. That is one strange race there in Glathriel."

"Yes?"

"We think she probably woke up in Ambreza near the border and, after seeing what she could only perceive as monsters, made a run into Glathriel. There they've developed some kind of deliberately primitive society that shuns all artifacts, machines, tools, whatever. That doesn't mean they are savages, though. Like some other races here, they went in the other direction, developing powers of the mind, realizing what might be just a slight potential in most of them, developing and honing it."

"Back on Earth I've seen men walk barefoot over red hot coals and suspend themselves on sharp nails," Gus told her. "And I've seen a lot of other strange stuff, too. Is that what you mean? They went strictly that way?"

"Well, I think it's a lot deeper than those types of things, but you get the idea. Ambrezan anthropologists believe that the Glathrielians have developed something of a group mind, a sort of insectlike social and mental organization without any hierarchy in which all of them are connected to one another. They convert their body fat into energy that can be used for things far beyond mere physical work. I think you've seen examples of that in her."

Gus nodded.

The colonel gave a mock clearing of his nonexistent throat. "I believe I shall go file my report. We have no interest in the girl, so I will leave her fate entirely in friend Gus's hands." And with that, the Leeming oozed out of the hospital lounge.

"You were saying they used fat to do things with their mind?" Gus prompted the doctor.

"Yes. Fascinating, really. Still, it's only the background here. What is really the point is that she walked straight into a place where the people were *organically* the same as she was but mentally and socially were far more alien to her than physically different races. She had no foreknowledge and no defenses. They co-opted her into their mental net. She would have seen it as an offer of friendship, security in her most vulnerable moment. She didn't resist, almost certainly expecting communication. She got far more. We think they literally rewired her brain. Not organically but electrically. The memories were still there, but they were no longer relevant or needed because the whole frame of reference was different. We can't say why, when she saw Brazil, she latched on to him with such tenacity, but we can guess that she knew he was someone from her old world and she wanted out. The problem was, she'd been rewired. She could leave, but she couldn't rewire herself. That would take the collective knowledge and power of a pretty large Glathrielian group. That meant she was suspended, neither here nor there. In our world she thought like and acted like one of them. But in their world she couldn't completely wipe away a lifetime of experience, memory, personality, and ambition to assimilate."

Gus nodded sadly. "Poor Terry. She deserved better."

"Then we get to the situation where you were present. She reached out somehow, using what must have been instinctive Glathrielian mental methods, and hooked into Captain Brazil's brain. Again, this is on an energy level, not physically. It was probably out of fear he might abandon her, but the link, once established, worked both ways. He gained access to some of her powers, and she gained a connection that might as well have been steel chains. With only the two of them, stuck for weeks on that island, more in her element than his, it's difficult to say what happened or if anything did, but it might have. Then came the eruption, probably a terrified leap into the sea and an attempt to get away, the big explosion, and, in the course of it, Brazil was seriously, horribly injured. The link between them, something like a telepathic bond, would have carried through to her as well. The shocks and his own physical and mental trauma, combined with what must have been sheer terror for her, overloaded her system. Linked to his more 'normal' wiring, going through all that with her Glathrielian wiring, the shock loosened and perhaps destroyed the careful patterns they'd built inside her. We think—and this is mere theory and probably can never be any more than that—the patterns were wiped out, as if the whole brain were flooded with a massive electrical charge. The Glathrielian powers, which are there now not because of wiring but because they'd been used so much, probably saved her life."

"I'm followin' about a tenth of this," Gus told her. "What is the bottom line?"

"Sorry. It's just such a fascinating study that I tend to run away with myself. The bottom line is that we haven't any 'normal' Glathrielian or Earth-type patterns for comparison— Brazil is hardly a good sample right now—but there are a dozen or more races here that share similar brain and nervous system structures with the Glathrielian physiology. More important, they share a lot of commonalities, so we can compare and at least build a *theoretical* model of what a Glathrielian brain pattern should look like and how it works. Your bottom line is that whatever was there was erased by the shock, and her brain then rebuilt what it could based on what it had left—the link with Brazil. We've tried all sorts of tests, always reliable on those others. Her memory isn't blocked by shock or brain damage—it's gone. The Glathrielian protective powers she had were constructed to be autonomic—automatic like a heartbeat. Those remained. So did the other basic autonomic systems. The rest? A simple vocabulary based on what little snippets of information were stored in areas closest to where memories are combined into thoughts—possibly her thoughts, possibly his. This has built up to more complex thinking by what she's able to get from the surface-level thoughts of others so long as those thoughts create holographic images in the thinker's mind. If you were to think of an image called 'boat,' for example, she knows what a boat is. I do not, however, see any real evidence of abstract thinking or much chance for it."

"Huh?"

"It's linear thinking, like we do, which means the pattern probably came from him," the doctor went on. "But it is very limited thinking, very limited processing of information. She has no patience and little interest in learning most things. If she decides she wants to learn something but doesn't get it quickly, she loses interest. She's entirely in the present; she has no concept of the future or any interest in it. She can be thrown a ball and is just as amused if she catches it or watches it drop and bounce. She learned to push down on latches aboard ship to open hatches but never could get the idea of closing them behind her, and she's been frustrated here because she's been trying to push down on doorknobs to open doors and it doesn't work. The woman you knew is gone. Accept that. What you have is a young child in her body. And there is no way of knowing at this stage if she will progress beyond where she is in more than very small degrees."

Gus felt the hurt of losing someone very close, but it wasn't quite like that. "Tell me straight, Doc. Can you say for absolute certain, beyond the shadow of any doubts, that Terry will never regain any of her memory? That it's a dead-on medical certainty that she'll be like this until she dies?"

The doctor considered her words carefully. "No, I can't. Not with absolute certainty. It is not like we've ever had a case like hers before or know exactly what we are dealing with. Not even the consulting Ambrezans really understand what's inside the Glathrielian mind. All I can say is, absent any evidence of physical trauma, it is a *very* remote possibility that much of anything would come back. And if anything were still there, it would come back in pieces, over a very long period of time."

"But it's possible? As possible, say, as Captain Brazil surviving all those wounds?"

"Well, yes, but—"

"She's tied to him, Doc. You said so. Maybe some of that immunity rubbed off as well. If I just send her back now, it's over, period. She can never come back. The door's closed forever. See, I just can't write her off yet, send her back to what is a certain life as part of a group mind living in the mud. She was so much more than that."

"But what else can you do?"

"Well, what are my options here?"

"Not many. She can't stay here. The law says that any-one likely to be a ward of the state must be returned to its native hex. Of course, she is free to go anywhere she likes as well, but I still feel that this is the best course to take. The Glathrielians could probably restore her to their state, but unencumbered by the baggage she brought in the first time. She'd live what for them would be a nor-mal life."

"Not yet, Doc. When I'm convinced, but not yet. There's still some options open, no matter how wild the odds. If nothin' else, I want to see what happens if Brazil wakes up."

The doctor sighed. "Well, as I said, I will get religion and go study the ancient gods if *he* recovers, let alone walks. But there's another reason for possibly sending her back. Perhaps a compelling one. It explains the other major mystery—why the Well preserved her pretty much as she was instead of translating her into another race as it did with you."

"Yeah?"

"She's pregnant, Gus. According to the Ambrezan material, about six weeks from normal full gestation. Counting back, that means she was pregnant when she came onto the Well World and almost certainly not much before that point."

"Oh, my God!"

"It's in the records, although extremely rare even in ancient times, it seems. The Well has no trouble taking one race and making of it another, but when you complicate it, give it what it perceived in its analysis as two in one, it didn't have an answer for that. So it pretty much optimized her for survival here but otherwise left her just as she was. She is going to have a baby, Gus, and she doesn't even know what a baby is or how it's made."

Gus sighed. "Jeez! *Now* what do I do?" If he sent her back, she'd probably be okay, but he'd be dooming forever any chance she might have to recover normalcy. But if he didn't, then what of the baby?

"Well, you heard the colonel. I'm afraid that since she isn't capable of deciding for herself, it's entirely up to you."

"We have exciting news," the colonel told Gus. "We have a real lead on the other one, this Mavra Chang. She is in the hands of an international drug ring whose headquarters are on the northern border of this very hex. A fair amount of money and death have gone into protecting them until now, but this changes just about everything, as you might suppose. The more things are different, the more they seem like home. Is it not so?"

"You should know," Gus muttered.

The colonel ignored the sarcasm. "Well, they are going to attack their headquarters in utmost secrecy, led by one of the few really honest policemen in Agon. With Brazil safely incapacitated, I am going north this very day to be in on this other operation. After all, if we have Brazil but not Chang and Chang can also access the well, then we have gained nothing. Still, I feel we are closing in and that this matter is about to come to a head. There are others from Earth in this raiding party as well, so it will be pleasant to have yet more of a connection with the old home. What do *you* wish to do, my friend?"

"Others? Anybody I know?"

"I don't think so. Someone *I* knew, at least for a little while, and two associates of Captain Brazil's who came in on his initiative, I believe, from Rio de Janeiro. One is a fellow countryman of mine—in the old life, that is. Two Dillians—

they are much like the centaurs of our ancient Earth mythology, I am told—and one Erdomite."

Gus sighed and shook his head. "I don't know. Much as I'd like to, the only person I *really* know well is right here, aside from you and the captain, anyway, and I'm just not too sure what to do with her yet."

"Someone I believe you may know *is* involved, after all," Lunderman commented, looking over reports. "Do you know a Juan Campos?"

Gus's reptilian head shot up, and the eyes blazed with a menace not seen before. "Yeah, I know the bastard! If it wasn't for him, none of us would be *in* this damned fix! He's in this group, too? Don't sound like his style."

"You misunderstand me, my friend. Campos is with the drug cartel. In fact, it might well be Campos who had Mavra Chang abducted."

That menace in the eyes didn't fade. "Same old Campos, then. He was dirty back home, and he's *still* dirty. Guess he just don't know any other trade. Figures. What'd *he* wind up as?"

"A Cloptan. They look something like cartoon ducks, but there is nothing funny about them or cartoonish, either." He paused a moment. "A Cloptan *female*! Most interesting!"

"He's a *girl*?" Gus found it impossible not to laugh, although a Dahir chuckle sounded far more threatening than amusing. "Well, at least he got *some* justice, the bastard. He won't be raping any more helpless women."

"Perhaps not, but Cloptan society isn't as traditional as most. Women have some real power there, in the government and in the rackets, too, it seems. I would say that whatever was done to him was compensated for by the society in which he found himself. He's come a rather long way to be influential in such an operation so quickly. Campos is the sort to have a deadly grudge against this Mavra Chang?"

"Yeah, he would, at least in his own mind. I was sick or drugged for most of it, but I remember enough, so I'm pretty sure he does, too. I want in on this one, Colonel. I want to see Campos squashed like the bug he is."

"I had hoped that you would say that. I should like to bring the girl along as well. Protected, of course, and well out of the action, but even if she can be of little help, the detective in charge says that he would like her up there."

"Huh? I hadn't really considered it much. Of course, I guess if I'm not gonna just send her back to that Glathriel forever, at least not yet, she has to stick with me. She trusts me pretty good, but—I dunno. I guess she could be sent back by *any* Zone Gate, so there's no real rush in that regard, but I'm not sure I want to get her exposed and active too much right now. Why would this drug agent want Terry?"

"He does not say. The only way to know is to go up there and ask him. But why do you have such concern over the girl now? She has certainly managed to take care of herself with minimal help so far, and even if she has lost her memory, she still has her unique abilities."

"Damn it, Colonel, she's gonna have a baby in like a month and a half. That's why. What if she goes into labor? What if she gets stressed or even accidentally hurt and the kid gets killed? *She's* no immortal."

The colonel thought a moment. "That *does* complicate things, I do agree. And yet Agon, and Clopta if we have to go there, are both high-tech hexes, and I believe she would probably be as safe as or safer in one of them than she would be back in that primitive no-tech homeland. You've seen the medicine available here already."

The colonel knew that Gus was only easing his conscience, that he very much wanted both to go and to keep the girl with him, pregnant or not. Gus would *have* to face the birth sooner or later anyway; it seemed pretty obvious he wasn't going to send her back to what was tantamount to oblivion forever. Somehow, deep down, it was obvious that Gus still clung to the belief that Terry, his old Terry, might well be down there someplace, buried deep inside that girl's head. Until he was absolutely convinced that this person was forever but a memory, if he ever was, he would cling to her out of honor, out of friendship, and because it was the only thing that kept the Dahir himself going.

There was, of course, no purpose in telling Gus at that point that what the Agonite cop wanted her for was bait.

SUBAR,
NEAR THE LILIBLOD BORDER

She knew Gus was troubled by something, something con-
cerning her, but she couldn't, or wouldn't, dig down to find
out why. It just wouldn't be *right* somehow, and besides, she
might not understand it, anyway.

She liked Gus a lot. She trusted him absolutely, maybe the
only one she'd met so far that she could say that about. Oh,
she trusted that nice doctor, too, but the doctor was way, way
too smart for her to really feel comfortable with. It was nice
being able to actually talk to somebody, but most of the time
she couldn't follow what the doc was saying, so it wasn't that
big a deal. Deep down she was just an interesting patient to
the doctor, but Gus really *cared* about her, although why he
did was still a mystery to her.

She had come to terms with the fact that most of the world
was and would remain a mystery to her; most everybody
seemed a lot smarter than she was, and after a while she realized that would be the way things were and accepted it. It
wasn't as if she had anywhere she wanted to go or anything
she wanted to do.

It would have been easier on Gus if she could speak, but
the doctor thought that the Glathrielian business had done
something to the area of the brain that controlled vocaliza-

tion. She could make some sounds, but they were just sounds, not words. This was something else that might or might not reconnect, depending on how she developed from this point. Because she *could* understand others, or *most* others—there were some creatures that seemed a total blank to her but not many—Gus had worked out what was still a simple sign language for her. It was okay for the obvious basics, but it would hardly serve as an alternative language.

Gus finally decided he had to tell her the situation, no matter how much she might or might not understand. The concept of pregnancy proved less difficult than he imagined; some mental pictures, along with a simple child's version of how it worked, seemed to get the message across.

She was fascinated by that. A little person growing inside her that would someday pop out and then grow up to be a *big* person. It made sense and answered a few questions she'd had about how all these people got there and why some were small and some were large, but she never wondered about how one got that way.

"Now that you know," Gus told her as gently and simply as he could, "you will have to be careful. Things could hurt you, or the baby, or both. You could go back to the people who are like you and be safe, or you can stay here. But if you stay here, there is a chance you or the baby could be hurt. You understand that?"

She nodded. She had picked up graphic images of what her people were like from Gus, the doctor, and others, and she didn't think she would like that life. Gus couldn't come, and she knew from his mind that if she went back, she couldn't talk to or hear anybody else but her own kind. She didn't like that idea at all. Not only did she want to stay with Gus, Gus's own thoughts about the way her people lived came through as something scary. She let him know that she understood he was worried about her and the baby and that he didn't want her to go.

It didn't ease his conscience, but it helped him go with the flow of events and accept that, risks or not, she was staying. He had the distinct idea that no matter what the colonel had said, they wanted her for something and wouldn't let her go in any event. He didn't want to be conned by these types; he knew them all too well. If she was going to be put in harm's way, then he was going to be there for her.

That afternoon they met the colonel at a sleek, silvery transport station and boarded a magnatrain for the north. She found the station itself to be a place of wonder, and the train was really neat.

"I spoke to Inspector Kurdon before we left," the colonel told Gus. "He seems quite happy to have us, and he's particularly interested in you. He thinks your little talent might well be very useful to him."

"Maybe, maybe not," Gus responded. "It's handy, yeah, but it's not as much as it seems to other people. If they have the equivalent of a television scanner, I'd show up on it, and I'll trip any alarms. This place has got to be guarded like Fort Knox. It's not like I can just walk in there and do what I want."

"Agreed. But I'm sure he has something in mind and knows all that. Well, we'll see this evening, won't we?"

They pulled into the northern terminus station at Subar about an hour after dark. The welcoming committee wasn't that hard to spot. Two Dillians and an Erdomese female stood out from the Agonite crowd as much as or more than they did.

"Oh, my! There's only that gruesome blob and that poor girl!" Anne Marie exclaimed. "I thought there was another!"

Julian looked at the Leeming oozing off the train and frowned. "I see that Colonel Lunderman hasn't changed a bit. It's just that you can see him so much more clearly now," she commented dryly.

"Greetings, my fellow expatriates, greetings!" the colonel said with his usual oily tones. Gus had wondered if Lunderman could say "Good morning" without sounding insincere. "I am Colonel Lunderman, and we might as well get the usual shock over with right off the bat. Say hello, Gus."

All three of the others were somewhat startled when the Dahir did just that. To have a huge dragonlike multicolored creature suddenly appear where one hadn't really noticed it before was always startling.

"Strictly defense," Gus assured them. "We're too big and bright to hide, so we have this ability. You'll get used to it. I can't turn it off."

Julian recovered first. "Whew! That's *some* trick! Could have saved us a lot of trouble if *we'd* had something like that!" She looked over at the colonel. "You've come a long way since we last met, Lunderman."

"And changed a good deal. I would not have known you at all, Captain Beard." While forewarned, the colonel in fact was amazed at the transformation in the person he'd known. In voice, tone, movements, manner—in virtually every category there wasn't a trace of the Julian Beard he remembered in the Erdomese female he addressed.

"Julian, Colonel. Just Julian," she responded, grim-faced. "Captain Beard is dead, or as good as dead. Think of me entirely as you see me. I have buried him forever." *Too bad the same didn't happen to you,* she added to herself. If she'd despised the human colonel, she positively loathed what she was seeing now. Gus, too, made her feel very uncomfortable. He was *creepy*. She turned to the third, silent member of the party and softened immediately. "And this must be Terry."

Terry smiled at her, capturing the sudden warmth inside the Erdomese. She was *very* pretty and seemed smart and strong, too. Terry couldn't figure out why Gus wouldn't produce the same friendly feeling, but it wasn't anything she could do much about right now.

The four-legged blond twins were also beautiful but not easy to catch thoughts from. Their thinking seemed to go back and forth between one and the other so that it was almost as if they were the same person in two bodies. Trying to follow it made her head hurt, and she turned back to Julian.

"Come," Julian told them all, even though her attention seemed to be drawn more and more to Terry. "This is not the place to speak of things. You never know who or what's around. Let's get to the people running the show, and then we can all fill each other in on everything."

Gus looked around the station with the experienced eye of a professional cameraman. It wasn't very crowded, and all the Agonese looked the same anyway except for size and dress, but he could spot the shadows and the tails. They had a way of not looking at a person and not being even curious about that person that made them stand out to a professional's eye in the same way they did in a crowd back on Earth. He wondered which were from the cops and which were from the bad guys, but there was no way to tell that. The breed was made in the same factory.

Inspector Kurdon proved to be another of the same type, but very dry and very professional. He greeted them almost perfunctorily, and Terry couldn't help but feel that he, too, had more of an interest in her than in the others for some reason, although there was no sense from him of the friendly, warm interest radiated by Julian.

"I know you all want to compare notes, so I won't keep you long," he told them. "My people will be able to provide appropriate if not very exciting meals for all of you. I'm not going to tell you to get an early rest because the later you go to sleep and the later you wake up tomorrow, the better. We are going in tomorrow night, but not until nearly midnight. Surprise will be very important to this operation."

"Surprise? With all these people and all this security you think you really fooled 'em, Inspector?" Gus asked him.

Kurdon looked at Gus with a bit more respect. "You are absolutely right in that sense. We can hardly hide the fact that something is up here, but our intelligence assures me that they still can't figure out what it is. My advantage is that they really believe the headquarters to be both politically and physically secure. Even if they *think* that we're moving against them, it doesn't mean as much as you might believe. First of all, we are not after drugs or even criminals of any sort. We're after their computer records, which are not easily transportable."

"Won't they just erase them the moment your people break in?" the colonel asked.

"Maybe, but they have no equivalent to this headquarters anywhere else. I'm sure they have backups, but they aren't linked because such a link can't be run through other hexes and they can't be stored here and be totally secure from us. Putting this headquarters out of operation will severely cripple their entire operation worldwide. It might be months, more likely years, before they get things running with any degree of efficiency again, and not without great cost in the interim. A lot of other hexes, not to mention the Patrol, have been wanting to move on this, but they couldn't so long as Agon and Liliblod allowed this center to continue. If it's destroyed, they will move, and the politicians in their pockets will scramble to be on our side all of a sudden. For that reason, I believe they will try *not* to erase the active records but rather depend on their own security to keep us from getting to the information. Then, when it blows over, they could have their own people mixed in with our crews and download and recover what they need. That is not going to happen. I believe we *can* crack their codes, but whether we can or not, the computers there and all their data will be either in our hands or completely destroyed."

"You sound pretty confident you can get it," Julian noted with skepticism dripping from her tongue. "What if you can't?"

"The drug business is the inspector's problem," the colonel told her. "*Our* interest is quite different. Some suitable prisoners, people who work there routinely day in and day out, should be what *we* need, although getting access to the records would make it simpler and surer. If our quarry is in there, we will have her. If not, we need to know where she might have been taken."

"If they don't just kill her when you break in," Gus put in.

"If they can kill her, she's not who we are interested in," the colonel responded coolly. "However, I have already seen enough evidence on my own to suspect that this is not a problem."

"Yes, but *Lori* isn't some superman!" Tony pointed out. "We could be killing *him*!"

Kurdon looked up impatiently at the Dillian. "We have been through this already. Everything we know suggests that if we cannot free him, he's probably better off dead. He is certainly addicted to a particular mutation of this drug in any event, which will cause enough of a problem. I am open to any suggestions on making it safe, but so far I've heard none. Until I do, this matter is closed. Now, if you will excuse me, I still have a lot of preparation to do. If there are no further questions, you should go and get acquainted and eat and finally sleep."

"Just one question," Gus said. "How you gonna get *in* there?"

The impassive turtlelike head looked straight at him. "Come tomorrow night and you'll see."

As Kurdon expected, the rest of the evening was much more relaxed, with a great deal of talking and comparing stories and experiences. For the first time Gus heard the account of the kidnapping of Lori and Mavra Chang and got a picture of the latter totally at odds with any memories he had of her back in the jungles. In fact, the Mavra Chang who emerged from the descriptions and tales of the twins and from Julian sounded to Gus an awful lot like a female version of Nathan Brazil. This at first glance seemed to make even more mysterious their estrangement from one another, but, Gus thought, often the pairs that seemed to work best together were ones one would never put together on one's own. A ship with two equally strong-willed captains was a ship that sailed forever in circles.

The colonel was something of the odd man out in the circle. There was something about him that made everybody who met him feel slightly uncomfortable, and aside from some reminiscences with Tony of their shared homeland in their original native Portuguese, the colonel did not participate all that much. He excused himself early, but the rest of them went on talking well into the night.

Terry liked almost everybody except the colonel. Somehow this group of very strange-looking creatures seemed very comfortable, very natural. It was something in the way they thought and interacted; no matter how alien they now were physically from one another, they were more alike in the way they thought than any of the other creatures she'd met, including the doctor. It was a familiar, relaxed feeling that was hard to describe, but it was comfortable to her. Somehow, in a way she didn't quite get, she knew that all these people were *her* people, the same way she'd felt about Gus from the start. She didn't really try to follow much of their conversation; it was kind of dull, and a lot of it made no sense to her. They seemed to be able to talk and talk and talk on the same topic over and over without getting bored, but it didn't matter. The underlying din felt like a warm, safe blanket, a haven from the unknown and truly alien world out there.

Finally, when it was quite late, they couldn't keep it up any longer. Gus told them that he would find a place suitable for himself and not to worry; Terry was physically best suited for Julian's tent, which had that floor of soft pillows.

Gus couldn't make Julian out at first. She'd been a guy, Mister Military Recruiting Poster, then was turned into a woman in a society that did not value females, had been rescued from it by Lori, and now, with Lori gone, seemed like a strong but dedicated man hater. It was almost as if she'd literally hated, disowned, and, as she'd told the colonel at the station, killed off every trace of who and what she'd been back on Earth. After hearing the colonel's description of the old Captain Beard on the train coming north, he hadn't expected this at all. In a very different way, Julian had reinvented herself as thoroughly as Terry had.

Terry, stay with Julian. I'll be nearby, he thought in the girl's direction. *She doesn't like men much, so if you see me inside and she can't, just pretend I'm not there. Okay?*

Terry seemed a bit confused but nodded.

The inside of Julian's tent was a veritable Art Deco wonderland of colors and exotic perfume scents, and it even had a full-length mirror tall enough for the Erdomite to see her whole self in. Terry found the whole thing a little dizzying and the scents a bit overpowering, but she got used to them after a while. It was the mirror that fascinated her the most, though.

She'd seen her reflection before, but never her whole body at once, and it fascinated her. She was still not used to that face staring back at her. The thing was, she had no comparison with what she was *supposed* to look like except Gus's mental images of the old Terry, and while she could see her in the reflection, it wasn't anywhere near the same. Chubby, bigger thighs, bigger ass, bigger breasts, and there, the tummy that kind of stuck out and didn't look like the rest. *That's where the baby is growing,* she thought, more in wonder than anything else. She felt it, much like a hard lump inside her, and every once in a while, when lying around or sitting, she felt it move.

Julian watched her for a little while, then came over. "I was told you're going to have a baby. You shouldn't be anywhere near here, let alone on this kind of trip. These men don't care about you or it. I was one of them once, and I know how they think. My husband was a woman once, but the Well World made her a man, and before long he started acting and thinking just like the rest of them." She sighed. "You're a fish out of water, just like me. You can't go home, and neither can I, even to our homes here. When this is over, I'm going hunting for a place for fish out of water. Maybe an island like the one you were stuck on, uninhabited. Maybe a little multiracial place where we could live our lives and just be ourselves without having to be what we're expected to be." She paused. "You just stick with me. I'll see they don't let you come to any harm."

Terry didn't think anybody meant her harm, but a place to just live and see the baby grow without all this other stuff sounded pretty nice.

Kurdon had his Agonite commanders there as well as the foreigners about three hours after sundown.

"All right, I've briefed the advance teams already, and some of this operation is already under way," he told them. "We've taken out every shadow and spy we can't control, so they're pretty well blind, and we're set up with the explosives, drills, and weapons in the forest above the headquarters complex. The raid is set for exactly midnight. At eleven fifty-eight the gang in the market will be out cold from gas being introduced there now, and a team will enter and cut all communications from the subbasement there to the headquarters. That will set off alarms, but at exactly midnight, only two minutes later, the charges and borers will start, and we will blow the main entrance, which is in Liliblod. This may cause a diplomatic problem later, and absolutely *no one*, and I mean that, is to cross the border. The charge should be enough to bring sufficient materials down on the entrance that it will be blocked. If by any chance it is not, we have sharpshooters just this side of the border to make certain nobody gets out from that end. The only emergency exits they have are into Agon, which will be easy to control since they're in line with the air exchangers. I want every unit in place behind the borers. Get in there as fast as possible. Stun or freeze anything that moves; kill anything you see that doesn't immediately surrender. Clear?"

The Agonese, mostly in black armored outfits with helmets and clear faceplates, nodded gravely.

Kurdon turned to the visitors. "There is no sense in risking the girl at this point. One of you should remain back here with her, and there will be a guard here in case there are any nasty surprises."

"I'll stay," Gus told him.

"No, not if you're willing to come at all," the inspector responded. "I need that cloaking of yours. The design is such that once we reach the main corridor of each level, we have to use it. Once the obvious resistance is taken out, you would be very useful in scouting ahead and spotting ambushes. Your background says you've been under fire before, which makes you even more valuable, since most of my men really haven't. That true?"

"Yeah, I guess so. If you really need me, I guess so." *Though if I'm gonna stick my neck out a mile, I wish to hell I had a camera and a network to send it to.*

"Julian, you can ignore a lot, but you have a personal objective in there, and if any of your old memories and reflexes remain at all, you've had real military training and experience. Am I wrong?"

"No," she admitted. "You're right. This is a little out of my line, though. I was an air officer." Julian was startled by the offer. She'd never even considered that Kurdon would want her anywhere but back in the rear. Now she found herself nicely trapped by her principles; if he was willing to trust a woman, she could hardly say no.

"You know when to duck and can anticipate how these men will move and how they'll operate, I think, and that's enough. For you it's all volunteer, though. Go or stay."

"I'll go," she told him. She didn't really relish this any more than did Gus, but it was do it or shut up about what she could or couldn't handle.

"Good. I can't armor somebody of your type, so you'll be in the rear of the formation, but I need your eyes, ears, any extra senses you have, and your experience. I'll outfit you with a small transmitter. Use the troops as a shield and move forward as they do." He turned to the Leeming.

"Colonel, as the other military man here, I'd like you up with the main corridor force as well," Kurdon said. "Remember, though, that you're vulnerable to energy weapons and there's no way I can armor *you*, either."

"We will do as we discussed," Lunderman replied. "I assure you I will be in no more danger than anyone else."

"I was in the same air force as the colonel," Tony pointed out. *Flying fat asses like him around with his cronies and equipment to make war on his own people,* he added to himself. "Dillians are also excellent shots."

"Well, maybe, but Dillians are also exceptionally huge targets," Kurdon responded. "If you want to come, okay, but you'll be in the rear. I'm not going to let you down there until things are secure enough that you have a chance to survive. Otherwise, you'll just be in the way. I may need you for interrogation or ID, though."

"Oh, dear! That doesn't leave very much for me, does it?" Anne Marie noted. "All right, then, I suppose I'm elected to remain back here with this poor child."

"You can monitor what's going on from the command post right here," Kurdon told her.

Anne Marie looked at Tony. "*Must* you go? I'm afraid I've gotten terribly used to you."

Tony smiled and kissed her. "Don't worry. As the inspector says, I'm going to be well out of range. But I *have* to go. You understand that, don't you?"

"No, but I accept it. Take care."

Gus turned to Terry, who clearly hadn't the faintest inkling of what the hell was going on. "You stay here. They want me and some of the others to go catch some very bad people and maybe save some very good friends. You can't come because you can't help and we might get hurt protecting you. Do you understand that?"

She frowned, then hesitantly nodded. She didn't like this at all, but if Gus said to stay, then she couldn't exactly argue. She suddenly realized that some of her new friends, maybe even Gus, could get hurt, though, and it scared her. He saw the somewhat sad, somewhat panicked look on her face.

"Don't worry. You'll be here with Anne Marie, and I won't let them hurt me. You have to believe that."

It would have been easier for her to believe it if she saw that Gus believed it, too.

"Where's the Dahir?" somebody asked, and Gus responded, "Here."

"Oh, that *is* kind of nerve-racking, isn't it?" one of the Agonese soldiers commented. "Wish I could do it, though, particularly now. Okay, any way to get this headpiece on you? It's pretty small and flexible. If you can, you'll be able to hear what we say and speak to us, even in a low tone. It will also be monitored here, so if anything goes wrong, a message can be relayed. Think you can handle it?"

"It's uncomfortable, but yes. Over the head and then below the snout on my neck. That will put the output mike right against the translator."

"Fair enough. You *have* done this before?"

"Yeah, but in another life and with a lot more equipment."

"Okay, people! Let's take a little walk in the woods!" Kurdon called to them all. "And keep it quiet, huh?"

Someone tried to hand Julian a rifle, but she refused, holding out a hand. "I'll make do with these," she told him. *I have to.*

It was a cloudy night, which helped conceal their movements but gave Tony some vision problems. Someone handed her an Agonese helmet, which was extremely loose on her and pinched her hair something awful in the back but which proved a little high-tech marvel. It probably would have been even more of one if it had been connected to the rest of the armor-plated suit, but the faceplate proved to have pretty good night vision abilities.

Basically nocturnal, Gus managed to keep position, and Julian needed no special gear, simply relying on infrared.

They walked for what seemed like a great distance through

increasingly thick woods and rolling terrain until at last they came upon a large unit already in place and surrounding what looked like a giant pencil the size of a small house on some kind of treads.

Kurdon went to the device, nodded to the technicians standing by it, and looked at his watch, then signaled for two of the technicians to move. They got up on the treads, pressed something, and a small room in the very rear of the thing was revealed. They got in, sat down, strapped in, threw some switches, and then the entry closed behind them. There was a dull whining sound from the device now, and Julian's eyes could see a sudden glow from not just the "point" of the pencil shape but from the tapered area as well.

"What *is* that thing?" she asked a soldier near her.

"Construction machine. It's used for tunnels on the railway, for reshaping rock formations, that kind of thing. There are only three of them in existence, and somehow he's got all three here tonight."

"You mean he's going to bore holes right into their roof? Can we follow? I mean, it's bound to be molten."

"It cools pretty quick. You have any feeling in those hooves?"

"No, not really."

"Then if we can go in with these boots, you can, too. Don't worry about it. We'll see that you make it."

The comment irritated her, but she stilled her tongue. No use pissing off somebody who was supposed to give her cover.

"Market is secure," Kurdon told them, the news coming through everybody's communicator at once. "Demolition team in place. Air exchange patrols check in by number."

They couldn't hear the responses, but apparently Kurdon was satisfied.

Nervous and scared, as he should be, Julian thought, *but he's having the time of his macho life. I bet he's dreamed of this moment.*

"Borer to full. Demolition team ready at my count. Ten . . . nine . . . eight . . . seven . . . six . . . five . . . four . . . three . . . two . . . one . . . *Now!*"

Just to the northeast of them a massive explosion sounded, shaking the very ground. Liliblod was a nontech hex; Julian had to wonder what the hell they'd found that would make that big a bang.

At the same moment the entire tapered part of the borer glowed red and then suddenly shot a blindingly hot white energy beam so powerful that Julian's eyes reflexively switched to day vision. It didn't matter. The whole forest was lit up, and nobody could watch that beam. Not far away, there were similar illuminations in the no longer dark wood.

Kurdon's plan was simple given the technology he had to work with. The first borer, almost on the border itself, would open up the main entrance to forces that could drop in and secure the hopefully trapped but panicked and confused denizens inside in one stroke. That done, they would move to secure all the security controls, taking command of them, then move a force back along the first level. The colonel would go in with this team.

The second borer, with Julian, would move in and secure the middle area, followed by a ground force larger than the other two. These would proceed in both directions, linking up with the first group on that end and the third group, with Gus, coming in the back and pressing forward. Once the first level was secure, they would use internal access if they could to go down; otherwise, portable borers would come in through the ceilings. The rear part of the second level was said to hold the cells; the forward part was the labs. Then the procedure would be repeated on the third and final level, where the computers, living quarters, and more cells were. *That* was the main objective and might possibly be the toughest—or the easiest. Few crooks bottled in so thoroughly liked to go out shooting; their chances were far better if they were taken prisoner. Or so it was theorized.

The borers cut off, and it was suddenly *too* dark once more, except for a dully glowing, perfectly symmetrical tunnel going down at an angle just where the borer had been pointed. The technicians moved the borer back on its treads; its job was done.

A small rectangular vehicle now moved up to the hole and, parked right in front of it, was opened by two soldiers. Water or something like it gushed out and down the tunnel, creating a cloud of steam that quickly cleared.

"Tunnels safe and coated," Kurdon reported to them. "Prepare to move in. Take it slow and easy. Don't slip. The angle's a good twenty degrees."

That worried Julian, with her hooves, but while the tunnel appeared perfectly round from a distance, up close it proved quite jagged and irregular inside. The first group had also strung a rope along each side and secured it, so there was a handhold to use if need be. She found it tough going but not impossible, and she was well in before it suddenly occurred to her that at the end of this thing there was bound to be one heck of a drop and there was no way she was going to be able to get down on a rope or temporary ladder.

It was eerie at the end, a dark hole filled with lots of lights—like dozens of flashlights waving around in a black cave—lots of echoing shouts, and the sound of both conventional gunfire and energy beams not too far off.

She brought herself as close to a sitting position as she could and was relieved when she saw an Agonese soldier on a ladder reaching up to grab her. They were remarkably strong for their size, she noted, accepting the offered hand and feeling not at all good that she had to do so.

There was the sound of muffled explosions both forward and in back of her. "Concussion grenades," a sergeant told her. "We're lobbing them in every doorway and opening we find. They'll knock most anything inside cold but don't do much damage."

She switched again to infrared and saw a well-organized

operation going on. It was also *some* headquarters for a criminal operation. The corridor seemed to be four or five meters high and carpeted, and the conventional lights from the soldiers' helmets revealed a place that looked less like a drug hideout and more like a luxury hotel.

"Entrance area secure. Lights coming on on level one only," Kurdon's voice came to them, and soon the whole ceiling flashed on, bathing them all in a soft but ample indirect light.

For the second time Julian had an ego-killing thought. *My God! What am I doing here? These people are more professional than I am!* If Kurdon had invited her along to prove a point, he was doing a damned good job.

She could still hear firing in back of them.

"We've moving out toward the back end with this squad, ma'am," the sergeant told her. "You can come, but watch it. As you can hear, this place is a lot bigger and more complicated than we thought."

She could only nod. "Shows you what you can do with unlimited money, doesn't it? Go on, I'll watch your back." *At least that's something I can do here,* she thought ruefully.

It wasn't until they had the lights back on that the officer in charge of the rear complex team called for Gus.

"These rooms go into rooms that go into rooms," the officer said in a mixture of wonder and disgust. "We can't be sure what's still in there. Just go ahead on your own and scout it. We can tell where you are by the transponder, so you won't get stunned or shot. Here's a pistol. You look like you can handle one. We need to find the location of a downward stairway as quickly as possible, so that's your objective."

Gus stared at the pistol but felt very uncertain about it. *I don't kill people; I take pictures of people killing people,* he thought, with a sense of unreality about it all. He didn't know if he *could* kill anybody.

But he still took the gun. It felt heavy and all wrong in his tiny, four-fingered hand, but he knew he could hold it and fire it. It was one of those Buck Rogers ray guns; no problems with recoil or ammo, at least so long as the battery held out.

He was appalled at the size and scope of the place. *Jeez! Don Francisco Campos was a two-bit piker, wasn't he? This place is the fuckin' Maui Hilton! Wonder where the swimming pool and saunas are.* He wondered how Juan Campos managed to fit into this kind of setup. For crime, this was strictly first-class, and classy to boot.

He was careful not to enter any of the rooms until after they'd tossed in the stun bombs. It was quickly clear, though, that the complex went off in both directions for some distance, and just tossing those things in the first room in a series of rooms didn't get too many people. Oh, there were a couple lying about in the first room he entered, but the others either stayed back out of that exposed area or came in after the blast, when the soldiers would feel safe.

Damn if some of 'em *didn't* look like real live Donald Ducks. Not too funny-looking, though; some of 'em looked real tough. Even so, there was a veritable United Nations of the Well World represented here. Gooey things and mean-looking suckers and women with goat heads and humongous breasts and a walking toadstool or two, not to mention a couple of two-legged alligators wearing pants and the biggest damned frogs he had ever seen.

He went from room to room to room, cataloging what he saw in low tones and warning the squad if any of the critters emerged with weapons in hand or lay in wait. He reckoned he was saving a number of lives, and that made him feel good, if not any less scared to death. With *this* big a zoo, there was no telling if he'd run into one or another creature that might not have a problem seeing Dahirs.

Finally, in one rear room that looked like a luxury suite at the Waldorf except for the fact that it was clearly built for some large humanoids with bull heads and horns and some of their cowlike girlfriends, whose unconscious forms he'd passed two rooms earlier, he found the jackpot. This was clearly a visitor's suite, and visitors could easily get lost in a place like this.

He couldn't read it, but it sure as hell looked like a map of the whole place.

Welcome to the Drug Lord Ritz, he thought with some amazement. *Man!* Had they ever been cocky and arrogant!

He made his way carefully back out to the main corridor and hunted for the officer. "Got something that will make life a lot easier if you can read it," he told the startled Agonite.

The officer looked at the maps, and his reptilian jaw opened in amazement. "I should say you did!" He looked at the first level map, then the second, then looked up and pointed. "Nine more doors up. Emergency stairs."

"I'm surprised they don't have elevators," Gus commented, still amazed at the place.

"They do, but they don't have power now. Besides, do *you* want to be in the first car when the door opens?"

"You got a point there."

"As soon as we do a linkup and get a first level secured, we go down. I'll radio command and control where the other access stairs are."

"How are we doin' so far?"

"Well, we knocked out about a third of 'em. The rest so far have been equally divided between giving up and fighting it out. We hope it'll be easier below, since they know they don't have a way out if we get down there, but you never know. A lot of their security people will be down there, and the bosses probably kept their loyalty with drugs. When an addict is faced with losing his drugs or is charged up on them, who knows?"

"Yeah. Thanks for the optimism," Gus commented dryly.

As expected, they had captured a huge number of the staff trying to flee out of the main entrance into Liliblod. The explosion hadn't completely sealed things off—there were more entrances and exits than they had thought—but it had trapped enough.

The colonel had come in with the first wave but didn't stay for the wrap-up. Instead, he pressed himself against the wall and slowly and carefully oozed up it to the ceiling, then began a slow but steady flow back toward the middle group well ahead of the commandos. A Zhonzhorpian with an energy beam rifle emerged from a doorway beneath the suspended Leeming, huge crocodilelike jaws open and dripping saliva, eyes blazing mad.

A pseudopod shot out and struck the gunman on his head. He dropped the rifle and roared in pain, clutching at his head, but his hands went into thick goo and seemed to be stuck there. With slow deliberation, Lunderman flowed down and around the man and engulfed him. He remained like that for a short while. There was a sort of hissing sound as if something were being dissolved in acid, and then a larger Lunderman reached up and flowed back onto the ceiling area. There was no trace of the very large gunman who had been there except his rifle, still lying where he'd dropped it. A few moments later various metallic and plastic pieces fell from the ceiling to join it as the Leeming rejected what could not be digested.

Far from being satiated, Lunderman was instead irritated. There was a limit to how many of this size he could absorb without going dormant and dividing, and this bubble-brained idiot had known nothing of importance.

Worse, Lunderman had no idea what his limit was. He hadn't ever eaten more than one a week until now, and that had been sufficient. Even dissolved, the additional mass of one was significant if not any sort of handicap. Judging from the added mass of this one, the upper limit might well be no more than five or six. If he doubled his size, he could not stop the process.

It was unlikely that there would be many of the cartel on this level who had any information except by sheer chance, anyway. He began to search for a way down. Best to find it quickly, anyway, lest some nervous soldiers spot him and not recognize him as a friend.

As he heard the concussion grenades going off not far in front of him and just as the lights came on, he found it. Some sort of service elevator, he decided, linking the upper rooms with perhaps the kitchen or even the labs. It didn't matter. The door was easy enough to dissolve with the extra energy he'd absorbed, and to his great relief the car was down at the bottom. He flowed along the tiny, meter-square shaft until he reached the second level. The automatic trip on the door was obvious from this side; he didn't have to burn through it to open it.

On the other side was a small room that possibly served as a crew lunch room or break station. Nothing special, and expected. It was deserted, and he moved to the door, listened carefully, but saw no crack or opening where he might extend a pseudopod to scout what was beyond. He flowed back up to the ceiling, reached down, and used the manual grip to push the door open slowly.

The room beyond was lit by recessed emergency lighting, giving it a dull orange glow. It was a big place and looked very much like a state-of-the-art, high-tech lab, which it was. There didn't seem to be anybody there, although some things were still cooking and bubbling away.

It *still* wasn't what he needed, but it was one step closer. Below this, if he could find another easy way down, would be the master computer room.

There was no way Tony could get down one of those tunnels, something Kurdon surely had known when he had agreed to allow the centaur to come along. Now she stood just inside the border, staring out into dark Liliblod.

"Damn! They say there's like *three* entrances out!" one of the soldiers commented. "We got the main one, but the other two are beyond our reach by this point. They say the complex is bigger than an office building! Crime sure pays some-times."

"Until now," Tony commented. "What about those other entrances? Anybody covering them now?"

"We sent a few people up there, but any of the big fish who wanted to get away are well into Liliblod right now, and our people are heading to shut them down from inside by now. One's just kind of a side door, I guess, for private com-ings and goings, but the other one's like a stable. They say they got some very strange animals in there."

Tony was suddenly alert. "Any of them with a body like mine? Animal head, perhaps with a horn, but a body like mine?"

"I dunno. I'll check. Hold on a moment." The soldier said something into his communicator and waited for the reply. "A few with bodies kinda like yours, but nothing with a horn."

"See if you can have somebody from the middle group contact Julian. That's the name. Report this to whoever you can get and ask them to get word to her. If he's anywhere around there, she'll recognize him."

"Who?"

"Just do it."

The soldier complied. "Message received and relayed, they say. That's all. I can't guarantee it'll be passed on. They'll be linking and going down to level two shortly."

Tony thought furiously, frustrated at not being able to get down there to see what was going on for herself. "How far is this stable? And how far in from the border is it?"

"About four leegs that way, and maybe just a harg inside, but that's far enough. Why?"

Four leegs was maybe half a kilometer, and a harg was no more than ten meters. "I was thinking maybe I could enter from there."

"Lady, you don't wanna do that. You got colonies of them Liliblodians right up there in the trees; I don't think they're real happy with us at the moment, and they don't give a shit about diplomacy and protests and all that other crap. They'd be on us like a plague if any of us went across that border, high-tech weapons be damned. They got sense enough to know they'd be wiped out, but they'd take a ton of us with 'em before they went and might figure it's worth it. They're probably so mad at us for blowing up the main entrance in their territory, they're just *waiting* for one of us to stray ever so slightly in."

"I came through there once before, and they didn't even show themselves. And I'm not of Agon. They *might* hesitate."

"Yeah, and if they don't, you'll be dead in ten seconds. Don't think your size will save you. Dozens of 'em will drop down on top and cover you, and you'll get enough poison in the first few seconds to kill half the world. Besides, even if you managed to get in, how would you ever get the heck *out*?"

It was a good point. Still, she was determined to do *something*. "Tell your men up there I'm coming and not to shoot. Don't worry. I accept your argument; I am not going to try it. But if I can be very close, perhaps I can be of some help."

With that, she trotted off toward the north.

Julian was frankly relieved to get the call. Frustrated and feeling useless, she was in no mood to follow them down to farther levels.

Assured that at least level one was now secure, she made her way forward toward the main entrance, from which someone would guide her to Tony. She was most of the way there when, just behind her, something came out of a doorway roaring with fury and charged right at her back.

She didn't even think, she just acted, shifting forward on her forelegs, rearing up the powerful hind ones, and kicking with all the strength she could muster.

The hooves struck the creature in the face and snapped it back. The thing gave a startled cry and then was flung backward against the far wall with the force of the blow.

Julian came down slightly unbalanced and with her hind legs splayed. She was a moment realizing what the trouble was and easing herself back up. Turning, still on all fours, she could feel her heart pounding in her throat and whatever the Erdomese used for adrenaline coursing through her. She feared a second attack, but the creature was not moving at all, just lying limply like a rag doll thrown to the floor by a bored child.

With some shock, she realized that the thing was dead. Looking around lest there be any more ugly surprises, she carefully approached the body as a couple of Agonite commandos ran toward her.

The thing looked like somebody's nightmare of a teddy bear, perhaps a meter and a half tall when standing. Those teeth and that fierce expression, now frozen in death, were never on any teddy bear *she*'d have around, though.

Two commandos approached the creature cautiously, then checked it out. "Dead," one said, and the other nodded.

"Lady, that's some *mean* kick you got," the first one commented to her. "I think you broke its neck and maybe its back."

"Yeah," the other agreed with grudging respect. "That guy must've weighed three times what you do, and he *flew*."

She was beginning to calm down a little and realize what she'd done. Now, where had *that* come from? It had been so natural, so automatic, she hadn't even had time to think before it was over, but she sure hadn't known she could *do* that.

Maybe *she'd* been the one to underestimate the Erdomese female.

The only thing was, she couldn't stand back up. She was locked in the four-footed position. She didn't mind that much; it was both comfortable and natural, and she used it often by choice, but now she guessed that it was part of the defense built into her. About the only problem was, it made her slightly shorter than the Agonese, even with her head up and forward on her long neck. Oh, well.

She felt suddenly *terrific*—euphoric, even. She'd actually done something! She wasn't as defenseless or helpless as she'd thought!

Not wanting to admit that at the moment she *couldn't* get back up, she said confidently, "I think I'll go the rest of the way on all fours, boys. I don't think my arms could take too many more bounces like that."

They watched her go on with obvious respect in their eyes.

"I hope my wife doesn't have any hidden tricks like that," one of them said.

The other felt his own throat. "Yeah."

Gus carefully scouted the stairway down to the second level. It was quite dark, and even his night-adjusted eyes had a problem with it, but there were small bumps of yellow lights running down both sides, powered by some internal source, that made footing not a problem. *Seeing* was something else again, but the sterile, flat walls carried sound well, and he could hear nothing close by.

If they were waiting for company, those on the second level certainly weren't doing it on the stairs or landing. Gus figured that they would expect a grenade to be tossed down the chute here, and with the echo, nobody would last very long. Most likely they would be waiting beyond the doors to this level.

While they might not be able to see Gus, they could certainly expect the door to open and probably wouldn't wait to find out who or what had opened it. He pressed up against the door and could hear voices which made him pretty sure that a nasty welcome awaited.

"Armed party probably barricaded just beyond the second level doorway," he reported into the mike. "No way I can open it without exposing myself. Stairs clear to level two."

"All right. Why not move down and check the bottom level, then," came a tinny-sounding voice near his ear. "If the stairs are clear, we won't give them a warning by blowing anything there. I'm sending down an advance party now to take out whatever's behind the door. If you can get into the bottom level safely, use your own judgment. Otherwise proceed back to two after the opening is secured."

"Okay. Heading down."

The bottom looked like the second level, but unlike there, he couldn't hear any signs of life on the other side. *Okay, Gus, how lucky do you feel?* he asked himself. *Are you Clint Eastwood or Mickey Mouse?*

Mickey Mouse, he answered himself, but he was still tempted to try the door. Once inside, he'd be virtually invisible to whoever and whatever was there.

He heard the commando team come down to the second door above him. There would surely be some explosions and shooting before too long. Maybe, just maybe, if he could open the door and get through quickly at the same time they opened up above, it would panic and confuse anybody with a bead on the door.

Hell, it was either that or get his eardrums broken sitting there.

He took hold of the door, then waited. *Come on, come on, let's get it over with!* he thought to the commandos above.

Suddenly there was the quick sound of an open door and a big explosion and then the nearly deafening din of weapons fire just above. He pushed back the door, standing to one side, and when it seemed as if nothing was coming out and nobody was nearby, he slipped quickly inside it, leaving it open.

There was emergency lighting here as well, only better than up top. It made the area glow a very dull red, but it was sufficient for him to see and get around.

If he remembered the layout, he was now in the area where they kept prisoners. Ahead would be the living quarters, the master kitchen, and then the computer complex.

It definitely had the look of a prison or, more accurately, a dungeon. He found why there hadn't been a welcoming party for him there immediately. The whole entrance foyer was little more than a giant cage of thick mesh with an electronically operated door at the end. There was no lock, latch, or knob on this side; it clearly was intended to be opened only from the inside.

That meant a guard or guards with some kind of surveillance system. He looked around the ceiling and upper wall area in the dim red glow and finally spotted where the camera just had to be. That left him with a problem.

If everything sealed when the main power went off and there was always a guard or two inside there, then the guard must be in a sort of in-between cage between prison doors. He might well be trapped in there. In fact, he was pretty sure he could hear somebody moving just beyond. How the hell could he deal with that guy?

He had a thought that was so nutty, it just might work. It was, after all, very thick mesh.

"Hey!" he called out. "You okay in there?"

The guard stirred and hesitated, unsure of who this was or whether to respond.

"Cm'on! I'm one step ahead of them bastards upstairs. They're gonna blow through here like butter with all the artillery they got, and right now I'm gonna be right in between 'em like the filling in a sandwich!"

The guard was more scared than suspicious. "You're with *us*?"

Gus gave a loud, impatient sigh. "If I was with *them*, this door would be blowing up about now. Cm'on, man! It ain't much, but it's the only chance I got!"

The guard still hesitated. "I got my orders. If the power goes, nobody in, period. Not without an okay from the boss or security."

"What the world you think this *is*, you dumb ass? It's the cops. It's a whole damn army. They already got the top level, and they're working on the lab level now. We're finished. All you can do is either make a break with me if we can or stay and die."

"Ain't gonna break out from *this* level!" the idiot said, almost with pride.

"No? Well, then we can fight or give up. If you gotta give up, you don't want to be the guy who's handy when they start checkin' the cells. Huh? Now, stop clowning and let me in!"

"I—I—I dunno. I don't know what to do."

"Anybody come up and reinforce you?"

"N—no. They all lit out for the front."

"Leaving you here to either buy 'em more time or take the fall. You're a sucker. I don't have any more time for this. I'm gonna open up on this door, and either it's gonna give for me or I'll run out of ammo. Maybe if I cut through this cage with this needler, I'll accidently hit the dumbest asshole in this whole complex."

"I—no. I, er—don't do that! Here!"

There was a fumbling sound and the turning of a manual key and a wheel, and the door swung open. Gus entered and found a sorry-looking little guy in a black outfit sitting there on a stool with a big energy rifle cradled in his lap. He was a little twerp, like an anemic otter in full dress, and he actually had a tiny pair of glasses sitting on his snout.

"W—well? Why don't you come in?" the guard asked, the rifle coming up.

"Right here, you dumb shit!" Gus shouted in his face, grabbing the rifle and bringing the stock down hard on his head. The guard collapsed in a heap, and Gus, rather than worrying if the little guy was dead or alive, felt a little thrill of satisfaction.

"Sucker," he said, checking the rifle and seeing that it was still in good shape. He decided it was handier than the little pistol if he could manage to hold on to it.

The inner door was easy to open, although the wheel was hard to turn with his small and relatively weak arm muscles. Finally the lock clicked and he was able to pull it open.

Inside was a long and ugly chamber of horrors.

LILIBLOD

He hadn't done it, and it made him feel worse than ever. He'd actually had the chance back there in Clopta, and he hadn't done it. He'd meekly gone back over the border and started following the same old trail, just as before.

What bothered him most was that he was well inside Liliblod before he realized that he hadn't done it or even remembered what he'd intended to do. It was almost as if he could have his opinions and dream his dreams, but he could only act on what he was told to do.

Maybe it's still going on, Lori worried. *Maybe just changing me physically into a packhorse isn't the end of it. What if even my brain is becoming more horse than human?*

The more he thought about it, the more certain he was that this was the case. He could think frantically and hard, even plan, but for how long at a time? Was he thinking slower, or were there very long stretches of time when he just didn't think at all? He'd made this trip countless times, over and over, but how many times and for how long? He didn't know. How long did it actually take him to walk the trail from Clopta to Agon? Again, he didn't know, not even how many days it might be. How long had it been since he'd meekly walked back in? Was it today? Or yesterday? Or was it further back than that?

He had no idea.

There were times when he was totally lucid, remembering a lot of specifics about everything, and there were other times when he couldn't remember much at all. Why, just back there, when he had thought of escaping, he had remembered most of a map and how to get around. He *knew* he had. But try as he might, he couldn't get that information back now.

He had been losing it little by little, piece by piece, and he hadn't even realized it until now. Maybe the process was speeding up. Maybe it was nearly done. How many facts could a horse's brain hold? Not too many, because it didn't need to hold all that many. He ate, he slept, and he walked the same trail. Could it be that deep down that was all he really wanted to do?

Or was it that he no longer had the *will* to do anything different and was making excuses? That his old self said "Fight!" but his current self wanted only peace and contentment? How much of him was gone, and how much had he himself pushed away so he couldn't make use of it?

He didn't even know how long he had mused on these depressing topics, but it was quite a while.

One thing he suddenly *did* know was that he wasn't far from the end now. Close enough from the scent that he could smell and taste the hay and oats and other good stuff they had at the headquarters, far better than just grass.

He usually stopped after dark and slept till morning, but he was close and he didn't really *need* to see all that much to make it. Not far, not far . . .

Suddenly, ahead, there was a massive explosion! The noise startled him so much, he reared back and shook his head in disbelief. And then came the sounds of guns firing and loud shouting by lots of people.

Suddenly terrified of what lay beyond, he stopped right on the trail and just stood there, unsure of what to do.

The tumult ahead died down after a while, but not the one *overhead*. The tops of the trees were alive with hissings and buzzings and sheer rage, and he heard those *things* begin to move along the treetops, move toward the border and the noise.

Suddenly two figures, a Cloptan man and a Zhonzhorpian, came running toward him on the trail. He tried to back up and back off a bit to let them by, but suddenly a flashlight beam caught him square in the face.

The two men were out of breath, were half-dressed, and looked to be in a terrible way. Soon they began arguing and then shouting at one another, and after a moment the Cloptan took something from a case he was carrying and a bright white beam caught the Zhonzhorpian full and enveloped him; suddenly the tall crocodilelike creature was no more.

The Cloptan then approached Lori, and he was even more terrified after seeing what had happened to the other, surely a companion rather than an enemy.

The Cloptan patted him on the side, trying to reassure him with the gesture and meaningless talk, and oddly, it *did* have a calming influence on him.

Then the Cloptan climbed up on his back and latched the case to the saddlebags while keeping the gun in one hand. Firmly, the rider turned Lori around, away from the end of his journey and back toward where he'd come from. Cloptans weren't horribly heavy, but this was going to be one heck of a walk.

He wished he knew what had happened back there, but whatever it was, it sure wasn't good.

"Lieutenant, I think you better get some men down to the third level as quick as you can," Gus said into the mike. "I left the door open. I think I killed the lone guard, but if he isn't dead, he's too dumb to do anything but give up."

"What's the matter? What did you find?"

"Monsters. Monsters in the basement. You might want the inspector down here as well. If Agon doesn't have capital punishment, I think it will by tomorrow."

There was silence for a moment, then the officer said, "All right. I'll send a squad down and relay your message. Will you wait for them?"

Gus looked around and shivered slightly. "I don't think so. The guard station at the other end is empty, but the door's locked. I think I can blast through it, though, now that I've seen how the doors are made. I'll report when I can."

"Resistance on the second level was light after that initial barricade. It's mostly labs, and it looks like they ran when things started happening. Watch yourself, though. Any of them that didn't come up to level one are pretty likely to be down there—and desperate."

The cells were of the highest quality for dungeon cells. High-tech, Gus thought. State of the art. Thick, shockproof, probably bullet- and rayproof doors made of some material that nonetheless was totally transparent save for the electronic locks and a small slit for feeding prisoners not otherwise restrained inside.

There were 1,560 races, it was said, on the Well World, and he'd seen only a tiny fraction of them. And even though many were bizarre in the extreme, none of them could be as bizarre as some of the *creatures* in the cells. Hybrids, genetic mutations, people whose own bodies were in the process of re-forming themselves into the visions of insane designers. Some screamed, some cried out, others sobbed, but he could not help them or look at them.

Now, what the hell does any of this have to do with a drug ring? he wondered.

Designer creatures. For what? Designer jobs? Animals with the smarts of humans to avoid detection, follow complex orders? Traitors, people who'd failed in their work for the gang, now forced to become monsters at the beck and call of their masters? Why kill them when they could be turned into something useful? Recycling taken to its ultimate degree.

There were a few that weren't like that, but they weren't much better off. Chained to walls, scarred, ripped open but still alive in agony ... They must have had information somebody wanted. At least it was more familiar. He'd seen this sort of stuff back on Earth in central Africa, in the Middle East, and in a few of the less pleasant Far Eastern beauty spots. In some ways the mentality was the same no matter where you went, even here. The others, the monsters—that was just a high-tech extension of the same idea. New toys for the depraved.

The idea of a Campos with this kind of power was disturbing. The original incarnation was bad enough. Gus remembered what a big-time syndicate boss had told him once. It wasn't about money. Money was rarely a concern after a short while. It was all about power.

"Hey, Lieutenant, you got a news crew here in Agon?" he asked through the mike.

A moment later, after a request to repeat the question, the answer came. "Yes. Several."

"Well, get 'em down here when you can. Let 'em see this, photograph it, broadcast it. Even though it'll make every viewer sick to their stomach, it'll legitimize this raid and your government more than anything else. Some of those corrupt bastards who protected this place all these years should watch it, too. And if they don't know how to cover it right, call me. I'm an expert."

He reached the jail door at the other end. Knowing where the locking mechanism was, he fired the rifle on full blast, holding it steady until the lock turned first black, then red, and finally white. He released the trigger, then reared back on his tail and kicked with both powerful feet. The door resisted the first time, but the second kick saw it move back. He had been so angry, he saw he'd actually bent the material.

The secondary door had been left open, since it was never designed to be more than a security lock for people wanting in. As he went through it, shots rang out all around and tracerlike needler rays rained down on him. For a moment he thought they could see him, but then he realized that they were just firing blindly at the sound.

"Hold your fire, you idiots!" somebody called. "Don't waste energy! Wait until they actually come through!"

Good advice, Gus thought with nervous release. They wouldn't have had to do much more of that before they'd have winged or even killed him. Blind shots were his worst enemy.

They'd overturned tables, beds, sofas, everything they had, and made a pretty fair barricade. This was *not* going to be easy, and he was suddenly acutely aware that he was between them and the commandos he'd just urged to come down behind him.

There didn't seem to be much of a choice. He picked a weaker and less sturdy part of the barricade, went over to it, took a deep breath, then simply charged in with a roar, making furniture and appliances fly all over the place.

The gunmen were so startled that the ones closest to him pulled back in total fear, while the ones on the other side again opened fire on the now-deserted corridor.

He didn't wait for them to figure out what was going on. He was, after all, a very large target even if invisible. He opened up on the fleeing men with the rifle, forgetting he still had it on maximum. The whole corridor was bathed in white energy, and those caught directly in the beam were disintegrated, while those farther away found their clothing and skin in flames.

He turned to the others who were just turning to bear on him and charged into them with a hideous roar that echoed terrifyingly down the corridor, so close in and so violent that they had no chance to use their weapons. There was no rifle this time; Gus's huge reptilian jaws opened and closed with savage fury as his targets futilely struggled and fought to break free. One down . . . Two . . . Three . . . Where the hell was four?

Running down the hall right into the cells, where he would undoubtedly find a welcoming party by now.

His mouth was dripping with blood in three colors, and there were pieces of people from three races all over the place, but nothing alive.

And the funny thing was, he felt *great*!

He looked around on the floor and didn't see his own rifle but saw a furry dismembered hand still clutching a nearly identical one and pried it away.

Staff living quarters and kitchens. He could just walk right through them to where he really wanted to go, but he didn't think he would.

He wondered what the current record was for the Agon commandos for killing these turds and also whether it was possible for him to break it. The ghost of his old Lutheran pastor shattered in his mind. Hell, he was really starting to *enjoy* this!

●　●　●

Julian's walk back to what they had called the "stable" entrance had calmed her somewhat, and she was finally able to relax enough to stand on two legs again.

She wasn't sure just what they were bringing her this far away to look at, and when she saw, she *still* wasn't quite sure.

"What *are* they?" she asked an Agonese sergeant.

"Beats us, ma'am. We were told maybe *you* could tell *us*. We ran 'em through our own system by shooting video up to the command center, but they can't place them, either, at least not by species or hex."

They looked mostly like horses and mules, but not *quite*. No two were nearly alike beyond the basic form, but no two rang exactly true, either. She could see what the Agonese meant and why they hadn't really been able to explain it.

There were tall ones and short ones, big ones and little ones. They divided first into two classes which she thought of as equine and elephantine. The equine had thin legs of varying lengths, balanced torsos, and heads on long necks. They tended to have camouflagelike colors, dull and mixed, with lots of browns and olives. Hair was short or long; tails were optional and of varying lengths and designs. The heads, though, were what caught her attention. They all looked different, and many of them looked unsettlingly like caricatures of the faces of some Well World races.

The elephantine were more bizarre, with very thick legs; wide, round padded hooves; and large, squat bodies that tended to be hairless and dull-colored, with pink or gray or mottled variations, as if they'd once had hair but it had fallen out. They, too, had faces, but the faces—again all different and with some hint of familiarity—were virtually looking out from the top front of the torsos without distinct heads or necks. She couldn't imagine how they fed.

The worst thing was, they all looked at her and the others with eyes that seemed very intelligent indeed and expressions, when they were capable of them, of extreme sadness.

"Did you capture anybody alive from this area?" she asked them.

"Yeah, but they haven't been too talkative yet. We asked them what these things were and why they were here, and all they said was that it wasn't their area but they thought they were couriers."

"Couriers!"

"Yeah. Apparently this is a fairly new batch still being trained. They have some that run through Liliblod to Clopta, but most of them go to other areas where they can run stuff by night through backcountry areas without being seen."

"Do they make sounds?"

"Uh huh, but they're just crazy screeches or bellows. Nothing intelligible, even on translator, if that's what you're thinking."

She was thinking worse than that. She was thinking of those two doctors she'd gone to see with their miracle experiments and records that had included information on Glathrielians and Erdomese.

I actually let them put something into me, too! My God! Am I going to turn into one of these things?

She told herself to calm down, that they wouldn't have been crazy enough to try anything like that and risk exposure, but she couldn't quite convince herself. *I'm going to be a paranoid hypochondriac for months,* she admitted ruefully to herself.

She tried to pull herself together. "Are they—natural? I mean, do they seem, well, normal in the sense of being put together right?"

"Well, as far as we can tell, they're all sexless," the sergeant told her. "Of course, with *those*, who could tell what's really missing?"

Julian thought of Lori and Mavra Chang. Couriers? Like *these* monsters?

"I want to talk topside if I can," she told the sergeant. "They told me that my Dillian companion couldn't get down here. I'd like to contact her if I could. I need to compare some notes. Is that possible?"

"Could be. I'll call the command center and see if they have a channel open."

Inside of five minutes she was talking to Tony. "Where are you?" she asked the centaur.

"If you're where they said you were, I'm probably about five meters on top of you," Tony told her. "What's the situation?"

As quickly and as adequately as she could, she described what she'd seen and her thoughts on the missing pair.

"I agree, but we must remember that these poor wretches were probably their own people being punished for failures, while Lori and Mavra were objects of revenge. I can see them perhaps making Lori one of these poor creatures, but I cannot see Campos doing that to Mavra Chang. If I remember Lori's account of his adventure in the jungle, I can see why Campos would want some revenge, but not the kind of long-term suffering that would be due to Mavra. I know something of the code and the way people like Campos think. It was that sort of person that caused me to stay away from my native country until democracy was restored there. Lori was a point of honor, a detail, even though an important one. But Mavra Chang by direct action impacted personally on Campos. She stopped his attempted rape, she kidnapped and drugged him in the jungles, and then she caused him to wind up here. No, Mavra Chang would be special, someone who would have to be in permanent hurt and humiliation, available for frequent lifelong scorn. Considering what you have told me, who knows *what* these people were capable of?" Tony thought for a moment. "A pet, perhaps. A dog or cat or whatever would be appropriate but not too obvious. Something that could be walked on a leash through a public park. You see what I am getting at?"

"Yes, I'm afraid I do," Julian replied.

"Someone should be able to remember Lori and what they

turned him into," Tony said confidently. "They are still in a state of shock, but interrogations should bring results. That is a big place, but it is not *that* big, and I would suspect that the permanent staff knows pretty much what is going on throughout the place. But Mavra—I fear that unless we can get into that computer and find out precisely what they did or unless we can crack those two butchers open, we will have to reach Mavra by going through Juan Campos."

"I've never met this person," Julian told her, "but I am beginning to think that I *want* to meet her. Preferably in a nice dark alley . . ."

In a hex with the kind of technology that could put a very powerful computer into something the size of a claw, the computer center was incredibly huge. How much information did they have here? What could these rooms of memory cubes, each capable of holding trillions of facts, possibly contain? More than merely all the data on the drug business, that was for sure. Blackmail on thousands of leaders in every hex they went to? Biological information on every single race, with details on how to make something for each that would addict them? Probably, Gus thought. At least that.

He was as surprised by the size of the place as he was by its emptiness. He'd expected at least a few people here, just to make certain that this stuff didn't fall into anybody's hands, but the place was completely deserted.

Or was it?

Over there—a terminal of some sort and something, something large but indistinct, sitting at it . . .

Colonel, what the hell are you up to?

Jeez! The Leeming was *huge*, a blob fit for the horror movies almost. At least twice the size he'd been a few hours earlier, anyway.

The large projection-type screen above the terminal booth was alive with flashing data. Gus couldn't read any of it and was surprised that the colonel seemed to be able to do so.

Come to think of it, even if the old boy *had* somehow mastered the writing, how the hell had he gotten past the security system and inside to the data?

And suddenly, with the cynicism born of covering countless wars and tragedies, it all fell into place.

"I always wondered how you got so much authority and power so fast, Colonel," Gus said loudly, his deep voice echoing slightly off the walls.

The colonel was startled. "Gus? How did you get *here* so quickly?"

"This is Education Day, Colonel, at least for me. Today I found out things about myself I never knew before, and I also found out why the Dahir have such a strict and pacifistic religion and don't want their people wandering all over this world. We're killers, Colonel. Natural killers. It's in the blood, in the genes, the hormones. We *enjoy* it. *I* enjoy it. It's a tough thing to keep down once you've started doing it. That's why the Dahir faith is so strict and life there so god-awful boring. It's the only way to keep us civilized. Nothing worse than a natural killer you can't see wandering around, is there?"

"You are a rational man, Gus. You only have killed your enemies."

"That's true, but I have a strange feeling that it's going to be very easy to be defined as an enemy of mine from now on. But I haven't told you the whole story yet, Colonel. Education Day is still ongoing. I learned the best part just by stepping in here and watching you."

"What do you mean?"

"Nothing this big, no operation this slick and this huge, could possibly get to be this way on its own, and I don't care what drugs they sell or how much money they spread. We ain't talkin' just a gang here. We're talking governments, or parts of governments, at the highest levels. Presidents and kings and dictators and probably South Zone councillors as well. Not that they were in on the details, of course. I doubt if they were ever here or even imagined how some of their money was spent, but in on the top levels of control. Not all of 'em, sure. Not even a majority, 'cause what sense would *that* make? They didn't care about the details. They were busy using that power to weaken and take over governments of hexes they didn't even know how to pronounce. Control economies, trade, you name it. Pretty soon the whole Well World's workin' for them and it don't even know it. It must've drove 'em crazy when they figured out they had to sacrifice this place, but their little underlings did something, and they can't afford to even let their own people know what it was. Uneasy lies the head, huh, Colonel?"

"Go on, Gus. You are quite entertaining."

"So it's going along really good, and then, suddenly, *wham*! Here's the legendary Nathan Brazil unmasked, and he's headed for the internal works sooner or later. They can't kill him, so they try and slow him down, make him feel comfortable, that kind of thing, while they consult and figure out what the hell to do. I mean, they can't let him get *inside*, can they? If they do, he'll see their racket right away and queer it. I can just imagine the nightmares. And then it's not just one of 'em but *two*. Either one's the worst thing anybody could imagine. Both together might be unbeatable. *Two* unkillables. But they're pretty clever. The two clearly haven't seen each other since the last ice age on Earth, so it's easy to make each of 'em think the other's out to get them. They won't get together then even if they could. But how to keep them from getting up to the equator? *That's* the other problem."

"It is quite an amazing fantasy you weave, Gus. You should have quit news and gone into the cinema."

"It gets better. You, for one, are there as a member of a race that was one of the insiders. The Leeming. Somehow, right off, they see you as just the kind of guy who's perfect for them, but you can create a friendly, human face. All the power, all the authority—and one job. Just keep Brazil happy and anywhere but heading north and always where you can find him. I don't know why you didn't just have him arrested and jailed right off, but I can think of a number of reasons."

"For one thing, Nathan Brazil is a legend, a part of mythology, like Odin and Jupiter back home. Bringing a sufficient number of leaders to the conviction that he was more than that and that he was a possible threat to the Well World's very survival takes time. The last is next to impossible, really. No one fears the repairman; they welcome him. They fear the demolition man, and they fear their gods. Ironically, Brazil himself tipped the scales on the required religious conversions merely by surviving what no creature of his makeup should possibly survive. And the more he recovers, the more nervous they will get. They will endlessly debate how to enforce any deal or bargain they can make with him, but who can truly make such demands of a god once that god is on his throne? So they will keep him locked up. There is your story. One day he may escape, but by that time they will be long dead."

"Uh huh. And who had your job with Mavra Chang?"

"You would not believe me."

"Try me."

"The Dillian twins."

"I don't believe it!"

"They didn't know anything about the rest, unlike myself. They were just given an all-expenses paid chance to see the Well World if they would simply make a few reports on the location and whereabouts of one Mavra Chang as things went along. They didn't know Chang, and they were made just aware enough that she was more than she seemed and something of a threat to peace, stability, and order. Armed with that, it was rather easy to make her miss connections, foul up her bank accounts, that sort of thing. And unlike the captain, who truly gave me the slip, she actually contracted with those very forces which wanted her out of the way to carry her here. It was Brazil we were worried about. We didn't give a thought to Chang. Now, though, we find that Chang is not here. Somehow she slipped through our net and into the hands of a minor player about which we know very little overall but whose mental profile in the records indicates that she would do almost anything to keep Chang out of anyone's hands but her own."

"That still bothers me, Colonel. You know where Campos lives. You could have gone there at any time and forced her to show you Chang, but you didn't. You went through all this, which must cost them plenty."

"It did. It is painful and a real setback," the colonel admitted. "But you still fail to appreciate both Campos and the man she ingratiated herself with. If one inkling, one *thought* that Chang might be another Brazil entered *his* mind or the minds of his associates, they would vanish, and Chang with them. The hold they would have over the entire international organization would be nearly absolute. Surely you must see that. Chang must never be the object of all this except to such as we. And when we bust them, headed by fearless and incorruptible policemen like Inspector Kurdon, even they will have no suspicion until Chang is in our hands and locked away in Zone next to the captain with the so-pleasant name."

"And now you're here finding out exactly what they did to her, what monster they turned her into, and precisely where she is. And after that, making certain that nothing in that computer will *ever* be read by the inspector or anyone else. Tell me, Colonel—how'd you learn to read that stuff so quickly? And how'd you learn how to use their computer system? You ain't been here much longer than me."

"Long enough, my friend. Besides, we Leeming have more than one way to learn things. In fact, with certain kinds of races, which make up close to ten percent of the south's racial makeup, we don't have to do anything more than feed. You can see by my size that I've been a very gluttonous soldier."

"You mean you can learn stuff by *eating* somebody?" Gus was incredulous.

The colonel chuckled. "Friend Gus, you are on an impossible world full of impossible creatures such as the two of us, turned into a big colorful lizard who can not be seen unless he wants to be, discussing a worldwide takeover conspiracy for which there remains no proof at all and which you only learned about because of a hunt for two demigods. And you find my alternative learning method unbelievable?"

He had a point there, Gus had to admit. He kept his rifle on the colonel, but he expected a trick any time now. The colonel hadn't moved, but did he seem suddenly more like his old self in size? Or was that imagination?

"You're a rotten son of a bitch, Colonel," Gus told him. "You had a second chance here, a real chance of a new life and a fresh start, and you decided to remain what you were back on Earth. Don Francisco must have paid you pretty good, too, I suspect."

"Not nearly enough, but after the return to democracy there were problems for many of us, and we had to find alternative sources of income to maintain ourselves and our families in the style to which we had become accustomed. This is not the same thing. This is the equivalent of military rule, which we imposed to prevent the communists from dominating our beloved land. In that I followed orders and remained true to my country. I am doing so again, and I feel that it *is* a new start for me. Again I have honor. Again I serve my country and my people."

That shimmery SOB *was* shrinking! Gus shut up and moved back toward the entrance. It was barely in time; a thin layer of goo rose up and grabbed for him as he moved.

Nice try, Colonel. You are better than I gave you credit for, Gus thought, nervously eyeing his narrow escape. If the colonel had kept him talking just another thirty seconds, he'd have been history!

"Gus? Where are you?"

Ready to take aim on your slimy guts the moment you pull yourself together, you fat pig, Gus thought, but he remained silent but vigilant.

"I'm sorry, Gus. I won't make another stab at you," Lunderman assured him. "Look, no one will believe your story, not even Kurdon. You have no place to go and no way to act on what you know. You can't win, not against this kind of power. But you don't have to lose, either. You are a very resourceful man, Gus. *Very* resourceful. Just as they found a place for me, they can find one for you. Anything you want. What have you to look forward to, anyway? You can't go home—particularly now. You know that yourself. The Dahir church would probably have you sacrificed to keep from corrupting the rest of the flock. You are both a man and a creature without a country, Gus. But with your unique talents and awakening appetites you needn't be an unhappy one."

I wouldn't be tempted if you were giving me a straight offer, Gus thought, *but I can see your puddly self flowing all around the floor and in between the consoles, feeling for me even now.*

The colonel had grown large, but not *that* large. It was relatively simple to keep out of his way if Gus just paid attention.

Gus could see a fair amount of him now, but too flattened and too spread out to make a real target. Still, Kurdon had warned the Leeming that he was vulnerable to energy weapons, and that happened to be just what Gus had in his cute little hands. Time for a continuation of Education Day.

Gus set the rifle on wide, aimed at the largest concentration of Leeming he could see, and pulled the trigger fast and briefly.

The colonel screamed an unholy scream as part of him fried and vanished. It suddenly occurred to Gus that this might have been the first real pain Lunderman had felt since becoming a Leeming. Reflexively, the rest of the amorphous creature withdrew inward toward the central mass. But where *was* the central mass now? Gus wondered. Not at the console.

Cat and mouse, Colonel? Gus thought. *Suits me fine, but I frankly didn't think you had the guts.*

Lunderman didn't. Suddenly, across the room in one corner, a great mass rushed upward with tremendous force and speed. It was so fast and so blended against the dark that Gus was slow to react, and by the time he got off a shot, the thing had vanished into the ducting above.

Gus didn't like the fact that the Leeming was around up there somewhere and nursing both a wound and a grudge, but he could hardly follow *that* exit. At least the colonel couldn't see him or anticipate his actions. Even so, the faster he was out of here, the better, he thought.

Still, he had to risk some communication.

"The colonel was working with the gang," Gus reported. "I am in the computer room. He was in here erasing records. I shot at him but only winged him. You can't capture him, but he's the only one of his kind here, and he can be fried. I recommend a shoot on sight, particularly since he eats people by absorbing them." Suddenly the magnitude of what he'd done hit him. "And get some people in here really quick," he added. "Lunderman's left the computer turned *on* with the damned security already deactivated!"

The sun had been up for hours when they struggled back to Subar, but all of them felt it had been worth it. Terry almost cried for joy when Gus came back and ran to hug him.

There was no sign of the colonel, but all the entrances and exits were heavily guarded and it was felt that he was still in there somewhere.

Inspector Kurdon looked exhausted but generally satisfied. "Sixty-eight of ours killed or wounded, but at least two hundred of theirs dead and almost a hundred in custody, and we broke that cancer that has been eating into the soul as well as the soil of my nation for far too long. It has been a worthy night indeed."

"What about the computer? Have your people learned anything?" Gus asked him.

"Not as much as we might have had the colonel not gotten

in there first but far more than I think any of them would have wished. What you caught him doing was unleashing what my computer people call a tapeworm." The term wasn't exact, but that was the way it got translated to Gus. "A program that goes in and finds and destroys specific information. A second was ready to load, and a third was found nearby, but thanks to you only the first was run."

"Any idea of the nature of the information destroyed? Or is that a ridiculous question?" Anne Marie asked him.

"No, it is not altogether ridiculous. We can deduce a little of it, although we have barely scratched the surface of the thing. It will be *months* before we get everything we can out of that data base, and we need to make certain that no one who does not have the most impeccable honesty gets in there in the meantime. I do not like it that the colonel is still at large in there, but we do not believe he could actually operate the computer. Rather, he knew how to run the tapeworms and where they were stored. In a sense, merely losing what we did is a fair trade for having the security system opened up. We might have learned far less over a much longer period had we had to attempt to crack it."

"And the erasures?"

"Oh, sorry. As I say, by deduction. Political names, big regional names, that sort of thing. We won't get a payoff or politician's listing from that, I'm afraid."

"It's bigger than you know," Gus told him. "You wouldn't believe how big. I got it straight from the colonel."

Kurdon gave a weary nod. "I believe I know how far this had to have gone just by looking at its scale and by the sheer number of hexes where deletions were made. Do not worry, Gus. It wouldn't matter if the entire council was corrupt, as they probably are in one way or another. This complex and the computer are in *Agon*. Agon alone has authority here. *And I know who is who in Agon.*"

"What about Lori and Mavra? Any word on them?" Tony asked, concerned over Julian's report.

"It is the first minute of the new information age," the inspector said. "Give us a little time. This is of the highest priority. Get some sleep, all of you! Even *I* am going to attempt it. By the time we awaken, they will have news, perhaps very exact news. *Then*, I believe, we will be on our way on a journey to the northwest."

"*Clopta!*" Gus breathed. "And Campos."

Kurdon nodded. "Also by that time I expect that I will have so many high Cloptan officials terrified of me that I will be carried to this Campos person on a litter with politicians as bearers." He smiled, the first time any of them could remember seeing such an expression on an Agonite. "It was a *very* good night."

By late afternoon, when they struggled back to the command center, most still half-asleep but unable to go any further toward resolving the problem, the trusted technicians inside the computer room had some answers.

"A bird and a unicorn," Inspector Kurdon told them. "Neither are monsters in the sense of the ones we discovered down in the cells. They are in their own ways works of art—if, of course, the results proved equal to the computer estimation. Your friend Lori was something of a compromise, it appears. The original order was for a grotesque, like what we saw. But when they saw the genetic potential and also discovered that Campos was just going to make him a courier like the rest, they had second thoughts. They made the monster part come out early, then later fade as the *real* program kicked in. Campos was apparently furious at the start but later decided she liked it after all. At least, there's no sign of any attempts to do worse again."

"You got this from the computer?" Julian asked him.

"Not entirely. Our doctor friends seemed to have pulled a very slick vanishing act in the middle of a cordon I'd have sworn was unbreakable, but their assistants weren't so fortunate. And the assistants know the medical computer quite well and helped with all the detail work. With what we got from the clinic, we were able to go to specific points in the big machine and get virtually a replay of the entire discussion and debate, almost a step-by-step explanation and tutorial. They were sick of making monsters. They wanted to make pretty, living works of art." He reached into a pouch and pulled out a picture. "Here is what your Lori looks like now."

The pretty beige pastel colors had been retained, and the hair, and much of the elements of the original Erdomese, Julian noted. Only the body had thickened, becoming less wiry and more equine overall, and the forearms and hands had become traditional horselike legs with fixed hooves much like the Dillians'. The head had been thickened, and the head and face reshaped into a rather cute horse's head, but retaining the curved horn in the forehead that was the mark of an Erdomese male. Compact, sturdy, cute.

"Kind of like a cartoon Shetland pony," Gus commented.

Kurdon cleared his throat. "The worst news, I fear, Madame Julian, is that the specifications set down by Campos included that he be a gelding. It was actually designed that way. There are no genitalia at all."

Julian knew she should have felt shock and grief for Lori, but somehow she felt relief. Still, she noted, "I wouldn't exactly be the proper mate for a pony, anyway, would I, Inspector?"

"Um, no. I hadn't thought of that. We also discovered why all the poor wretches we found made only unintelligible sounds. It seems the practice was to install within them a type of artificial translator that intercepts both incoming and outgoing language. Only someone with an identical translator tuned to each individual's code will be understood by the—pardon—creature, and vice versa. That way, if something happened, if one of them escaped or fell into the hands of the law, they could never reveal anything they knew. And the total sexlessness made them docile, passive, easily trained, and nearly incapable of rebellion. No aggression, no initiative.

They may hate it, but they'll do exactly what they're told to do."

Poor Lori, Julian thought, and somehow that very senti- ment, spontaneous as it was, made her feel a little better about herself. "Where is he now? Do you know?"

"He was on the Liliblod route, and he was due in Agon ei- ther the day we hit the place or today. So far no sign of him, and we can hardly go hunting in Liliblod for him, not for *quite* a while."

"They won't *eat* him, will they?" Tony asked worriedly. She'd already decided to make a run in to see that stable area for herself when a soldier had given her a pair of night vision glasses and shown her the denizens of Liliblod. That had talked her out of any such foolishness. Giant furry spiders with glowing white death's-heads dripping with venom ...

"Tony!" Anne Marie scolded.

"No, it's a fair question," Kurdon said. "My feeling is that they will not break their own end of the bargain. They are a strange lot, but they have an odd sense of honor and consis- tency. In all these years they never once touched anyone who stuck to the agreed-upon routes, although frankly, I'd not like to test them *too* much right now. There's some evidence that a number of higher-ups had emergency escapes down to the stable area just in case, and since we didn't nab them, we must assume they got away into Liliblod as well. Best case I suspect is that he'll eventually turn up, possibly after getting over confusion over all the new people there. Worst case is that he met up with some of these fleeing bigwigs and was turned around and pointed back toward Clopta. If that is the case, he should be snared when we move on the gang there. They can hardly send him back again. To what purpose?"

"They might kill him!" Julian said worriedly.

Tony shook her head. "Not Campos. She's not the type. She's more likely to put him in a horse stable, if they have such things in Clopta, and ride him around the park on nice mornings."

Kurdon nodded. "That is our assessment as well."

"But what about Mavra Chang?" Tony asked him. "You said a *bird*?"

"Yes." Again a hand went into the case and brought out a picture. "Probably something like this. It's an even greater work of art than this Lori, in a way. You see, that's a real creature, albeit a rare one from a hex far away from here. A real bird. The only thing that's different is the size of the braincase, which was accomplished with some clever bio-engineering. Campos wanted her mentally intact, to *know*."

"Odd-looking thing," Gus noted. "Kinda like an owl, but with a long bill and pretty colored feathers."

"It's flightless," Kurdon told them. "The wings have completely vanished. It is also quite large—about a meter high, and it can weigh upward of thirty-five kilos. It spends basically all its time rooting with that long, curved bill and sticky tongue, eating mostly insects. It needs to eat a great many of them, but it can also eat raw meat and even a little grain if need be. It is nocturnal, practically blind in daylight, which, aside from its size, is its only defense. The legs are too short and stumpy for speed. I doubt if it can run at all. Sort of like walking on your knees. They made certain she wasn't going to go anywhere."

"The poor dear!" Anne Marie exclaimed.

"Will you be able to do anything for them, all things considered?" Julian asked him. "I mean, you said this was genetic data here, and I went to those—those *doctors* myself. They said doing it more than once could lead to instability, deformity, death."

"Hard to say, with our two most knowledgeable experts among the missing," Kurdon noted. "Probably we can do very little. What we *can* do is outfit them with translators that restore their communication with the outside world. At least that will give them some voice again in how they want to cope and some help in doing it."

Julian thought about the pair. *Another couple of one-of-a-*

kinds, she thought. The population of her mythical dream island was growing.

"Well, we should be able to get them when we get Campos," Kurdon assured them.

"Shouldn't you send ahead and have them arrested now?" Julian asked him.

"Too risky. Clopta is not Agon, and without a bit more authority from that nice big computer, it's not dependable. Remember, even the two maniacs who created this managed to escape us, and that was *here,* in our own backyard."

"Shouldn't we be off, then?" Tony asked him. "I mean, it's likely some of those escapees are even now heading toward Clopta with the news of the raid. They may go underground before we can get to them."

"Liliblod is the same size as Agon, and they are on foot," Kurdon reminded them. "We, on the other hand, will bypass Liliblod and sail directly into Buckgrud, the Cloptan main port city, which is where our quarry happen to live. Besides, even with what happened here, I am pretty sure they'll still feel safe in Buckgrud, which the cartel more or less owns and operates, and under the protection of their own bought politicians."

"I hope you're right," Julian said, looking at the photo of the new Lori. "It must still be awful for them now. I'd hate to get this close and lose them."

"Don't worry about it," Gus said confidently. "I mean, hell, the hexes aren't really huge, and outside of their native hex they'll be easy to spot. Hell, I bet Juan Campos looks like Daisy Duck."

Julian nodded. "A very dangerous Daisy Duck."

BUCKGRUD,
CLOPTA

Juana Campos was made up and dressed to kill—if one was a Cloptan male. In fact, it was the large eyes and pliant over-sized bills that gave Cloptans a ducklike appearance, but they were not related to ducks, nor were they exactly birds in spite of the featherlike covering—rather, they were egg-laying mammals that incubated the eggs in the marsupial-like pouches which both males and females had. Aside from the oversized heads, the body shape was quite humanoid, the fe-male's particularly so, although the males tended to be more pear-shaped and actually rather dull-looking. The females even had thick, lush hair growing from their heads, while the males were universally feather-topped and rather bald. The females even tended to be taller than the males, but while short, squat, and fairly ugly as a rule, the males were built like tanks and abnormally strong for their size. Much of their bodies was protected by invisible but quite effective thick, bony plates right down to the genitalia.

In Clopta, women were literally soft and men were literally hard.

Gen Taluud was built like a bank vault and had a face to match. Ugly, raw, with a curl on one side of his bill that re-vealed the otherwise seldom visible sharp teeth lining the inside. He looked like the kind of Cloptan who might walk right through a wall, and he radiated that kind of toughness even when saying nothing. He had spent twenty years doing all it took to become the top man in Buckgrud, the man who owned the mayor and the provincial governor and whose very word was law. But it hadn't been merely by strong-arm tactics, bribes, double crosses, and murders that he'd risen to the top; he was anything but the stupid muscle he appeared to be.

He'd initially gotten interested in Campos simply out of curiosity, someone who had once been something entirely different. That made her exotic and interesting, and the fact that she also had a hell of a figure didn't hurt. Campos had initially been appalled at the circumstances the Well had forced upon her but also realized that this was a golden opportunity, maybe a chance to rise high and fast in spite of the changed circumstances and in a way overcome the sexual change and get both power and protection. She'd learned, observed, and played the part Gen Taluud expected of his mistresses. Campos recognized the Taluud type immediately as the same sort of boss his father and other cartel members had been back on Earth, and she also understood the business. The only one who'd stood in her way once she'd accepted the situation and her own self as permanent had been Taluud's longtime existing mistress, who wanted no rivals. But when she'd tried a hit on Campos and failed, thanks to Campos's own experience, she had become easy to handle. Campos had pulled the trigger on the woman herself and disposed of the body in a time-honored way so that it would never be found.

If Taluud suspected or knew, he never said, but instead of being upset, even forlorn about the loss of a longtime companion under mysterious circumstances, he'd given Campos a free ticket to the top and treated her with a fair amount of respect, in some cases giving her the authority usually reserved for his lieutenants. Campos understood the bargain. So long as she was at his beck and call, jumped when he snapped his fingers, and served him loyally, she otherwise had nearly free rein within the organization. Still, service to him could be unpleasant sometimes, as the big man was fond of rewarding certain underlings and bigwigs with his girl's services for an evening or two. But with no assets other than the body and a shared ruthlessness, she'd learned to use that, too, to build a ring of powerful friends in the organization that might well outlast even Taluud.

But no matter what else she had planned or what she felt like or wanted to do, when the big man called, which he could at any hour of any day, she was expected to drop everything and show up, always looking her very best. This was just such a time. The fact that it was three in the morning on a weekend did not mean anything particular to her.

Taluud was in his penthouse, clothed in a fancy dressing gown, sitting in his big, overstuffed chair and puffing on an imported cigar. The cigar was as much a badge as a habit; he went through a dozen a day, and a box of them was close to the average annual wage of a Cloptan. Around him were a half dozen fully dressed lieutenants, all of whom she'd known intimately in the past, and one fellow in the chair opposite who was anything but properly dressed and looked like he'd just crawled out of a sewer after battling angry crocodiles. Other than Taluud, he was the only one seated, which was unusual only in that usually nobody sat in Taluud's inner sanctum but he. She stood there, taking in the scene and wondering what it was all about.

Taluud in turn looked straight at her and took his cigar from his mouth to use as a pointer. "Glad you could get here so fast, doll. This guy here is Sluthor. Up until a few days ago he was transport chief at the complex. He tells me a god-damned *army* just blew it to shit."

Campos's lower bill dropped a bit. "But Genny, that's *impossible!*"

A clenched hand came down so hard on the coffee table that the table almost broke. "You *bet* it's impossible! Not only was that place a fortress, but we *owned* the Agon military!" he shouted. "But it *did* happen! And only a few of our people got away. They're struggling in now from Liliblod in ones and twos, all looking at least as bad as Sluthor here. I been on the communicator the last two hours to the capital, and you know what, nobody's in who knows *nothin'*! You hear me, doll? *Nobody's in!* To *me!*"

"I—I don't understand." Campos had a very bad feeling about this that had little to do with the mere loss of even such a wonder as the complex.

"Well, neither do I. I got one of our people in the capital to go into Zone and get some face-to-face answers, but he ain't back yet. Too soon to get many details, but we got some basic stuff from Sluthor and the others straggling in. It ain't just the loss of the complex—we can always build more— and nobody there was so important we couldn't afford to lose 'em, but *how* in the name of the six hells of Dashli did they have the fuckin' *guts* to do this?"

Slowly, through the big man's tirades, what little was known came out.

They'd suspected for some time that something was up, something not at all good, but they'd never expected anything on this scale. This kind of scale would take approval by and the active support of the council, yet nobody on it had warned them or tipped a hand. Instead, they'd given full authority and support to the raiders under an overzealous cop who'd been neutralized, or so it had seemed.

Campos thought it over. "Sounds like somebody very big and very powerful but not on our side got the idea that some of the council was bent," she suggested. "And the ones that were had to save their own tails by letting this go through. If they'd tipped anybody, it would have been a sure sign they were bent, so they had to let it go. It's the only thing that makes sense."

Taluud nodded approvingly. "That's what I figure, too. The question is, Just how much and how many are they willin' to sell out to cover themselves? They had their own man, one of them jelly blobs from the south, in on it. Probably to get in there and protect their asses by deleting the records. That we know because we knew about him before, and he suddenly shows up there just before the raid. The question is, What are the others doin' there?"

She blinked. "Others? I don't understand."

"Them two horse-assed girls, the goat girl with the four tits, and, with the jelly blob, some unknown type ape girl who don't say a word and somebody else we never got a handle on. Thing is, our people reported to the complex that all these critters had one thing in common: They all knew each other. Even the jelly blob. Word was that every single one of 'em had come in from offworld and gone through the Well. Just like you."

Now she understood why she was here and what this was about. "You mean they're *all* there? Together?"

"Pretty much. Who knows if there are any missing. We already had run a check on 'em. The two horse asses and Four Tits got there on one of our courier boats. They been snoopin' around for months but weren't much of a threat. Seems they were there lookin' for somebody—God knows why else you'd stay in that lizard heaven. Somebody snatched off the same courier boat. Another of their own, most likely. Sluthor did a check on the ones that stayed in Agon. None of 'em seems to have come in with you, and none of 'em seem to have any connection with you other than comin' from the same planet once. That goes for the jelly blob, too. That's in your favor. But I know you went down there and did a lot of checking a while back. Where's the ones who came here with *you*?"

She thought a moment, realizing that there was great danger here. The whole truth might cause nasty problems, but a lie could be deadly—or worse. She needed time, and Gen wasn't giving her any. Maybe a half-truth was best . . . for now.

"I was a prisoner when I was dragged here. You know

that," she reminded him. "Right at that time I hadn't realized how good I had it, and I was boiling for revenge. Two of the sorry bitches who got me into that fix were on one of *our* boats and heading right here. I couldn't resist. I'm sorry, Genny, I just couldn't resist, particularly after I visited the cells and saw what they were doing down there. It seemed like heaven had delivered my enemies into my hands. I . . . persuaded Arn Gemalk, who was head of security then, to divert the boat, have them taken off at the pickup point, and delivered to the docs at the complex. I wanted revenge, and just killing them seemed not nearly enough at the time."

Taluud nodded, interested but not apparently upset at this. "And what did they do to them?"

"Turned them into couriers, I suppose. The idea was to make them live out the rest of their miserable lives as cut-off monsters serving what they hated."

"And you don't know what they became or where they are now? The odds are they were the trigger for this—now, don't worry your pretty self about that! You didn't do nothing to them I wouldn'ta done myself. Thing was, though, the horse asses were doin' a favor, trackin' one of 'em for the council, so when they were lifted, it went straight to the top. There was too much heat, and after a while they couldn't stall it anymore. Yeah. This all fits together now. Shit, I wonder if we can find that pair and give 'em to them. Might take the heat off. Otherwise they're givin' the cops and patrol and all the excuse to take us out base by base, station by station."

"Beg pardon, sir, but even if we *could* track them down, they will hardly be in a condition to be recognized. Would it make any difference?" one of the lieutenants asked worriedly.

"Yeah, yeah, it would. They wouldn't like gettin' back two freaks, but they'd have what they was after, anyway. Provin' who they were is just a matter of a new translator. Even if somehow they could talk or they got one of them mind-reader races to get through, what could they tell? We're still in the clear, right? And they get what's left of who they're after."

"Wouldn't they soon be in agony from lack of their variety of the weed?" Campos asked him. "It might not be much of a victory to hand them over."

"Even dead, they'd be found," Taluud noted. "But the weed's no problem. We found that the ones who go through that monster stuff get immune to it over time. Don't matter. We got much better control by that point, anyway."

So they don't need the drug anymore. Interesting. "But how would you tell who and what they were, let alone where?" Campos asked him. "I mean, once they're processed, I thought they were just assigned and all traces of them erased."

"Yeah, well, they don't exist, true, but people got memories. Maybe they can't be found, maybe not," the boss responded. "How many we done of these? A hundred, give or take. Not too many, and there was always a contingency plan just in case for a lot of things, including them doctors. Sluthor says they were in their clinic on the coast and not at the complex when it was raided. If they managed to give their tails the slip before the cops moved in, they'll be on a courier boat right now headin' for a safe hideout west of here. They may have to dodge some patrols, but they should be there before any muscle gets in these parts, and maybe they remember these two. Neither of them was from races we see anywhere in these parts, if I remember. You remember what they were, doll?"

"One was a male from somewhere far off; I think it was Erdom or something like that. The other was still the same as when she left our old world. I understand they're called something here, but nobody seems to know much about them."

"Glathrielian," Sluthor said tiredly. "I've been trying to think of it myself. That's what they called the apelike female who came in with the Leeming."

Campos was suddenly *very* interested, enough to dampen her fear although not enough to make her disregard the sense of danger. "This was a female of the same type? Dark skin, perhaps, no body hair to speak of except on the head and crotch?"

"Yes, that is pretty much a good description of the pictures I saw. Do you know her, then?"

"Yes, I know her. She is the one I *truly* hoped to get my hands on, but she was not with the others."

"Well, you lay off her now, period!" Taluud told her firmly. "She's untouchable. History. They may even have an idea that she'll draw you out. You don't go near her, you hear me? We may all have to disappear for a while until this blows over. Keep your bags packed and be ready for a call. They lure you with her and nail you, the next stop's right here!"

"I doubt if I'd get the chance at her unless it *was* a trap," Campos sighed. "Still, it's too bad. I could have had such *fun* with her."

"What's the point? Sluthor here says she don't talk and is like some brain damage case. Besides, it's gonna be a while before we can use those docs again no matter what."

Campos nodded. "I know. But she's unchanged, and I know from the other that the weed will work particularly well with that kind. Make her an addict, put her on a leash, walk her around like a pet . . . It would be *very* satisfying."

"Yeah, well, get that out of your head now. No personal vendettas while we got bigger trouble. Besides, you already got a pet. That big ugly bird, right?"

"No, I gave her to the zoo," Campos told him, suddenly nervous that two and two would be assembled in the room. "They are quite rare, and the zoo is going to breed her."

Fortunately, it never occurred to the gang leader to consider that the process didn't always create monsters or sterile mules, either. "Yeah, well, no more of that. We got enough trouble from this missing pair if we're guessin' right. All we need is a third to vanish and we may have to bury ourselves, and I do mean bury."

"I wouldn't *dream* of doing anything without your permission, Genny. You know that."

"And you better hadn't, not anymore. Still, bad as it is, we got a few days to play with here; let's not panic. Ain't no raiding army in Clopta yet—they couldn't keep *that* from me. Figure if they didn't find their friends in the complex, then this is where they'll head, though. Take 'em a few days to sweat the details, a few more to get here by boat, a few more than that to set up things so's they can move here. We got at least a week. If they got away, them docs should be in before that, so we may get a jump on the law in finding that missing pair. Also send out the word. Anybody who remembers them when they was in the complex or being seasoned, they tell us just what they are and where they might have gone. Get on it!"

There was a chorus of "Yes, sirs!" and it was clear that the meeting was over.

Campos remained for a bit, wondering if Taluud had anything else for her and hoping to get more information, but the boss dismissed her. "Get lost, doll. Go home, pack, and stay close to the phone. I got calls to make."

She turned and walked out.

By the time she emerged at street level from the private elevator, she'd already started to think about things on her own. What if somebody remembered that she had been there for the whole process? What if the doctors had backup records or clear memories of just what they had done? Taluud was no dummy; he would figure out that she'd been holding out on him and already knew the information he wanted. *Then* life would get *really* unpleasant. But she didn't want to turn them over, particularly not Mavra Chang. Campos wasn't fooled by the drooling servile act, not now that she knew that the bird bitch wasn't even addicted anymore and had never let on. Chang in the zoo or under her control was one thing; Chang with a voice and a mind was something else, even if she stayed a bird. There was something too familiar, deep down, about that bitch. Given the chance, Mavra Chang would spare nothing to arrange a similar fate for Juana Campos.

But why was the council, the kind of United Nations of

this world, so worked up about Chang and the Erdomite? The Erdomite was just somebody with that news crew; he *couldn't* be important in the long run to anybody. But Chang—that "goddess" stuff, playing jungle Indian high priestess . . .

She had been pretty damned sophisticated when she had gotten here.

Those Indian bitches had thought that she was immortal, that she'd been there like forever. Stupid superstition from the dumb-ass Stone Agers? It had seemed so. But what if . . .

What if those rumors of her being some kind of creature who could work the whole damned Well World had been true? They'd recalled the wanted bulletins, said she was just a minor player for the guy they were really looking for, but maybe that was a blind.

First they said she was some kind of real god if she got inside, then they said she wasn't really. What if the first story had been true? What if Mavra Chang could somehow get inside whatever ran this world and do pretty much whatever she liked to everybody and everything? And they got afraid that somebody else, somebody like Genny, would snatch her and somehow make her do what Genny wanted when she was there . . .

That would explain everything that had happened, wouldn't it?

If they find out my birdie is Mavra but don't figure out the rest, they'll give her back. Sooner or later she'll get away, get in there, one way or another, but they won't care what she orders for a Juana Campos.

In the hands of Genny and the cartel things might be even worse. Even if she could somehow talk her way around the deception, which was highly questionable, *they* would be playing for all the power, not her. A world remade by Genny wouldn't be a fit place for anybody. Not with that kind of power. He'd go nuts. If he made a deal and they ran things together, it would be even worse. Two nuts. And no place at all for Juana Campos.

But what to do? What to do? In a couple of days, a week at best, it would be out of her hands if she just let events take their course.

Wait a minute! Maybe there is *a way out of this!* She walked down the darkened, rain-slicked street, deserted at this hour, the only sound the sound of her heels clicking on the hard pavement.

What if she did her own vanishing act? By the time Genny figured it out, the shit would be hitting the fan here. And if she had her two treasures with her, there'd be nothing to stop the cops. They'd come after the organization here like that army'd gone through the complex she'd thought impenetrable. Looking for her, most likely. If she'd checked up on them, they *had* to know that she was here. They had probably already figured it out; they just needed the clout to come after her.

But what if neither she nor they were here? The cartel would be underground for quite a while, particularly in this region. But to where? And how?

Liliblod would be out of the question. She'd never felt comfortable in that creepy place, anyway, and right now it'd be even worse. Likewise, nowhere in Clopta would be safe. By ship? Too risky, and if they tracked her, she'd be trapped with the goods. Due north was Quilst. She didn't know much about it, but it was nontech, so it would be damned hard to trace her, and she was pretty familiar with roughing it in primitive conditions far worse than she'd seen here. Lori ate mostly grass and shrubs now, and Mavra ate bugs and carrion. Not a real supply problem. Lori could haul stuff, and if it got so Mavra couldn't find anything to eat, then Lori might be a good feed if need be.

But what if the Quilst was as nasty as or nastier than Liliblod? She needed to know. There were semitech hexes to the east and west, which *might* do. She needed information, and the first thing to find out was if Lori was an option at all. She didn't have much time—maybe a day or two. First thing to do was to check on Lori. If he wasn't in when she was ready to leave, the hell with him. She'd get a real horse or something like it. A few weeks, or maybe months, away, just marking time, would be worth it. After they'd scoured Clopta and Genny and his gang were history, she could come back. Maybe not to Buckgrud but to one of the other big cities where she could lose herself or, better yet, to the northwest, where there were farms and ranches. She had a number of IDs in the system. Cut and dye her hair, do a few other things, and she might just get away with it.

If she had Terry in her clutches, it would be just *perfect*, but one couldn't have everything. Not yet, anyway.

The clicking of her heels sounded for all the world like the ticking of a clock. A clock counting down the window of opportunity . . .

She had a lot of calls to make.

Lori had tried to keep track of how long the nightmare journey had taken, but either exhaustion or the creeping dullness in his mind had made it impossible. It certainly *seemed* like forever, particularly with that very heavy bastard on his back urging him on and making him miss needed water and food stops.

Still, the guy had to sleep and drink, too, so there'd been just enough of a break to survive. How much did these ducklike things *weigh*, anyway?

Still, once in the warehouse, he'd slept the sleep of the dead, and when she woke up, still feeling pain in every joint, he was at least able to eat and drink.

Still totally confused by what had happened and why he was back *here* instead of *there*, he nonetheless started to get the idea that things weren't normal on this end, either. There were lots of Cloptans around, including many he'd never seen before. They were all frantically loading stuff into huge vans that pulled up one after the other, and he realized that they were emptying the place.

Maybe the good guys finally won one, he thought hopefully. Not that it would do him much good. They were clearly just shifting operations for a while, and where did that leave him? Either they'd shoot him or they'd take him with them to put on some other courier run. It wouldn't even matter if somebody found him. What would they see? A nice little horse with a horn, that was all. Too small for real horse work and, as a gelding, not handy for any other reason. How could he even contact somebody else to tell them he was more than he seemed?

More important, would it make any difference? It was getting harder and harder to remember things. Not just little things, big things. Before he was a horse he'd been a man, but a man who did what? He had memories of a desert and some tent towns and a city by a big wall, and he remembered a woman of the same race, but even she was kind of blurry. And before that there had been someone, something else, but that was so distant and so confusing, he wasn't sure about it. He tried frantically to think, to remember. *I'm not a horse! I'm a* . . .

But he *was* a horse. He couldn't get around that. No matter who or what he'd been, he was now a horse. He was always going to *be* a horse. What was the use of fighting it, of dredging up those old memories, of worrying about things that he could not do anything about?

Someone . . . somebody else . . . had struggled with a big change, and it had driven them nuts. The woman. And when they'd stopped fighting and accepted who and what they were, they were finally able to find some happiness, to stop torturing themselves.

Maybe that was it. Maybe he should just stop trying to be anything else and accept it. Stop the thinking, the remembering, the deep thoughts. Just . . . live. If he *was* going to just be a horse, what would his wants be? Food, water, sleep, and maybe a little care and grooming by somebody nice. What else could he ever want or need? Nothing *these* men had. Nothing *anybody* had that he could imagine.

Then why did he feel such a sense of loss? That was why he'd been searching around in those memories, but while he could come up with all sorts of memories, episodes, and mental pictures, he couldn't come up with anything any of those past lives had offered that seemed at all important or interesting to him now. All it seemed like was an endless search to find things he hadn't had. But he'd never really found them, he knew that, because he had never been sure what he wanted.

And now, here he was, and he knew exactly what he needed and wanted, and the simple things on the list didn't go beyond the basics. Maybe what he'd lost were all those problems and worries. His big problem now was that he hadn't been thinking like a horse.

With that idea in mind, he drifted back to sleep, but it was a lot easier to decide on this course than to stop the dreams.

The Quilst were a kind of cross between animals and plants, it seemed. The pictures made them look like walking, talking turnips who ate dirt. They weren't said to be particularly hostile, but they didn't really build roads and seemed to spend most of their time training hordes of insects to do stuff. Maybe the data was true, but the fact that the Quilst hadn't even put a Zone ambassador down south in recent memory meant that if the information was out of date, she was up the creek there.

The Betared were those horrid little bear things. They were well involved with the cartel at the highest levels, but they all had the temperaments of Genny on a bad day. The Mixtim looked like giant multicolored grasshoppers, but they supposedly had taken steam energy to its highest levels. They were so totally omnivorous that they could, and did, eat almost anything, but aside from often disturbing visitors with their culinary tastes, they weren't threatening and were very civilized, if specialized, like lots of insect cultures. She'd never seen or heard of one with the cartel, though, and they certainly looked like the best of a bad lot. Even if it proved less than inviting even for a getaway, Mixtim was well located with a variety of other hexes available.

They'd also take international credits there, which they used for trade, so at least it would provide options. Mixtim it was, then.

Now a haircut, and a dye job, some practical working clothes, and a bit of an identity switch, and she'd be ready to reclaim her little living treasures. She hoped the zoo wouldn't be too sticky about it, but if they were, then there were other ways.

First, though, she went down to the warehouse, which was getting pretty well cleaned out. "Moving the stuff offshore mostly, to islands and to boats, until this blows over," one of the supervisors told her.

"I called earlier. They said you had a courier come in, looks like a pony?"

"Yeah, he's in the back there. We have no instructions on what to do with him."

"I'll take him," she told them. "Mister Taluud is looking for specific couriers for some reason and doesn't want any harmed or lost until he finds what he's looking for. I'll take full responsibility."

The supervisor shrugged. "Fine with me. One more worry off my shoulders. But what are you gonna do with him, lady? You can't put a horse up in downtown Buckgrud, and you sure can't take him into an apartment."

She laughed. "Let that be my problem. Just show me to him."

Lori was only half-asleep when Campos walked into the rear stall area, and when his vision cleared and he saw who it was, he felt sudden fear and loathing. This was *not* the kind and gentle groom of his needs!

"Hello, Lori," Campos said, almost as if she were greeting an old friend. "Time for us to go."

It was so strange to hear words, whole sentences, that he could comprehend that it shocked him out of his stupor for a bit. "Go where?"

"Oh, you can still *speak*! Well, that will make things even easier."

But he couldn't, not like before. He no longer had the physical equipment to make the variety of sounds necessary for the translator to pick up. Still, the device worked by direct implant into the brain, so as long as *something* came out, however much it was like a whinny or a gurgle, the whole thought came through.

"We have to leave this place soon. Tonight, I hope. I have much to do myself, but I have a place for you to stay until I am ready. I'm taking you to a nice park where you'll be tied up but able to eat and drink and relax in the open air. There's a nice old fellow there who'll see that you're all right until I can come back for you. It's a very nice day to be outside, anyway. Later on we're going to take a train ride, at least part of the way. Right now, just you, me, and our old mutual friend."

"Friend?"

"Yes, indeed. I wouldn't *dream* of leaving without the pride of my little collection!"

Mavra Chang was not having a very pleasant existence, but she was in far more command of herself than Lori had been.

Then again, Lori had never been this low before. Mavra, as she was remembering, had been so low sometimes that this seemed downright optimistic. And of course, Lori might not have much of a future. Mavra knew she'd have that, or at least she hoped so, depending on where the hell Nathan was.

That was her greatest fear. If Nathan had made it inside the Well, maybe she *was* stuck like this and doomed to die. Somehow, though, she didn't believe it. She was still getting information, memories from the Well data base as she thought of them, and going over bits and pieces of her past long forgotten. Nathan sure as hell would have cut that if he'd already been there.

Maybe he was having as much trouble as *she* was, she thought hopefully.

Still, this was not a promising beginning. The Buckgrud Zoo was state of the art, but that meant that she'd been placed in a large area with few places to hide. A large, fake, hollowed-out tree was the only real place of escape, but it had little in the way of maneuvering room inside it. Around it was an area about ten meters square with a heavy glass or glasslike window on one side and very dark walls on the other three. The lighting let people see inside but to her looked like a cloudy night.

The glass was coated with some sort of nonreflective substance, and she could not see herself in it or see much beyond, although if she went up very close, she could barely make out a variety of overdressed giant ducks gawking at her. She couldn't help wondering how many times, if any, Campos had been by just to gloat. There was water in a simulated spring and small pool, and there was food.

That was the worst part, the food. Live insects, mostly worms and crawlers, were introduced several times a day, along with an occasional carcass of something that might have been an unfortunate zoo accident or roadkill for all she knew. The problem wasn't that she was going around gulping down the squirming critters or picking at the festering dead meat. She'd long since passed the point of being revolted at that aspect.

The problem was, she really liked them.

What she didn't like was how even the apartment and its window had offered more attractions than this dump, which was so boring, it risked driving her into the madness she'd been fighting all this time. The only entrance or exit was at the top of the cage, a good four meters beyond her head. The occasional cage attendant would come in now and then on a rope ladder, which was impossible for her to manage, without arms to hold on to it with. The ladder was taken up when they left, anyway. The glass was as thick and unbreakable as she'd ever seen, and there wasn't a chance of getting through it.

She was even more worried that they were going to breed her with a male, as Campos had threatened. It was what zoos did, after all, but what would it do to her? She still had her mind, she could think as a human even if the thoughts were dulled by who knew how long in this incredible boredom, but if she just let her mind wander into fantasy, the bird genes just took over. What if they brought in a male whatever it was and she got knocked up? Would she start building a nest and sitting on eggs and thinking about little squawkers?

The Well was notorious for not making it easy, but damn it, it shouldn't make it *impossible*. But try as she might, she hadn't been able to see a single way out of this mess.

What was even more depressing, was that if there *was* a way for her to get free, flat out she could make maybe a hundred meters an hour, and not for very long. She would also need to spend a lot of time keeping the metabolism going with food. No wonder this bird was rare. Figuring at maybe a kilometer a day if she was lucky, she could make the Avenue and the equator in, oh, maybe three or four years under absolutely perfect conditions.

Yeah.

And so she was quite startled when, in the early evening after the zoo had closed for the day, she heard the cage door open and saw not the usual attendant or the vet but the new model Campos climb down the ladder.

"Hello, my pretty birdie," she said with mock concern. "You needn't play with me. I know you don't need the drug anymore, and I'm not someone to trifle with right now."

"Are you here to taunt me?" Mavra asked her, despondent as ever.

"Oh, my, *no*! In fact, I am here as your liberator, believe it or not. It seems that you have become too popular for your own good and are far too valuable to be left in a musty old zoo. We are going on a little trip, you and I, along with my other pretty little treasure, and we will not be back for quite a while."

"You're taking me *out* of here?" Mavra's heart soared, even though she didn't expect to be going to a nicer place.

"Yes, indeed. In fact, Algon, he's a nice attendant here, will help you up out of the cage. He is a sucker for a pretty face and a few credits. Here. Get into this netting, and then I will tell him to pull you up."

Mavra suddenly felt a little contrary. "You can't lift me. What if I refuse?"

"Refuse? You mean you *like* it in here?"

"Not particularly, but they feed me regularly. You wouldn't go to all this trouble if you just needed to skip town. Somebody's got a line on what you did to me, haven't they?"

"You are quite sophisticated for a jungle primitive, aren't you? Yes, my precious, they *are* looking for you, but it will do you no good to hope. Even if they found you, you would just be kept here in a cage much like this. They might even keep you right here, although with a *much* better lock. I suspect, however, they would take you south, perhaps *very* far south. *I*, on the other hand, am going north, at least for now. Better the devil you know than the devil you do not." Her tone grew suddenly lower, more menacing. "Besides, you little shit, if you don't do it right now I will take one of these rocks, beat you into unconsciousness, and *roll* you into it. Now, *get in!*"

Mavra didn't have any doubts about Campos doing exactly that, so she complied. *Out and going north . . .* There was some hope again. Maybe she was too hard on the Well. One had to have patience with the gods before they answered one's prayers.

Algon took her, still in the netting, and placed her in a box with air holes that sat on a rolling cart. Soon they were out into the night air and, with Algon's passkey, out of the zoo and onto the street. The air felt good, although she was frustrated at being so completely and literally boxed in.

For somebody sneaking out of town, Campos certainly had a lot of help that could reveal her plans no matter what bribes she'd paid. First she was put in the back of a small truck that was certainly driven by somebody else, since Campos remained with her. There were also a number of cases and a steamer trunk.

They stopped after a while and shortly loaded on what certainly sounded and, from the tiny bit visible through the air holes, *looked* for all the world like a small horse.

"You're sure you're not too conspicuous?" Mavra commented, but it was ignored.

More hands unloaded them, and then the box was opened, but only to cut away the netting and transfer Mavra to an even larger box, one apparently designed to transport live animals. Inside was a fair quantity of raw meat and a gadget that would give her water in small amounts.

"Just relax," Campos told her. "You will be in there for a long time, but we shall meet up again before you run out of food and water, I promise you."

"Meet up again? Where are *you* going?"

"The same place you are, only by a different route. I have no time for questions or need to give answers to such as *you*." And with that, the box was sealed and began moving again.

Mavra could hear Campos speaking with others, but since the conversation wasn't directed to her, it wasn't picked up by the translators.

She was puzzled, no, totally confused. What in the *hell* was this maniac doing?

If Mavra was confused, Lori was even more so. For one thing, two female Cloptans had shown up in the park later that day and had set up for what looked like a horse bath and rubdown. It turned out to be a dye job; his pretty beige and all the rest were now jet black, and his mane and tail were snow white. Even the horn had been painted black, and it still smelled awful.

Then Campos had come with the van, loaded with a number of cases and baggage, and eventually had unloaded it at a freight stop on the Cloptan high-speed train line. He was collared there, and a whole bunch of routing tags were attached to it, then he was led onto a livestock flatcar which also contained a large number of animals that looked like a cross between a cow and a camel but with a kind of rounded, platypuslike bill. In a very short time the train began to pull out into the darkness.

The first time they unloaded Mavra Chang's box and reloaded it onto another train, she had a glimmer of what was going on.

She was being transshipped over half the damned hex, on one freight, then on another, in a pattern that probably looked like a baby with a crayon had created it. All of the other stuff was being shipped the same way, but on different trains, and it all seemed to be designed to eventually wind up somewhere together. Shipping agents, working from wired instructions, would reroute the packages so that no one would know the final destination or be able to easily trace them.

It was amazing what money and a computer could do, she thought.

The fact remained, though, that if she was attempting a getaway with everything, including Mavra, then she was traveling very heavy, and if she stayed in a high-tech hex, they would eventually track her down. That meant lowering the technology standard, but to do so with this much stuff would be pretty rough for a Cloptan female on her own. That one horse certainly wouldn't do the job.

Mavra's train reached the end point first, and she sat there, now inside a warehouse, the only sounds occasional trains whirring past outside. She wondered what was coming next and how Juana Campos figured on pulling this off. She didn't mind the wait; that was all she'd been doing for a long time, anyway, but that had been waiting for nothing. Now something was happening. Things were *moving* again, and so was she.

That was worth waiting for.

Just before dawn some automated equipment unloaded several cartons, and they were placed very near Mavra's box. She guessed they were the rest of the stuff from the van. Now all that was lacking was the horse.

It wasn't lacking for long. Just as the sun was starting to come up, Mavra heard the sound of hooves clicking on the hard floor of the warehouse and picked up the unmistakable scent of live horseflesh.

Lori, now tied up to a metal stake near the boxes, was totally confused. All night it was on one train, then onto another, going back and forth, and sometimes, he was sure, on the same train over and over. Unlike Mavra, he didn't like it or understand it one bit.

None of them had long to wait after Lori at last arrived. Whether on a schedule or because the loadmaster didn't like having a horse fouling up his nice warehouse floor, a crew entered and began transferring everything once more.

In the daylight, even with his poor vision, Lori could see that they were at some kind of border stop. On the other side of the sleek magnetic strip that served as Cloptan train tracks there was a very different looking building and beyond it a very different looking terminal. It was a little hard to see as well, as if he were looking through a discolored gauze curtain.

A hex boundary! And not the one to Liliblod, either!

The Cloptan crew and its robotic equipment moved everything across right to the border. The boxes were then put down flush with it and pushed across slowly by small rams that came out from the equipment. Lori alone was led through, feeling the familiar tingle as he passed into a new hex, and then he could see more clearly what was beyond.

It was suddenly chilly. Not cold, but there was a definite chill in the air, and signs of light frost were still around, slow to melt in the rising run. Lori didn't really feel the cold, but it was still something of a shock.

188 • JACK L. CHALKER

More of a shock was the crew that awaited them on the other side.

They were bugs. *Huge* bugs. And not just huge bugs but bugs of just about all shapes and sizes, the smallest still the size of an alley cat.

They were quite colorful creatures, and the two that were enormous, at least two meters long and standing taller than Lori, looked like nothing he'd ever seen even in a nightmare or in the Amazonian jungles. They seemed closest to praying mantises.

He was scared, nervous, and yet somewhat excited and didn't even realize all the old memory connections he was suddenly making again.

A big beetlelike thing crawled up to the pallets on which the boxes rested and with two whiplike hind limbs took the lead pallet and started pulling it effortlessly toward the station beyond. Other, similar creatures did the same with the rest. Finally another, who looked more like a bipedal grasshopper, approached Lori, who shied but couldn't pull away, being tied to a post. But the thing didn't eat him; instead, it wordlessly untied him and began to lead him after the boxes.

The railroad warehouse was a wonder of cogs, levers, belts, pulleys, and other such automation, all of which was apparently driven by external steam plants and which rumbled and hissed and gave off occasional steam through vents. Steam also seemed to heat the place, at least somewhat; it was certainly warmer here.

Overcoming his fear and revulsion at the sight of the giant insects, Lori began to watch them work with fascination. They all looked so very different, yet he began to wonder if in fact they really were. Each seemed to be physically designed almost as a tool would be designed, to do one or two specific tasks well. The big low ones were the strong-arm types, the longshoremen who could move and lift loads much larger and heavier than they. Sleek, small, fast bugs went up and down the conveyors and pipes, oblivious to whether they were right side up or upside down, apparently checking to make sure that everything was operating properly.

The big praying mantis types were primarily lifters, almost like living dockyard cranes using huge mandibles that form-fitted into specially designed containers.

Suppose an insect society, many of which had different specialized varieties anyway, could really breed and design to order or need? Each individual hatched, shaped, and endowed with the capabilities to do specific jobs and serve the whole? That obviously was what was here.

It was an ideal thing for a nontech hex, but the steam power and degree of automation said this was semitech. The bugs of the industrial age, adapted to fit the new requirements.

If they were as durable and as prolific breeders as most bugs, this was a race that might well be able to survive and even thrive anywhere, under almost any conditions.

Outside, both Lori and Mavra could hear the shrill sounds of steam whistles large and small going off and the rhythmic *chug chug chug* unique to one kind of mechanical marvel moving about.

Steam locomotives.

Neither was aware of the other's identity or proximity, although there was little they could have done about it had they known, yet both suddenly shared the same thought.

The crazy dance of the trains might not yet be over.

ANOTHER PART
OF THE FIELD

Gen Taluud was very uncomfortable in the presence of the colonel, but he needed information and needed it bad. He might have some business to do with this jelly blob if the answers were right.

"It was a complete disaster," the colonel told him. "They even managed to prevent me from destroying a great deal of the computer files. Fortunately, I *did* manage to eliminate information on certain major figures and also some details of the divisions within the hexes such as yours."

"You think that'll help *me*?" Taluud thundered. "Hell, everybody there knows me, and so does everybody here. I ain't in the quiet part of the business, you know. If they'd flush something as big as the complex down the toilet, they wouldn't think twice of flushin' me along with it." He bit off the end of a cigar and spat it out with such force, it traveled halfway across the room. "So what's the price, Colonel? What in hell will get 'em off my back?"

"As you surmised, the pair kidnapped by Campos, and particularly one, Mavra Chang. Find them, turn them over, and you are likely to find the pressure turned well down, so much so that you might well be back in business within six months to a year at best."

"Then we'll find 'em!"

"Um, yes. *That* is a priority. The question is, Do we really wish to turn them over to the council when we do?"

"Huh? What in hell does that mean? Of *course* we do. You think I want to be ruined?"

The colonel had considered his course on the journey here, accomplished mostly by sea and not without its own danger. Leemings had great power on land, but in the water they were helpless, and in salt water they could not help but absorb great quantities and sink like stones. Even these amorphous creatures needed to breathe oxygen, and they were not equipped to fashion working gills.

"Mister Taluud, have you thought beyond what's happening to consider *why* it's happening? Why our mutual bosses would allow such a catastrophe?"

"Savin' their own asses, that's all, just like everybody else."

"In more ways than one. They are scared. They are frightened of something so much that they are willing to pull down an important part of what they had built with such care and patience. This Mavra Chang isn't merely someone with a lot of friends. They would *never* have sacrificed the complex for as simple a reason as that."

Gen Taluud really hadn't thought about it, but what the creature had said made a lot of sense. "Go on."

"Let me tell you what they firmly believe about Mavra Chang," the colonel said calmly. "And I'll also tell you about my experiences with a man of the same race. A man named Nathan Brazil."

Taluud listened, fascinated, not knowing whether to believe this stuff. Still, it was clear that the big shots, the rulers and politicians behind all this, were totally convinced, and they had greater resources than he did. Still, it was hard to swallow.

"You really believe all that crap about her, Colonel? Honestly? And this guy who they think is some kind of ancient god, too?"

"Does it matter, sir?"

"Huh? Whatddya mean?"

"Let's assume it's all true. Every word of it. You could never make a bargain with that sort of creature. Even if you thought you had a deal, once inside, at the all-powerful controls, what would bargains with mere mortals count for? How would you enforce the bargain? You see what I mean. There is no way we can allow her to actually get in, so it doesn't matter if I believe it or even if it is true. It doesn't matter if *you* believe it, either. *They* believe it. The raid and the massive actions still to come here prove that."

"Yeah, so what? What's that get us?"

"Perhaps a lot. If *they* got her, they'd just lock her away under guard with Brazil and try to keep them there until all that we know passed away. But what if *we* had her? You and I, together. What if we had her and she was salted away safely in a place only we knew? Think of the possibilities. What do you want to be? Emperor of Clopta? Governor general of the district? Permanent chief councillor? No running, no fear of the law at any time because you *are* the law, secure in the position because if they don't give you everything you want, if they even *dare* to act against you, you can give one order and Chang will get into the Well. You see the potential? You are a powerful man, but only in this city and to a lesser extent in Clopta. Like me, you still take orders from those higher up. The kind of people who are now selling you down the river, as it were. Isn't it tempting to turn the tables and have *them* deferring to *you*?"

It was a masterful scheme, absolutely brilliant. Taluud's estimation of the colonel went up a great deal in just that one moment. Only one thing made him hesitate.

"All very well, Colonel, but what do *you* get out of this? What's to stop *you* from just eating me and becoming ruler of the world yourself?"

The colonel was ready for that one. "For one thing, I don't want to be ruler of the world. I think it would be far too much work to be fun. Much better to be an adviser to that ruler and have his ear when needed. No, sir, I don't want that. But you see, all my life I have taken orders. All my life I have served governments and cartels and bowed to Don Francisco this and General Hernando that. It's been no different here. I do their dirty work, I cover up their mistakes, and still I am dependent on others. I am a man of modest and humble beginnings. The army of my native land on my native world saved me from poverty and starvation. I worked my way up, doing whatever was necessary, whatever could advance me. I did not have the relatives, the connections, or the old military school ties that counted. Finally, with the air corps, I managed to attain basically the level I am at again here—but I was *still* subject to miserable pay and the whims of my superiors, always with the sword at my neck. One of those—those high-and-mighty generals could in an instant declare me dangerous or push me aside. When I got here, I had certain unique qualities and experience and managed to achieve this level rather quickly, but I am still the servant, the outsider. I am not a native. I can never be at the top."

"What do you want, then, Colonel?" Taluud asked him with growing interest, wondering if he could trust any of this.

"I want to be the grand leader of Leeming, the most supreme general and president for life. A modest position of power compared to what *you* might attain but more than enough for me. There are certain—characteristics, if you will—of a Leeming that have the potential for me to live a very long time and for a part of me to live on almost forever. Within my own land I would be absolute ruler. You would have all the rest."

Taluud thought it over. Maybe the slime was telling the truth, maybe he wasn't, but Gen Taluud hadn't lived this long without being able to judge when a fellow as unencumbered with morals as he himself told stories like that. Besides, he could always get the bastard fried if it looked wrong.

"Very tempting, Colonel. Very tempting, indeed. But we're missing one thing to make such a deal, and that's this what's her name. We don't even know where she is or, at the moment, *what* she is."

"I know. Both from the computers and from the medical records of those curious doctors. She is an *anuk*, a very large wingless bird. They were quite proud of her; the genetic remake was so complete, she is said to be capable of reproducing—as an *anuk*, of course."

Taluud's cigar almost dropped from his fingers. "A what? A bird? How big a bird do you mean?"

"Oh, a meter, give or take a bit. About this high, I would say." A pseudopod shot out and hovered in the air.

"Why, that lyin', double-crossin' bitch! I'll fry her ass for this! *Nobody* does this to Gen Taluud!" He picked up the communicator. "Get me Campos. *Now!* No—wait a minute! Go over there and pick her up—*personally.* I want her here in ten minutes, you hear?" The communicator slammed down.

"I gather you already know the location of our quarry," the colonel commented. "How convenient."

"Yeah, maybe. Seems to me she said she'd given it away to someplace, but I can't remember. Don't matter. She'll tell me anything I want to know soon enough."

The communicator rang, and Taluud picked it up. "Yeah? *What!* Well, what about the other two broads? Them, too? *Shit!*" He looked back at the colonel. "They flew the coop! All three of 'em flew the coop! Like they can hide from *me!*"

"I would not underestimate this Campos. I have information that on the old world Juan Campos was in some ways an equivalent to you here."

"Yeah, yeah, I know, but he ain't got no control. I never trusted guys who got to be big because their father was big. You work yourself up, you don't have to prove nothing."

"My point exactly with my own case," the colonel noted. "We agree on a great deal, sir. I believe this could be an excellent partnership."

"The zoo!"

"I beg your pardon?"

"She gave the bird to the zoo!"

A few calls brought the news that the zoo, too, had some-one missing. He was back on the communicator again.

"Look, how tough can it be? Three broads and a bird the size of a teenage kid. You put the word out. Naw, they prob-ably are outta here by now, maybe on a ship—check all the docks and passenger and cargo manifests. Also check the trains, border controls, you name it. *They got to be some-where, and I want the 'where' and fast, hear?*"

"I admire the way you move on things," the colonel said approvingly.

The communicator signaled, and Taluud grabbed it. "Yeah? Well, you get movin' on this other thing. As soon as you find 'em, you get a dozen of your best men and meet me. We'll go after 'em personal. *Then* we pull the plug. Hear? First we want them girls. Period."

"What was that about, if I might ask?"

"Your buddies from Agon are here. They're in the capital right now, armed with lots of information on certain political types, and they're gonna have a pretty free ride by tomorrow. The rats are deserting the ship up there and fallin' all over themselves to be helpful."

"My—'buddies,' as you call them. I assume this is the cen-taurs, the Erdomite, the Dahir, and the Glathrielian girl?"

"Yeah, yeah. Them and that holier than thou Kurdon, too. I *knew* we shoulda made him have an accident years ago! Well, that's what I get for bein' a softy! No more!"

"This—bird. It was well known?"

"Yeah, around here, anyways. It was so weird-lookin', any-body who saw it remembered it. *Shit!* Right under my nose! Right under my fuckin' *nose!*"

"If even the more common elements in your own organiza-tion will remember it even slightly, it is serious. And she was last in the zoo, too . . . Probably on display. That means even more will remember. Honest, upright folks. We will not be too far ahead of them, I fear."

"Maybe not. But if it's always ahead, I'll settle for a few

steps. The only one's gonna laugh at the end of this is the one who winds up with the bird, right?"

"I would say that was a fair statement."

"Then *we* get there first."

"What of these other two females? Might they be with Campos? How much of a problem might *they* be?"

"They're all looks, no brains. Campos was the one with the looks, brains, and guts. I don't know how she even got the other two to go along, but they're dumb enough to fall for a lot of stuff. Well, I'll fix all three of 'em when I get a hold of 'em!"

The communicator signaled. "Yeah? What? *Oamlatt?* That's on the border with Mixtim! You *sure* she crossed over there? Absolutely positive? Yeah, well, it's a lead. Let's get on it. We got anybody in Mixtim that's handy? Shit. Well, it shouldn't be brain surgery to find information. See what you can find out, if you can find anybody there who remembers a *second* woman, or a big bird, or whatever. Call me back." The boss turned to the colonel. "Mixtim."

"Problems?"

"One of the girls—not Campos, one of the others—arrived this morning. I said the other two weren't all that bright. She made a call back here just so's her sister wouldn't worry about her. They're sure she went over into Mixtim at the Oamlatt border crossing. It's a rail intersection and trade center. Makes sense."

The communicator buzzed.

"Yeah? A black pony? That don't sound like no bird!"

"Wait a minute!" the colonel said in an urgent tone. "Ask them if the pony had a horn on its head."

"Hold it. Did the horse have a horn on its head? How do I know? Stickin' up, I guess." There was a pause. "It did!" Taluud looked over at the colonel. "Okay, it did. So?"

"The other one. She's taking *both* of them with her!"

"You get to work on the Mixtim side. See if you can get any information on trains and such. I want to know where they bought tickets to, hear?"

He pressed a button on the communicator, then redialed another number. "All right, we're on 'em. Have your team meet me at Central Station. Call ahead to Oamlatt and make sure we have supplies for a long trip and the firepower we'll need that'll work there. Yeah, Oamlatt. They went into Mixtim, and we're gonna have to go get 'em. You meet me at the station after gettin' that set, you hear? I'm pullin' the plug."

He looked at the colonel. "You like bugs?" he asked.

"Depends. Raw, boiled, or fried?" Colonel Lunderman responded.

"Everybody's flown the coop," Kurdon told them. "It was to be expected, but I am still disappointed. At any rate, we've broken the main connection for this entire region for quite some time, and we have enough on the local boys both here and in Agon that it's unlikely to be restored on a scale like this in the near future."

"You mean you've actually destroyed the cartel?" Julian asked, somewhat awed at the concept. "Because of *us*?"

"Because of you we have hurt them, yes," the inspector agreed. "And we have given two hexes and perhaps many more in the area a breath of fresh air and cleanliness, which is more than I dared to hope when this began. As to the cartel, though, no. It is damaged but far too large and too spread out to be killed. To truly kill it we would need a means to get at the ministers of many governments, to clean house at the very top. What we have gained is a bit of local joy and some pride; we have finally hurt them. But destroyed them? Hardly. You cut off a few heads from this kind of monster, it still has far more heads than it needs. You cut off *all* its heads and somehow it grows new ones. Just winning a battle of this magnitude is incredible, but the war? No. Take it from a career policeman. So long as there are greedy and power-hungry people at the top and corruption festers, you cannot win. You play to tie, that is all."

It was pretty depressing looked at that way.

"What about Mavra and Lori?" Gus asked him. "I mean, that was part of the reason for all this."

"Yes, it is, and the council is still very anxious to have them. But there is a limit to what I can do myself, and I am already overburdened here. My main concern is my own country, as you must understand. If I cannot cure the world-wide cancer, I can at least try my best to ensure that Agon becomes fully cancer-free. You will have whatever funds and authority you require and the aid of any official that you contact. It would be better to work through the locals on this, anyway. They know their own territory."

"That certainly helps," Tony told him, "but I gather you mean that we're on our own from this point."

"Hardly. As I say, this remains a top priority with the council. You will find cooperation along the line in most civilized areas, and we now have descriptions and bulletins going out from Zone to governments throughout the Well World. Make no mistake—we will find them."

"I want Campos," Gus said with a low growl. "I want Campos *bad*."

"Then your next stop is Mixtim," Kurdon told them. "Take the train to Oamlatt. I'll arrange for Cloptan authorities there to brief you on what we know so far. After that, you will have to pursue. Please do so. If they are chased, then they cannot stop, and if they do not stop, they are bound to be seen and reported. If they *do* stop, you will be on them. I have seen you all work now, and I have every confidence in your abilities to do the job."

Gus sighed and looked at Terry. Damn it, he *knew* he should stop, but they were so very close. And for Terry's sake as well as his own, he *wanted* Campos.

He wanted to eat her alive.

In the ancient times when the Well World was operated as a biological and social laboratory rather than simply existing, there was the problem of simulating the limitations of real planets that would logically evolve such races and ecosystems. In many cases that meant placing limitations within the hexes on everything from the losses in electrical signals over a distance or whether certain levels of technology would work at all. The semitech hexes had the most variations, but in all such places the great emphasis had been on steam. Mixtim had a generally flat landscape and a somewhat dry continental climate where the rains were seasonal and the rivers broad, fairly shallow, and winding. It was a land best suited for growing hardy crops, mostly grains, but without the practical use of rivers to move large quantities of harvest from where it was grown to where it was needed.

The answer had been a vast network of steam-powered locomotives pulling long trains of produce to and from major population centers and also to ports of entry with neighboring hexes, where it could be traded for goods either impossible to manufacture or not worth the trouble to make within the hex. They were sleek, fast trains like nothing ever seen on Earth, but they had the unmistakable sound and fury of the classic steam engine. The network was particularly remarkable because of the inability to use a telegraph or maintain the integrity of an electrical signal through the tracks. Nonetheless, they had a fine safety record, and the trains of Mixtim ran on time.

In fact, it almost seemed as if the whole population were involved in running or servicing the trains. While the trains occasionally passed clusters of high twisted mounds filled with teeming denizens of the insect world, after more than two hours there wasn't a sign of a major city and the villages they passed were more likely trade centers and farming communities. On the other hand, there appeared to be one every time two different rail lines crossed, and there were an *awful* lot of rail lines in Mixtim. Juana Campos was counting on that and the fact that they had little in the way of computers or even written records for nonroutine shipments. Everything like that was more or less off the book.

The natives crammed into cars and resembled festering colonies, but there was little provision for visiting travelers. On the other hand, the Mixtimites had plenty of surplus boxcars along every siding, and it was no problem at all to hook one on for special purposes.

The society was, as expected, totally communal, so there was no money or other favors exchanged for services, but outsiders were in fact valued and expected to pay, the fees going to whatever local jurisdiction for the purpose of buying imports. Some of these were specialized or customized farm tools and implements or finely machined parts for irrigation systems, and some were as simple as candy and other delicacies.

The largest import, however, was chemical fertilizer, and *that* made Mixtim and its railroad less than ideal for visitors. The Mixtimites, it seemed, either had no sense of smell or liked the smell of it. The stench of fertilizer was everywhere.

"This is totally gross," said Audlay, one of the two former roommates with Campos back in Buckgrud, as they sat on a layer of wheat or some kind of grass on the floor of a boxcar heading into the hex.

"Look at it this way. At least we won't have to worry about gaining weight here," Kuzi, the other roommate, responded in a tone just short of I-think-I-have-to-throw-up.

"Quit complaining!" Campos snapped at them. "I don't like the smell any more than you do, but what do you want me to do about it? You knew it would be rough when you decided to come along. You also knew when you came that there was no going back. Not for a long while. Now, make the best of it!"

"Yes, Juana," Audlay responded, sounding almost like a small child.

Campos had dominated the other two since she'd moved in six months earlier. They were of an all too familiar type, very much the kind of people the old Juan Campos thought most women were. They seemed to live in fear of almost everything, and in spite of their protests, they *liked* being dominated. What power and confidence they had they drew from another, and that other was the one whose power they feared. They were both afraid of Campos, but it wasn't just out of fear that they'd agreed to come along. They both felt that this was the only way out of an existence they didn't like and one which had no real future.

Audlay almost defined the word "bimbo." If there were two thoughts in that head of hers, they were jumbled from being blown around by the air passing between her ears, Campos thought. Still, she had just enough pride and sense to realize when she was being humiliated, even if she didn't understand the joke. The men had her do silly, ridiculous things and played all sorts of pranks on her when they weren't insulting her or slapping her around. She had found herself oddly attracted to Campos from the first, though. There was something inside the strange woman that radiated the power, the authority, and occasionally the attitude of the men she'd known, yet Campos wasn't a man. The newcomer had often defended Audlay against some of the more oafish lieutenants. A woman capable of standing up to the men and protecting others had been an unbelievably attractive individual, and Campos had shown her all sorts of new and different positions and turn-ons she had never dreamed of before. She would do just about anything Juana said, but not without whining and complaining about it all the time.

Kuzi was different. Older and tougher, she was very much the product of a rough and morally ambivalent life and had taken everything she could get. She, in fact, had only one fear, and it wasn't Campos; she was getting older, and while she was still attractive, every time she had looked at herself in the mirror for the past year or two, she'd seen more and more bloom coming off the rose. Her man was coming by less and less, and fewer others were interested in coming around when they had other, younger women to fool around with. She'd seen the handwriting on the wall and hadn't liked it one bit. The guys also weren't exactly young chicks anymore, either, and where did they get off dumping her? She didn't like Campos all that much, but she saw a lot more there than the men had. The strange newcomer had hated the life almost from the start, and it was clear that she'd been biding her time until she could do something about it. Well, now that the time had come, it was time for old Kuzi to fish or cut bait.

Campos regarded Kuzi not much more than she did Audlay, but she did recognize the armor plate that was there. A gun might be as dangerous to them as to anybody else in Audlay's hands, but there was no question in Campos's mind that Kuzi could and would blow away anybody she had to.

Still, Campos wished that she had a couple of better and stronger allies than this pair. There just hadn't been enough time to build the kind of alliances she really knew were necessary before it had fallen apart, and these two were the only ones she could depend on upon such short notice. Still, sitting in a boxcar that smelled like warmed-over shit going through a landscape that was kind of like the Argentine pampas over-run with human-sized grasshoppers and cockroaches, she was under no illusion that she was biding time until something came up that would give her more of a plan.

"What are they all so scared of that damned birdie for, any-way?" Kuzi asked after a while. "And why load ourselves down with that pair?"

"The horse will be handy. He carries things, remember," Campos responded. "Besides, there is no other animal of that type who can understand a complicated order. As for the birdie, that's the prize, and I did not really realize it. They are all afraid that my precious little birdie can walk inside this world and play God. Would you believe that?"

"*That* thing?" Audlay commented, her upper beak rippling in disbelief.

"She was not always 'that *thing*,' as you say it. Inside is still the brain, the mind, of the person it used to be."

"So you gonna take her up north, let her go inside, and fix things for us?" Kuzi asked her.

Mavra, still in the box but well within earshot, could not help but note that she was being talked about. "Don't believe it? Take me up there and I'll show you how it's done," she offered, knowing the response.

"She says she can do it," Campos told the other two, to whom Mavra's words were just unpleasant squawking. "The trouble is, what would she do to *us* if we let her, eh? *That* is the problem. That is *everybody's* problem with her."

"So where are we goin' and what're we gonna do?" Audlay asked her.

"We are going to change trains a few times just for insur-ance's sake, and then we are heading for another border. This is a nice place for a getaway, but it is hardly the kind of place where I think any of us want to spend more time than we have to. Have either of you ever been this way before?"

"I went down to the place in Agon a few times and once or twice to the islands, but that's about it," Kuzi told her. "I don't think Audlay's been out of Buckgrud since she ran away from the farm. Right?"

Audlay nodded.

"That makes us all strangers, but I have more experience being a stranger in a new land than either of you," Campos told them. "Still, I admit I have never been in *this* strange a place before. We need some information. We need to know what is in the hexes that are around this place."

In a way, Clopta hadn't been nearly as alien as she would have expected if she'd just heard of it. The buildings were odd, some of the customs were very strange, the people looked different and had in some cases different needs and comforts, but overall, it really *hadn't* been that different from Earth. That was what had made it easy for her to fit into it. Deep down, they were the same *sorts* as those she'd known back home. Agon hadn't been all that different, either, no matter how different the look of the people or what they ate or what their houses looked like, and some of the other races she'd met at the complex hadn't been alien enough where it counted to really worry her. *This*, though, was unexpected. There *were* places, nearby places, on this world where things were so alien, she could not fit in. It had added a layer of difficulty almost from the beginning that she hadn't counted on at all.

"Find one with power, a real bathroom, and running water," Kuzi said, half in jest.

"It will get harder than this, I think!" Campos warned them. "We cannot use the modern hexes. Modern hexes have computers and electronic identity checks and efficient policemen and probably corrupt officials with ties to those we left behind. No matter where we go, we stick out. We are a different breed. Best for the time being to stick to places where it is difficult to find people who do not want to be found, where news travels very slowly, and where the government is a three-day ride. We need food, and shelter, and privacy. We must move until we find it."

"What then?" Kuzi asked her. "We just sit and hope they bust Taluud and his whole rotten lousy crew?"

"For a start," Campos told her. "Still, I feel that there is something else, something valuable that I am missing here that will be the answer to all our problems."

"Yeah, well, so long as you have something they want, they'll keep looking for us," Kuzi noted.

Campos's head snapped up, and her long lashes almost hit her forehead. "What was that? What did you say?"

"I just said that so long as we have the birdie and they want it, they'll keep coming."

"Yes! That's *it!*"

"Huh?" the other two both said at once.

"I wonder what price, what guarantees we might get at the highest levels for her. I have been an idiot! We have a treasure this whole world wants, no matter what the reason! It is simply a matter of making sure we can safely cash it in!"

"Yeah? How are you gonna do that?" Kuzi asked her. "You know Gen and his mob. Would you trust them on any deal once they had what they wanted and didn't need us no more?"

"Not a bit," Campos admitted. "But if it were from the government, in writing, and public, then perhaps it would be honored, no? A full amnesty, a full pardon for anything we might be charged with first and foremost. Some money—reward money—for returning what was lost. Quite a lot of money. Enough to buy all the finer things. A villa, perhaps, or a ranch, and some strong-necked, simpleminded men to carry out our orders and see to our needs. It has possibilities, does it not?"

"You think you can get 'em to buy that?"

"Over time. It will have to be well thought out and carefully done, but yes, I think we can get at least that. But first we must have that place I spoke of."

"You mean the ranch with the cute dumb guys?" Audlay asked.

Campos ignored her. "We need to hide out for a bit. Make them uncomfortable, even desperate for a solution. *Then* we can make any sort of deal with confidence."

She needed more than ever to find out about the hexes farther on. Somewhere on this crazy world, where every country seemed no larger than Ecuador, there was the kind of place she sought.

"Yes, three Cloptans, a horse, and a lot of baggage," the colonel said. "We know they came at least this far."

"Oh, yes," the stationmaster responded, standing on her hind legs and looking very much like a parody of a human. "I remember 'em. They *did* change here. Kind of odd, two groups of foreigners coming through. We don't get much of that here, you know."

The colonel and Taluud were counting on that. It had been frustrating to stop at every transfer point and make the queries, particularly with the train crews so insistent on keeping the schedule so perfectly, but it had paid off.

"They took another train from here?" the colonel pressed impatiently.

"Oh, yes."

"Which train? Going where and in which direction?"

"You know, we've been hoping to replace the roof on the main silo over there before the rains come," the stationmaster commented.

"Just let me have a few minutes with the little bug, boss," one of the gunmen whispered to Taluud. "I'll find out what we need."

Taluud slapped the man hard in the face with the back of his hand. "Idiot!" he commented. He could estimate the number of bugs within shouting distance, and he didn't like the mental image of what would happen to them if they roughed up the key official in town.

"So you need a new silo roof?" the colonel responded. "And how much will it take to get one made for you, say, in Clopta?"

"Oh, not a lot, but more'n we got," the stationmaster responded. "Maybe six hundred units."

Lunderman could hear Taluud choking slightly in back of him, but he knew how much cash the man had in those suitcases. "You'll have your new roof, sir. Now, as to the others?"

"Train 1544," the stationmaster responded. "Eastbound."

"When is the next train due in that direction, if I may ask?"

"Oh, there'll be one by in an hour and forty-one minutes," the station master responded, looking at the enigmatic station clock.

"Then we'd also like passage on it when it arrives. How much will that be?"

"Can't say," the Mixtimite told him. "I don't know how far you want to go."

"How far did *they* buy passage to?"

"End of the line. That'd be the Hawyr border."

Gen Taluud saw a long string of such transactions ahead and groaned.

"Don't worry so much," the colonel told him. "After all, they don't have nearly the cash with them that you do. They can't keep this up for long."

"Long enough," Gen Taluud growled, turning to one of the gunmen. "Pay the man. And add six hundred for his damned roof."

For a society without money, they all sure seemed to have a good knowledge of the finer points of the system, he thought ruefully.

"These documents from your own government railway commission tell you to give us full cooperation as well as free passage," Julian argued.

"I see it," the stationmaster told her. "Trouble is, we haven't been on the friendliest of terms here with the Mother Nest. Been hard to get materials."

"He's sayin' that the government's all well and good, but his three hundred babies all need shoes," Gus commented. He turned to the stationmaster, who had reacted as everybody always did to Gus's sudden and fierce appearance.

"Tryin' to scare me poppin' in and out like that?" the stationmaster asked nervously.

"It's a habit. We understand what you are getting at, but they didn't give us a great deal of cash, just enough to get by, and we may have a long way to go. We've spoken with other stationmasters here, and they have understood the problem. What makes you think we can give you more?"

"Got a new silo roof out of the last bunch."

"The *last* bunch? You mean there's more than the Cloptan women?" Tony asked.

"Sure. *Was* they women? Can't tell the difference myself. But first the one bunch comes in, and they buy tickets for themselves and freight for their stuff. Then this second bunch comes in, also Cloptans, but with a real strange character like nothin' I ever saw before—as strange as all of you. And *they* seemed right interested in payin' whatever it took to find out where the first group went. Guess I shoulda held out for more than a roof, huh?"

Julian thought a moment. "What did this other one, with the second group, look like?"

"Didn't look like anything at all. No, I mean it. Just a giant ball of goo. Nice manners, though."

"The colonel! The colonel's after 'em!" Gus hissed. "Okay, look, we could give you a paper that would authorize you to go to Clopta and place a prepaid order for something if you want, but we can't give you cash."

"I dunno. We don't work like that here."

"Yeah, well, I'll tell you how *we* work. We try and be reasonable and hope for cooperation," Gus told him, some menace creeping into his already intimidating voice. "If we don't get any cooperation, we note who didn't give it to us. Then we have to send a message to our people and to your government that we could not do our jobs *because we couldn't pay his bribe*! Might not get us what we need, but it sure brings us satisfaction."

"Oh, goodness, yes!" Anne Marie put in, getting the drift of things. "I wonder what happened to that last one who did this to us. We never did find out because when we had to backtrack to check, they were marching out the whole population of his town somewhere. It was *most* distressing!"

The stationmaster's limbs twitched a bit, and the antennae atop her head seemed to cross.

"Give me a sheet of the official notepaper with the seal," Gus told Tony. "I'll put it on the next train to the Mother Nest. Then all we'll need from you, sir, is your name and title and the name of this lovely little town here."

The twitching continued, and finally the stationmaster said, "First batch took 1544 eastbound. The second group followed 'em."

"And when is the next train?"

"Sixty-four minutes."

"We thank you for your cooperation," Tony told her. "We will report our satisfaction with the line to the authorities."

"No, just leave me out," the stationmaster responded. "They'd just come and take away the money I already got . . ."

"*Amateurs,*" Gus hissed contemptuously.

"Hawyr is out," Juana Campos muttered, looking at a map which she couldn't read but which she'd marked up in Spanish. "High-tech and reported not very friendly anyway. Karlbarx is nontech, but they're said to be some sort of giant rat thing and they eat meat. I don't think they sound too great, and there's not much trade there or a line going all the way to the border, anyway. Quilst I'd already ruled out, so that leaves Leba. I don't like it, but that seems to be the best choice."

"Are they all full of flesh-eating monsters or what?" Audlay asked plaintively. "I mean, gee, it sounds like a horror show."

"Well, the Lebans are plants, and they supposedly don't need much except dirt and water, so that's something," Campos commented. "They're also semitech, but the only use they seem to make of it is that they've allowed the Mixti-mites to extend a few railroad lines through."

"*Phew!* More smelly boxcars?" Kuzi said rather than asked.

"Maybe. We'll have to see what it looks like. The trains are basically through to the other borders and don't seem to have many stops in Leba. I doubt if a plant that gets all its nourishment from the sun, rain, and soil needs much from anywhere else. Trouble is, we go up there, we can get boxed in fairly easily. There's only one more hex to the equator, which, I am told, cannot be crossed. The Leban trains don't go there; they head for Bahaoid or something that sounds like that, which is a high-tech hex to the west that they *do* trade with. So we got this plant hex, and then a nontech hex up against a wall, and a high-tech on both sides. Not great."

"We could turn around and go back," Audlay suggested. "Maybe they wouldn't figure that."

"The *last* thing we want to do is go back toward Clopta, believe me. We'd be in jail or worse, and most of them in there with us would be part of the old organization and maybe not too keen on seeing us, either. No, I don't think so. Not now." She sighed. "Leba it is, then."

"You say they're *plants*?" Kuzi asked her. "I just can't imagine that. A flower garden that talks back."

"Somehow I don't think it's going to be like that," Campos responded. "We can only go and see. And I hope we can arrange for some fresh food for our little troublemaking prize here. As an insect eater, she's probably been going nuts being unable to eat this whole population."

Low hills began as they traveled north toward the border in Mixtim, and soon the countryside began to be broken and interesting once more. Along the rivers there was lush green vegetation, but beyond the hills were covered with grassland, too arid to really farm effectively, considering that the water had to come uphill, but sufficient to provide sustenance for a few small villages that seemed to exist primarily for the railroad.

There were no border controls as such there, but the station and small yard right against the hex barrier were used to rewater the engines and give them a checkout as well as to change engines and crews for the haul through Leba. The steam engines used had a different look to them; they were much larger, with long boilers, and had huge coal tenders just in back of the engine in place of the wood carriers of Mixtim. While the engines were prepared and checked out, there was a two-hour layover.

"Figures," Gus commented. "You wouldn't want to burn wood in a land where the people were the plants. They might take it personal."

"They must mine the coal elsewhere," Tony noted. "There didn't seem to be any signs of such mining or of coal, period, anywhere we passed." She sighed. "Well, time to at least find out some information. Excuse me."

Anne Marie stood looking at the ghostly border and what was beyond. "Looks rather ominous," she commented. "And certainly wet."

The skies within Mixtim were bright, with just a few clouds, while the skies on the other side of the border were a low uniform gray. The place was certainly green, though; it seemed like an endless forest, perhaps a rain forest from the looks of the fog and mist curling through the tops of the trees beyond.

Tony returned a few minutes later. "News good, not so good, and in between," she told them. "First, no more switches. They went into Leba, all right, and so did the colonel's bunch following them. The ladies went through many hours ago, the second group only on the train before this one. We are certainly catching up, but I fear to the wrong group. I am *most* worried about the colonel, Gus."

"He's a slick meanie, all right," Gus agreed. "but I handled him."

"Yes, once. I remember thinking when we spoke to one another of Brazil and Carnivale and old times that I was glad he was on our side. Now that it seems he is not, my fears are realized."

"I still say he can be handled."

"In a high-tech hex, yes. He is as vulnerable to the energy weapons as we are. But the energy weapons do not work here, Gus, or in Leba, either. Regular guns, crossbows, that sort of thing, *they* will work, but what would be the effect on a creature like him of shooting him full of bullets and arrows? Not much. He can drown, yes, but we are far from the ocean, and I doubt if we will be able to entice him to jump into a deep lake. We need a way to counter him or we might rue catching up to him."

Gus considered it and nodded. "I think I see what you mean. In this kind of hex you gotta think like you're in a western, and they didn't have Colt .45 disintegrators back then. There's gotta be *something*, though, that'll get him. If those things weren't mortal, they'd have eaten this whole damned world by now!"

"That is a point," Tony admitted. "But what?" Her eyes looked around the rail yard, not really knowing what she was looking for but hoping for some kind of hint, something that would give them an edge.

"What is that little beetle doing with the small tank up in front of the engine there, dear?" Anne Marie asked.

"Putting oil in the headlamps for the dark, I would say," Tony responded.

All three of them suddenly said at exactly the same time, "Say! Why not?"

"I wonder how much they can spare and how much we can safely carry?" Anne Marie mused at last.

"Yeah, and don't forget the matches," Gus added.

Tony sighed. "That is still a worry. It looks *awfully* damp in there."

"Look on the bright side," Anne Marie said with a smile. "If they are all intelligent plants over there, at least we won't be executed for starting any forest fires."

There is a sort of train service area and such right here, in the middle of the hex, just before the line branches off to the east," Juana Campos noted. "That is where we must get off."

"What're we gonna do about all our bags and stuff?" Audlay asked. "I mean, we can't carry all *that*, and not even your cute little pony can take all that much."

"Yeah, we're gonna be in the middle of nowhere," Kuzi agreed.

"I had hoped we could take more by hiring natives or animals when we needed them," Campos told them both. "It seems like we can't count on anything being what we think of as normal up here, though. We're just going to have to go through the stuff, see what we *have* to take and what we *can* take. Anything else will have to be left."

"You can leave that bird for all I care," Audlay commented. "That thing's gonna be what takes up a lot of room."

"We can use some of the clothing to make a kind of brace, and she is light enough to be able to be carried by our pack mule here. If she is truly charmed, she won't starve. With all these plants there must be insects by the millions, so if we just tie her to a stake at night with a very long rope, she can go find her own food. The Mixtim say that the natives here are not hostile but demand respect and that fruit and such are available if you do. We will have to depend on that."

When the train stopped for the servicing in a wooded glade near a rushing waterfall, it was already very late in the day. They had spent a full day and night going back and forth on the trains of Mixtim and now, at the end of a second day, were in the middle of nowhere in Leba. The two companions were not at all thrilled with this adventure anymore, and Campos was beginning to wonder if she hadn't made a mistake herself.

It was gray and depressing, there was a light rain falling— there *always* seemed to be a light rain falling—and they were in a wilderness setting surrounded by mountain-sized rolling hills. Where there wasn't grass or puddles there was mud.

"You sure this is a good idea?" Kuzi asked her. "I mean, we're gonna go off in this *muck* toward who knows what. And we don't even know if anybody's really following us! If they just got an all-points out, hell, we oughta go on to that high-tech place at the end of the railroad and be comfortable for a night or two until we can figure out what to do next."

"Sounds good to me," Audlay chimed in, looking at the mud as if it were acid about to swallow her up.

Campos shook her head. "No, I have been hunted before. You get a feeling for it. Still, we cannot do much, starting this late in the day. Perhaps before we *do* figure out anything, we ought to see just who we are up against. I propose that we stop here and camp out, no matter how miserable that sounds, but not close to here. Up there, overlooking these yards, might be far enough if we can fool these Mixtim staff into thinking we went some other direction. Then we wait for more trains and we see who gets off. There is one late-night train and then not another until morning. There is also no question that we can hear them when they come. If we look and no one gets off of either train, or no one gets off who does not then climb back on, we can decide what to do, perhaps even take something of a risk and catch the *next* train after that toward civilization."

"But what if a bunch *does* get off?" Kuzi asked her.

"Then *we* will be in back of them rather than ahead. Then, if they do not discover that we remain near here, they will go off into this wilderness in search of us. If they do figure out our plan, then we will have to deal with them. Come. We are in for some very heavy lugging that will take all of us and Lori to do and then a more miserable climb and a miserable dark, wet night. But by tomorrow we may well be able at last to act."

Kuzi looked around nervously. "I wish we'd seen some of these Lebans. I'd like to know what we're dealin' with here."

"Oh, *yuck!*" Audlay said with obvious disgust as she sank ankle-deep into thick brown mud. "I don't think I'm gonna be able to take this!"

"Just pretend you're back on the farm you ran away from," Campos told her. "You weren't city born and bred."

"Yeah, but that was *comfortable*! I just didn't realize it till now."

Campos grew alarmed. *"Don't you cry on me, you silly wimp!* Give me a hand with this—*now!*"

It was said in the Campos tone of voice that few ignored; those who did lived to regret it.

They had managed, with Lori doing some pulling, to get what gear they'd saved a hundred feet up the mountainside, although it was exhausting work. Mavra was finally out of the box and on a rope tied to her ankle, but she was expected to walk, and she managed, her feet actually able to dig into the mud and turf, although she moved slowly.

Although near exhaustion, Campos made sure that they had a tent up and that the gear was either repacked or sufficiently hidden from view. The station crew had paid them no real attention, but they were certainly bound to be remembered, so after all was said and done, leaving everything on the bluff overlooking the yard, the three of them and Lori managed to make a show of going down, through the whole yard, across into the darkness beyond, and off toward the northwest. They then circled around, came up below the yard, crossed the tracks, and at last made it back up to the camp.

If anybody in the yard was asked, he would swear that the trio had gone off in that direction.

It was enough, but it had been done only with Campos threatening and cursing. In the latter stages she was pretty physical with them, particularly Audlay, but it was accomplished.

Now there was nothing to do but huddle in the tent, in the sleeping bags, and wait for the sound of a steam locomotive.

The late-night train had brought nobody familiar, nobody suspicious, and nobody who didn't look like a large insect. Campos didn't know whether to be relieved or worried, but she decided that finally she might be able to get some sleep.

It seemed like only an instant, but somebody was shaking her, and hard. She resisted, then started, reflexes taking over, and grabbed the nearest strange arm.

"Take it easy!" Kuzi snapped. "You was out like a light! I heard the train and went down and took a look, and you'll never believe who got off."

Campos shook herself awake. "Who?"

"Your jilted lover, the great himself!"

"Gen Taluud? *Here?* But he never goes *anywhere*! And he *never, never* does his own dirty work! This isn't his style!"

"Well, it's him, all right. Think I could mistake that son of a bitch, fat cigar and all? And he's got five guys with him; looks like Pern and the whole bodyguard."

This was an even more unexpected curve. Campos hadn't expected to be chased by Taluud at all. "Anybody with them?"

"Maybe. I dunno. There was this—this *thing* with 'em, and they all seemed to be talkin' to it, but I couldn't tell you what it looked like even now. I *will* tell you they got *horses* with 'em, but the horses sure don't like whatever it was."

Campos pulled herself out of the sleeping bag, every single muscle aching, including some she had never known she had. "Are they still there?"

"Last I saw, yeah. I figured I better get back here and wake you up fast."

"You did exactly right. Stay here and keep Audlay quiet if she wakes up and don't tell her about this yet. If she hears it's Genny in person, she'll panic. I'm going for a look myself."

Kuzi was right; it *was* Taluud in the flesh, and she really couldn't make out what the hell that thing with the boys was, either. One thing was for sure: he'd come in style. Not only horses for all the boys but pack animals, too. He must've spent a fortune on that outfit. This wasn't personal anymore, that was clear. She knew him too well. He'd have ducked underground under most circumstances and just sent out feelers to everywhere to report to him if the girls were found. No, for Genny to do it himself, there had to be more to it.

There was only one possible explanation: Genny had found out or figured out who the bird was and had come to the same conclusion she had. He'd have stayed in character if he just wanted to give them back as he'd said. No, clearly he knew of Mavra's value and was determined to use her to work his own deal.

Back on Earth her brothers and father had always teased her about thinking too small. Maybe they were right. What would amnesty mean to Genny? He was so crooked, he'd have new charges in a week. And as for riches, he probably had enough stashed away to buy his own hex. She'd had a certain admiration for him from the start for what he'd built and how much he'd accumulated and how comfortable he was with all of it—very much like her own father. Now that admiration was justified. That fat old SOB was rolling the dice for all the marbles, winner take all.

What *was* that thing with him, though? It kind of flowed or oozed, but sometimes it looked almost like a very large man—an Earth-type man. What could one do to stop it if it found one? she wondered. It would be like shooting into a giant wad of gum. It would be best not to find out. Genny alone would be bad enough.

She watched, worried and impatient, until they finally mounted and rode off slowly in the direction they'd faked the crew out on the night before, leaving one of the bodyguards at the station just in case. The *thing* with them had gone, too; although the animals hadn't liked it, it had assumed its manlike shape and managed to mount a saddle.

They'd be back because they lost the trail, because there wasn't one, or because they would finally figure out the deception. Still, where could they go? What could they do at this point? Where they were was as safe as anywhere else around here, and it would be pretty tough to surprise them.

At least it wasn't raining. It was still as humid as the jungles but much cooler, and there was still a lot of fog and mist around. Without the rain there seemed to be something saying that not everything was hopeless.

Audlay was up by the time she returned, and Kuzi had made a small fire with the camper oven, really just a metal device with a chemical fuel that could be used to heat one thing at a time. It didn't give off a lot of smoke; Campos decided to let them eat something.

Both Lori and Mavra looked wet, muddy, and miserable, but they were still there and still secure.

"You are very popular," she told them. "We will see who gets who, though, in the end. Do not get your hopes up. No matter *who* winds up with you, you will still be what you are and they will still lock you away. In a way, you are both very fortunate to be with me and not them. *I* need you. I need both of you. They only want my little Mavra."

Lori's head jerked up. *Mavra!* So *that* was what all this was about! If only there was some way to communicate directly with her and not just through Campos!

"Yeah, I'm real popular," Mavra responded. "And hungry. There were some pickings around here, but not enough."

"You will have to eat what you can. I have nothing to spare right now," Campos told her. "Would you prefer I shot my pretty pony here and let you feast on *him*? He's another like you, you know."

Mavra turned and looked up at the pony and for the first time noticed the horn, painted black though it was. *No. Couldn't be,* she thought. *But then again, maybe it could . . .* Like Lori, she tried to think of some way of communicating.

An hour later there was the sound of another train pulling in, but it turned out to be going in the opposite direction. For a moment she was tempted; that certainly was one option, considering their fix. But if Genny had left one man here, had he also left others elsewhere? There was that long layover at the border coming up; there was probably a similar one going back and nowhere at all to hide.

After another hour there was no sign of Taluud's party returning, but another train was coming up from the south and it stopped at the station. More people did indeed get off, and they stuck out worse than Cloptans.

Two centaurs—blond and beautiful, Campos thought approvingly. And an unmistakable Erdomite female. Probably the little bitch they said was with Lori on the boat.

And then, suddenly, her bill opened in complete amazement. It couldn't be! It just *couldn't* be! But it *was*!

Theresa Perez, naked as the day she was born and fatter than a stuck pig but otherwise looking much the same.

Campos couldn't take her eyes off the girl or fight the

near lust for complete revenge that was rising within her. *I could have them all! Even now! I could have them all to play with . . .*

But how?

She saw the Cloptan left behind start to walk out toward the train, spot the other foreigners getting off, and quickly duck back behind a shed, pulling his pistol.

Shoot them all, you idiot! Just leave me the girl . . .

He looked as if he might well be going to try to do just that, perhaps to all of them, but just as he steadied his arm and aimed, *something* had him. Something that somehow hadn't been visible before but now was a huge, monstrous lizard, wide jaws chomping down on the man, who struggled once and was still. The pistol fired once, a totally wild shot that seemed to go nowhere, and that was it.

Campos was upset less at the scene than at the sudden appearance of their savior. Where had that creature come from? And for that matter, where was it now?

This was going to take a great deal of thought.

"Sorry to mess up your station. It was not intentional," Anne Marie told one of the Mixtimite workers. "I'm afraid he was going to shoot us."

"We have an absolute dictum neither to judge nor to interfere in the strange customs of other races," the creature responded philosophically. "Please just clean up any messes you make before you leave and take only your memories and what you brought in with you."

Gus stared at the large insect as he walked off, apparently unconcerned about what had happened. Finally he said, "Why do I feel like I'm about to be arrested by Smokey the Bear?"

"Forget it," Julian told him. "Good job. How did you spot him?"

"Just luck. Even Dahirs have to take a leak now and then."

"Well, we ought to be more careful from now on," she

warned them. "Tony, see if you can find out what this was all about from some of these workers. I want to know what Cloptans are doing here trying to take us out."

"You aren't the only one," Tony agreed, and trotted over to some of the workers who were tending the water tank.

Julian looked around at the high mountains and dense forest with its puffs of fog and frowned. "I don't like this. I feel very exposed here."

"You went through that whole nasty business at that underground nest of cutthroats, and *this* beautiful spot makes you more nervous?" Anne Marie responded, a bit amused by the contrast.

"We were attacking there, and *they* had to contend with *us*," Julian reminded her. "Now *we're* the sitting targets." She looked around and above them and then seemed to see something. Her Erdomese eyes adjusted for the long view, bringing the bluff into clearer view as if through mild binoculars.

"Something?" Anne Marie asked, a bit nervous again.

"I thought I saw something on that bluff, but I can't be sure. Whoever it was is gone now, though." She kept watching the area just to make sure.

Anne Marie twisted around and rummaged through her saddle packs, bringing out a medium-bore rifle with a scope and a clip of ammunition, which she inserted into the stock. She checked it, then raised it to her shoulder and panned the area, looking through the scope.

"Can you really shoot that thing straight?" Gus asked her worriedly.

"My great uncle Reggie used to sit around and tell the family stories about his war in Burma. I'm not sure we believed them, but he was a member of the Aldstone Downs Shooting Club, and he took me with him once when I was still rather young. Took pity on me, I suppose—young girl in a wheelchair and all that. I watched them shoot some clay pigeons, but it looked rather silly. They had a rifle range there, though, and Reggie wanted to show off how good a shot he was to his unbelieving niece. He was *quite* good, I might say, and just for a lark he let me try it from the chair. It proved quite a good platform for small-bore. He'd take me back now and then because I liked it so much. Finally stopped, though, when I began outshooting him." She sighed. "He's long dead now, but these are stronger arms, better eyes, and a *much* better platform."

"I wish I could hold something that would shoot," Julian commented, still looking. "My own abilities seem to be purely defensive and useful only close in." She finally looked away, and after a moment Anne Marie lowered the rifle.

"You are *sure* you saw someone up there?" Anne Marie asked her.

"I'm sure. But who knows? It might be one of the elusive natives for all I can tell about them."

"Stay here, all of you," Gus said. "I'm going to go look for myself."

Terry started to follow, but he cut her short. "No! They can't see me, but they can see *you* now."

Tony came back over, noticing the rifle. "What happened?"

"Julian thinks someone is up there. Gus has gone to check," Anne Marie told her. "In the meantime, I thought we'd be ready just in case."

"Interesting," Tony said, thinking and looking at the bluff. "The Cloptans—almost certainly Campos with what might well be Mavra and possibly Lori as well—arrived just before dark last night. They went off in that direction, toward the northwest, leaving much of their baggage behind one of the train sheds, and weren't seen or heard of again. The colonel and five Cloptans came in this morning, fully armed and with horses and pack mules, left that one back here, and set off after the first group. They, too, haven't returned."

Julian shook her head slowly from side to side and said, "I wish Gus was back from his scouting. I seem to remember him saying Campos was from a pretty wild area, maybe the jungle, back on Earth."

"So?"

"Nobody with *any* survival experience would go into an unknown wilderness at nightfall. No roads, no trails to speak of. It doesn't make any sense. And why northwest? Why back yourself up against the equator, which I am told is a solid wall like the Zone wall in Erdom? I kept trying to think what *I* would do in their place." She clicked her two hoofed hands together. "That's *it!*" They never went *anywhere*! I'll bet you they're right up there in a solid defensive position!"

"We should know when Gus comes back," Tony said optimistically. "Until then I suggest we move a bit more toward some protection from that bluff just in case there's a rifle as capable as the one Anne Marie has up there."

"I agree, but I wouldn't worry *too* much. After all, they can't see Gus, you know," Anne Marie reminded her.

"I wouldn't get overconfident," Julian warned. "That is Gus's one big weakness. I do not think that this Campos is any pushover. If she saw Gus in action . . ."

Mavra had been trying to figure out a way to communicate with Lori. She walked over to the black unicorn pony and looked at the ground. There was a fair amount of mud there, and slowly she began to smooth it over with her broad bird's feet. Lori, on a short rope tied to a stake, was nonetheless able to come over to the area and watch.

Language . . . What language? Greek had worked before. Try it.

The feet weren't adequate for writing, so she leaned over and began writing in the mud with her sharp, slightly curved bill. MAVRA.

Lori understood what she was trying to do but couldn't make out what it was. Once he had known these things, once he'd read many languages, but it was so hard, so hard to remember . . . He shook his head no.

Mavra was elated that she'd gotten any reaction at all but disturbed at his inability to read what she thought looked fairly clear. She wished she had been able to learn this English tongue the others knew or at least the alphabet it used. English ... England ... England was a part of Britannia, right? The Portuguese had hated the English and spoke as if they were not distant in their native lands. So England, Britannia ... Conquered by Rome, as had been most of Europe and north Africa. Latin? If something was wrong with learning Greek, he might not remember Latin, either. But what if the alphabets were the same thanks to the Roman conquest? It was worth a try.

M - A - V - R - A.

Lori twisted, took a look at the letters, and tried to remember, tried to bring *something* back. A, B, C, D, E, F, G ... The old rhyme came from somewhere, and out of the depths of his brain he saw MAVRA there.

A nod of the horse's head.

Mavra felt better. Something was better than nothing. But how was Lori spelled? Did it matter?

LOWREY?

Lori thought he was losing it but got hold of himself and read it again. Lowrey? *Lori!* Enthusiastic nod. He'd grade for spelling later.

This next one would be harder. Mavra looked over, but if the two women with Campos saw anything odd there, they surely gave no sign that they noticed.

ESCAPADUM, she managed, with a *lot* of effort. It looked awful, but maybe it would come through.

Again Lori puzzled over the word. What the hell did *that* mean? Escapa ... *Escape!* A very enthusiastic nod.

He moved his head and managed to almost grab the rope around his neck in his mouth. Mavra watched, got the idea, and went over to the post. It wasn't much of a knot, more a casual loop, but since she had only a bill designed for digging out insects, untying it would not be that easy. Still, looking over at the two Cloptan women, she started to work on it.

It didn't matter where they were or what they were. As

Campos had pointed out, they were self-sufficient in most surroundings and had no real needs beyond food and water. They had been coming north, so they were still headed for the equator. If they could make it, what difference did it make if they were on their own as animals and would have to take some time to get there?

She almost had it when Lori gave a deep neigh and shook the rope. Mavra turned to see Campos coming back and knew she had to back off.

Lori didn't feel too disappointed. If they were going to have to walk in this place, then Mavra would probably be stuck up on top of her somehow, because otherwise they'd move at a crawl. The first chance they got, he'd make a break for it no matter what. If they could make it into the woods at any kind of speed at all, those three Cloptans would never catch them. They would be forced to give up any real chase after they realized that their supplies were also gone atop Lori's back.

Maybe what Mavra had claimed was all true. Coming from such depths of despair and hopelessness to a point where they not only were brought back together but might actually make a break for it in a region better suited to them than to any pursuers had been too much to hope for. It had taken Mavra to make him realize it, though.

For now they had to wait. He looked over at Campos. What in the *world* was she doing with that machete?

"Just some vines and those metal cups," Campos was instructing the other two. "That will do, yes. Kuzi, get the pistols and put clips in them, then bring me one, and *fast*!"

Quickly Campos sliced through a small tree so that only a small stub remained above the ground. She twisted some thread from Audlay's sewing kit around it, secured it in a notch, and tied the two metal cups to it so that they touched just off the ground. She then unreeled the thread over to another stump so that it crossed the most obvious path. She then tied it off to another cut trunk on the other side.

Kuzi brought the pistol to her, looking nervous. "What is this?"

"Just get back behind the tent and keep Audlay out of the way," Campos whispered. "There's something down there you can't see until it is too late. If those two cups hit each other, stand and just fire as fast as you can anywhere between the threads. Straight out. It's taller than we are."

"What is it?" Kuzi whispered back, suddenly scared. "That thing I saw?"

"No. Something else. Like a big lizard from hell, only for some reason you cannot see it until it is eating you, so just *shoot*! I will be over by the rock and doing the same. If we fire quickly enough, we may get it or at least knock it back."

"Gee . . . she really does know this stuff," Audlay whispered, terrified but still confident in Campos—more now than ever.

"I hope so," Kuzi responded. Giant blob creatures, invisible killer lizards . . . This wasn't exactly the picture she'd had in mind of the trip.

In spite of his confidence at not being visible, Gus still proceeded cautiously. The mud was slippery, and if he lost his balance and fell, he'd be seen, all right, by just about everybody, maybe before he broke his fool neck.

He reached the bluff where Julian thought she'd seen something, and sure enough, it looked as if somebody had been there, maybe for quite some time. What was that— some kind of root there? He'd seen Cloptans chewing on that stuff, but only the menial types. Somebody said it was some kind of mild drug, he remembered, more a habit than an addiction. He picked one up and sniffed it. It smelled like, well *root beer*, sort of. He dropped it and looked around. Well, if a Cloptan had the habit and was stuck here watching things as a lookout, that would be about what one would expect.

They couldn't have gone much farther up, not in the dark. There were certainly signs of some kind of boots or shoes, and was that a hoofprint or two? Maybe.

He moved on up, being extra careful, and as his head cleared a flat area just above, he saw the tent and campsite and, over to one side—holy smoke! Could that be *Lori*? The horn was right and it was kinda like the picture Kurdon had shown them, but the colors were certainly all wrong.

They could dye the hair, but they hadn't cut off the horn.

And over there near the pony—a meter-high ball of feathers that kind of gave off a whole riot of colors. Looked like a damned big owl, though, except for that long pointed beak. Could that be Mavra?

His heart started pounding with excitement. This close! Here they were!

With nobody else in sight, he moved swiftly to get up to the top and try to introduce himself when he suddenly felt something catch on his foot. There was a dull chatter.

Suddenly, the whole place seemed to explode. He felt something slam into him like a hammer, and he fell backward and then began to slide down the slope, bits of grass coming off as he slid farther and farther down the mountainside toward the freight yard below.

"Did we get it?" Kuzi yelled.

"We're still here!" Campos pointed out. This was the most excitement she'd had since waking up in that burg. The sense of danger coursed through her and invigorated her in a way she'd felt only briefly since becoming Cloptan, that having been when she'd disintegrated that bitch on the docks months earlier.

"*Now* what?" Audlay squealed, uncharacteristically excited more than scared. She was actually *enjoying* this!

"I don't think that thing will be climbing up here anytime soon again," Campos told the others, "but there are three more down there, and now they'll know we're here. Get together what you can! Never mind how it's stuffed in! Roll it all up, tie it off, and get it somehow on the horse! We are going to have to move fast! Keep the ammo out. Get me another clip and take one for yourself!"

Kuzi threw Campos a clip, and she ejected the old one and inserted the fresh clip in the pistol. But even as she moved with Audlay to strike the tent and get everything together, she called, "Move? *Where?*"

"Into the forest and then down!" Campos told her. "Get down toward the tracks if we can, I hope. I'll keep us covered while you get packed! *Move!*"

Terry had followed Gus mentally all the way up, and when he'd been hit, she'd cried out and started toward the trail. Julian moved to try and stop her, but Tony called, "No! Let her go! It may be the only way we'll find him! Stay here! I'll get him if he's still worth getting! Anne Marie, keep me covered. If they start shooting again, shoot in their general direction. Keep them back!"

But Juana Campos had no intention of exposing herself again, only of blocking anyone else from coming to the camp level.

It was also pretty easy to find Gus; he was totally visible, sprawled out, covered with mud about halfway to the bluff, and from his side a pool of yellowish liquid gathered.

Terry reached him first. He groaned and tried to get up, but it was too much for him. Tony was there only seconds later.

"Gus! Are you all right?"

The Dahir's eyes opened, and he took in several deep breaths. "You've got to be kidding."

Tony examined the wound. "It looks like you've taken a bullet in the side. Small caliber, but a mean-looking wound. Can you stand? I will try and help you down the rest of the way."

"I—I dunno. It ain't really hurtin' yet. Here . . . pull me up—*Jesus!*" He stiffened and sank back down. "Man! It hurts like hell *now!*"

"Well, we are going to have to get you down somehow. If I help you, do you think you could get on my back and just cling there?"

"I—*augh*! I'll do it! Gimme a moment . . . Okay—*now*!"

The female centaur's arms, so weak in Dillian terms compared to the male's, were more powerful than anybody else's they'd met along the way. Pivoting around at the nearly universal hip joint the Dillians had, she pulled Gus to a standing position, then grabbed him and pulled him up onto her back. He was barely on, and sideways, but by force of will he managed to turn himself around. Tony immediately started down, Terry following worriedly.

Once back on level ground, Anne Marie helped Gus back down, and they turned him on his side. "Looks like it passed clean through," Julian noted. "That's actually a good sign. Trouble is, we can't tell if it hit anything vital internally because we don't know what 'vital' *is* to a Dahir, and the only doctors I know of in this whole region aren't ones I'd recommend to friends."

"We should wash off both the entry and exit wounds," Anne Marie told them. "We can get buckets or something from the Mixtim, and there's plenty of water around here, goodness knows. Stopping the bleeding, though, is going to be a real problem, and there's still shock and infection to worry about. The best we can do is use some of the big bandages in the kit and tape him up and then wait."

"No! Stop! You *can't* wait!" Gus gasped. "Too close! Too close!"

"Just take it easy," Tony soothed.

"No, you don't understand! *They're up there!* Mavra and Lori both! I saw 'em! *Ow!* God! This hurts!"

"Mavra and Lori both?" Julian responded, looking up again toward the bluff and beyond.

"And a lot of guns and a willingness to use them," Tony reminded her. "One thing at a time! Where can they go? They are on foot now, as it were, and Cloptans would have a lot more trouble in this landscape than *we* would. If they can get off there at all without coming back through here, they will be off trail and going down into a wilderness. Our biggest danger is that they will come down, guns blazing. You and Anne Marie see to Gus. I will ensure that if they *do* come down, they will not get far. Do not worry about them. At the moment I would rather be in our position than theirs, actually."

"I don't know about that," Julian commented. "This Campos seems to be a devil, almost supernatural in the harm she can cause. What if they *do* get down? What if they flag down a train?"

"These trains do not stop for flags, I don't think," Tony assured her. "The Mixtim will allow nothing to interfere with their punctuality."

Gus was no ideal patient while the wounds were washed and dressed, but after a while he passed out, and that helped a lot. They rigged up a kind of litter from wood and a freight station tarp and got him under a shed which held maintenance tools. It was all they could do.

Julian sighed. "Look, I'm going to go down the tracks and see if I can pick them up. Oh, don't look so alarmed! I'll be careful, and I won't *do* anything, only locate them and get back here. They won't be expecting anybody to do it, anyway."

"I don't like it. We've already got one wounded member, and he was in many ways the handiest of us all," Anne Marie said, shaking her head.

"You said it yourself about Campos," Tony reminded her.

"I know, I know, but don't you see? It's something I can *do*. Something that makes sense that I can do better than either of you. And of all of us I'm the most expendable, anyway. You two have futures when you finally get back home, and even Gus has the girl here in a kind of sweet, Platonic way. I can't go home, and you know what they did to Lori. Mavra Chang might be my only way out of this. Don't worry." She paused, then added, "But even if for some reason I don't come back, don't give up. I'm going to do what seems best at the moment. I don't intend getting caught or shot, but no matter what, you find them. You find them and get them to that Well."

They knew that nothing they could say and nothing they could do short of tying her up would change her mind, so they let her go.

Once outside, Julian looked around until she found what had to be the messiest, gooeyest mass of dark brown mud anywhere and then got down and rolled in it until she was literally covered with the stuff. There was a heavy mist starting up; it wouldn't dry out very easily.

Then, on all fours for maximum traction, she started off up the tracks in the direction of the end of the line somewhere far off, searching less for individuals than for hope.

Juana Campos was thinking as they made their way slowly and laboriously down the mountainside, almost tree by tree. The girls had acquitted themselves well in their first real trial; for the first time, she was beginning to have actual respect for their potential.

All along I have been thinking like a woman, she told herself. *I have been thinking like the mistress of the local don. I am more than that. That I am a woman I cannot change, but I am also Juan Carlo Rodriges Campos de la Montoya, son of Don Francisco Campos, the greatest man of modern Peru. If I am a woman, so be it, but I will not think like one. Taluud, you will not be the one to rebuild in Clopta, this I swear! Before I am through, they will bow and scrape to me as they did to you. Here begins the future of power in Clopta!*

No more thinking small, of amnesties and rewards. Those who truly had the power in this world would have to acknowledge her, or a certain little birdie would go visiting the Well. Take it or leave it.

Those amateurs hunting for their friends would not climb up the mountain again, and the only real threat from them had been taken out. Gen Taluud would not be so timid. He would send his *men* up there and find them gone. Then they would see the signs and figure out what she'd done, and they'd come hunting. Hunting on their big, fat horses. If they could shoot an invisible thing, then how much easier to shoot them off their mounts! Hell, just potting Genny would probably do it.

Once down the hill, she'd find the perfect place, and there they'd camp and lay their ambush. They would wait until the others came. *Then* whoever was left would have to deal with *her*!

And part of that price would be completing the set. *Then* it would all be right. *Then* this world would also dance to a Campos melody!

It was easy to find the railroad; a train came by every hour by day and every two or three by night. Whatever they traded, the Maxtim sure traded a lot. Finding the spot in a light rain before darkness fell would be more difficult but not impossible. The trees and rocks around there were almost made to be natural fortresses, and she knew how Genny and his men thought.

The other two listened in amazement to the plan, but with growing excitement. Not just Kuzi, the new supreme lieutenant, but even Audlay was saying, "Can I have a gun this time, Juana? *Please?* I been wanting to shoot some guys for the *longest* time!"

"Pretty one, if I thought you could even hit a *mountain* with a gun, I would gladly let you," Campos told her. "But you can be just as important and cover the one area that neither Kuzi nor I can. Just be patient. We must find our spot and prepare it well tonight. I think they will come tomorrow."

Julian had worked her way slowly along the tracks until well after dark before she decided that she had to have gone too far and started back.

At that, she almost missed them. They were quite well dug in and nearly invisible from the road. It was only the fact that they expected their trouble to come from the southeast that betrayed them at all. Once or twice the one on guard looked out from this direction toward the freight yard, and when that happened, Julian's infrared vision abilities caught a glimpse of a head.

Now that she *had* found them, though, she didn't know quite what she was going to do. Something inside her told her that no matter what situation she was in, she simply could not take offensive action. It was something inside her that was part of what made her a very different person from the one she'd once been. She could instinctively defend herself—that she'd discovered in the complex—but to go in there and harm someone not trying to do immediate harm to her—it just wasn't in her.

She had no weapons, anyway. In fact, she had come with nothing at all, her earrings and nose ring being the only artificial things she had. That and her brain, which was at least working efficiently—or was it? She'd had this idea to come here and find them, but that efficient thinking machine hadn't a clue as to what to do with what she'd discovered.

She wondered if she could get around them and spot where Lori and Mavra were and what their situation was. It might give her an opportunity. She moved into the forest and up and around the Cloptans' camp.

They had picked their spot very well. No matter what the angle, Julian couldn't quite get in back of them or above them with any kind of clear view. She knew better than to try to get in really close. They'd trapped Gus somehow, so what chance would *she* have?

She realized she was making excuses for herself, but it didn't matter. She was still too much the Erdomese female to be capable of aggression or even of doing most things on her own. It was like knowing everything there was to know about flying a plane and then discovering that she had acrophobia. In fact, although she knew that the only rational course was to go back and warn the Dillians, she found herself unable to bring herself to risk detection by the ambushers. For all the false bravado at the complex, she still had nightmares about it, in particular about being jumped from behind. She'd done it once, because that had been the group and she'd gone with the group, but she doubted she could do it again—especially on her own.

I'm as much of a freak as Mavra, Lori, and those poor things back in the complex, she thought miserably. *I'm still the same scared, wimpy little Erdomese cow I was before, only they made it impossible for me to like guys who can defend me.*

She tried to figure out some way to actually act, to make something happen, and came up with a hundred different things, but she just couldn't do any of them.

She wondered what she would do if the Dillians came walking up the tracks into the ambush. Would she have the nerve to warn them, or would she be forced to watch them be cut down?

Shortly after dawn there was a change in the camp. Voices and the sound and scents of things being prepared for a breakfast.

Women's voices, unmistakable even with that Cloptan rasp.

Julian envied them even as she hated them. It wasn't *fair*, she thought, finding tears of self-pity rising within her that she was also powerless to stop. *A bastard like Campos gets to act decisively, and I can't even work to save my friends!*

About two hours after dawn came the unmistakable sound of horses, and Julian feared she was about to witness what she'd worried about all night. However, it wasn't the Dillians who were coming up the tracks but somebody else. Those voices were definitely all coming from men.

"Only three Cloptans!" Campos hissed. "Three and that blob thing." She looked over at Kuzi, who had her rifle out and poised, and then back at Audlay. "You ready?"

They both nodded.

"Hold it! I hear a train coming—from the south, I think!" Campos whispered. "Wait until the train is almost to them.

Then take out the two on this side first. The noise might keep the other two from even noticing the shots. They won't have a clue where we are or even that we're here until the train passes, and then we've got them cold."

Gen Taluud heard the train as well. He and the colonel were on the far side of the tracks, and the other two were on the near side. As the train approached, he said, "Let's all get over there and let the train pass! There's not much maneuvering room for horses over here!"

Campos could hardly believe her good fortune. "Back two first! Same idea!" she hissed, and Kuzi nodded again.

Suddenly the train was upon them, belching steam and smoke, the Mixtimite engineer sounding the whistle as a warning.

Campos and Kuzi fired their rifles from braced positions dead on, and the two gunmen in back fell off their horses. One of the horses bolted forward, startling Taluud and unbalancing him, and Campos's squeezed-off shot caught him in the shoulder instead of the head. He whirled in the saddle and screamed at the colonel.

Kuzi's shot struck the colonel dead in the "chest" area of his manlike riding form, but it passed right through and didn't seem to do much more than knock him a little off balance.

Campos had expected that, but now she actually stood up, fully exposed, as the train rumbled off into the distance, and shouted, "Hey! Genny! Over here, *baby*!"

The big boss of Clopta looked up from nursing his wound, saw her aiming directly at him, and shouted, *"No! Doll! Wait!"*

She fired, and his head nearly exploded, with brains flying as he toppled off the horse in a heap.

"That is very impressive," the colonel shouted to them. "But you may shoot me as much as you like. It is very difficult to find my vital spots, you know, and I am coming up there to embrace you all!"

The shape got off the horse, and Kuzi pumped five heavy-caliber shells into him before his manlike shape dissolved and he began flowing toward them up the side of the sheltering rock.

Suddenly it was not the two shooters but Audlay, teeth showing, who stood atop the rock holding a pot filled with something. "Hey! Blobbo! Want a little bath?" she asked, and emptied the contents of the pot on top of the colonel.

The colonel froze, then asked, "What is this? Do you think this will stop me?"

Campos and Kuzi emerged from either side of the rock outcrop. Both of them were holding torches.

"No, sir, it is more like a relative of kerosene," Campos said. "Would you like a light?"

The colonel didn't have a ceiling or corner to run to, and he had no knowledge that Audlay wasn't at the top with a torch of her own.

"No! Wait! You need me!" he cried out.

"How do we need you?" Campos came back, hesitating and wondering if she was a fool to do so.

"I had a deal with Taluud! He was going to run everything! The whole show! I was to get my own home hex as absolute ruler!"

So *that* was it. "So why do I need you now?"

"You don't know who to talk to! I do! I know who pulls the strings up to the councillor level! You can only deal with the government up front!"

"Oh, yes? And perhaps we put out these torches and you eat us, huh? I think perhaps we do not have enough guarantees. We will do this ourselves!"

"My word was always good to a Campos!" he retorted. "I am Colonel Jorge Lunderman!"

"Lunderman? The one who worked for my *father*?"

"Sí! Sí! Yo siempre encontré su padre para ser un hombre más honorado! Y él, a la vez, tuvo no razón para me dudar. No una ves!" the colonel said urgently.

Campos was impressed. *"¿Yo tengo su palabra ahora,*

*como estuvo con mi padre, tan estará entre nosotros
también?"*

*"Sobre el honor de mis ascendientes y antes de el Dios y
el Virgen Santo, sí!"*

"Colonel, this may be the one fatal mistake I make, but I
believe you," Juana Campos told him. "Kuzi, it is all right.
Put out your torch. The colonel and I have just come to an
agreement."

Kuzi looked hesitant. "You're sure? What was that you
were saying in that funny language?"

"Nothing is certain, but I think so, yes. I asked the colonel
if he was willing to pledge his service to me here as he did
for my father back where we both come from. He agreed and
took a most solemn oath to that effect. Now, go see if you
can get the horse back. We can use them. It is all right."

The colonel oozed nervously back down the rock and re-
formed facing Campos. "I am honored that you would trust
me still," he told the Cloptan. "I am, however, a bit amazed.
At this very moment I could reach out in a second and swallow you, and what could you do about it? No, no! Do not
worry! I am a man of honor. I ask of you no more than I
asked of Taluud, and I might tell you that I feel that things
will be much better in your hands than in his. I am just curious as to why you trusted me at this point."

Campos gave a Cloptan smile and looked up atop the rock.
"It is all right, Audlay. You can put your torch out now, too!"
she called.

The colonel started quivering like gelatin in an earthquake,
and soon peals of laughter issued forth from the mass. Finally
he said, "I do believe, madame, that this is the beginning of
a most wondrous partnership."

The Cloptan nodded. "Where are the other two men who
were with your party?"

"Back at the freight yard. The Dahir's in pretty poor shape
from your shot, and the others remained with him. They are
now, I should hope, disarmed and well under control. I don't

think either the men, who were only bodyguards, or the Dillians will give us any trouble from now on."

"And the girl? She is there, too?"

"Oh, yes. She is of no consequence, however. She had some strange powers at one time, but she appears to have lost her memory and control of those powers. She appears able to read surface thoughts but cannot speak. And she is very much pregnant."

"Pregnant! By one of our old kind from that place here? Or from before?"

"They think before. They think it is the reason that she was not changed physically into a different race by the Well. Is it important?"

"It *could* be. Before they brought us to this place, they had us more or less service many of that cursed tribe. I was drugged; I do not know for sure which ones. It might well be someone else's, but it might, just *might*, be my own child!"

"It might be obvious in at least general terms once it is born. The features . . ."

"Yes, it might at that! Well, well, this puts an entirely new complexion on things. We will want to ensure that she has that baby before we think of other uses for her."

"And where are the other two in this little drama?" the colonel asked her, still reeking of flammable oils and nervous about the fact.

Kuzi was bringing up the horses, which had not gone far, when they all heard Audlay give a shriek. All of them headed for the camp behind the rocks.

"They're *gone*!" Audlay cried. "Them no-good animals lit out on us durin' the fight!"

OTHER PARTS
OF THE FIELD

Long before the gunfight Mavra had started to work once more on Lori's rope. Being a nocturnal creature had certain advantages, one of which was seeing quite well in the dark, even if not quite in the same way she used to think of as clear vision.

It was clear that the women were setting up an ambush; the odds of all three of them being required to pull it off were equally good. She and Lori were virtually ignored once they had been staked out.

Campos was very smart, a lot smarter than Mavra had given her credit for in the past, but the Cloptan was not without some basic human failings, one of which was that she'd clearly begun to regard both Mavra and Lori as the animals they appeared to be, forgetting the minds buried within. This was often a fatal mistake on the Well World, and while it couldn't, unfortunately, be fatal here, it meant that Campos never thought that Mavra would be able to untie the slipknot holding Lori or that Lori, with a patience and dedication no horse could maintain, would simultaneously be chewing through the rope tied to Mavra's leg.

By morning it was merely a matter of pretending to still be restrained and hoping that the women would be too concerned with the coming showdown to check on the pair, who were in any event within clear eyeshot of them.

When the sound of oncoming riders was heard and the three Cloptans scrambled for their positions, Mavra looked at Lori and Lori just nodded. When the first shots rang out, Lori went down on his forelegs and Mavra scrambled aboard as best she could, then grabbed the rope still around Lori's neck with the claws on her feet and held on for dear life as Lori took off.

Watching nervously, Julian was startled to see the break and immediately moved away from the ambush and followed them.

Mavra could stay on only for so long in that precarious position, particularly with a trailing rope, and fell off two or three hundred meters into the woods. Lori felt her slip, stopped as soon as he could, and turned back to help her. Suddenly a ghostly, filthy mud-caked shape moved from the trees toward Mavra, who was struggling to get up. At first Lori thought it had to be one of the mysterious creatures who were the dominant race in Leba, but she soon realized that it was someone far more familiar, someone she knew . . .

Julian put up a hand to Lori to reassure him, then examined Mavra, who'd stopped trying to struggle to her feet when she realized somebody else was there.

It was easy for Julian, even with her hard mittenlike hands, to get the rope off Mavra's leg and then set her on her feet. She then gestured to Lori to approach, put Mavra on his back, then used the rope she'd just freed to secure the large bird to the pony's torso.

"Can either of you understand me?" she whispered, as only a few voices could be heard in the distance, the train and shots now long past. Getting no immediate response and not wanting to waste any more time, she pointed to Mavra's bill and then to the other rope around Lori's neck. Holding on with the bill and relying on the wrapped-around torso rope to keep her body on, it looked like she might actually be able to ride.

Julian pointed farther into the forest, away from the sounds in back of them, and they proceeded onward. Mavra was uncomfortable but fairly secure upon Lori's back, and Julian reverted to all fours to set a steady but not exhausting pace that covered ground without risking more spills.

They did not stop for hours, not until Julian's thirst was too much to ignore. As soon as she passed a pool of water off to their right, she slowed and headed for it, Lori following, and together they drank. Then Julian untied Mavra and set her down so she, too, could drink and perhaps exercise or feed.

In the darkness of the thick forest Mavra had some reasonable vision, although nothing like what true night would bring. Everything was there but washed out, as in a faded photograph. She was exhausted and felt like she was starving, and her back was killing her from riding like that. And yet . . .

She hadn't felt this good since she'd reentered the Well World.

She was free again! It didn't matter what she was or where she was; it only mattered that she was again delivered from her enemies.

Different insects were out in the day from in the night, but she had enough practice now to figure out where they were and find them. She wanted to make sure that she didn't get out of sight of the other two, but she also wanted to eat as much as possible. She hoped that Julian would discover by herself or somehow be made to understand that they should travel long and hard but only at night, when they would have the advantage of better vision.

After Julian ate some fruit that she found on the forest floor, she went into the pool and tried to wash out as much of the mud as possible. It usually wasn't a good idea for an Erdomese to take a bath of this scale, but once in a while didn't hurt and this was certainly necessary. It was also damned cold water, which meant she had no urge to linger.

Still, she did feel better when she got out and was more her old self again, although there did seem to be places where the mud would *never* wash out. What she really needed, she thought, was dryness, the heat and near absence of humidity for which her body was designed. Thoughts of the desert and its feel and its beauty had crept into her mind off and on of late, particularly while she was just sitting there in Agon. As much as it would kill her, she could not banish Erdom's call to its own. She very much wanted to go back there, but not like this and not while that foul system endured.

She wondered if Lori felt it, too, or whether he felt much of *anything*.

Clearly the two of them had hatched this escape plot, but did that mean that they could understand each other? Somehow she doubted it, at least on a verbal level. They hadn't exactly been making bizarre sounds at one another, anyway.

Think, Julian, think! You may not be much good at anything else, but you are very good at thinking!

That had been her trouble in the beginning, she realized now. Unable to face her position and limitations, she'd stopped thinking and started to let others do all her thinking for her. That was exactly the wrong way. Thinking things through, learning all that could be learned, solving problems and delivering solutions—these were things not everybody was very good at. If she couldn't physically, psychologically, or culturally carry them out, there was always someone who could.

What about writing? Translators did nothing about writing ability any more than they covered up one's previous language skills. They were an enhancement to vocal communication, that was all. She looked around for a stick, found one, and went back over to Lori. She might not be much at writing with those hands, but she sure as hell could block print.

In the mud near the pool she scratched, in English, CAN U READ THIS?

Lori watched, then came over and looked down at it. It was so *hard* to dredge up those old skills, but he managed. It was a little easier than it had been with Mavra; at least this was English. He nodded his head.

Julian was excited. At least there would be *some* way to get through.

R U OK?

Yes. It was an absolute answer to a relative question, but there wasn't any way to add qualifiers.

WHAT DO U WANT TO DO?

That was a deliberate attempt to provoke him into finding some way to get a more complex answer back. He understood its purpose but wondered how the hell he could do it. He tried writing with the stick in his mouth, but it wasn't any use. Then he tried scratching in the mud with his hoof, but that didn't really produce anything intelligible, either. Finally, he gave a big sigh and shook his head negatively.

Maybe Mavra would be better for this, Julian thought. But what language did they have in common?

In an instant she realized that would be a good test of whether they actually had a chance or were just adrift until caught or killed. If Mavra knew the commercial standard language that Julian had spent so much time in Agon studying . . .

It was some time before Mavra had her fill and wandered back. She couldn't help but wonder at how those two were reacting to one another. Julian needed the old Lori, and the old Lori was gone. She approached where they were resting and saw the regular scratches in the mud. She hadn't thought Julian capable of it; maybe she'd changed personalities yet again since the last time they'd been together.

Julian had been dozing but awoke when she sensed someone nearby. Spotting Mavra, she reached for the stick and then went over and smoothed out the mud. The basically ideographic Well World standard commercial language was versatile but not easy, and she had only a limited command of it. Still, Mavra could have no better command of it than she if Mavra were just another person from Earth. But if she was who she claimed to be . . .

CAN YOU READ THIS? Julian scratched, then carefully placed the stick in Mavra's bill. Mavra went over and looked at the writing and was so surprised at what she saw that she almost dropped it. How the *hell* did Julian learn *that*?

Don't ask stupid questions you can't get answered, Mavra, just answer if you can.

I CAN READ IT, Mavra scratched back. It looked awful compared with Julian's, but it was sufficient.

WHAT DO WE DO NOW?

Mavra wrote back, RUN LIKE HELL.

Julian laughed. If somebody could give an answer like that after being like *this* for so long, she was something special indeed.

THEN?

Mavra took the stick. HEAD NORTH THEN WEST TO AVENUE.

Avenue? What was an avenue here? It was a formal and distinct ideograph all its own; that indicated an important noun, a real place.

WHY?

GET IN WELL. MAKE THINGS RIGHT, Mavra wrote.

Make things right ... Right for whom? Julian wondered. Still, it was the answer she had both hoped for and expected.

GO BY NIGHT, SLEEP DAYS, Julian suggested.

THEY WILL BE WAITING FOR US.

They? Campos? The colonel? The Dillians? WHO IS THEY?

EVERYBODY. ARMIES. WHOLE WORLD.

That was alarming. NO OTHER WAY IN?

MANY. LONG WAY. TOO LONG.

HOW FAR?

ONE HEX LENGTH N, HALF WEST.

That meant maybe 250 miles north, give or take, and half that west. A *really* long way to go on foot, and with nothing but themselves and their wits. She had thought, or at least *hoped*, that they had traveled farther by train, but she hadn't really paid attention to the map, and Mavra probably was guessing, too. It could be less.

Or more.

YOU WILL GET IN, she scratched to Mavra. *Somehow or another we have to.*

They'd be coming for them, that was for sure, but even Julian knew that the odds of catching anybody in this environment were as slim as the odds of their actually pulling this off. On the other hand, at least there wouldn't be a lot of talkative natives.

Or would there? All this way and she still hadn't the slightest idea what the natives of this hex really *were*.

She got up and started looking around. They hadn't come very far, that was for sure, but they'd come *some* way inland. Did the natives leave the forest as wilderness and cluster in places off the beaten track?

The trees were huge, creating a vast canopy of green above. There were scads of insects, both crawling and flying, and while they looked suitably bizarre and like nothing on Earth, they were clearly recognizable as insects. There *might* be birds, but if so, they remained pretty high up and weren't apparent.

About the only really odd thing was a kind of vine that seemed to grow in thick clumps down the trees, giving them almost the appearance of wearing skirts. She wondered how strong the vines were. The rope solution for keeping Mavra on Lori's back wasn't a good one, but the vines might give her more flexibility. Julian went over to a low-hanging mass of them and examined them.

The vines looked back.

She was so startled, she backed away. There were *eyes* of a sort on the ends of those things! Or at least they sure *looked* like eyes, one per vine ending.

And now the vines moved in a cluster. Quite slowly and lazily, yet as deliberately as snakes, which they reminded Julian of.

She walked a bit to the right, and the clump of eyes slowly followed her. Back to the left, the same. She *wasn't* imagining it!

Were they all part of a single organism, part of the tree, or parasites on it? Some sort of plantlike worms, perhaps? She'd better find out, she decided, because now that this bunch had blown their cover, as it were, all the vines on all the other trees were looking at her, too.

This may be the dumbest thing I've ever done in a lifetime of dumb things, she thought furiously, *but it's worth a try.*

"Hello," she said. "We are strangers here, brought here by others. Bad people we are now trying to escape from. We don't want to harm anything, but we do not know the rules here. Are you the Lebans?"

Did translators work even on plants? Or was she talking to a common variety of parasitic worm with no more intelligence than any other worm?

The vines got very agitated and seemed to speed up their motion, curling in and out, back and forth among one another until it looked like they were caught in some sort of windstorm. The other clusters on other trees were doing much the same.

It's almost like they're talking with each other, discussing me, she thought, still not sure if she wasn't just imagining this. She looked nervously upward into the trees for perhaps a giant open mouth at the end of the tendrils, but while they did vanish into the upper reaches of the tree, there was no clear body to them.

But *how* were they talking, if that was what it was? While the translator might be able to get through to them if, presumably, whatever they were attached to had some way to hear or feel vibrations, what if they communicated by a totally different means? That was *still* assuming that she was talking to Lebans. *Now is the kind of time when I wish I could confer with the others,* she thought.

There was suddenly the sound of a wind, although she could feel no air moving against her skin.

Then there came a deep, melodic bass tone that seemed to come from within the tree itself. Incredibly, it seemed to be forming words, although they were a bizarre-sounding monotone, like trying to listen to conversation from the world's largest one-note tuba.

"You may pass in safety," the voice seemed to say. "Do not

touch the vines. Do not harm the trees. Eat what you will of the forest floor but pick nothing."

She *wasn't* crazy! These *were* the Lebans! "We will obey all of your rules. I promise," she told the clusters of eyes. "We go north by night to the equator beyond your lands."

"We have heard what the others have done," the monotonous horn responded. "They will not find you in Leba if you give Leba respect."

"It is a very pretty place," she said, trying to butter them up a bit, still wondering if they were the vines, the trees, or something inside the trees and out of sight. "But it is not our place. We would not harm it, and we need to leave it. Um . . . You wouldn't happen to know which way is north?"

The vines swirled, curled, and then pointed off in one direction. "Thank you," she told them. "I must get some sleep now. We have a long way to go."

"You will not be disturbed," the voice promised.

The vines slowly subsided in their rhythm, then hung limp and still once more.

It was very odd, but she felt like she *could* sleep here now. She wasn't exactly sure why and she probably could never explain it to the others, even if they'd believe it, but she felt suddenly more secure, no longer watched but rather watched over.

If you are polite to the Lebans and show respect, they are very friendly . . .

Somehow she'd just have to make do with the ropes.

She wondered what would happen to somebody who *wasn't* polite and respectful. The ones who would be after them might be such people. One could certainly outrun a Leban, but one couldn't run out of them. She wondered just how strong those tendril-like vines could be . . .

Somehow Anne Marie was not surprised to see three Cloptan men and the colonel ride out and three Cloptan women and the colonel ride back in.

"Ever the Talleyrand type, aren't you, Colonel?" she said with acidic sweetness.

"What's she talking about?" Juana Campos asked him suspiciously.

"Talleyrand," the colonel explained, "was a pragmatist in royalist France. A minor functionary, he saw the French Revolution coming and, when it happened, helped the revolution find royalists and arrest them. He survived the reign of terror, survived the excesses, and in the end supported a young officer named Napoleon who became emperor himself and made Talleyrand a count. When Napoleon faced defeat, he negotiated with the old royalists and brought them back to power. He died a wealthy and respected statesman, in bed, of old age, but he never betrayed those he served or lost his honor, which is why they all trusted him. I do not consider her comment an insult but rather a compliment."

The two gunmen were more shocked and not as understanding. *That* had to be put right immediately.

"Listen, you two, you are very fortunate to have been here!" Juana Campos told them. "You are still alive and you have futures, if you wish to take the colonel's example. Taluud is dead. His empire in Clopta is even now being crushed. You have a choice to make. Serve me in the same way you served Taluud and you will prosper and be high in the *new* organization I will build when this is over. Choose wrongly and I will allow you to enjoy the colonel's embrace. I do not *need* you for controlling this lot, but I can certainly *use* you."

The two men didn't like it; their own world was being turned upside down in the same way their captives' had been. Still, the alternative was certainly worse. "All right, ma'am. We'll stay with you," one said.

She nodded. "You will take orders from me and from Kuzi here as if she were speaking my own words. You will keep your manners intact as regards all three of us and will keep your hands off. Be faithful, and your rewards will be great. Hesitate, foul up, or betray us, and you will be dead. Remember that if you are testing any of us with your *manly* strength, you are also testing that strength against all of us, including the colonel. You understand that? *Do you understand that?*"

"Yes, ma'am," they both said.

"You call *them* 'ma'am.' You call *me* 'boss.'"

"Yes, boss."

Campos looked around and saw Terry. For her part, the girl was totally confused as to what had gone on, but she understood that Gus had been hurt and that those who had hurt him were now in control. Of them all, though, it was Campos who terrified her. There was something there, inside her, something *awful*, particularly when she looked at Terry. It was not something that could be explained but rather something that was intrinsic, something ancient, something rarely glimpsed. The colonel had elements of it, and so had the duckmen, but in Campos it was not hidden, it was not partial, it was the essence of her, and it was frightening.

It was pure, uncompromised, unequivocated evil.

And yet somehow, while she felt Campos's particular evil whenever she looked at her, she also sensed that at least for now, that evil was not a direct threat. Not yet. For some reason Campos did not want to harm the baby.

Campos felt such satisfaction at finally having Terry in her clutches that it was a moment before she realized that something was wrong. The two Dillians, the girl, the big monster in the shed . . .

"Where is the other? The Erdomite?"

"These were the only ones here. We checked the whole place out thoroughly," one of the gunmen said.

Campos turned to Tony and Anne Marie. "All right—where is she? And no games!"

"We don't know, and that's the truth," Tony told her. "She left us yesterday evening to go to scout for where you might be. She thought you'd head for the tracks and perhaps lay an ambush. We haven't seen or heard from her since. When she didn't come back with you, we thought perhaps she was a casualty."

Campos shook her head. "So that was how it was done. While we fought with Taluud, your friend came in and liberated the others."

"Likely," the colonel agreed. "We had no knowledge of it. I wouldn't think she'd be much of a threat otherwise, though. Their women don't have the proper hands and are not otherwise built for fighting. You are certain that the other two cannot understand each other or anyone but you?"

"I am certain of that, yes. They cannot talk, which means they cannot plot with each other. I see your point. But they are going to be very difficult to track and to catch in this terrain."

"Perhaps. Perhaps not. They will *feel* us at their backs no matter where they run and whether we are there or not. They will zig, and zag, and perhaps get lost a few times, but eventually they will get their bearings. In the end, we know the direction in which they *must* go. They *must* go to Verion, then west, to the northwest corner of that place. They have no other choice."

Campos looked at the Leeming and frowned. "You believe it, then? That if she can get inside, she can become like a god?"

"Until I got to know Captain Brazil, I thought it was nonsense," Lunderman admitted. "And then, after, when I saw him survive what would have, *should* have killed anything alive, I was nearly convinced. But it was when talking with Tony here, back before the raid, that I became certain that this is not nonsense."

"Why?"

"*You* were dragged here. So was Gus. Lori and even the girl here were more or less brought here by Mavra Chang. I and our missing Erdomese fell through by accident. But there is no getting around it. Nathan Brazil walked here, knowingly, of his own free will. He invited these two to come along. He promised them what they achieved. And Mavra Chang, too, took great risks to voluntarily come through. Of all of us, only Brazil and Chang came freely, knowingly. Why? Because they *knew* what they would find here. And of all of us, only they and the girl here, whose pregnancy prevented a change, remained Earth-human. All the rest of us were dramatically transformed. No, it is beyond chance. And where does that pair try and head once they set out separately, independently? To the equator. To the door inside the world. No, it more defies logic to deny their true nature than to believe in it, however fanciful. They are not human. They have merely chosen to appear that way. Brazil may heal, but he is out of this. Safely away. That leaves Mavra Chang, and I do not believe that she will let any obstacle stand in her way."

"She could just wait. Bide her time and wait for Brazil to save her. After all, she cannot know he is a prisoner."

"No, I believe we took care of that possibility. They are rivals. Each is convinced that the other means to assume total and sole control. As far as Chang is concerned, this race is still on. She cannot afford to wait."

"She'll know that we know this, too. Is Verion the only door?"

"No, there are many, but she will be forced to go for Verion because it is closest. Any other choice means more travel, more hexes, more chances of discovery, and, most of all, much more time."

"Will it be guarded?"

"There is a token force there. There is one at all of them. Nothing that cannot be handled, though. I have authority with some of the council even now, and those two have authority with others. A nontech hex, a boring and routine guard assignment—it should not be much of a problem."

"What makes you think we'll help *you*?" Tony asked him.

"Several things. First, it is your only hope of returning to

Dillia alive. Second, there is still one of your number that you might well be able to help, and that is all you were ever promised. And third and finally, your friends here will need you. We can transport our party and supplies, but Gus either travels with you or he must be disposed of here and now. I would like to keep him around because it will keep the girl in line and certain to stick close to us as well. By the same token, concern for her safety will keep *him* in line, even if he fully recovers. But you must understand that you are the most expendable of us all."

Campos looked at the centaurs. "Think about this, Dillians. It would take very little to spoil those pretty looks for good. You will do *nothing* except what you are ordered to do. You will take no hostile action against us. You will say nothing to others except what we tell you to say or both of your tongues will be cut out. Do anything, *anything* that displeases me and I will blind you. You are packhorses to me, nothing more. Raise a hand or a weapon against me and you will lose both weapon and hand. Try and escape and I will kill you. If you make it, the ones who remain will suffer your punishment. The girl, for example, does not need eyes or ears or hands to do what I am interested in. She will not leave her strange paramour, and she will be kept close to me and the colonel at all times. Do we have an understanding here?"

"I believe we do, yes," Tony said gravely. *But if I could kill you, even at the cost of my own life, I think I would do it.*

"Well, get the big lizard ready to move, then," Campos instructed. "Even as he is, I want him tied down to the litter at all times, and one of you must always be watching him. With these horses and supplies, where they can go, we can go; where we cannot, I doubt if they could, either. We will track them if we can. If we lose them, we go for Verion immediately. Now, *move!*"

VERION

Julian had no way to mark time in Leba, but it had seemed an interminable journey, made all the more so by her inability to really *talk* with anybody.

Sure, she did some questions and answers with Lori, who seemed to need some mental contact anyway, and some more bits-and-pieces discussions with Mavra by the stick method, but those were almost always to ask specific things or just to keep from going nuts. The Lebans remained friendly and true to their word, but they weren't exactly conversationalists, either.

The journey had been an extremely rough one, and it wasn't over yet. The whole place was mountainous and wet, much like the Olympic range of Washington state but without the trails. The Lebans could be counted on to recommend a route or keep them pointed in the right direction but not for much else. They were certainly friendly, though, in their own way; as they'd gone on, the Lebans would often shake fruit right off limbs when nothing obvious was available to eat.

Still, there had been no distinctive landmarks or anything to mark the progress of their journey. After a while one stream valley looked like another, and all the mountains looked pretty much alike as well. It was impossible for someone with her build and hooves to walk bipedally and not lose her balance over and over; still, she'd been walking on all fours so long by this point, she wasn't sure she remembered how to use just two. Once she'd threatened, even prepared, to go off and live in the wild alone. How stupid that seemed now!

Thus, when sunrise neared to mark the probable end of yet another day, Julian, like her companions, was just silently trudging along, coming over yet one more rise. Suddenly she saw something she hadn't seen in so long, she'd almost forgotten what it looked like.

Sunlight. Sunlight just creeping over the landscape, a little bright on this side, much duller beyond what seemed like a vast semitransparent curtain.

The border! It had to be! And if the Lebans hadn't been playing an enormous practical joke on them, beyond lay Verion.

She shrieked with such delight that Lori stopped, and both he and Mavra looked over, concerned that Julian might be in some trouble. Julian turned to them, put out her forearm, and pointed.

She felt like rushing to it, and the hell with the daylight, but she knew that would be the worst thing to do. If there was sunlight in Verion, then perhaps there were Verionites who were not as friendly as the Lebans.

Best to remain on the same regimen, she knew, although it was hard, really hard, not to push on. That boundary didn't just mean that they were passing into a new climate, a new land, but the *final* land, the destination point. And even though it would still take them a great deal of time to reach that destination, they had been safe, almost protected in a way, in Leba, with the natives watching out for them and with plenty of food and water and at least reliable help with the directions. That, out there, was more than just another unknown land and people.

Somewhere beyond that final curtain was the enemy.

They had no illusions about that, Mavra the least of all. It didn't take a genius to figure out that the Verion Avenue was the only practical choice they could make, and so they'd be waiting there, right near the end, waiting for them to walk into a trap.

That was another reason Mavra had insisted they not go elsewhere, though. Verion was a nontech hex; nothing but muscle, water, and wind worked there, as in Erdom. That also meant no radios, no instant communications, no tracking scopes and sophisticated monitoring systems. The enemy knew *where* they would wind up but not when. *They* could pick the time and the opportunity.

A lot, then, would depend on the Verionites, whatever they were. Would they be searching for them with a reward for their capture? Would they be hostile to everybody? There was no way to know in advance.

In fact, Mavra had been almost insistent on finding out something about them. If the Verionites were nocturnals, for example, they might do better moving by day and remaining just this side of the border until they were close to the Avenue.

The Lebans knew, but it was no use asking them directly. Simile wasn't always effective in a translator conversation, particularly when one party didn't have one.

Still, she tried. "Are the Verionites animals?"

"Yes."

"Do they eat meat or grain?"

"Anything."

"Are they larger or smaller than we are?"

"About the same."

"Are they friendly to visitors or unfriendly?"

"Unknown. They seem all right to us."

Not exactly a great deal of help.

"Will we be able to find food over there?"

"Probably."

"Are they day creatures like you or night creatures like us?"

"Day mostly."

"Is there anything else we should know?"

"Yes. Remember to look up."

She was startled. "They fly?"

"Some do."

She hadn't figured on that. Flying in a nontech hex meant some kind of bird or other winged creature. That wasn't good at all. *Definitely* a night crossing, and with extra attention given to concealing them from the air.

Still, she couldn't help but feel excited. Although there were many long, dangerous days or weeks to come, it was the first measure of real progress since she'd taken up with Mavra and Lori.

"One last question. Do you know the way this world usually measures time?"

"Yes. The railroad is quite punctual."

"Do you know how long it has taken us to reach this border?"

"Yes. Fifteen days."

Fifteen days. "Sorry—one more and then I thank you for all your assistance. At this rate, how long would it take us to reach the Avenue?"

"Another twelve days to reach the equator, then ten. If you can go exactly northwest, ten to twelve days for the whole journey."

"I thank you. I will always hold the Lebans in my heart as true and trusted friends. I have had very few since I came here."

"We are pleased to know this."

It was time to make some plans.

Mavra was all for heading straight for the destination by the shortest route. Lori wanted to take it slower and more cautiously, not feeling the same sense of urgency.

In the end it was up to Julian, of course. Their opponents might *expect* them to take the shortest route, but then again, how would they know when she and the other two would emerge from Leba and where? In a sense, straight to the goal was the safest course; it meant the least distance to move, and that lessened their chances of being spotted and reported. Mavra didn't like the idea of fliers, though, any more than Julian did. Fliers could cover pretty good distances in short periods of time, vital for reconnaissance in a no-tech hex. But if the Lebans were right, and Julian interpreted their answer to mean that the Verionites probably saw about as well at night as Earth-humans, then they had a chance if they could conceal their day camps.

It was an all or nothing roll of the dice at this point, but it seemed like the only way to play it.

Near sunset they moved out, down and through the final valley and to the Verion border. Just looking across it, even though the hex boundary made it dark and hazy, they could see a dramatic change. Many rivers and streams crossed boundaries, as did landforms, but clearly Verion was a much drier place. The hills continued, but the trees almost completely stopped, replaced with grasslands and occasional bushes and other small shrubs.

Not a lot of cover, Julian thought worriedly. Still, there was no other way to get it done. She stepped through the border, feeling that now-familiar tingling sensation, and into Verion.

It was suddenly very hot and surprisingly humid for a place that far from an ocean. There wasn't much transfer between hexes beyond the immediate area of the border, where some convection was inevitable, so this was probably how it was going to feel.

They proceeded in, although intending only to find a reasonable place to camp out of sight and wait until the next night to begin their real journey.

The sky was clear, although there were some lazy-looking birds off in the distance which Julian hoped weren't the local equivalent of vultures circling over a kill.

They traveled down the first hill, into a ravine, and then

back up the gentle slope of the next, slightly higher one, which revealed a whole new vista.

Beyond, the land flattened out considerably, although there were various isolated landforms standing like bizarre sentinels as far as the eye could see. The lowlands clearly had eroded away over great periods of time, leaving pockets of harder rock, possibly volcanic.

In the middle of this strange landscape of bizarre shapes and flat plains were clearly developed areas. There *were* trees here, but they were far different from the ones in Leba: tall, thick, but without branches and with leafy growth only at the very tops. Julian thought they looked like palm trees that had fallen off their diets.

More important, they were clearly planted, both for ornamentation and in groves. Nearby were large fields that showed definite signs of cultivation. A fair-sized river cut through the middle of it, leaving a jagged canyon that looked pretty formidable. There were, however, two clear suspension-type bridges over it, showing a great deal of nontech sophistication.

Well, none of us are tree climbers, Julian thought, *and those trees aren't going to conceal us too much, but the fronds will give us air cover.*

The real problem was going to be the canyon. The only practical way across was over one of those bridges, and during that time they would be exposed with absolutely nowhere to run or hide.

She wished she knew more about the people here. She wished she knew a lot more about everything having to do with this place.

By the time they reached the first of the trees, it was clearly too close to dawn to consider risking either of the bridges that night. Best to camp, get some rest, and watch and see if any of the natives showed themselves. She wanted to see them, but not all that closely.

It wasn't long after dawn, just as they settled in under the trees, when she got her wish.

The sound of what seemed to be a wagon drew her, and she crept over to the edge of the grove, making certain to keep as well hidden behind a tree as possible, and looked out. What she saw was one of the strangest sights yet on this bizarre world.

It was a wagon, all right, and it was huge, with two big solid wheels that had to be two meters high holding it up. What got her was that it appeared to be pulled by two oversized, very fat Earthwomen, and on top, on a tiny seat trying to keep his balance, the one who held the reins looked for all the world like an Earth-human-size pig in a very wide brimmed straw hat and wearing a pair of overalls.

A closer look with her ability to magnify things showed that her first impression of the creatures pulling the wagon was wrong but that her notion of the driver was pretty well dead on, although Porky Pig it wasn't. That was one *ugly* hog up there.

The creatures pulling the wagon did have a humanlike shape, were bipedal, had enormous rear ends and thighs, and seemed to have breasts as well, but the faces were very apelike. Their backs and sides were covered with brown fur, while their fronts appeared a hairless purplish skin color. For such large creatures, though, they had remarkably scrawny arms, and if those were hands, they weren't much more useful than Julian's, if that. They looked to be at least seven or eight feet tall and proportioned to that height save for the arms and huge hairy feet. They weren't pulling the cart by walking or ambling but by a kind of slow jogging canter that seemed almost horselike.

The draft animals had been the startling things, but the driver was more interesting because he didn't match what she expected at all. He certainly had no wings, and if pigs could fly in this hex, it surely was by some means not obvious to her.

Were the Lebans wrong, or was there more here than she could see right now?

She knew she should go back and stand a better guard as

the first watch—Mavra and Lori couldn't speak, but they could surely wake the others up in a hurry if need be, and their judgment was the important factor in a watch—but she wanted to see how that thing got across that bridge.

The answer was that it didn't. Instead, several more pig creatures—*hogs*—emerged from a lemon-drop-shaped hut near the bridge and began operating an oddball system of pulleys and gears that revealed strong cables strung parallel to the bridge. When the cart reached them, Verionites climbed up and began stringing cable through slots along both sides while the driver unhitched his odd "team." Another set of cables was then attached to another series of poles with gears and pulleys, and the "team" was hitched to a circular master gear on these and started going around and around slowly.

Julian watched in amazement as the entire cart body was lifted off its carriage and huge wheels and into the air, suspended by the cables. An operator at the far end and another at the assembly right at the rim of the canyon threw a series of giant wooden levers, changing the gearing, and the cart began actually to move along the cables down to the second set of gears and poles and then out over it, powered by the team on the far end.

It's a cable car system! she realized. A very clever and elaborate cable car system using the sheer muscle power of those beasts. More interestingly, it was also a kind of basic container system; they didn't move the carriage and wheels, only the container and its cargo.

Once the container was across, the team was unhitched from the system and led across by the driver, the bridge swaying a bit under the weight of the two behemoths but hardly stressed. On the other side the process was reversed with a new carriage. It was slow but efficient.

The other, parallel bridge did not have such an assembly and was probably built later for routine foot traffic, which would not have to be held up waiting for teams to pass. With those draft animals and the rather imposing girth of the

Verionites, traffic was pretty well limited to one way at a time, anyway.

The natives were clever, quite modern, and industrious; that much was sure. She had the opportunity to take a magnified view of a couple of them while they were setting up the cables, and while the faces were ugly and their figures matched the sort bipedal hogs might be expected to have, their arms and hands seemed quite muscular and flexible, and their feet, supporting that form and weight, more resembled those of a hippo or an elephant than a hog's. Large, wide, and flat, almost like tree trunks, they provided pretty good balance and flexibility.

But if those suckers could fly, she wanted to see it!

She wondered if perhaps such clever folk might have hot air balloons or something like that which the Lebans would consider flying. That was a thought, although it wasn't at all something she would have thought common in a hex like Verion. Like Erdom, Verion was against an impenetrable barrier, in this case the equator, and so wasn't hex-shaped at all. Balloons might well be practical in a compact hex-shape, but unless they were pretty well staked down and used only for lookout purposes, they were unlikely to be practical for travel here.

Still, after seeing those bridges, the cable car, and the container apparatus in action, she wouldn't put anything past these people. In a sense, she admired them from what little she'd seen. Most of the nontech hexes seemed to have accepted their lot and mummified their culture and society. Erdom was a perfect example of this—static, with change considered a threat. The Verionites, though, had refused to accept their limits and become at least in part a culture of engineers. It was almost as if they'd said, "Okay, here are the limits, and here's what we want to do. Now figure out how we do it!"

That made them dangerous as well. They couldn't afford to treat this society as a standard, lazy nontech culture.

Remaining in the groves all day, Julian also noticed one other characteristic of the hex that seemed quite odd. Everything animal appeared to be bipedal for some reason; even the insects ran around on two legs, looking almost like miniature varieties of Mixtimese. Yet another very odd place, but not nearly as strange as Leba or even Mixtim.

That night they had to face the problem of the bridges.

There was no way around them; who knew how long this canyon was or how far it stretched? And even if it didn't go on forever, what of the river at the bottom, which certainly seemed large and wild running? There was a sort of tollbooth, but both it and the cable crew and shack seemed to shut down shortly after dusk; they had watched the creatures lock up and leave. Lights indicated a town not too far on the other side, probably a farming center and way stop for bridge travelers, and everybody on this side seemed to cross the bridge and go off in that direction. Whatever justified the whole system was either to the east or to the west of them; they certainly did no traffic with Leba.

There was no way to be completely safe crossing the bridge, but nothing in the infrared showed that they had left any kind of guards around, although Julian had half expected to be barked and growled at by bipedal dogs or something. The big problem would be that they had no idea what was on the other side. The guards might be there, where the bulk of the people were, since a barrier on either side would do to block passage, or they might ring alarm bells over there by merely shaking the bridge up and down as they walked. Although Julian had heard nothing specific, an alarm system might be hooked up when they closed, or it might be something she wouldn't recognize as an alarm but they would.

What they found was a solid wooden gate, a sign, and a large bell. The sign was in Verionese, not commercial, so it was impossible to read it, but they could all guess what it said: "To use bridge, ring bell for attendant."

There *was* an opening on either side of the gate, but it was much too small for either Lori or Julian. Mavra went to it, looked in and up, and saw that the gate was secured from the other side with a large wooden bar. This was one time when her lack of arms might be an asset, although not for actually moving the thing. She was, however, able to wiggle through the opening at ground level with minimal loss of feathers and get on the other side. That left the bar, which was a bit above her eye level. It looked to be a simple enough system, but how to move that bar when she didn't have any arms?

Ultimately, she pressed her back against the gate, got her head under the bar, and tried to straighten up as much as possible. The bar moved, but not enough to come out of its latch.

After several frustrating attempts, after which she realized that she needed to be about her old height, small as that was, to get it high enough, she decided to step out and look at the thing.

It was just a board, nothing spectacular but effective enough. She finally decided that the only chance was to lift the thing as high as she could and then, when the weight of it, which was not inconsiderable, was on her head, to move sideways and hope she could slide it enough so that it would fall outside the latch on one side.

Several attempts failed, but finally she managed it, her head hurting like hell, and the end of the board fell to the floor of the bridge with a *clunk*! The other end remained precariously balanced on the other latch.

Dizzy and with a whale of a headache, she nonetheless stepped back and gave off a single low squawk. Julian heard it and slowly and carefully pushed against the gate. The board jammed a couple of times, but Mavra was able to help free it, and finally they had it open enough for Lori, then Julian to squeeze through.

The trouble was, if word had reached here about them and the Verionites were on the lookout for signs of strangers, the open gate would be a signal. Julian pushed the gate closed and strained to lift the board back up into place, but she just didn't have the strength. Lori, seeing the problem, didn't stop to wonder why she was doing it but came over and put his head and neck under Julian's arms and lifted slowly, giving her the added strength she needed. It wasn't neat, but the gate was again locked and bolted.

Julian helped Mavra onto Lori's back but didn't bother to tie her. At the speed at which any of them could cross the swinging span, it was unnecessary and would take time they couldn't spare.

The roar of rapids came from far below, masking out much of the sound once they were out over the chasm, and the bridge rippled and swung back and forth as they crossed. But it was a sturdy and well-built structure that had seen much traffic. At least the idea of alarms rigged to the bridge seemed remote; there was a distinct night breeze that caused it to sway slightly entirely on its own, making it more difficult to keep one's own balance on it but possibly explaining why the crossing was usually restricted to daylight.

There was a small house at the other end with a light inside, apparently the toll keeper's house. Before they even reached it, the pungent smells of Verion's masters hit them, and it wasn't much more pleasant than the odors of Mixtim, although it was more varied—the scent of massive sweat, garbage, and pungent spices all rolled into one unappetizing and somewhat sickening perfume.

Just before they reached the other side, somebody came out of the house and started fooling with something unseen on the side of the building. They froze, and for a brief nightmare moment they had the swaying, the winds, and the odors all at once.

Then whoever it was went back inside, and they finished the walk slowly and quietly, trying to keep hoof sounds to a minimum. They were relieved to see only a small wooden crossbar on a pivot where the bridge again reached land. As quietly as possible, Julian raised it enough for Lori to get through, then ducked under it herself.

The wind really started up on the other side; while unpleasant, it had the effect of masking their own sounds as they moved between bridge and town, across the road, and around the main settlement.

Well over a hundred more miles of this, Julian thought nervously. Too long in such a civilized country. They had gotten lucky this time, but there was no way of knowing what other obstacles this land had in store for them before they reached the final and largest obstacle of them all.

Beyond the town the bizarre mixture of twisted landforms—spires, pinnacles, tiny table rocks—grew even more dense, and the Verionites had planted virtually every available space in between. Here and there were virtual herds of the huge, lumbering bipedal draft animals just wandering about or lying around sound asleep and snoring loudly. The wind rippled the grains and grasses as if they were a gigantic sea and made its own series of groans and moans as it twisted in and out and all around the natural statuary.

As morning approached and false dawn was illuminating the western sky, Julian searched for a good camp. She was beginning to wonder if perhaps she had misunderstood the "up" warning of the Lebans or if there were Verionite sentinels, like shepherds, atop some of the broader rock forms as watchmen. It was still hard to see, though, how they'd get up or down without wings.

They would have to camp at the base of one of them, though—a particularly large tower of twisted black rock that had shallow cavelike indentations at the base that would provide at least some cover. There was no choice; it would have to do.

Julian, as usual, took the first watch. Mavra's own sense of time from watching the shadows seldom failed her here; her second watch was as reliable as Julian's. Only Lori seemed to have little sense of time, so he took the last watch, since it was fairly difficult to miss the sun going down if the others weren't already awake by then.

For Mavra, so long out of the chase, every step took her closer to her goal. Somehow, some way, she would get inside. Nothing and no one was going to stop her this time. Lori, on the other hand, was going through the motions with little hope; everything that could go wrong up to now had, and he fully expected, after such an epic walk, to wind up caught and back in the hands of the enemy when they reached wherever it was they were going.

It hardly mattered to him anymore if they even got there. Seeing Julian and being so dependent on her all this time could only remind him of what he had lost. Considering how she'd handled herself so far, she needed him or anything he might do other than carry Mavra about as much as he needed a sewing kit. He didn't even have desire, only a sense of guilt and loss.

For Julian, although taking it one day at a time, there was a sense of the endgame in this. She hadn't the slightest idea if they could get Mavra into this Well place or not or what would really happen if they could, but either they would or they would not. If they did, then at least victory would be denied the evil people both from Earth and from this world. If they couldn't, she was pretty sure they'd not be given a second chance at it.

Anything you desire. That had been Mavra's promise to them. *Anything you desire.* A nice phrase, that, but what did it mean? Was it like the ancient genie, granting wishes? That was always an easy one in fairy stories. They wished for wealth and romance and happily-ever-after endings. It wasn't that simple in real life. It particularly wasn't simple for her. She'd had a series of shocks and psychological changes that almost outdid her physical ones, and they'd even messed with her mind with her own consent.

What did Julian now, today, really desire? Not to go back, to become Julian Beard again. For all his glamour, she hated his stinking guts. Still, why had that earliest incarnation wanted to become an astronaut? Because of a need of adventure, of challenge, the excitement of the new frontier. That much remained of him, she thought. She didn't want a happily-ever-after ending; she wanted new challenges, new chances to do something different, worthwhile.

Erdom was hardly the place for that, permanently and happily stuck as it was in a kind of bizarre variation of the permanent twelfth-century Earth.

And yet she'd come to like who she was and what she was and dreamed of the desert lands that she'd hated when she'd been there.

It seemed as if there had always been something tearing at her since she'd been here. Male, female, master, slave, rebel, wife, loner, lover of the herd.

The way they'd rearranged her head, she could never go back; the society would burn her at the stake as a witch. But if it could somehow be countered or removed, she'd become that servile little wimp again, and *that* she didn't want, either. What if she could go back as an Erdomese man? It solved most of the conundrums, but the trouble was that she didn't want to *be* a man, not anymore. She'd been one once, and while he'd loved it fine, she didn't think very much of him now, and that was just what she would become. Look at what it had done to Lori, whose own contrasting Earth background was the opposite of hers. She didn't exactly want *that* guy back, either, let alone want to become another one.

There was a real catch in that three-wishes business that the fairy-tale writers hadn't ever faced. In order to make decent use of them, one first had to know what to wish for.

On the third day they passed near another small town and then another. The roads, which they stayed off but which they watched carefully, seemed to grow more frequent, wider, and better maintained, not to mention more crowded.

And on the third day they also saw that pigs could fly.

The last thing anybody would have expected to come across in even the most sophisticated high-tech hex was an airport, but that was exactly what it was. There was even an unmistakable wind sock on a large reflective pole. Making camp in some trees not far from it because the timing was right more than because they wanted to be this close in, they actually could watch it in operation.

There were two types of fliers: the aircraft and the kites.

Watching a kiter take off was something of an amazing sight. Strapped underneath a massive width of a canvaslike material, the hoglike Verionite was then placed on a wheeled dolly. Then a team of the big, lumbering creatures that Julian had dubbed bigfoots were brought out, hitched as if they were pulling a cart. When the omnipresent wind was right, someone gave a signal, and the four-bigfoot team would start lumbering down a cleared path, gaining speed until they were running flat out. This plus the wind would catch the leading edge of the kite, and it would rise into the air, the dolly dropping away, and up it would go, breaking free of the ropes or whatever they were that the bigfoots used to pull.

In fact, once aloft, the kite fliers seemed to have some sort of rudder control and perhaps ways of seeing the wind currents aloft, which must have been pretty tricky from what Julian could see. She had been a pilot once, too, and had done some hang gliding off Maui, so she knew that this would have been nearly impossible, no matter what the design of the kite, under Earth-type conditions.

But this wasn't Earth, nor was it supposed to simulate the Earth. It was simulating some other world somewhere else.

At any rate, once aloft, the pilot had lift, could get up farther, and could clearly steer. The amazing thing was how the device kept climbing until he was just a speck in the distant sky. Watching the aerodynamics of the thing, though, Julian had to wonder if under these conditions a skilled and highly trained pilot might not be able to stay up there for hours and possibly cover a fair distance.

Even Mavra, who piloted spaceships and other craft far more sophisticated than anything Julian had ever more than dreamed of, was impressed. Even with the level of automation in her day, there were minimal atmospheric flying skills that had to be learned before one was allowed to pilot a massive spacecraft.

There was another kind of flier as well. This was an oblong gondola supported by a matching hot air balloon suspended over the top of it. One Verionite was in the gondola, controlling the flame, although it was unclear just what the source of that heat might be or how they managed to get a sufficient amount of it in a controllable and obviously compressed form to allow for the level of controlled blasts he could give it.

And then there was the bigfoot pedaling the bicycle.

It was an absurd sight, but its logic was pretty clear. Once the gondola lifted off—with the bigfoot, obviously trained to do this without panicking, sitting strapped in the seat at the front—the man at the flame gave a command and the creature began pedaling. This in turn started a large propeller at the rear, sheltered in a frame with a vertical rudder that the man at the flames appeared to be able to control using a long pole.

Once aloft, with these winds, the balloon would have been at the mercy of the currents and would have picked up speed; the bigfoot, however, was able to overcome this, and its energy and the prop in the back provided a forward momentum that looked as if it might reach, oh, three or four kilometers per hour in the face of the wind. Altitude was controlled by the fire and the master gave the craft direction by manipulating the rudder poles. The thing could actually travel. Julian suspected that the winds blew at different speeds and levels at low altitudes and that, again, an expert pilot could find the right one for wherever he wanted to go, attaining maximum speed. At that rate, he could make the equator in just a couple of long days or almost anywhere in this land in four. Not fast, no, but that thing could carry a limited cargo, such as mail, packages, and news, at a speed that a nontech civilization could hardly match on the ground. Such a system would be vital for emergencies and would make communication practical. It bound the hex together, she guessed.

It also meant that if there *was* a wanted poster out on them, as there almost certainly was on Lori and Mavra, the odds were that there weren't many in Verion who didn't know about them.

It also made travel by night a good decision, virtually essential, as they were clearly moving toward a denser population center.

On day five they were on the outskirts of a major city, where the skies were filled with flying pigs in variations of the two devices they'd seen at the airport but with such a variety of color and design that it was clear that the Verionites had a far different aesthetic sense than Julian.

More dramatic, off well beyond the city on the farthest horizon, was a solid dark line, easily seen through the more prairielike and less obstructed land that the hex was becoming. It wasn't much, but it was too regular and too consistent to be either natural or an optical illusion. Still forty or fifty miles from them, it was nonetheless visible.

The equator!

The position of the sun told them that they had been heading more or less true northwest, which meant that as of now, they were less than a week away from the Avenue.

Mavra had given up trying to explain or describe the Avenue to Julian in scratch writing. Apparently she would just have to go there and see it for herself. The only thing Julian got was that it was sunken, like a very broad culvert, flat on the bottom, smooth on all sides, and that it led to one of the doors into the Well.

That meant no cover and low ground at a point when forces could be all along both sides shooting down at them. All kinds of technology would work there, but it wouldn't matter. When they were exposed on the floor of the thing, Julian knew that rocks could get them, never mind bullets. Nor, Mavra informed her, could one just enter the Well even if one made it to the doorway.

"Automated. Opens only at old shift change," she told Julian. "Midnight."

"Can *anybody* enter it at midnight?"

"No. Only authorized. You come in with me. I am authorized."

"How long does the door stay open?"

"About fifteen minutes unless I close it first."

Julian sighed. "So we have fifteen minutes to get down there, run a gauntlet, and somehow get inside without them killing or capturing us. It's *impossible!*"

"See layout, defenders first. Then we'll see. I think I may have a way."

"You want to give me an idea of how you're going to do it?"

"Wait. When I know it is possible, then I tell you."

Julian shook her head, wondering if any of this was worth what she'd gone through the past couple of weeks. If it was anything like it was described, it was absolutely insane to even attempt to enter. Even if Mavra Chang were who and what she claimed, it made no difference. Until she was inside, she was just a big, heavy helpless bird who couldn't outrun a child. This whole business *had* to have driven her insane; that was the only explanation for why she even could think that she might get in there.

Mavra understood Julian's attitude, but she could *feel* the Well, feel the contact with its power and even some of its knowledge at this point. The Well *knew* where she was, *knew* that she was close.

And the Well had gone to a great deal of trouble to get her here. With Nathan out of it in some southern hospital and Mavra this close, it wasn't going to let her get away now, of that she was certain.

THE AVENUE

Campos and the colonel had tried every means that they
could think of to find some sign of the missing trio in Leba,
even bringing in expert trackers from other hexes that the colonel knew about, but to no avail.

The Lebans themselves had seemed singularly unimpressed
by their problem and had declared themselves neutral and un-
interested in the affairs of other creatures. Not even Campos
or the colonel could think of anything to offer them that
might tempt them into cooperation.

There were times when some of the animals brought in
seemed to pick up a scent, but it always led to a dead end,
with the creatures going around in confused circles. At one
point the colonel swore that if he didn't know better, he'd
swear that someone was pulling a drag over the "foxes'"
trail, confusing the scent and leading them away, but he
couldn't imagine why anyone would do that or how he could
without betraying himself. He finally decided that the land
was just not conducive to finding the fugitives' trail.

Score one for the prey, they both were forced to admit. On
the other hand, the endgame was what counted.

The colonel had hoped, though, to avoid the endgame simply because he was none too secure about showing up in his

old role. Kurdon had certainly put out the word on his betrayal at the complex; it was unlikely that he'd have real authority even if his friends in Zone were able to keep the law off him with some cover story.

More than that, they would have to deal with armed soldiers whose loyalty was to their own hex and then to the Zone Council and not to any third parties. And there was always the chance that in spite of threats with real teeth in them, their captives might be able to betray their real status as prisoners to the army personnel at the Avenue.

Campos, too, wasn't pleased with that prospect. "I think perhaps we should get rid of them now, before they can cause trouble later," she suggested. "All except the girl, of course. If we cannot control the likes of *her*, no matter *what* her wishes, we do not deserve to be in this game in any case."

The colonel, however, didn't like the idea of finishing them off. "We can't do it *here*," he explained. "The executions would be witnessed by Lebans no matter where we did it, and the Mixtim are under their protection as well. I don't know what all those tentacles could do, but I *do* know that if we got out alive at all, a message would somehow be sent to Zone, and we would be as wanted as the ones we chase. This isn't Clopta, after all. There are times when diplomacy and a light touch might yield better results than the heavy boot. Bring them along. If they cause trouble, we can dispose of them when we get to Verion. But consider this: The Dillians and the Dahir still have the official weight of the Zone Council on their side. *They* can legitimize *us* with the army. So long as one or more of their companions are within easy range of either of us, I think they will go along."

Campos frowned. "You are not playing both sides again, are you, Colonel?" she asked suspiciously.

"I took an oath and I meant it! This is not some sordid drug business here; it is for the highest of stakes! This will be very, very tricky no matter what we do!"

Campos thought it over. "All right, Colonel, I will play it

your way for now. Please just make certain that I do not see you changing sides once again."

"I *swear* to you . . . !"

"Never mind. We have wasted far too much time here. Let us get the party together and head out for this Avenue, whatever it is. But remember, Colonel, if they betray us at the last moment, they have nothing on me at all of a criminal nature. What have we done? Fled a drug baron and defended ourselves against a monster and the baron and his henchmen? Gone where I have a right to go? Taken these people where they wished to go, anyway? You see?"

"You are forgetting that the condition those two are in was your doing," the colonel pointed out. He did *not* point out that the only witness to his treason was Gus, who could hardly afford public charges and testimony in Zone because it would mean leaving Zone and exiting in Dahir, a place that very much wanted him back to ensure that he would not leave again.

"So? Even if they can prove that, which is not a certain thing, how could the poor mistress of a gangster have such authority in the gang in so short a time on this world? It is hardly an international crime like the running of drugs. Even kidnapping is a local crime here, did you know that? Had I kidnapped or held prisoner a fellow Cloptan, *that* would be a different story, but *these*? No, I think not. And as I am certain that you, as usual, always have a way out of a tight situation, the fact is, the way this world is set up, neither of us has committed crimes for which anyone is looking for us other than those we directly committed crimes against." She considered that and found it highly amusing.

"Come, come! My friend and son of my patron!" the colonel said. "What are we *doing*, passing blame back and forth to one another? I believe there were 160-odd nations back on the Earth we left, perhaps a few more. There are *780* sovereign and independent nations here, each with its own unique race and needs. Consider how little could get done back on

Earth and you have only a shadow of how little can truly get done of an international nature here. Without this unpleasantness with Brazil and Chang, they could not have even *touched* the cartel! What have such as we to fear from such as them?"

"Yes, you are right," Campos said after a moment. "Well, we will let them live, at least for now. As you say, what can they do?" She paused a moment. "Of course, if those army people get our birdie, then we *might* just have to commit one of those crimes, you know."

"True," the colonel agreed, "but if that happens, we'll have Mavra Chang, so what difference does it make? If the king—or queen—is the state, can that person commit a crime against themselves?"

It was a *most* amusing idea, and both of them laughed.

For the first time on the journey Terry felt really frightened. The images in that Juana's mind about her were bizarre and nightmarish. She couldn't imagine what she might have done to deserve such complete and utter hatred, but Juana Campos was scarier than anything she could imagine, even in her surface thoughts. They were also so inconsistent as to be totally crazy. How could Campos on the one hand imagine blinding and maiming Terry and treating her like an animal and at the same time look upon her with genuine concern?

It took a couple of days before she realized that Campos's gentler nature, what there was of it, was directed not at her but at her coming baby.

Gus was improving but still in no condition to do very much, and the travel didn't help his healing at all. There were times when the pain was such that he was very much afraid that he was going to die and other times when it was even worse and he was afraid he wouldn't die. Still, Terry's presence kept him from giving up and provided the determination to heal no matter what.

He had never expected to still be here this close to the birth and headed away from the kind of medical help that she might well need. He knew of women who still *died* in childbirth, particularly in Third World countries, and he'd seen too much infant mortality for one lifetime already. He cursed himself for ever agreeing to leave Agon with her as well as for being stupid enough to get shot.

Now it was clear that Kurdon had wanted her handy as bait in case Campos had to be lured out of some underground hiding place in Clopta. Well, Kurdon joined a lengthening list of people, including Gen Taluud and himself, who had underestimated Campos. Trouble was, it was no skin off Kurdon's ass what happened; Gus had paid with a painful, debilitating wound and capture, and Taluud had paid with his life. But it was Terry who might well pay the biggest price unless somehow he could get well enough to save her.

The Dillians, too, felt less than noble about the help they'd been in all this and were pretty well defeated and resigned. A few times one or possibly both might have escaped, but they could hardly have taken Gus and Terry with them, and they had no doubt that either Campos or the colonel would make them pay for any transgression by Tony or Anne Marie.

In point of fact, Tony for one was surprised to be alive at all. It didn't make a lot of sense not to have killed them, but since they hadn't, there was at least the possibility of getting out of this with a whole skin. Whether the same could be said for Terry, Mavra, or Lori remained to be seen, but as Anne Marie had commented, "We started this as grown-ups. It would be maddening not to be there at the finish."

On Taluud's sturdy horses and with well-provisioned pack mules, they made the Verion border in just three days.

"It would be tempting to run our trackers all the way down this border and see if there is a scent now," Campos commented, "but whether or not they have gotten here yet is something we cannot say. We wasted so much time back there trying to find them that it is not worth it at this point. Let us push on to this Avenue; I want to see what the devil this setup is."

"Shall we cross over to Ellerbanta? They are high-tech over there, you know. It would be much easier to travel. We might well be able to ride up on something that has real power and eat decent food again."

"It *is* tempting," the colonel agreed, "particularly considering what these Verion hogs think of as high cuisine, but I think not. Our odds of making headway with any guards are far better on this nontech side than on the other, and they will *have* to come this way."

In another three days they reached the point where the Avenue intersected the equator. None of them had ever actually seen a Well World wall before; its scope and sheer sense of permanence awed them all. It rose from the ground as if placed there by the hand of some enormous giant, rising up, up, as far as the eye could see. There *was* a top limit, of course, but it was impossibly high up, and beyond that there rose an energy barrier that still stopped any sort of passage across it.

The southern hemisphere of the Well World was dedicated almost entirely to carbon-based life; the few exceptions were primarily silicon variants that still required much of the same ranges of environment for life and sustenance. The northern hemisphere, on the other hand, was entirely non-carbon-based and in fact had so many varieties that they had their own separate lexicon up there. Most of the northern races, it was said, were so alien that they made little sense to those in the south. Ammonia breathers gazed out on methane oceans, and sulfur oxide breathers found it chilly at a mere ninety degrees Celsius. There were whole regions up there where even crossing from one hex to the next would be lethal to the native of the first, and not a single condition there would support any of the life in the south without an artificial environment.

The only way back or forth was by a special gate in the two Zones, north and south. The equatorial barrier kept everybody else, and everything inside the hemispheres, from mixing.

If it wasn't for the Avenue, there would be no way to tell

that this was any sort of unusual place along the otherwise totally smooth, impenetrable wall. The Avenue simply went up
to it and essentially merged with it, with no apparent sign of
a seam. It was almost as if it continued on through, although
there was nothing to show that it did or didn't.

When they reached it, it was certainly impressive. The border ran right to the edge of the Avenue entrance, and there
were cuts every few kilometers where sloping ramps switch-
backed down. Campos went a little down one ramp, through
the border, and found that the other border, for Ellerbanta,
was along the opposite side. The Avenue was a place all its
own, broad, smooth, and finely machined, which showed the
otherwise invisible artificial nature of this world.

Campos took out one of the energy pistols she had, which
hadn't been anything more than a weight since leaving
Clopta, and fired it at an angle to the opposite wall, which
was impressively far away. The shot hit and seemed to be absorbed by the material. There was no ricochet, not even of the
light from the energy beam.

Impressed, Campos tried it on a section of wall right next
to the ramp. The same thing occurred, and she then gingerly
touched the spot, which showed not even a scorch mark at a
beam level that would have atomized the horse. It wasn't
even warm to the touch.

There was no question that even by the standards of the
Well World, the Avenue was beyond any of the technologies
here and stood like an artifact, perfectly preserved, running
straight as an arrow due north as far as the eye could see.
Campos had had the same sort of feeling when seeing the
great Incan cities and those of the Aztecs and Mayas as well,
somehow out of place in their junglelike settings, suggesting
another world, another time, and a civilization that could
barely be imagined.

At night the Avenue glowed with an eerie light, this one a
golden yellow, revealing a pattern in the Avenue floor and
walls not so obvious in daylight. By night, by this internal

glow, the "street" level seemed to be made up of hexagonal blocks of absolutely uniform size.

"Gives you the creeps, does it not?" Campos said to the colonel, looking down in the darkness.

"I find it astonishing. What incredible creatures they must have been! So far beyond us that we could probably not even imagine their civilization and way of life. This whole *world* nothing but a laboratory for them. It must have been like Mount Olympus or the angels around the throne of heaven."

"But still they died out, just as the Incas, but not by conquest," Campos noted. "Maybe things were not so heavenly, after all, I think. They are dead. Gone. All we are doing is looking at their toys."

The colonel wasn't so sure. "Perhaps. But if they left at least one gatekeeper, as I believe they did, then they didn't think they were going to die out, and they certainly didn't die out due to external or accidental forces. To reach *that* height, they had to have destroyed themselves somehow. What was it that they did, I wonder, and why? *They* certainly didn't think of it as an end, else why leave a gatekeeper? I wonder if we can even *conceive* of what they did. I doubt if we could understand it even if one of them explained it to us. Why build a laboratory, set it up this way, and then leave? And where did they go? And why?"

"Such power they had," Campos breathed. "They would never have given it up willingly. Still, we will never know, eh? Not unless your Captain Brazil wakes up and decides to talk about it."

"Oh, he has. Gus told me all about it. He claims he's nothing more than a man who accepted a bargain with the previous keeper, who was so sick of immortality that he simply wanted to die. And that our captain finally had reached that same point himself and had chosen Mavra Chang as a candidate replacement. Apparently she flunked the initiation."

Campos thought about it. "You know, if that is true, I almost wonder if we could *still* make some sort of deal with her. What does she owe *him* or the builders? Think of getting inside, in the control room of this whole thing. It must be like nothing we can imagine, yes?"

"Indeed. But I hardly think she'd be in any sort of mood to keep a deal struck with you, not after what you did to her," the colonel pointed out. "Even if she kept her word, it would be, I think, like making a deal with the devil. She might make you a queen, all right, but a queen who looked like she does now and with the same limitations. No, I don't think I'd like to trust her on that. Our original plan is far more practical. In that case, we *know* the sort of minds we are dealing with and the limits on their power and authority."

"I think you are right," Campos agreed. "Still, I have to admit that if your captain is telling the truth, then perhaps he did not pick so badly, after all. Consider how far she has come and under what circumstances she has managed to do it. I keep wondering if, considering all that, she will not somehow manage to slip inside."

"Not if we get there first," the colonel responded firmly.

The soldiers stationed here were Verionites; there had been a larger and more mixed force earlier, but it had been discontinued because of its expense, because of the complaints from other races about the tedium and lack of amenities to no apparent purpose, and because the Verionite government wasn't exactly thrilled with the idea of any foreign troops on its soil for any length of time.

They were almost laughable, these troops, except that they had a certain imposing look about them up close. Those pig snouts and big, ugly hog faces and tiny, nasty-looking eyes were atop large mouths from which lower canines often protruded, giving them a very fierce look indeed. Their arms were thick, powerful, and muscular, and their hands had very long fingers that ended in sharp black nails.

They were, Juana Campos decided, really *mean*-looking.

They wore metal helmets that came to points and uniforms of a filigreed wool-like material that included crimson jackets, gold buttons, and black trousers with gold stripes. There were perhaps fifty of them at any given time, under a single officer and two NCOs, and they were rotated frequently.

And they considered their orders to be a very big joke.

"We're to stop anybody from going in *there*," Major Hjazz, the current officer in charge, told the newcomers. "As if they could!"

"There is nothing really there at the end of the Avenue, then?" the colonel asked him.

The major chuckled. "Well, yes. Every night at midnight you'll see it. It'll click on, a kind of glow—the usual hexagon, you know. But you can go up to it, bang on it, butt your head against it, anything you want at all. It won't make a damn bit of difference. It's still just wall."

"Indeed. But tell me, when this light is on—can you see anything? Anything inside?"

"You can see for yourself any midnight. There's tourists come up to see it all the time, both from our own people and from Ellerbanta. Most of the nonlocal races, they come in on tours through Ellerbanta, though, where they got that stuff that makes you soft and lazy. When it's turned on, you can *sort* of see something in there, but you can never really make out what it is. They been tryin' since a lot longer than I been alive, I tell you! Hey, it's just a light on one of them timers like they use in Ellerbanta. It turns on, stays on maybe fifteen minutes, it turns off again. No big deal. Most folks don't come back. It's not much of a show."

"Well, with your permission, we'll camp near here for a little while. We were supposed to meet some others here, and it is pretty clear they haven't shown up yet. They were coming in via your country and on foot, so it might well be a few days, even a week or so, until they get here. It's vital that we speak to them, so would we be in the way if we stayed around a bit?"

"Naw. Feel free. It's the off season, anyway. Still, if your friends are recognizable, I could see if they've been spotted anywhere along the way and how far they might be from here."

Hardly, I think, the colonel said to himself, but aloud he said, "Indeed? Any runners or riders you might send might not cross their path, and we don't know their route in any event. We might ask if things drag on, but it's not necessary at the moment."

"Oh, we wouldn't send runners or riders," the major replied. "We send and receive mail every day by air."

"By *what*?"

And thus it was that the party learned of the aerial accomplishments of the Verionites.

It was the source of endless fascination to the party to watch them take off and fly like that, and the bored soldiers were more than overjoyed to show off, explain things, and particularly emphasize the problems and dangers of doing it so near the barrier and the border, where wind and such could cause serious problems or even disasters. "We've scraped up more than one from the bottom of the Avenue," one private told them. "Messy."

"I'd think you'd just sail right over to Ellerbanta," Tony commented.

"Oh, sure, that's what you *try* to do, but it's not that easy 'cause you don't have a lot of height from this point. That area right in there between the borders ain't all that wide when you're flying, it's true, but it's dead air. You start to sink like a stone, and you don't have much tolerance between those walls for landing. You hit one, or the barrier, and it's all over."

Tony and Anne Marie had been given a good deal of freedom, and they made some use of it. Even Campos seemed to have tired of them as prisoners; she and the colonel more than once tried to talk them, rather nicely and almost as equals, into simply heading over to Ellerbanta, taking a train to the capital, and using the Zone Gate there to go home. There was nothing more here they could do and very little that they could do to Campos or the colonel, in spite of all.

"And Terry and Gus?" Anne Marie asked them.

"Gus knows that as soon as he's recovered enough, he's out of here," Campos told her. "As for Terry, she remains here with me. We are old acquaintances, she and I, and I feel sorry for her."

"She of all people should be sent home now!" Tony argued. "She's going to have that baby any day now!"

"She is a strong, healthy girl. She will do all right," Campos told them both. "Back home in Peru I have been at many home births. It is the way of my people in the backcountry. More than once I assisted doctors of Shining Path with such things. What few things are needed I have had brought here thanks to the ingenuity of our host countrymen."

"Well, I'm not about to leave until she's through it!" Anne Marie told her adamantly.

Campos shrugged. "Suit yourself."

Terry had ridden with them and watched all this in growing confusion and uncertainty. At least Gus seemed better, although still in great pain, and it almost seemed as if the two centaurs were completely out of danger. She knew *she* was still in danger, but she could do little about it. Running away wouldn't do anything but maybe make them hurt Gus. Besides, she couldn't run or even ride right, not anymore.

She had trouble sleeping; every time she changed position, it woke her up. She couldn't walk far or easily; it was more like a waddle, and it was very tiring with this big, hard, increasingly heavy lump in her belly. Her nipples hurt, her breasts seemed swollen, and she had to pee every ten minutes. It didn't take anybody smart to see that she wasn't going *anywhere*.

She, too, was getting pains and the weirdest feelings down there, where they said the baby would come out. She couldn't imagine a baby coming out of *that* little place, but if they said it did, then maybe somehow it did.

After a day or two the pains got worse and more frequent,

and those strange feelings got even stronger. It was a kind of pain like no other she could remember, and she got very worried about it. Anne Marie tried to reassure her, telling her that it was all normal and that all women who had babies went through this. But Anne Marie had never had a baby. She'd been too sick. Even she couldn't know how *awful* an experience this was turning into and how it seemed to keep dragging on and on.

Early one morning, when she was walking from the pit toilet back to the tent for the umpteenth time, she felt something different, and all of a sudden all sorts of smelly, gushy, yucky watery stuff was flowing out and down her legs. She knew that she hadn't peed again and that it hadn't come out of *there*, and it confused and frightened her enough that she went to Gus, who was just lying there as usual, and pointed.

Gus hadn't much experience in this himself, but he knew something had happened, and he called for Anne Marie and Tony.

"Why, I believe her water's broken!" Anne Marie said happily. She turned and looked straight into the concerned Terry's eyes. "That means the baby will come very soon now. Not much longer. Hold on, girl! Hold on!"

That was going to be really hard, because the pains were coming back now full force, a *lot* stronger and a *lot* more often.

"Shouldn't she be lyin' down?" a concerned Gus asked Anne Marie.

"If she wants to," the centauress replied. "Otherwise, let her stand or sit or whatever. In one sense she's better off than in some hospitals where those stupid male doctors don't let women stand up or sit and treat this like it's some kind of illness. It's not an illness, it's the miracle of birth, quite natural, and about as amazing as anything that has happened to us."

Over the next few hours the pains got even worse, and they just kept coming and coming. She was getting to the point where she no longer cared about anything, not even the baby. She just wanted it *over* with.

"Get Campos in here," Anne Marie instructed.

Tony looked at her oddly. *"Campos?"*

"He claimed he could deliver a baby and had before. I haven't. *You* certainly haven't. And I don't want that nasty colonel within a mile of this."

"But—the way Campos thinks of her! She could *kill* the child!"

"She won't. I've talked to her. She thinks the child is hers. Don't argue! *Get him! Now!"*

It was the most miserable, painful time of Terry's brief memory, worse than anything, worse than dying. The pain, the exhaustion, the people yelling at her—she began to hate them all. And it went on, and on, and on . . .

"Push! Now push!" someone was telling her, and she felt as if she didn't have enough energy to do anything else at all, but she pushed . . .

And then the girl who never said a word, never uttered much in the way of sounds at all, screamed. Screamed with a length and depth that were almost unbelievable and sent panicky nearby Verionite soldiers running for their weapons.

It felt as if she had passed a stone the size of a watermelon, but now, suddenly, it was over. Somewhere off in the distance she heard the incongruous sound of a baby crying, but then she simply passed out.

"Santa Maria! It's a boy! A *big* one, too!" Campos shouted with unrestrained glee. She carefully clipped the umbilical cord with a small clamp she'd gotten from the Verionites, then washed off and wrapped the baby, a rough and tumble type who clearly didn't want to be out in this weird, cold new environment at all. Anne Marie took care of the placenta and otherwise cleaned up the mess.

"Poor dear! She's passed out, totally exhausted."

"Shouldn't wonder," Campos commented. "Twelve hours. *Ai!* But here is the result, and not a blond hair or blue eye to be seen. These are Latin features on the child! You see? No Mister Gus with his lily-white north in *him!*" She laughed.

"Even here, in this place and in this muddled mess, a new Campos is born!"

"Well, don't kill him by taking him all over and showing him off!" Anne Marie scolded. "Give him to me. He should be here when she comes to, and she will have to nurse him, considering the conditions here. You can go brag all you want. I'll take care of things at this end."

Actually it was Tony, who had remained nearby through it all, who had the worst reaction. She wasn't at all sure now that she wanted to have children, not one bit.

Gus was not one to be put off by the fact that it wasn't his child. In fact, it had never once occurred to him that it might be. He'd almost injured himself all over again when he'd heard that scream, but when he heard the baby's cry, he'd sat back down again.

He wasn't at all sure if it was or wasn't Campos's kid, either, but he was glad that Campos thought so. It would keep Terry safe for quite a while longer.

The fact that mother and baby were doing fine was enough for him.

It took another three days for Mavra, Lori, and Julian to reach the camp at the end of the Avenue, but they'd managed an epic cross-country trek without, they felt, once being detected, and that was something of a victory in and of itself.

By that time Julian had a very good idea of what Mavra had in mind, and she wasn't at all sure that it was any crazier than simply rushing the place.

In the wee hours of the morning Julian crept in and examined the soldiers' little airport. It was dead quiet, the bigfoots asleep out in the field and everything quite still. There wasn't even a guard on the place, because what purpose would *that* serve here?

There were several of the kites in a storage shed, and all of them looked like they'd seen a lot of work. Still, they looked about as reasonable as one could expect, and the belts and such would probably hold Mavra if, of course, she could steer it by head movements.

She brought Mavra in to examine them, and the bird woman looked at them long and hard. Finally she nodded.

They would not do it tonight, but they would certainly do it quickly. It was *much* too dangerous around here to stay long.

The other question was how to launch and how to get Lori and Julian in with her. In that regard, there was nothing much she could do except use them to get her aloft, and then, if she managed to gain altitude in the darkness and make the proper turn, they would just have to rush full speed through the camp and down the ramp as soon as Mavra vanished inside the Avenue walls. If Mavra was through, they'd get through. If she wasn't, what difference would it make?

The next morning they tried as best they could with the writing system they'd developed to make whatever plans they could.

"You are sure you can fly it?" Julian wrote.

"I am sure I can. I understand the principle. If I can maneuver the front struts with my head and beak, I can do it."

"This is crazy," Julian told her. "We could do as well by just rushing them with you on Lori. They are sloppy, not on guard."

"No," Mavra scratched. "Too risky. Bad guys will try anything to stop me, even killing you. If I am not with you, they won't. They will be trying for me."

"When do you want to do it? We do not even have a watch. How do we know when it is time?"

"Guard changes," Mavra told her. "Last night they had two after dark. Second was at time the door opened. We go on second guard change."

"The odds are very poor."

"The Well will not let me fail. Watch out for yourselves, not me."

She was so confident that this insane, harebrained scheme would work that Julian almost believed it.

Even so, it was hard as hell to get to sleep just thinking about it. All this way, all this accomplishment, and for what? How much training and experience did it take for those Verionites to fly those flimsy things? What did they know or what might they see in the wind currents that was unknown to Mavra? Could she and Lori even provide enough speed to get lift at all?

And most important, what was she most afraid of? That she'd fail? That Mavra would fail? Or that Mavra would succeed?

What then?

Would the wonderful wizard have a heart, a brain, and courage to give away? Or would it just be a small woman behind the curtain pulling levers?

At least Dorothy had had an idea of what she wanted, as had her companions. And she'd never had to fly an unfamiliar aircraft just to get there. She'd even missed the balloon, hadn't she? And all she'd had to do was click her heels together three times . . .

This was gonna be a hell of a lot more complicated, and who knew what all the assembled wicked witches would have ready to stop them?

They'd seen the centaurs, of course, Campos and her bunch, and the colonel, as well as the brutal-looking if rather sloppy soldiers. At least nobody seemed to want to camp out down there at the bottom of the Avenue. It was just too lonely, too spooky, and too bereft of water and other necessities.

There had been no sign of Terry or Gus; they could only hope that nothing bad had happened to either of them.

Maybe that was enough reason for this crazy business, Julian thought. It's too crazy to work, and it's too risky as well, but if it does . . .

At least they might be able to get even.

• • •

For all the agony, Terry had delivered quite cleanly. Campos had been ready with a borrowed and boiled scalpel, but it hadn't been needed. When the baby had decided to come, it had come, with Terry sitting mostly in an oversized Verionese chair, gravity doing much of the final work. There was also no real sign of tearing, although there almost had to be some inside.

The girl, they decided, was a hell of a quick healer.

She awoke about an hour after the birth, feeling as if she'd just delivered boulders. Then she was handed the baby and the baby was placed gently to a breast, started to suck, and really gorged himself.

By the next afternoon she'd slept off a lot of it and was feeling remarkably better and a *lot* thinner and lighter to boot. She kept the baby with her at almost all times, except when Campos wanted to see it or show it off, and, wrapped in a soft blanket, the baby seemed quite content.

The second day, as she grew more ambitious, walking with the baby along the barrier, always accompanied by someone, she seemed to grow more and more interested in the Avenue. That evening, after dinner and feeding the baby, she went out accompanied by no less than Campos and Tony, the latter just because she didn't trust anybody around the girl. Terry surprised both the guardians by going through the barrier and partway down the ramp, holding the baby gently.

Campos stared at her, wondering. "Sometimes I think she can see inside there, see what we cannot," he remarked as much to himself as to Tony. "I wonder what draws her to it. Does she see or hear something, perhaps?"

"Hard to say," Tony responded, but she, too, had noticed it. The girl hadn't shown the slightest interest in the wall or the Avenue in all the time they'd been there, but now, after the baby had been born, it was, next to the child, the *only* thing that really fascinated her.

Later on Campos discussed this with the colonel. "You

would almost swear that she saw inside," she told the Leeming. "That she thought that she could just walk right through."

"She is such a strange one," the colonel responded.

Campos was not ready to let it go at that. She'd watched her face staring into that blank wall too often now.

"I wonder what would happen if we *did* take her there when the door opens," she mused. "What if that 'rewiring' or whatever they did to her back in that so-called human hex tuned her to the signals in there? What if it is some sort of mental signal, some frequency that is denied those of us created by its machinery?"

"You are actually suggesting that she might be able to walk through?" The colonel thought about it. "I find that highly dubious, but even if she *could*, what good would that do us? She is such a simple sort now. She wouldn't know what to do once she was in there, I shouldn't think. I often wonder if *we* would or if even the controls would be so alien or so beyond our ability to understand."

"I grow very tired and very bored here," Campos told him. "I began to think that our quarry is never going to appear or certainly that they are not going to appear here. Perhaps they have more patience than we thought. Or perhaps they weren't as good as we thought they were. There have been no signs, no signals, no reports. It is as if this world swallowed them up."

"I share your frustration, but what can we do? If we give up now, it has all been for nothing."

"Perhaps. Perhaps I am just playing mental games with myself to keep from going insane with boredom. I just wonder, though, What would it hurt to take her down there when the door opens up tonight? If she walks in, she walks in *with us*. With *all* of us, perhaps. As you say, it is probably incomprehensible to us, but what of that? If she could just walk through, and we with her, in front of the amazed stares of the guards! Think of *that*! We would not need Mavra Chang at all to work our will! Inside, then out. We two and the girl. That alone would be enough to cause terror in the highest places, yes? And only *we* would know that we did not do a thing!"

"It is foolishness. You are simply letting a poor unfortunate girl throw you."

"Still, think of it. If she could, and we did, I would be right, would I not?"

"Well, yes, but . . ."

"But what? She is almost certainly not going to be able to do it. I admit that. But where is the harm in trying it? Just once?"

"And who would be down there with her?"

"Just us. She, we two, and the baby, of course, which she, as a good mother, keeps with her. If we can get in, I would like that baby to go in as well. Think of the possibilities. Think of what powers we could claim for that child! Why, there would be *cults* built around the child! More power to those who control the growing child than from any drugs, because there is no product to move except belief. Campos the god-child! And Madame Campos, the only creature known in the history of the universe to be both a father *and* fully female! And you, the high priest of it all. Makes you think, does it not?"

"Well, I will only say that if you want to be humored, I will go along. But do not be too crushed if nothing at all happens at midnight. I still believe Mavra Chang will eventually show up here and that she, not this foolishness, is the key to it all."

"Worth a try, though, no?"

"Whatever you say. On the other hand, on the off chance that this impossible idea actually works, have you considered that we might not be able to get back *out* of there?"

"You do not need to come."

"Oh, no, I did not say anything about that. I will be there with you, I assure you. If there is the chance of *anything* happening, even a change in the texture of the wall or the transparency of its opening, I should like to be there to see it."

Tony watched the evil pair talking and went over to Anne Marie. "I don't like it. Those two are up to something, and whenever they are up to something, it is always bad for everyone else."

Anne Marie looked over at the two, perhaps ten meters away, and nodded. "I agree. And anything they might be up to might well not be good for Terry and that sweet little baby, either. I think we'll keep a good watch on her tonight."

The Well had sent meteors to summon them and bring them through; it had slowly, subtly manipulated probabilities to ensure that at least one Watcher would come to it. It had used all its tricks, major and minor, to accomplish the simple goal that its ancient, automated instructions required of it, and because it was a machine, it had used a circuitous route that would be inexplicable to the linear thinkers who had been the targets of its convoluted, bizarre program. Now all the sequences were run; now all the mechanisms were in place. Even Nathan Brazil, who knew it best of those alive, had tried to fight it in the past and failed, but while patient, the Well would never be denied. Now all the means and methods were in place, the players assembled, each well suited to do what was required to accomplish the Well's own ends, although they themselves were unaware of it. And only Mavra Chang had confidence in it even though she could not feel its hand.

It was time.

The wind was up, blowing directly in their faces across the flattened field. Mavra Chang had examined and even played with the large kite under which she was now strapped but had refused a test flight. Much too risky, too much chance of a crash, and no chance then to make another attempt. One shot for everything. Fifteen minutes of window, fifteen minutes to win the game, set, and match in spite of all the forces arrayed against her. The only thing she was certain of, though whether the knowledge came from her own ancient experience or had been fed to her by the Well, was that a hang glider was guided not with hands and feet but with subtle shifts of the pilot's weight. She was lighter than any of the natives of the hex, but she was sure she weighed enough to maneuver the craft, perhaps higher and faster than even the creatures for which it had been designed. It was more than a hope; it was a necessity that it was true.

Julian watched, only half-concealed in the brush, and frowned as she saw Terry come out, carrying something indistinct in her arms, flanked by both the colonel and Juana Campos. The latter was even smoking one of Taluud's cigars, the puffs of smoke rising and dissipating in the wind.

She was happy to see Terry; it allayed one of her worst fears. Still, what *were* those villains doing with her? And— *what*? They were walking through the border, down the ramp to the Avenue! *What the hell?*

She checked the guards who stood overlooking the vast alien entryway below, bathed in the night glow of the Avenue's strange luminescence, and saw them getting nervous but not yet moving.

Now the *Dillians* were moving toward the Avenue rampway! One of them halted, then the other, and they conferred for a moment. Then one trotted over to a large tent nearby and entered, the other waiting at the start of the ramp, dividing her attention between the tent and what was going on below.

The one in the tent emerged with something large and strange-looking on her back. Could that be *Gus*? Why take *him* down there? And why was he so visible?

Something was definitely wrong. There were four Cloptans as well, two males and two females, and they began heatedly conferring with each other, then they checked their guns, and they, too, were heading down!

My God! Julian thought. *Who's next? The whole damned Verionese army?*

Her eyes went back to the guards, who were visibly nervous at the sight of so many people going down into the Avenue. One of them shouted something, but if there was a reply, Julian couldn't hear it.

Over to one side there *was* activity in the Verionese army camp.

She thought of calling the whole thing off for the night, but Mavra was already strapped in, Lori was hitched up, and it was all ready to go. Mavra would never understand or forgive her if she didn't launch now, but maybe this was all just as well. If Mavra saw the assemblage down there, she might abort the thing herself. At least, Julian hoped so. This was getting ridiculous, and there was no way to warn *anybody*!

She frantically considered trying to write something that Mavra could read, but now the activity from the army camp revealed itself as the changing of the guard; two privates and an officer or sergeant were marching over to relieve the two agitated guards.

She had no choice and no time! There was absolutely nothing she could do about this!

Oh, my God! Here we go!

MIDNIGHT
AT THE WELL OF SOULS

Julian raced for the field, saw where Lori was set up, and barely checked to see if Mavra was okay. It didn't matter anymore. Either it went right or it was over.

She pulled up next to Lori, fumbling with the stupid makeshift pull strap. She finally got it, took a deep breath, and tried to get hold of herself, then clamped it around her neck and shoulders. She turned, lined up with Lori on all fours, then said, *"NOW!"*

Lori might not have understood the word, but the intent and emotion were clear. He kicked into action, and the two of them suddenly felt the straps tighten and then something dragging along behind them. There was no chance, no way, to look and see if it was working; they just had to keep running at full gallop and hope for the best.

Mavra wasn't as prepared for the yank and the move forward as she had thought, and the pull tab that would release the straps fell from her beak. She strained forward, tied into a kite never built for somebody like her, trying to get the last little fingernail-width distance to grab the ring again while rolling forward on her stomach, bouncing on the makeshift carriage.

She felt the kite's leading edge bite into the wind, start to

296 • JACK L. CHALKER

lift, and then come down again. Then it caught once more, and she felt herself rising free of the carriage and of pressure below. With a last desperate attempt that felt like she was tearing her neck from her shoulders, she got the ring, pulled it, and then, with her head, forced the kite up, up as the straps dropped away.

It was a *lot* trickier, bouncier, and rougher then Mavra had thought it would be. No time to look down, no time for bearings; she had to keep it into the wind and with sheer head and neck motion force it up, up, like climbing stairs in the air. Once or twice she almost lost it and had to use the controls rigged to her feet to roll and stabilize while losing altitude, and it took every single ounce of strength and will to fight the thing and get another updraft and climb, climb, climb all over again . . .

Suddenly she was well over the whole field and banked south, trying to gain more and more altitude so that she could get some feel for the craft and sight her objective. The nearly absolute blackness had been the equatorial wall; now she was up, maybe several hundred meters, and angled so that she could see much of the landscape beyond.

For a moment the view, the tiny lights, torches, lamps, and glow on the horizon of the capital were hypnotizing. She had forgotten what it was like after all this time . . .

From somewhere, something was giving her more and more the feel of the thing with each moment aloft, how it steered, how it angled, climbed, and dove, and she didn't fight it. The glider was controlled with very subtle shifts of body weight, and the greatest problem was resisting the urge to overcompensate. As her skill at maneuvering increased so did her confidence. This wingless, flightless bird was soaring now!

She banked back across the field and turned toward the camp and the Avenue. Below her, she could see Julian and Lori going much too slowly, trotting toward the camp. *Hurry up! Hurry up, you idiots!*

It would be tricky, but she decided to make a single trial pass and see what she was dealing with inside the Avenue if she could. The border kept vision a bit dimmer and less clear than she would have liked, but she thought she could see *people* down there. That was bad, but she couldn't afford to risk a second pass. There was some commotion in the Verion army camp, and a lot of soldiers seemed to be rushing to the edge of the abyss, even though some of them were half-dressed.

She couldn't worry about any of this. Something inside her, or perhaps beyond her, from beyond that equatorial wall was saying, *"Now, now! You must come to me now!"*

She took a wide swath around the camp, the airfield, and beyond, proceeded a bit south again, and steeled herself to make the attempt at the door. It would be dead reckoning, and she would have to guess the distance and descent right the first time. The only sure and reasonable way in was to cross the border, straighten up, and fly directly at the door, hoping she sustained enough lift to reach it and did not crash against the wall or drop like a stone.

Below her, Julian had taken her time to get her breath and to disconnect Lori and herself from the other end of those straps. Then she'd started off toward the Avenue, but slowly, at not even a brisk trot. Lori matched her but wondered what was wrong. The messages he'd read said that they had to move quickly at this point and that time was of the essence once Mavra was away. What was holding Julian back? Why was she almost slowing to a dead stop?

Suddenly he sensed that she was afraid. After all this, she was afraid to take the last gamble herself!

Lori had neither much hope nor ambition for all this, but he damned well wasn't not going to see it through. He dropped back, reached over, and nipped her on the ass right near her tail. She started and involuntarily speeded up, and now he raced forward, taking the lead, charging as fast as he could go right into the middle of the Verion army camp.

For some reason Julian found herself unable to take her eyes off him. She just ran after him, and ran, and ran, right into that camp herself.

The major, the sergeant, and several troopers were all arguing and grunting over jurisdiction and procedure and what the hell they were supposed to do. Nobody had ever *really* gone down there without permission before, and nobody wanted to take the responsibility for doing anything at all. Everybody kept making excuses and passing the buck, with the result that nothing was decided at all.

Suddenly somebody yelled, "Watch it! Animals coming!"

And the brave helmeted troops of Verion scrambled to get out of the way as first a pony and then another—*pony*?—ran right through them and to the Avenue ramp.

Lori found it hard to put the brakes on, but there were four turns and no guardrails in the ramp going down. He only hoped that Julian was behind him and that she wouldn't push him over.

She *did* almost fall over the first turn and down into the hard culvert below, but while one leg slipped off the edge, she managed somehow to keep a grip with the other three and scramble back up. She wasn't thinking at all; she had this irresistible impulse to follow the horse ahead of her, and she was going to do it come hell or high water.

Ellerbantan monitors on the other side were far more comfortable but no less bored than the Verionites opposite. Two of them sat watching control screens more or less, dreaming about anything but being there, when one of them suddenly jerked up and punched the other with a tentacle.

"Look at that! It's a whole *mob* going down there from Verion for the midnight show!"

The other one devoted all three eyes to the scene, then relaxed. "Don't worry about it. See how many races are there? It's just one of those damned tour groups."

"Yeah, I suppose you're right," the other agreed. "Still, it's funny they didn't follow the usual routine and come over and warn us."

"Aw, you know those Verionites. Walk all the way down, across, and back up here just for that?"

"Yeah," the other sighed in disgust. "If there was something wrong, they'd be here in a flash, shoot off one of those flares or something. Heck, if those were anything more than tourists, they could take 'em out with arrows."

"My point exactly. So relax," said the first one, and went back to its daydreaming.

On the Avenue floor the colonel and Tony flanked Terry and the baby and watched with curious apprehension as the great yellowish hex switched on just in front of them.

Terry seemed to think it was funny. She gave a kind of delighted giggle and went right up to it, cradling the sleeping baby as she did so. She approached so closely that she could see her reflection in it, as well as the ghostly reflections of the pair behind her.

"She's going to *do* it! She's actually going to *do* it!" Campos breathed.

"I think she may *try*," the colonel agreed.

At that very moment Mavra Chang, hoping that ancient instincts and the Well's own aid hadn't failed her, crossed over into the Avenue's space and tried to center herself as she felt the lift give out. She was going forward still and reasonably straight, but there was no way in hell she could climb or in any way pull out of a shallow but definite forward dive.

Ahead, she saw it. *The door to the Well! Open! Waiting for her!* If she could only stay airborne long enough to make it!

It was going to be very close, and ahead now she could see figures standing there. A Cloptan? Could that be *Campos?* But who, or what, were the others? Jeez, that almost looked like a human woman just at the door itself. She hoped she wouldn't crash behind them; that would be the worst result of all, to fail so very close to the goal. But if she didn't, she risked knocking down the woman.

Well, the hell with it! Precious little she could do about it now!

What the hell? Suddenly the two *Dillians* were there, and one of them had a big lizard on her back. *Get out of my way! Get out of my way!*

She gave a horrendous, panicked screech that echoed through the whole of the Avenue. All of the ones inside heard it and turned, as much in curiosity as in fear. Eyes widened as they saw the huge kite coming, and only Campos had the presence of mind to realize what it must be.

"It's Chang! *Shoot her! Shoot her down!*"

Mavra Chang came over the Dillian's head, so close that Anne Marie's hair was blown by her passing. The four Cloptans who'd just reached the floor themselves drew their weapons when they heard Campos cry, but the thing was too low. Not only did the Dillians block any decent shot or view, if they shot through them, it would be too late.

The colonel sent out a pseudopod that actually touched the kite, wrenching it a bit, but even though he had hold of it, he was too close to the door and the thing still had too much momentum for such an unthinking chance grab.

The girl, having seen what was coming, moved to one side and crouched low so that first the kite went through the door with Mavra Chang still tied under it, perhaps a meter off the Avenue floor, then the colonel was dragged in, too, still clutching it.

Campos had hit the floor when she'd seen that the kite couldn't be slowed. As she got up, she watched in amazement as the girl looked at the baby, smiled, and then stepped into the hex opening and vanished.

"*No!*" Campos cried, and lunged forward, and was herself swallowed up.

Tony and Anne Marie looked at each other quizzically.

"I don't care if you have to throw me, get me the hell in there!" Gus growled at them.

Anne Marie shrugged, and Tony shrugged, and the two galloped right at the opening and went through.

The four Cloptans were totally confused by all this, and finally it was Kuzi who screamed, "I don't give a damn 'bout *nothin'* no more! I say we follow the boss!"

The others nodded, guns still drawn, but as they ran for the door, they were almost knocked down by two horses, or something very like them, running at full gallop toward the Well access. First Lori, then Julian ran right into the thing and disappeared amid some wild but inaccurate firing by the Cloptan guns.

Finally Kuzi started for the door, and the others followed, all angry, confused, but determined to go through and find out what the hell was on the other side and why everybody else had disappeared and to where. Kuzi marched right up to the still-outlined door and right into a solid wall that knocked her down and sent the others sprawling in back of her.

The door remained visible for about another minute and a half, and the Cloptans tried just about everything from firing energy weapons and conventional pistols at it to pounding on it, but it did no good. Then it winked out, and they were left alone in the suddenly silent and very deserted Avenue.

"It ain't *fair!*" Audlay cried. "Everybody got to go but *us!*"

THE WELL
AT ENTRANCE HALL 9

The colonel was totally disoriented, and it took him a few moments to disengage from the kite which lay, crashed, nearby and re-form himself into a practical shape.

He was most conscious of the silence, sudden and absolute, but he was too experienced to dwell on it at the moment. Instead, he went over to the kite, put out two strong armlike pseudopods, and turned it over.

Its struts were splintered, and it was virtually broken into two pieces; whatever had ridden in on it must have taken a terrible jolt.

But there was nothing in the harness. It looked in fact as if the straps had been *burst*, as if by something suddenly enlarging to a point where the straps could no longer contain it.

If so, where was it?

He looked around and saw the door behind him, as transparent as glass. He saw the girl check the baby, smile, and walk through into the chamber where he now was, the invisible surface parting as if it were a thin curtain of water.

The girl stopped, then looked around in wonder at the whole of the enormous chamber. Then the baby moved and made a sound, and all her attention came back to it.

Now Campos, looking very comical, picked herself up and

almost *stormed* through. She spotted the colonel immediately, paying little mind to the girl. "So? Where is she?" Campos asked, eyeing the broken kite. Her voice echoed in the vastness of the hall.

"She's not here," the colonel responded, gesturing toward the underside. "I can't explain it. It couldn't have been more than a matter of seconds, a half minute at most, until I was able to regain my composure and check it. I still had hold of it!"

Campos reached into a pocket, took out another in the dwindling supplies of Taluud's cigars, and lit it. "I don't like this. I say we go with the original plan and all get the hell out of here before it closes on us!"

The colonel looked around at the eerie, empty hallway with its incredibly high, nearly endless ceiling and vast expanse, and said, "I tend to agree. I—"

Suddenly, the Dillians burst through the door, Tony with Gus on her back.

"Who the hell said you all could come?" Campos snapped at them. "And why bring *him*?" It was clear she meant Gus.

"Because he asked us to," Anne Marie answered matter-of-factly. She looked around the great hall, as did Tony, and both gasped at the scale. It made all of them seem like a speck of dirt on a nice, clean floor.

"Well, everybody can turn around and get out right now!" Campos thundered. "All of us!"

"Lost your nerve? So soon?" Gus taunted, then frowned. "Hey! I don't hurt no more! In fact—"

He rolled off Tony's back and onto the smooth floor, then looked down at his side. Almost on impulse, he tore off the bandages. Underneath there was nothing but smooth, undisturbed skin. Not even a scar was visible.

"Well, I'll be damned! I'm beginnin' to *like* this place!" he said wonderingly.

Campos was growing increasingly nervous. "Well, *I*, for one, do not! We go! *Now!*" She looked at the other Cloptans coming toward the door. "If we don't, it's going to be an even *bigger* mess! About the only ones missing are—"

At that moment Lori and Julian came into view behind the Cloptans; they could see but not hear the Cloptan group scatter as they passed and saw the Cloptans firing wildly, but then first Lori and then Julian were inside the hall, their hooves abruptly clattering against the smooth floor.

"I had to open my big mouth," Campos said grumpily. "All right! *Out!*"

"Who's gonna make us?" Gus asked him. *"You?"*

"Colonel, I am suddenly very weary of that one. He has been a burden for too long," Campos said to the Leeming. "Will you please see to him?"

The colonel moved close to Gus, who had no armor and no defense and was still all too visible to everyone there. The Leeming hesitated just a moment, and Gus asked him, some obvious nervousness in his voice, "Well, Colonel, you and I gonna finally finish it here, huh?"

"Gus, I don't really want to kill you," Lunderman said with apparent sincerity. "Just take the girl by the hand and let us leave."

"No, Colonel. I don't think so. For some reason, I got this funny feelin' that the rules are different here." He didn't sound very confident, but he wasn't going to move, that was clear.

"Finish him, Colonel, and get out!" Campos screamed.

"Sorry, Gus. You chose it yourself," the Leeming said, shooting out a pseudopod and flowing a part of himself up and around Gus's midsection.

Gus's tooth-filled mouth opened in amusement and obvious relief. "That tickles, Colonel. If I'da known that was all there was to it, I wouldn'ta bothered to waste a shot on you back in Agon."

The colonel withdrew rapidly.

"What is wrong?" Campos asked, sounding nervous herself now.

"It didn't work, that's all. It was as if there was something, some very thin barrier surrounding the whole of his skin. I could not get through it."

"Leave him, then! Get the baby and the girl and let's go!"

"I wouldn't be all too certain that leaving is an option, Campos," Tony commented, gesturing at the door, where even now the other Cloptans were trying as hard as they could to penetrate without success.

Campos broke for the door, ran to it, and reached out as if to show that it was just a thin piece of nothing.

It was hard as a rock.

"Sorry, Campos. I want you right where I can see you," came a voice unfamiliar to most of them but very recognizable to others. It was a deep, melodic woman's voice, and it came to each of them in his or her native language.

"Mavra! Is that you?" Tony called, her voice echoing like all the rest in the vast chamber.

She gave a low, gusty laugh. "Yeah, it's me. I made it! Against all the odds, I made it! Me! First in and in control. Hey, *I* didn't call the Well to get here; *it* called *me*! When I got this close, I knew that whatever the odds, it would provide whatever I needed to get inside. I got to admit I was doubting it myself there, particularly at the last minute, but I'm here now. I'm not sure why all of *you* are here, but it seems appropriate somehow."

"Where are you?" Campos yelled at her, defiance still in her voice. "Why do you hide yourself from us?"

"Well, you know, when I get in here, I'm really not myself," Mavra responded. "I guess I wanted a little time for you to settle down. But if you want to see what's become of your little birdie, then so be it!"

All the lights inside the chamber came on, illuminating them as if in daylight. "Oh, my *God*!" Julian gasped. They all turned toward where she was looking and had a similar reaction.

The creature that was approaching them was over two meters tall and reminded most of them of nothing so much as a huge beating heart, skin a sickly blue and red, pulsing rhythmically, moving forward on six powerful-looking, sucker-laden, squidlike tentacles.

"I *told* you I wasn't myself in here," Mavra's voice came from somewhere within it. "You see what I mean about the shock value. It's a pretty practical form, really, for this sort of thing, although it's not exactly current fashion. This is what they looked like, the people who built this place, at least at the end. By then they'd advanced far enough that they didn't need all the handy stuff evolution had provided earlier. I can't describe it to you. I'm doing a thousand different exchanges with the Well right now, each perfectly clear, while I'm using just the tiniest part of myself to hold this conversation with you. I'm running and checking out math and diagnostics on a scale even I can't believe. I'm also seeing everything the Well is sending me, and I have 360-degree sight and absolute hearing through all the frequency ranges. And even with all that, I couldn't *begin* to build something like this. Imagine a whole race with this kind of capability. It's staggering."

"You—you really *were* one of *them*, then?" Julian managed, amazed.

Mavra laughed. "Oh, no. I couldn't *imagine* being one of them, or how they lived and thought. The Well just re-creates me in the image of its makers, so to speak, because otherwise I couldn't work the controls here. I guess by *their* terms I'd probably be a low-grade moron, but the capacity and speed of the brain are such that I can handle the routine stuff."

"Everything—the whole Well World—is maintained and controlled from here?" Gus asked, losing his abhorrence of her form and becoming more the old reporter again.

Again Mavra laughed. "No, that's just one tiny little area here. A kind of microcomputer, compared to the whole thing, that does relatively simple jobs. The *main* job of this thing, if you must know, is keeping the universe running."

It was so staggering a concept and so impossible to believe that nobody had a follow-up on it for a while. Finally Gus said, "So God is a computer?"

"You *might* say that. I get the idea that this isn't all of it, but there are limits on what I can understand or do here. They didn't want their repair personnel playing too fast and loose with the universe. We're just dumb lunkheads. We make decisions that are basically moral ones, ones the Well isn't programmed to make for itself. If the fabric of space and time itself is damaged, the way it was the last and only other time I was in here, *we* have to choose to push the button and reset the universe. It's a mean responsibility if you think about it. I wiped out whole worlds of civilizations last time, probably killed multiple trillions of beings from all sorts of races, not just the ones on the Well World. They didn't think a machine should ever have to make decisions like that, so they assigned somebody to do it. The closest translation to the job would be 'Monitors,' but it often comes out as 'Watchers,' 'cause that's really the job, too. We just exist, and watch things, and make sure they don't fall apart, while waiting for the phone to ring."

Campos was appalled. "You mean *that* is what all this is about? A stinking *computer* calling its *repairman*? And for *that* all of *us* were wrenched from our lives and twisted and reshaped and dropped into this nightmare of a world?"

"Something like that," Mavra admitted. "It *does* have a way of making its summons a bit dramatic if we can't get to one of its doorways in space, and I'm afraid a lot of people *often* get dragged in. It wasn't designed that way. I doubt if it ever occurred to the builders that people like you even existed, Campos, let alone that they'd be hauled over here to cause even more misery. I doubt if it ever occurred to them just what trouble it might be for the Watcher to get in here, either; otherwise they would have made it easier. But I'm here now in spite of the best efforts of quite a number of people to prevent it, including some of you here. The only ones

I *expected* and *invited* were Lori and Julian. Ummm . . . Yes, minor detail to set right."

Lori's body was suddenly misty, then distorted, and when it was again clear and distinct, Lori of Erdom, fully restored, stood in their midst. He shook his head as if clearing something out of it, something rattling around inside. Finally he sighed and said, "I feel like I'm waking up from some awful nightmare. I have all these crazy memories, impressions, but most of them don't make any sense."

"Well, you were a horse," Mavra pointed out. "I'm afraid all that information in your head couldn't always fit in that horse brain, but your spirit, your drive, remained, and in the end you still did what you had to do."

"Julian, I—" he began, and stopped, seeing something in her eyes and manner. It was readily apparent that Julian was less than fully thrilled to see her husband back to normal.

"Lori, Julian's going to be a little bit complicated, so just hang on for a little bit," Mavra told him.

The colonel spoke, although they all were awed at the display of power Mavra had just performed. "You—you can do *that*? With your mind alone?"

"I just order it. I don't bother with how it's done any more than you bother with how the electricity gets to the lamp when you turn it on. It's easy in specific cases, but it gets more complicated if you have to do something on the scale of a hex. When you get beyond that, to whole civilizations and worlds, I'm not so sure I'm up to it. Still, we may see."

Gus, too, was awed and fascinated, but not to the point where he didn't want to press things a bit to satisfy his curiosity. "So what's wrong?" he asked her.

"Huh? What do you mean?"

"Well, we all got stuck here for *some* reason, right? I mean, it called you and the captain, and that was to fix stuff. What's broke?"

Mavra seemed disturbed by the question. "I—I've been trying to find out. All of the diagnostics so far are turning up just fine. The universe isn't in peril, no world is about ready to die, nothing appears wrong. Still, we were called here for *something*. The Well went to a great deal of trouble to get us here. I guess I haven't hit it yet, although that *is* rather odd. If something's broken enough to summon us, then something in the Well's diagnostics routine should have told me straight away. So far—nothing. It's very strange."

As if in response, she began to receive a data stream from somewhere deep within the Well. Something about a "Kraang Matrix Formula," but it didn't make any sense. It didn't correlate with anything in the Well's operational system, in the symmetry of its physics and mathematics. What the hell was a Kraang Matrix Formula?

Before she could even request research information on it, another signal broke in, one she'd heard only once before but one that had provided a major motivator for her to reach the Well.

"Mavra! Mavra! You've done it! Now free me! Free me!"

"Obie? Is that really you? Can you really live again?"

Once, in the past cycle of existence, before the last reset, she had roamed the universe with Obie, a moon-sized computer built by some of the most brilliant minds of her own time, a self-aware computer that could in a limited way do some of the things on a vastly smaller scale that the Well could do. She could never explain Obie, but having to see him—Obie had always been a "him"—wiped out with the rest of that universe had been the most horrible thing she had ever had to face because of its permanence.

"How can I do it, Obie? I don't know a lot about working this thing."

"I'll send you the instructions. I already knew a lot, so I could follow what was being done here. Just pass the instructions along exactly as I give them to you, no changes, no hesitations, and I'll once again be formed in orbit around this world. Think of it, Mavra! The two of us together again!"

No more horrors of existence on that grubby Earth, no

more crawling before the likes of Campos, no more pettiness and Earthbound strife . . . Together again, with that power, no matter how limited, roaming the universe, exploring, learning, helping out . . .

"Brazil never told you because he wanted me to die," Obie sent to her. *"He thought that my power was too great a potential disruption to the Well. He couldn't help it, but he did it, Mavra! He killed me, Mavra! And now you can bring me back! Now you are in charge! Take the data stream and command the instructions! Free me! Free me!"*

"Go ahead. Send. I'll try, Obie. I'll try!"

All the exchange, her internal debate, and the final decision, had, to the others, taken place within the blink of an eye. They barely knew that something was going on.

"So what will you do with us now?" the colonel asked her. "Revenge? That seems a rather petty thing for one in your current circumstances."

"You are right," she answered him. "Revenge is something beyond a superior creature such as this one. When I am human, I am very vengeful, but not like this. Not now."

She could see Campos seem to relax, and the colonel, more suspicious, also seem a bit more comfortable. "What will you do, then?" Lunderman asked her.

"Justice," she answered, sending new fear into them. "Justice is the highest calling of a higher intellect."

"Sequence completed and program running. Done. Input accepted. Result nominal," the Well reported to Mavra.

But what did that mean? Was Obie reconstituted, alive again in orbit? All the Well's local sensors showed no change. Nothing but the usual random debris up there. What had she just done?

"Obie? Where are you, Obie?"

"Obie couldn't come," said a strange, commanding, powerful voice that seemed to fill the whole of the great hall. "So I came instead."

"Holy shit! It's *another* one!" Gus exclaimed. "And this one sounds like Darth Vader!"

And from the center of the hall another shape appeared, very much like Mavra, but not *quite* like Mavra. It was bigger, more than three meters tall and half again as thick, and it seemed to be bathed in a radiant glow.

"How *wondrous* it is to be free once again!" the Kraang exclaimed. "I did not believe that it would ever happen in spite of my best efforts!"

Mavra had no conception of who this newcomer was, but she knew pretty damned well that it had been the result of her commands to the Well, which was now reporting a return to "nominal" status, meaning no more repairs were necessary.

Mavra Chang tried to retrieve information on this newcomer, this bizarre new creature who seemed to have come from nowhere, but she couldn't. Suddenly she felt the Well closing off from her as if a series of switches were being thrown one by one, shutting her out, diminishing her . . .

She tried to fight, but the Kraang was out of her league. Suddenly, for the first time, she realized that it *had* all been for nothing, that she'd been played for one of the biggest fools in the history of the cosmos.

She stood there, suddenly just Mavra Chang again, a tiny Oriental-looking woman, slightly built, naked, and looking very, very small indeed.

"Don't feel so bad," the booming voice of the Kraang said to her. "I have been most impressed with you. *Most* impressed. You couldn't know about me because I was outside of the entire system, outside of the entire Master Program. It was designed that way so that I would drift forever in space, neither fully alive nor dead, never intersecting or interacting with anything. Designed that way over five billion years ago."

"*You!* It was *you* sending me those messages!" she said, openmouthed, never feeling more like a sucker in her whole life than right now. "And *you* were what was wrong! You were what I was called to fix!"

"Clever. Yes, it is true. You know the principle of the fifty million monkeys. That sooner or later fifty million monkeys at fifty million typewriters will write the works of Shake-speare if given an infinite amount of time. Well, *my* condition was like that. Eventually, in a coincident situation during the last reset, the Well was supposed to give a course correction that would have continued my endless lonely isolation. At that moment, however, the reset was executed, and that command was not completely given. Eventually, an intersection was made in spite of it all. I was able to tap into the data steam, although only in limited ways. I've been watching you—all of you—since you were processed through the Well and became part of the minor data stream. I've seen it all through your eyes, heard your thoughts, monitored your dreams. But it was all for naught. All for nothing if someone came here who understood the problem and corrected it. For-tunately, you made it in first, my dear. That will stand you forever in my favor."

"Nathan," she said guiltily. "If Nathan would've gotten here first, he would have been able to deal with you."

"Yes, that's true, I suspect, although I am still not terribly clear on who or what he actually is beyond being a patholog-ical liar. Severing him from the data stream will take consid-erably more work, but there is no hurry now, is there?"

"You are one of the founders? An original of this race?" Lori asked.

"I am."

"Then why did they imprison you so? And where did the rest of them go? Will you tell us that?"

"As a race they went collectively mad," the Kraang re-sponded. "This insane project, this march to oblivion, began with nobler motives, but eventually the infection was com-plete. Only I stood against them. Even those who agreed with me were eventually won over, co-opted. Those who thought as I but did not have the courage to speak or act against it were carried along in its momentum. They did not exile me. They came to kill me. They came to put me through the Well, to make of me what the Well did to you. *I* was the one with the courage, and I was too smart for them. Deep below here, in the workrooms and stations of the Well, I arranged my own exile. *I exiled myself* rather than be forced into their madness! And I did it in a prison of my own devising, one that was controlled by an endless loop that the Well itself could neither monitor nor touch. I suppose they might have been able to break it in time, but they apparently decided to let it go, seeing how perfect my exile was. To them, I had committed a racial sin, and I had devised my own punishment, my own hell, as it were, and sent myself forever to it. They did not know that I was in a suspended state, shut down, all but the most minute part of myself in semioblivion so that the passage of such a great amount of time would be as nothing to me."

"But then, you must have known that somehow, sometime it would break down," Lori noted, fascinated as they all were, even if still terrified of this strange specter from out of ancient epochs.

"I was a mathematician," the Kraang explained. "I knew of randomness, of chaos, of the infinite amounts of time before this universe. *Would* it happen before the universe began to contract in upon itself once more and finally die as quietly as it had been born so noisily? *That* I could not say. It was nonetheless a vast amount of time in which, even with the Well, almost anything could happen. I must say that it never occurred to me that it would be this soon. Now, though, I am here and they are gone. Now the Well serves me and me alone. Overall, this universe is a patchwork remade by amateurs. *I* shall proceed to perfect it. Not right away, not so frighteningly dramatic, but slowly, with subtlety, with conscious interaction. I will provide the way, and the universe will choose to follow me and perfect itself. That portion which does not will be destroyed. My vision is a challenge to me, to the Well, to all the peoples and worlds of the universe! Those who see and accept me and my vision and follow shall inherit it under me!"

"It sounds like you're thinking of becoming God Almighty," Anne Marie said somewhat scornfully.

"I AM GOD ALMIGHTY, MASTER OF THIS UNIVERSE AND ALL THAT IS WITHIN IT!" the Kraang thundered.

Then, in still thunderous but more moderate tones, he added, "That happened the moment my program was canceled. How can I explain it to your puny, primitive intellects? The moment I returned to the point where I had left was the moment that the Well came under my total and complete domination and will, an instrument of myself. You are honored to be present at the coronation of the one and only true God of the universe. Now and forever."

"Amen," Gus said a bit sourly.

Mavra just sat there, head down, thinking over and over, *What have I done? What* have *I done?*

The Kraang, however, was going on. It was, Gus supposed, the first time he'd had a captive audience in billions of years.

"What is God?" mused the Kraang. "The *ultimate* leader. Immortal, all-powerful, able to call up any fact, any bit of information, no matter how large or how small, as he chooses. One able to reward those who worship him and follow his instructions and to punish those who transgress his will, his whims, no matter how petty. You all had gods—at least, virtually all of you—and one, Mavra Chang, played goddess for centuries to a bunch of people even more ignorant and primitive than she. The god of the Jews slew whole populations because one person transgressed. He punished individuals who did nothing more than slip once in an otherwise pious life with death and damnation. He set down a list of rules so arcane, so complex, that no one could truly follow them all. And yet he could take someone who murdered, who committed adultery, who violated almost every one of his commandments and make him a beloved king in spite of all that. Now where is the logic in that? Yet on your world that god became god of the Christians, god of the Moslems, the most influential and important god on the planet. The Hindus—we won't even talk about the destroyer of universes; it is self-explanatory. They perhaps had the clearest idea of the system as it truly was, but to what end? So that a rigid class structure could always be maintained on the people by the ruling elite in which even social climbing would be a mortal sin. The Buddhists—they saw through everything. Existence proceeded stage upon stage, until you reached the That Which Is Beyond. Oblivion. And that's just *your* world. You cannot *imagine* what some of the others came up with! Am I so much worse than the gods you *did* worship? The gods you tried to follow? Or am I merely a threat because I am real, I exist, you cannot deny me or my power or doubt it? You—none of you can rationalize *me* away!"

Mavra's head came up. "This is an unlikely group of prophets to begin your reign," she noted.

"Not at all," the Kraang responded. "Why, right now I can see that you are contemplating either suicide or some futile and fatal heroic gesture to ease your conscience. The colonel is trying to figure out the best way to ingratiate himself with me, as always the pragmatist. Campos is a bit torn between her Catholic upbringing and her lust for power which she finds potentially vast in my service. The Dillians are aghast but fatalistic. Lori and Gus are curiously similar in their desires to just be out of all this, although Gus is far more offended by me than Lori. And Julian—my pretty Julian has been on the verge of suicide since she got here and is still confused about her purpose, her role, and how she could possibly fit in anywhere at all. Let me demonstrate how easy it is."

Julian was suddenly bathed in an unearthly glow, a radiance that gave her a nearly supernatural look. Subtly, she was changing, not from being an Erdomese but into the absolutely ideal image of the Erdomese female, a change so perfect, so precise, and so beautiful that even those who weren't Erdomese could see it and even feel it. And upon her face was a look like no other, an expression of total and abject worship, of complete and utter innocence and joy. She fell down and prostrated her new self before the Kraang.

"And you shall henceforth be called *Sowacha*, which in Erdomese means 'Daughter of Heaven,' and all who see you and speak with you will know that your name is of me and my power and that you wield it in my name and with my authority," the Kraang intoned. "You will seek counsel only of me and return to your land as my servant and agent. I shall bless and protect you, and you shall be unsullied, without blemish or sin, and the church, and the land, shall know you as one who is my own. You shall lead the people in my name, and in my name you shall remake the land and people as I command."

"Yes, my lord and master," she responded, never getting up or looking up.

"You see?" the Kraang said to the others. "It really *is* that easy. I do not *need* or *require* your loyalty or your consent. It is merely a matter of reprogramming your rather simple minds."

The others were frightened to death by the demonstration, but Mavra Chang was just consumed by anger. She moved to rise but found she was frozen, stuck where she was. She couldn't outthink the Kraang; he had the whole damned Well at his beck and call thanks to her.

Damn it! The bastard had won! When he finished his ego trip, they'd all march out of here like Julian, slaves to the Kraang, devoting all their lives and thoughts and energies to whatever he wanted. And there wasn't a single damned thing they could do about it!

Suddenly, out of the darkness, the baby cried. They had all forgotten about Terry and the child. Even the Kraang for some reason hadn't included her in his survey of the group. Now, though, all the attention was diverted to the small, dark girl with the infant.

She walked steadily out of the shadows, looking expressionlessly at the Kraang. When she got to Anne Marie, she stopped, looked up at the Dillian, and said, "Anne Marie, take the baby. I think I've had just about enough of this ego-maniac's bullshit."

If anything could shock them more than the Kraang and his demonstration of pure power, it was Terry speaking and speaking so determinedly.

"Terry?" Gus managed, but even though it was Terry's body and Terry's old voice, it just didn't *sound* like Terry. It sounded like . . . like . . .

The girl went up to a stunned and frightened Juana Campos, reached in her pocket, and pulled out the last of Gen Taluud's cigars, biting off the end and sticking it in her mouth. She didn't strike a match; she just pointed at the end, and it burst into flame.

If anybody was more shocked than all the people present, it was the Kraang.

"Ahhh . . . That's *so* much better," said the girl after a few puffs on the cigar. "You can't believe how I missed these. Pure Ambrezan. That Taluud was a scumbag but he definitely had good taste."

The Kraang stood there on its tentacles, saying nothing, moving not at all, but the heartlike pulsations of its body were reaching a fever pitch.

"Keep trying, Kraang. If you try hard enough to control me, then you might just bust something. You're still flesh and blood, you know, renewable or not."

The Kraang was suddenly aghast, his enormous triumphal return spoiled by an anomaly his great brain could not understand, comprehend, or get data on. Massive quantities of data were going by at the speed of light itself, but the Kraang was coming up totally empty, as empty as Mavra had been in trying to find out about the Kraang.

"You weren't the only one, you know," Terry said, letting some ash fall to the floor. "*I* took a different route. I always was a better programmer than you."

"*YOU! It's—impossible!*"

"Not impossible, just damned hard. I just gave birth to a goddamned *baby*, for Christ's sake! Not even Mavra's had to undergo *that* wonderful experience! It was hard as hell switching in and out to keep me out of the data stream you were monitoring. Fortunately, the Well measured the probabilities of Mavra getting here first and factored in a few extra wrinkles. Those damned Glathrielians thought they were going to control me with their powers, but all they did was hand them to me to use. Handed them to me just as the Well figured when I rotted lazily back there in Ambreza instead of coming immediately to answer its call, in the person of one very fascinating and exceptional young woman named Theresa Perez. And it still had to explode a damned *volcano* under me to get me to do what I should've done right off! I'm as crazy as you are, Kraang, and just as much a shirker of responsibility, but *I'm here now*!"

Mavra's head came up, and she stared at the girl. "*Nathan? Is that really you?*"

In an absolute instant, without any sense of any time passing between, the girl was suddenly gone and in her place stood another being, a being slightly smaller than but otherwise identical to what Mavra had been and what the Kraang was now.

And in one tentacle it still held the burning cigar.

The tentacle shot over to a frozen Juana Campos and stuck the cigar in her mouth. "Here," Brazil said. "I don't like to see cigars that good go to waste."

The Kraang was appalled at the vision. "It really *is* you! How—how is it possible? I had everything, *everything* factored in! There was no mistake!"

"Sure there was. As soon as you bought my line on the life history I gave to Gus the same way Mavra bought your disinformation about Obie and Brazil," Brazil responded. "I was just another *amateur*, just like her, only more experienced. Isn't that what you said not long ago? A universe re-created by amateurs? Did you really think I'd leave the Well so unprotected? I never did figure out what happened to you, but I always figured that if *I* beat the system, then others must have, too. In a way I'm glad it was you this time. Mathematicians are so damned *logical*."

Only Gus among them had the nerve to inject himself into a discussion between two gods. "So what were *you*?" he asked.

Brazil chuckled. "Me? I was an *artist*!"

"This is more an inconvenience than a defeat," the Kraang told him. "I have full access to the Well. If I cannot touch or harm *you*, neither can *you* do anything to *me*! At the moment we are at a standoff. But I know from your own histories stored here that you cannot exit the Well on your own as you are. *I can!* You must remain here, imprisoned in the Well alone, forever, just to retain your access and retard my project. Every god must have a devil, I suppose. We will play a game. I will go everywhere, and you will try to stop me from doing anything you do not like. But *you* must do it *from here*! *Yourself!* I, on the other hand, will be free to ride the whole of the trans-spacial nets and roam the stars! I can be anywhere, anything, any time I wish to be. And eternity is a *very* long time."

"Tell me about it," Brazil said sourly. "Still, as much as I *hate* to spoil your godhead and coronation or even your lofty dreams, I'm afraid you're going to be in for a very, very big shock. Still, you want to leave, leave. Go ahead. I won't even try to stop you. You know where the exit is and how to use it. Go on, go ahead. *Try* to be a god. You'll quickly see how boring and silly it gets."

The Kraang thought that Brazil was being too smug and overconfident, and he knew enough not to trust anything the other said or claimed, particularly now. But try as he might, cross-indexed and fully researched, the Kraang could find absolutely nothing that Brazil had left as any sort of trap.

"Lost your nerve, have you, Kraang? Pretty poor performance for a god to lose his nerve. Of course, you can stick around here. Plenty to do, I suppose. Been five billion years and then some since we matched wits with some of those games that are still in the core system. Or do you remember that you used to beat me all the time when we were setting up but after a while you couldn't beat me ever again? That's because you never were willing to take risks. You had a grasp of math that's truly godlike, but you never, ever went against the probabilities. Even your clever exile trick was done with a keen eye to probabilities, given the limits placed on you. I cost you this round at the last minute by taking some risks, but maybe you'll win the next time. It'll relieve the boredom, anyway."

The Kraang seethed with anger and frustration, but he had been trying any number of combinations and at no time could he supersede Brazil's command of the Well. While they had been talking in normal time, a massive battle of intellects throughout the computer that took up the entire inner surface of the Well World had been going on, a battle of such speed and complexity that those who watched could never have comprehended or described it.

Mental thrust . . . parry . . . access denied . . . *backdoor . . .* access denied . . . *wall off . . .* sector not available . . .

Even in his enhanced form, the battle wasn't easy for Brazil nor was the outcome certain. In a sense, both he and the Kraang were equals here, equals before the Well computer, equals in knowledge, skill, and the ability to use the vast power and ultra-complex engineering of the master world, at speeds and on dimensional planes that were far beyond mortal comprehension. It wasn't one parry, one thrust, one end-around attempt, but thousands . . . millions . . . *quadrillions* all at once, like some vast chess game at superlight speeds with unlimited pieces.

Whole lifetimes of mental battle had taken place in the space of one second in real time. Brazil realized that he'd been far too cocky, far too confident in his power here. He'd forgotten what it was like to come up against an opponent of his native race, one fueled by eons of hatred and a lust for power. *I've become too much a man,* Brazil thought worriedly. He could not sustain a defense against the level of sheer emotion that had been stored up in the Kraang for so very, very long.

Equal! Equal, damn it! Dead even! Brazil began to see this as an eternal struggle in which strength of will was paramount and patience everything. There was no way he could keep this up forever and he knew it; more, there was no purpose to doing so. There *had* to be an answer! As it stood, neither he nor the Kraang could make use of this vast power beyond the automatics that served them both. Equals. . . .

There just *had* to be an answer! Some way in which they were not equals. Some way, no matter how minor, in which Brazil had some kind of edge.

And in the countless moves and countermoves between two more ticks of the clock, he had it. It was too obvious; it had been handed him on a platter right at the start. That was why he'd had to endure so much before he suddenly realized that it was there. The one thing that separated the two of them. The one thing that made the Kraang vulnerable. The one thing anyone not so desperate or so close to the problem would have seen immediately.

The Kraang eased back to where he'd appeared, which they now saw was a hexagonal plate embedded in the floor. He moved onto the plate, shimmered, and was gone.

Brazil waited there a minute, saying and doing nothing, then relaxed. "Well, I'm glad *he's* gone! Yessir, ridin' those hyperspacial nets . . ." He seemed in great spirits, as if enjoying some little private joke. Then he saw Julian, still the radiant daughter of heaven, although at the moment a wee bit disoriented. She suddenly lost her radiant glow, although he let her keep that perfect Erdomese form. It wasn't bad, he thought appreciatively. Maybe the Kraang *did* have a little artist in him, after all.

"Go on back over with the others, Julian. You've just been unconverted," he said lightly.

Mavra could not see why he was in such a wonderful mood. "You—you can just let that *monster* roam at will out there? After seeing what he can *do*?"

"Oh, come on, Mavra!" Nathan Brazil scolded her. "You know when a con's working as well as *I* do. Or at least you used to. I begin to wonder after the one you fell for yourself. Talk about *amateurs*! You fell for the worst, most basic, most obvious con I could think of—and it almost cost us everything. You've got to know deep down that this was one *hell* of a lot closer than I let him think it was."

"I understood that much," she responded. "And I'm aware that an awful lot more probably went on between the two of you than we'll ever know. Did you *really* set up the Well so that you'd have to be here if any other Markovian managed to survive?"

"Well, not exactly, but I think I'll add that capability now before we leave. You see, the time when we were in here together so long ago, I added a condition that so long as I was around, alive and kicking, you couldn't enter the Well except in my presence. Until we got here, I had no idea that the Kraang was still around, let alone that he was potentially loose, until you did."

"You *what*!"

"What are *you* so sore about? If I *hadn't* done that, look at what would have happened!"

"You didn't *trust* me!"

Nathan Brazil chuckled. "Hey, kid, you only had your learner's card. Still do, in fact, considering how *this* turned out."

"But—but—what *about* the Kraang? He's still *out* there! And he's still connected to the Well!"

"Yeah, he is, I guess," Brazil sighed. "Only even *he* knew a con when he heard one, and he *still* fell for it once I realized what his weak spot was. And he'd *told* me—told us *all*—just what that one weakness was. He really *was* a god. He'd almost always *been* a god, or at least a god, junior grade. Man! Anything you wanted—the energy-to-matter transformers made it for you just like you imagined it! Anything you wanted to *be*, to *experience*, to use, to own, to look at. There it was. That's how I conned 'em during the Great Transmigration. I became Nathan Brazil, or a reasonable facsimile thereof anyway, in Glathriel, which was a kind of pet project of mine, anyway. I conned 'em into thinking I'd gone the whole way, that I'd *become* a Glathrielian. The way I worked it, I showed up as just another guy, even to the Well. The only thing was, the Well had special instructions and links to me. I conned 'em. Designed it right into the program."

"But the Kraang—"

"Is *not* designed into the program that way," Brazil told her.

"Wait a minute," Lori put in, feeling an immense weight slowly lifting from him. "If he's not designed in like you or Mavra, then . . ."

"You got it!" Nathan Brazil responded lightly. "There's hope for you yet, Lori."

"Well, *I* don't get it!" Gus said, "and I don't see nobody else gettin' it, neither."

But Mavra Chang suddenly did, and she started laughing, and the laughter grew so loud and long that it echoed through the great hall and woke up the baby again.

"Mind letting us in on this, since you woke up the kid?" Gus called to her.

She got control of herself. "Let me see if I got this right. When he left, he rode the hyperspace nets as he said, whatever the hell *they* are, and he came out someplace, just as he always did when he was back in ancient times. But all those worlds are dead now. They've been dead for billions of years. So he's going to come out on a lonely, barren, incredibly ancient world of the Markovians, and he's going to see only artifacts and death. He's probably doing that right now. And then . . ." She started to laugh again and tried to fight it. "And *then* he'll have no choice but to move on! He'll probably have big, big plans, but to do them he'll have to use the gate that's there! And when he *does* . . ."

Lori suddenly saw it. "He'll wind up back here!" he finished, openmouthed. "But in Zone. North or south, just like *we* did. And the only way he can get *out* is to use the Zone Gate, and *that* will process him just as it was designed to do so many years ago!"

"Wait a minute!" Gus put in. "Are you tellin' me that the only place that egomaniacal bastard can go is right back here? And that when he comes through, his only choice will be to be transformed into one of the races here, just like *us*? So he'll be as mortal, as ordinary as *we* are?"

"Unless he figures it out, sitting there on that world," Brazil replied. "He might. Probably will, in fact. He was never a dummy, even back then. But then, so what? What's his choice? To live like he did before, with everything at his beck and call, but alone, on a deserted world, not comatose but fully awake, looking at the skies all the time and not being able to do a damned thing about it. Totally, completely, thoroughly alone."

"Until somebody comes along in a spaceship," Mavra said worriedly. "He's waited this long. He can wait."

"It's a pretty big universe," Nathan Brazil pointed out. "But we can check and see just where he wound up. And maybe, before we leave, we'll kind of nudge the probabilities of his ever being found a little more toward the infinite. Besides, even if he got off that world by conventional means, he'd be off the net, out of the loop. He wouldn't dare ever go through a Well Gate. His data links will only be as good as his proximity to one of the ancient worlds, so what will he be? Not a god. At best a very smart freak. I think we can deal with the Kraang. The one absolute guarantee we now have is that at worst he can never be more than a local menace. He can't get back in here, and he can't get back on the net. He's back to reality, just the way he was before he took himself out of the loop. All the old rules apply again."

"Maybe you're right. I hope so," Mavra said.

"And now we can go on to lighter fare," Brazil told her.

"You mean taking care of this bunch?"

"No, no, something far more of a puzzle than *that*."

"Huh? What?"

"Why'd you walk out on me in Babylon?" he asked.

CONTROL ROOM 27,
WELL OF SOULS

"I want you all to come down with me to my control room," Nathan Brazil told them. "Just follow me. It's not a long journey, not after the one you all have taken."

Nobody objected. Nobody was in a position to object much to anything, having seen what one creature like Brazil could do.

"Do you really want to know?" Mavra asked him as they crossed the great hall.

"Huh?"

"Do you really want to know why I left you in Babylon, or were you just being your usual self?"

"Yes. Of *course* I want to know."

"You can read it from the data stream."

"Not really. And that's only the facts, not what's inside you."

She thought about how to explain it. "Nathan, you really were comfortable there. And in all the other civilizations and cultures we passed through and lived in."

"Well, a few were new to me, but mostly, I'd been there before," he admitted.

"No, that's not what I mean. You were in your element there. I'm not just talking about it being primitive, I'm talking about the fact that in spite of it all, you succeeded. You talked to tons of people, you ate and drank and sang songs with them, you had no trouble worming your way into their societies and getting what jobs you wanted. You'd already been captain of two trading vessels, one in the Red Sea and the other in the Mediterranean, before we ever *reached* Babylon."

"Well, it takes some practice to—"

"No. You're not connecting in spite of that super brain of yours at the moment. Don't you see? While you were off with the boys drinking and carousing and telling tall tales, which is where *I* wanted to be and what *I* wanted to be doing, I was stuck back in wherever we were living. Or I was stuck with the other women—most of whom were ignorant, dull, and had never been out of the confines of their native cities or towns—doing the only stuff women were allowed to do. I didn't fit with them; it's not my style at all. The roles were so stratified that there was just no way to break out, really *do* something, interact with the *interesting* people, who were almost always men because the men got to do the interesting things. After a while I just couldn't take it. There was a lot to see and do even in that ancient world, but I wasn't allowed to do it, and your secondhand recountings only made it worse. Women were *property* in those societies; even at our levels they were expected to stay home and be protected and do womanly things. Break the rules, try something outside of those roles, and you got stoned, burned at the stake, or raped. You've never *been* a woman in those times. You can't *imagine* what it's like."

"I've been a woman for part of *this* trip, even pregnant, and while it's *different*, I can't say as I can see the problem."

"You experienced some of the physical aspects but not the social. Nathan, the only man of Terry's race that you interacted with was, well, *you.* In fact, it's *much* more liberating to be a woman here, particularly if you're *not* in your own home hex. To all the other races you're just another funny foreign creature. They may have hang-ups about their own men or women, but they don't apply that to other races. You never *once* had to face the simplest challenge for a woman back on Earth, walking down a dark street at night in a strange city alone. I can't describe it. I can do the same thing here, just like this, and it's totally different. Both Julian and Lori understand what I mean, even if Lori kind of forgot it in a power trip that I find totally understandable. Even Campos had a taste of it, for all she learned from it. In my own era I lived with elements of it, but I had more freedom, more opportunity; I could become a spaceship pilot, go where I wanted, and be one of the group singing the songs and telling the stories. On Earth I felt shut out—and there was no relief in sight! It wasn't any one thing, it was a lot of things. I walked into hell when I walked out on you, but it was no worse than the hell I was stuck in. That's why, when I finally did get away, I didn't come back. I couldn't take that role again. *I couldn't live my life through your experiences.*"

Brazil was silent for a bit, thinking over what she'd said and sifting it in his mind. "In primitive societies I don't see a way around it, really. With their lives so very short, they built their societies to ensure propagation. 'Women and children first' was the old rule, and women were noncombatants because each woman could bear a child only once every nine months while one man could impregnate one woman a day. It's ironic, really, that much of this evolved more than anything else out of the basic social realization that men were expendable. Even conquering armies would slay all the men but carry the women off. There were exceptions, of course—there always are. But we can't be the exceptions in any of those societies; sooner or later somebody will notice that everybody else is aging, growing old, and we aren't. The exceptions—Hypatia, Cleopatra, Joan of Arc—*they* get written up in history books."

"Yeah, and most of them die violent deaths at young ages, anyway," she noted. "I looked for the Amazons in Greece but never really linked up with them. I think I'd have been a little small for their lot, anyway. The only place I *did* find any peace and equality was on a little island off the coast of southern Greece that was an all-woman society, but it turned out to be a lot more boring and more a matriarchy than I figured. Besides, I didn't 'look' right to them. I was accepted as a guest, but I couldn't stay, not with *these* features. I began to wonder, though, whether you had to have an all-female army or an all-female society to just get some sense of freedom."

"And when you found it, however basic, in the Amazon rain forests, you just stayed. Yeah, I can understand the situation, but it's not quite the good and easy life being a man, either. Still, you should have come out and taken a look once in a while. Things changed, dramatically. Not all the way, but a *lot* better, even in my namesake Brazil and more to the north in America and in Europe."

"I found *that* out with Lori and Julian. A woman astronomer and professor, a guy who flew in spaceships . . . It was so damned *slow*, and then everything seemed to happen in a hurry. But by that time I was so isolated, so set, and had been doing it for so long, I barely remembered any other life. And all I saw there was women's pain, and heard stories of more of it, and I had no desire to move."

"Um, excuse me," the colonel interrupted. "I hate to intrude, but just where are we going? And why?"

"Just come down the moving ramp here and follow," Brazil said in an irritated tone. "We're going down to the control room so we can decide just what the hell to do with all of you."

Campos crossed herself.

The moving walkway went down into the bowels of the planet. Every once in a while it would take them right through a hexagonal portal of deepest black, as if going into a tunnel, only there was no tunnel there. They quickly became aware that every time they did that, they moved a tremendous distance in a very short time.

Finally they reached Brazil's destination, going through a

bizarre workshop whose size was on a scale that dwarfed their imaginations. Everything was massive, was apparently working, and looked as if it had been built two days earlier and cleaned just before they arrived.

There were openings all around in a massive hexagonal shaft, not just on their level but going up and down as far as they dared look. The openings were marked because they were not hexagons but great semicircles, and inside each was darkness—darkness but not inactivity, as countless small bits of energy flew and routed and shot around almost as if they were tiny galaxies in accelerated motion.

They went in between two such openings and down a short corridor and found themselves in a room that bore no resemblance to any they'd seen before. The wall was filled with tiny triangular shapes, each with a unique code on it in some kind of luminescent dots. In the center were two very strange looking pedestals, and as Brazil glided to one and crawled into it, it was suddenly obvious that these were in fact chairs for the race that had worked here.

Mavra, still human, pulled herself up on the other one and sat cross-legged on it, looking at the others. They in turn all stood looking back at them, both fearful and nervous.

"You'll pardon me if I have to remain in this form," Nathan Brazil said to them. "I need to do that to interact with and control the machinery with any precision. I think we ought to conclude our business as quickly as possible now, and we'll start with the easy ones. Tony? Anne Marie? You got what I promised you back in the hills west of Rio that night. You got yourselves involved early with the wrong folks, but you also stuck with Julian and saw the consequences through. I can only ask you what you want to do now."

Tony and Anne Marie both frowned. "Just what exactly do you mean, Captain?" Tony asked.

"Just what I said. Would you like to return to Dillia? Would you rather go to where the Dillian project wound up?

A world still a bit primitive but civilizing fast, much like our old one in that regard, in which your present kind are the dominant species? Or would you rather be someone, something else? Tony a man again, perhaps?"

"Oh, dear. This is for real and forever, isn't it?" Anne Marie responded. "I—I'm afraid I don't know what to say. I'm quite satisfied the way I am. I'm young, healthy, and attractive, and other than being young before, the other two are still very new to me. I hardly feel like second-guessing your computer."

"I have but one regret," Tony told them. "I regret that in this form I cannot fly again. I *did* love it, you know. But this is not a bad form, and it has a great deal to recommend it. I never did put much stock in what people looked like on the outside, anyway. Anne Marie is my dearest friend, but I would never even have met her had not misfortune sat so heavily on us both. As opposites, we would of course marry, and our course would be fixed, and that perhaps would be a shame. We would never know our potential or be able to become *individuals.* I think this machine is perhaps wiser than we. I would never have dreamed of this solution, but it is the one that is right for both of us. As for the Dillian world, it would be fascinating but not, I think, as fascinating as the endless variety right here." She took Anne Marie's hand and squeezed it, and the other smiled knowingly.

"Let's go home, dear," Anne Marie said softly, and she meant to Dillia. She took the baby and gave it to Gus, who looked *most* uncomfortable with it, and after he did what he could to support the child, he looked back to complain to Anne Marie that maybe he wasn't the right one for this job.

But the two centaurs suddenly weren't there anymore.

"And now we have you, Colonel," Nathan Brazil said with a stern tone creeping into his voice. "You have a *very* warped view of honor and duty, I think. Anne Marie compared you to Talleyrand. I *met* Talleyrand once, and I checked to make sure I still had my purse when I left. Still, everything he did, beyond ensuring his own survival, was because he believed that he was doing his best to serve his country and its people. In a sense he was a pragmatic anarchist. He knew that his nation was going to have a government, and he firmly believed that no matter what that government was, it wasn't the one France truly needed. He was trying to save what he could through it all, and he did a reasonable job, considering the obstacles. But you're no Talleyrand, Colonel. You never cared about your country or your people. You climbed up from virtually the bottom, and then you forgot what it was like to be there. You didn't just sell your service to get out, you sold your soul. You never even *thought* of the people you hauled in during the dictatorship as real people. And you sold your services and honor on the side to some petty drug lords of a neighboring nation whose product infected your own people as badly as those to the north. Then you got here, and what did you do? The Leeming accorded you rank beyond anything a newcomer deserved, and you sold it again—*to the same damned types of people*! And then you rationalized every single bit of it. You're amazing, Colonel. You're the only man I know who sold his soul twice to the same bidders."

"You are unfair! I *never* betrayed my country! *Never!*"

Brazil gave a big sigh. "That's the tragedy, Colonel. You can't even understand what you did. 'I didn't gas the Jews! I just followed Himmler's orders!' My, I heard *that* one enough! No, Colonel, you didn't betray anybody. And all those homicidal fanatics in Peru got a lot of their money because you arranged transit to Venezuela for their goods. And then those goods went all over the planet and poisoned thousands, tens of thousands. But *you* didn't do it. Like those death squads you allowed to go through Rio and São Paulo and the other cities of Brazil, killing off all those poor children—*children*, Colonel!—because they were bad for business. Just tidying up. Doing your duty for God and country, going to confession once a week to be absolved of all your sins. Take the Eucharist on Sunday with a clear conscience."

"Do not lecture me! You! The mighty immortal! How can *you* know what it is like to have to fight and starve and claw your way to anything before you die? You *know* you will survive, ageless, through the generations!"

"Oh, I've seen death, Colonel," Brazil told him. "Death is a very old friend. I admit he's never come for me, although I had a little glimpse of him when I thought I might not make it here. I've seen death clearer than almost anyone. It's all around me. *Always!* I see it take everyone, the rich and poor, young and old, innocent and guilty alike. Sometimes I have to run from it. I have to make myself hard in order to stand the view. But I hate it. I hate it more than I hate anything else. Maybe I can't understand what made you this way, not really, but I *can* understand that for everyone in your position when you began, most did not make the choices you did. No, Colonel, I reject your thesis."

The colonel drew himself up and became the semblance of the man he'd been, impressive and ramrod straight. "Then we can never resolve this. I am your prisoner. I die with *dignity*, like a *soldier*! I will not crawl or beg!"

"I'm not going to kill you, Colonel," Nathan Brazil told him. "I'm not going to kill anybody here, not even Campos, who deserves it more than anybody. I'm going to give you an opportunity you never gave *any* of your victims. I'm going to give you one last chance to get your soul back."

The colonel vanished.

Campos was increasingly nervous. "Where did he go?" she demanded to know. "What did you do with him?"

"I sent him back."

"Back! Back *where*?"

"Home. To Brazil. In a little while he'll wake up and discover where he is. He'll find that a few things have left him. The knowledge that comes from education, reading, writing, a wide vocabulary, other languages, that sort of thing, but he will *know*. He will know even though where he will wake up is in a corrugated box in a garbage dump on the outskirts of São Paulo. He'll be a child again, but this time an orphan dressed in rags, along with all the other such people who try to survive day to day on the garbage of the well-to-do whose homes they can see way off in the hills and in the downtown high-rises. The original child died of exposure and malnutrition the instant he went into the body. *He* won't die, though. Not right off. Not if he moves fast enough and hides well enough. It's lower than he's ever been. It's about as low as you can be. And I've given him an added little factor, an added degree of difficulty, so he can have a real appreciation of those he never saw in life except as victims. The child I chose from far too many available to me is a nine-year-old girl."

"You bastard!" Campos cried. "And what will you do to me? The same sort of miserable thing? Well, go ahead! No matter what you do to me, I shall always be a Campos! Not even being a female *duck* could stop me! You better kill me or I will rise from *whatever* depths you plunge me into! And unless you wish to bathe your own hands, or whatever they are, in innocent blood, remember that there is *still* a Campos here!"

"No there's not," Brazil responded. "The baby's father is Carlos Antonio Quall, a sergeant in the Brazilian Air Force, and the union wasn't even forced." Before Campos's expression had even fallen at this, Brazil added, "And I just *love* challenges!" And with that, Juana Campos vanished as well.

Mavra looked at him. "Well?"

"Well what?"

"What did you *do* to the SOB? I think he was right, by the way. *I* didn't kill him when I had the chance, and look at the horrors he caused here. I was never really positive before, but now I know that there really are some people so totally evil that you just can't teach them."

"Who said anything about teaching? Maybe I'm wrong, but he gave me a challenge and I accepted. I sure wouldn't put *her* in a box in São Paulo. In ten years she'd probably have the most vicious girl gang in that city. Still, let's see."

"You're not going to tell me?"

"Later. We have other business before we can get to *our* business."

"At least—the kid *really* isn't his?"

"No. That's how Terry diverted attention from the meteor while you and the others got through. It was your own plan, remember."

"Um, yeah. I'm not feeling so great about that now. Still, I'm glad to know it hasn't got any trace of the Campos bloodline."

"Yeah, what're you gonna do with this kid?" Gus asked them. "I'm getting real nervous just trying to hold him right, and he's pissed all over me once already!"

"Patience, Gus, we'll get to you," Brazil said lightly to the Dahir, and then turned his attention more to Mavra. "Well? *You're* the one who made the promises to Lori and Julian."

She shrugged and looked at the Erdomese, who both felt that they were present at the Last Judgment. "I promised you two anything you wanted if I got here. Well, I'm here."

"Yeah, but I don't know what to ask for," Lori responded. "I'll tell you what I would *want*, or at least I *think* I do, but I can't say how. I put a lot of time and effort into my field because I loved it. Maybe I was trying to prove something to myself, maybe I was trying to excel as a woman in a man's field, all that, but the bottom line was that there were a *lot* of places I could have done that. When I got here, I *enjoyed* being a man in a man's society for once, but it was a society I didn't want to live in. I could *look* at the stars, more than I'd ever known, through Erdom's bright, clear skies, but I couldn't *study* them. I couldn't work in physics at all. The most I could be, under optimum conditions, was muscle. A strong arm with a sword. I wanted more than that. I had more than that back home. I *like* this form, its strength, its power, the absence of the kind of fear Mavra told you about, but what good is it if it's all you are or can ever be? The only thing of *real* value I got out of Erdom was Julian."

Julian gave him a humorless smile. "And that's what I am, even to you. A 'thing' of value," she noted. "I can't blame you any, really. When we came through that hex, that matriarchy, where the women ruled supreme and the men were no more than objects, there was no real difference. I'm *still* not even sure if I think like a woman, really, or like a guy who was forced to take what he dished out. I know that most women can't see the serious problems that men have in society—their lack of freedom—and part of that is that they don't want to. When you're down, you resent the ones that are higher up. When you're a higher-up, you forget what it was like to be down. And neither side can ever really come together. Me, I've got the impossible problem. I finally came to terms with this shape and form and sex. I *like* it. I like the way I look, the way I feel, and I've found I can do things many of the men couldn't. But I don't want to go back to being a piece of property, a 'thing of value,' without a voice, without rights, without even the freedom to think serious thoughts. *I* was a scientist, too, you know. I kept faith because I needed Lori, and he needed me, but, let's face it, I don't need Lori anymore."

Lori seemed shocked at the statement Julian made and shook his head sadly. He didn't understand this at all.

Mavra shook her head sadly at Julian. "You're wrong. You're *still* wrong. You've been through all this, more experiences and more damned personalities than most folks could ever imagine, and you haven't really learned a thing. A person alone who needs nobody else isn't a whole person at all. Even the plant creatures here interact. And I don't know anybody, except maybe Nathan and myself, who needs somebody more than you do. In a sense, the Kraang was right about you. What don't you like about Julian Beard? That he was self-centered, egotistical, that he saw everybody else as kind of props in his life? I got that much from you the moment you stepped in here, but he wasn't a bad man, just vain and selfish to the core. The Well took that away from you, and in a vain and selfish fit you decided death was better than not being the center of the universe. Lori rescued you from that, but *he* didn't make you the center of the universe, either. Within the limits of that atrocious society he tried to make you a partner, but you couldn't stand it in the end. You couldn't survive that way, or at least you didn't *want* to, and you couldn't survive any other way. You were so desperate to break free that you let those butchers mess with your mind even though you had a pretty good idea that they'd mutilated Lori and me. You were *relieved* when you found Lori as a horse. That put *you* in the center again, the one controlling *him*. Even then you needed his guts to get here."

Mavra sighed and looked over and up at Nathan's pulsating bulk. "Well? You got the big brain right now. What do you think?"

"I think that while we're going to have to correct Erdom a bit, these two just don't belong in a nontech environment," Brazil commented. "On the other hand, a kind of compromise that *you* sort of suggested with your comments and a few things said elsewhere here present a possibility."

"That *I* suggested?" Mavra came back, puzzled.

"Yeah. It's going to take some really *major* work here, though. Let me see. Gus? You've been the most solid one through this whole mess. If there's anyone I'd want with me in a nasty situation, it would be you. You've also got more moral sense than the rest of the bunch put together."

"Nice to hear," Gus told him. "But it don't count for much, does it? I'm a big, fat lizard holdin' Terry's baby, but all that time I thought I was stickin' by her, it turned out to be *you*."

"No, you're wrong, Gus," Brazil told him almost tenderly. "She was there. I had to hide myself so thoroughly that not a trace of my true self emerged. Occasionally I had to switch back and forth between that damned rehab tank in Agon and her body. She *knew*, Gus. She was there all along."

"Until your comin'-out party. Where is she *now*?" he asked.

"In that body, my old body, which has healed with astonishing speed, at least from the point of view of the medical people there. *They're* the ones keeping her sedated for the moment. In fact, they've taken it out of the tank, restrained, still sedated, and have transported it to the Agonese capital for shipment through the Zone Gate there. I'm afraid they're in for a nasty shock this time. That body's linked to *me*. Everything they've done to it I've known, felt, just as if I were still in it. I've deliberately kept it alive and healing. When it comes through the Gate, oh, almost any minute now if my timing's right . . ."

One of the hexes in the floor of the control room turned black, and a figure was suddenly there, as if faded in. It was Nathan Brazil's own body, with long, wildy flowing hair and beard, lying stark naked on the floor.

The body stirred, sat up, and looked around, a very confused look on its face. "What? Who . . .?" it asked in his voice, then saw Brazil in his native form and scrambled backward.

"Come on, Terry! We didn't go through all *that* together to be put off by looks, now, did we?"

The figure frowned, then got unsteadily to its feet, eyes on the pulsating creature. "You—you're—*him*? You *are* him!" Then, suddenly aware of the beard and other odd feelings, it said, "Or am *I* him? This is *crazy*!"

"You played around inside me before," Brazil reminded her. "Now we'll have to keep you there for a little bit. Don't worry, it'll all work out."

"Terry?" Gus said hesitantly. "Is that *you* in there? I mean, if it is, you can *talk*!"

"Yeah, I—what happened to me, anyway? I followed those signs into that swamp, and then there were these people, and then everything seemed to be all different all of a sudden. I—I remember *all* of it, I think, but half of it doesn't make any sense! Neither does *this*, for that matter!"

"I had a tough time figuring out the Glathrielian system,"

Brazil admitted. "If we hadn't spent all that time together on the island, I might never have gotten it to the level where I could manage what I did. When that volcano blew and I got conked by the tree keeping you from drowning, there was a moment when my human part and all of you merged inside that head. The only part of me that was left in your body was this, the part you could never reach. It took a couple of weeks of healing in that hospital in Agon before my—*our*—brain began functioning well enough that I reestablished contact and was able to sort us out. Now that *my* old brain, which repairs itself like the rest of the body, is functioning normally, all that was you can use it. You're back, even if not quite as you were."

"I, uh—" Terry reached down and shook his head. "I'll be damned. I always *wondered* what it felt like to have one of *those*."

Gus cleared his throat, which was a somewhat menacing sound although not intended that way. "Um, Terry. You remember *this*?"

He went over and looked down at the baby and smiled. "Yeah, I do. Whose is it, anyway? I'm not my own kid's father *and* mother, am I? That would be too much!"

"No, I'm sterile. I have to be," Brazil assured her. "Remember your diversion at the meteor back in the Amazon?"

"Oh, *him*! Damn! Still, he *is* cute. Let me hold him!"

"Gladly," Gus responded, handing over the child. "Um—do you remember me, Terry?"

"Yeah. You could flip in and out, like, so folks couldn't see you. For a while you were my only real friend."

"Terry, that's Gus," Mavra told her. "I'm Alama, and that tall furry creature with the horn on his head is Lori."

Terry gasped. "Oh, my God! *Gus? Lori?*" He laughed, and it wasn't at all like Brazil's laugh. If one knew both Terry and Nathan, one could see Terry in every move and hear her in every spoken word. Finally, still gently cradling the baby, he said, "So we're all kind of scrambled up here, and we're all standing here before a talking turnip with tentacles and the queen of the Amazons. If I ever got this story on the air, they'd lock me up in an asylum."

"Well, that brings up our situation," Brazil said, finding even himself a bit disconcerted talking to, well, himself. "We have four—actually, now *five*—people left here, all of whom have problems. The child was born on the Well World to a creature who'd been processed. Because of the laws and limits of probability, the only way I could send you, Terry, and the baby back without making a real mess of things would be to Earth at a point in time *after* the gate closed. Nine months plus a few days, to be exact. As far as reality was concerned, you'd have spent the whole time as you'd originally planned, in the Amazon jungle with the People. That's the way the math runs here. Terry alone I could deal with in any way I pleased, but the baby complicates it beyond belief. From your standpoint, you wouldn't have made that last jump. Instead, you would have stopped short. You wouldn't remember anything that's happened here, and you would have spent nine months with the People and had the baby with them."

"The baby's a boy, so you'd have to give it up to one of the regular tribes or leave the People," Mavra pointed out.

"I'd leave," Terry said flatly.

"I know," Brazil told her. "But you would never go back to civilization. You'd join one of the tribes there, and both you and the boy would remain with them. You know that if you ever went back to civilization, you'd be a freak, a ten-minute story for two or three days on your own old network, and then that would be that. You'd stay, you'd have many more children, and you'd grow old watching them grow up as members of the Amazonian tribe."

"That's not much of a future," Terry noted.

"It's a choice. If you stay here, you'll be racially Glathri-elian, but you won't be rewired again. What limited powers you can use without that, you will retain. Your baby will be safe, too. I'll see to that. I'm going to keep tinkering with that bunch until I get them right! But they've got a long way to go even to get beyond the Amazonian stage themselves."

"You're saying it's jungle or swamp? My choice? *Some* choice!"

"Not necessarily. I'm going to attempt something that is very, very difficult here. I've never done it before, but there's no reason it can't be done. In fact, in theory it should be easier than most other things around here because it's built into the old mechanism. When we started off here, the hex attributes were symmetrical. High-tech to semitech to nontech in repeating radial patterns. Over time, as races proved out, we moved them out the worlds and built new races that often required different limitations than the previous tenants. Over time it became a jumbled mess like today. But the mechanism for switching them around is still there, still accessible. The effect will be so unnoticed in most places that it'll take some time to discover it's been done. Only one of them will know right off, and it'll most likely destroy their current civilization. As far as I'm concerned, it's worth bringing them down a notch. Anyway, they're clever people. They'll survive."

Mavra stared at him. "Nathan? *What are you going to do?*"

"After we make a few adjustments in the Glathrielian Way, ones that will start them on a new track. I'm going to upgrade it from nontech to semitech. Since doing this would cause the Ambrezans to contemplate genocide, I'm going to downgrade the Ambrezan hex to semi-tech as well. By the time the Glathrielians rise, the Ambrezans will have reworked their own system to adjust. They're agriculturally based, anyway; they won't suffer in the long run from this." He paused a moment. "And I'm going to upgrade Erdom to high-tech."

"What!" both Lori and Julian cried at once.

"The same lovable climate and people—changing *that* is a lot more complicated—but with a major difference. And, oh, yes, it seems that there's going to be an epidemic there soon. It won't bother most people more than a bad cold. But it won't be curable by partaking of the women's curative milk supply. It's going to infest the males mostly, with their lack of natural immunities, but it's going to find itself allergic to testosterone and related substances the males have naturally. All, of course, except the castrated ones. I'm afraid it's going to be *very* fatal to them very quickly."

"You—you're wiping out the *priesthood*!" Lori said, mouth agape.

"I'm afraid so. They've kept that place in the dark too long. Now, if a couple of people, one male, one female, maybe married so that they're socially acceptable, *knew* this and also knew that high-tech works there now, well, who would be the only two there who really understand the new technology that will be brought in? And what is needed? Who will have to be the founders of the first university of the new electronic age? If you're sharp enough, and clever enough, and work together on this, you might just pull it off. You might not, and things aren't going to change overnight, but they *will* change. You two want a challenge?"

"It—it's more than we could hope for," Lori told him. From minor associate professor to founder of a new technological civilization. Not bad.

"That's what I always went for," Julian told them. "Challenges. It sounds like a big one. I hope it's not *too* big."

"Well, these things seldom work out the way you plan, but sometimes they work. Give me a week and then check it out. I'll send you a little gizmo when I throw the switch so you can know it's started."

Julian winked out, but Lori stayed. "What—where'd she go?"

"Suspended in transit. I wanted a word with you alone. When she emerges, she's still going to be that bombshell Kraang made her, but I've removed that stuff that idiotic pair of butchers did to her head. You saw how he made that attitude adjustment, too. I don't think Julian can ever completely conquer her own egocentrism, not on her own. I decided the hell with it and did it for her. It's nice to be able to shortcut these things. She's going to be just as smart as she ever was—smarter, I think, than before—but she's going to forget that she ever was a man. She's going to find us males as inscrutable as every other female. And the next time she sees you, she's going to realize that she's maddeningly, passionately, completely in love with you. She won't question it or reflect on it as any sort of change; she'll realize it's been there all along. *You*, on the other hand, I *want* to remember your life as a woman, what it meant. You won't ever forget it again. You forgot it once, and it didn't help Julian's mental health or your own. That race is the most sexually interdependent on this planet. Use it when you go about re-forming the system."

Lori stared at him. "Thank you," he said, and vanished.

Mavra nodded approvingly. "Well, you did *that* pretty well. I hate to put building a new society in the hands of two *physics* majors, but what the hell. I guess you work with what you got."

"What about us?" Terry asked. "What happens to *us*?"

"You have the biggest job of all. Both of you," Brazil told them. "Gus, you remember what you told Kurdon? Bring in the press? Take all the pictures? Let everybody see what this filth is all about?"

"Yeah, I remember."

"Well, that's your job. Yours and Terry's, and others, from many races, if you do a decent recruiting job. I'm sending you both—all three of you, actually—to a place you haven't been. It's called Czill, and the creatures there are walking, talking plants. No kidding. But they have one great purpose—they've assembled the most massive, highest-tech library and information resource on this planet. They're going to know you're coming—their computers will tell them. And they're going to know just what your job is going to be. The idea will be so fresh, so new to them that they'll love it. They'll fall all over each other helping you get it going."

"Yeah? What . . . ?" Gus asked, not really following.

"An independent news source. Printed where it has to be, broadcast where it can be. Carried all over with the same speed and efficiency with which the cartel dealt its poison. You've already got a few stories, including the hex changes and the cartel. You'll have more right off. A number of very high-ranking councillors are going to have serious health problems very soon, and some of their associates back home are going to suddenly find that there's a lot of evidence in the open on just how corrupt they were. But that won't stop the evil. It'll flare up again in a different form. It's endemic. If everybody here is a reflection of his or her creators, well, you've met the Kraang."

"You mean a syndicate? A worldwide *news* organization?" Terry gasped. "And *we'd* be *running* it?"

"That's right. And training others and sending the scholars from all the races who come to Czill to study back with the knowledge of what a free press can do. You two think you're ready for that kind of job?"

"Are you kidding?" Terry responded. "Jeez! From naked little twerp who couldn't even talk to Ted Turner!" She turned to her old friend. "And with you right there, just like old times!"

"As much as the Dahir's talent for hiding is handy, I don't think being a Dahir is right for this job, though," Brazil continued. "If you can't go back to Glathriel, at least for a while, maybe it's better if you were a pair."

"You mean I get to be *me* again?" Gus exclaimed. "Yeah!"

"Well, not quite. But if you don't like it, go through the Zone Gate in Czill any time in the next seven days and you'll be pretty much as you were born. If you don't, then my revisions stick. Okay?"

"Yeah, well, I guess that's fair enough."

"Good luck, then. I'm counting on both of you. *All* of you! Oh—by the way, Dillia's not that far from Czill. You might check in with our friends there from time to time."

"Okay, we will. Hey! Wait!" Terry called. "I'm not gonna be a *guy*, am I?"

"No, you'll be who you want to be. I promise. Farewell."
They winked out, and Nathan and Mavra were alone.

"What did you do with them?" she asked him.

He adjusted the program and put her back into the matrix.
Almost immediately she became a smaller version of him.

"At least the stool fits now," she said. She looked into the
Well and traced Gus and Terry and the as yet unnamed child
to Czill. "Wow! Gus is nothin' to complain about, is he? I
may go to Czill myself!"

"You can't. The only way out for us is back out into the
universe."

"Oh, yeah. But where'd you get *that* stud's picture from?"

"Terry's mind. It's her idealized fantasy male."

"I see you didn't make *her* any different."

"No need. He loves her. She already *is* what he wants. Besides, she has absolutely no competition."

"You got that right." She sighed. "So here we are again,
sitting here just like before, doling out happy endings like
some fairy tale and solving all the problems of the universe
except our own."

"Seems like," he agreed.

"Nathan—you're remaking all sorts of parts of *this* world,
but you keep putting *our* universe back the same old way
again."

"I can't help it. *This* world's easy. It was designed as a lab.
All the controls and instructions are available. But Mavra, I
wouldn't have the first idea in the *cosmos* of how to rework
something as complex as an entire planetary civilization and
ecosystem, let alone all of them. It took the whole damned
race working *together* with this thing to do *that*. I'm a button
pusher. If I can push a button and do something or throw a
switch or issue a command, that's fine. Even the Kraang
knew better than that. He was going to be god, but he needed
disciples to do his dirty work."

She sighed. "I see. So it's back to that crummy old Earth
again, is it? After we fix up a few more things here?"

"Pretty much. Now, we *could* go other places, of course,

but there's no guarantee they'd be any better. I tried it once, and it was worse, if you can believe it. Don't think about all that past, either. Where we'll be going they'll have electricity and aircraft and video and all sorts of stuff you haven't seen in ages. It's still violent, and it's hardly close to perfect, but it'll do if you watch your back. The same evil strain that shows up here sometimes shows up there as well. Besides, it *will* be different this time in the long haul. The Kraang's interference seems to have caused some rifts in the usual probability program, at least for Earth, and I'm sure as hell not going to push the reset over *that*!"

"You mean—you don't know where things are going, either, this time?"

"Not really. I was shocked at the changes in the Well World from last time. You saw those streamlined Dillians, for example, and many of the others were equally refined."

"Yeah, so?"

"They're evolving, Mavra. Changing. Becoming something newer, maybe better, maybe worse, but different. Even here change is coming. Back on Earth—well, I no longer know the specifics, but in general things will work out. There'll be wars, and violence, and hatred, and drugs, and things we haven't even thought of yet, but science is already on the fast track, technology is already running wild. Eventually they'll pick up the pieces, put themselves together, and head out for the planets and then the stars. They have to. It may take a while, but we'll be a little more comfortable getting there. They already have women captains of aircraft, so you've got some potential right off. It's no more or less dangerous or risky than it was, but it's a damn sight more *comfortable* at this stage."

She sighed. "Well, okay, maybe. At least we can play for another tie, huh? Accelerated change, everything, everywhere, even here. Everything and everybody but us and this big old machine."

"Well, somebody's got to be around to appreciate it. That's

what's so damned wrong with all this, all this time, I think. The worst possible sin happened to me long ago, and I just couldn't deal with it."

"The loneliness?"

"No, even worse. This endless, unchanging perspective turned me from an artist into a damned art critic!"

She laughed. "You never told me what you did with Campos. I'm going to see."

THE JUNGLES
OF EASTERN PERU

Juana Campos woke up as if from a dream and shook her head as if to clear it. She suddenly remembered what had happened and started, then sat up and checked herself.

She was still female, but she was *human* again! And, well, if she had to be a woman, *what* a body! This figure was a killer; she knew that without having to examine it further.

She felt her face, and it seemed normal, too, not horrible or disfigured. Her skin was smooth but copper-colored, and it looked rather nice.

She got up, still puzzled that Brazil would have made her like *this* and looking for the snake. There *could* be one here, that was for sure. It was jungle, dense and deep, much like back home.

She walked on a little way and then stopped and gasped. It *was* home! There was the airstrip over there! And there the house where, as Juan Campos, she'd been born!

A truck full of her father's men roared toward the back end of the airstrip, when somebody looked over in her direction and shouted. The truck stopped at once, and suddenly they were all piling out, staring at her.

"*Ai!* Would you look at *that*!"

"That is the most stacked Indian bitch I ever seen!"

"I think I'm in *love*!"

She didn't turn. She knew them all. Pablo, and Carlo, and Juan Pedro, and Pipito Alvarez . . .

She started to shout to them, to tell them she was not what she seemed, but when she opened her mouth, nothing came out! She tried again to shout, to talk, to make any sort of sound, and she couldn't do it! She was *mute*!

They started coming toward her, leering.

Writing. Maybe something, *anything*! But how? And what to write? How did it go, anyway? She couldn't remember!

They were still coming, and now Carlo started into a running trot and the others followed. *No! No! I'm Juan Campos, you fools!* she wanted to shout, but nothing came, nothing at all.

Suddenly she was filled with panic. She turned and started to run back into the forest, back to where she could hide.

But she'd waited too long. They were too close, and she knew it.

They already had their pants off by the time they caught her, and they took an awfully long time, before they picked her up and took her back toward the compound, exhausted, bleeding, and nearly unconscious.

Hell, *this* bitch was good for the whole damned bunch of *campañeros*! With a little more seasoning and discipline, why, she might last for *months*! Don Francisco wouldn't mind. The only danger was that the old boy might take her for himself!

THE BEACH
NEAR CANNES

Mavra Chang came out of the water, happy but exhausted, and looked around for Brazil. It wasn't great yet, but *this* was definitely more like it! And with the film festival only three weeks away, she could look forward to some real glamour around.

She spotted Brazil and still had to chuckle. Nathan Brazil, infallible god, provider of happy-ever-after endings, always the same old stick-in-the-mud himself. Wise as Solomon, ancient as history itself, always confident.

For the first time in his five-plus billion-year life the great man had goofed. A *minor* goof to be sure, but from her standpoint an absolutely *perfect* one.

They'd spent the week redoing the hexes, adjusting, tinkering, fine-tuning, trying to think of every little detail that they actually *could* do something about. They'd taken several days to check it out and run simulations to ensure that they'd gotten it right.

Nathan had even remembered to send Lori the sleek, motorized camera and reflecting telescope.

Everything was just right. The Glathrielians were set on a new course with a fine subtlety, the Ambrezans were going absolutely bananas but they'd ensured that nobody would starve or die when all their high-tech stuff just stopped, and Gus, who had *not* chosen to revert to form during his week's trial—and little wonder—was settling in with Terry and little Nathan, a touch Brazil had loved.

And finally, they'd gone down to the exit gate and set the positions and the probability adjustments so that they would have real identities when they materialized back on Earth in their base forms. Brazil had already stayed too long as the Egyptian David Solomon, so he'd specified that a new identity be created consistent with his base form and relative to Mavra, who, not wanting to become a jungle goddess again, was getting an extensive identity makeover. It was so automatic, he just did it without thinking, issuing the bare minimum commands needed to accomplish the goal.

"Well," said Nathan Brazil, "that's about it. We're actually in pretty fair shape, although it's interesting that the Kraang's interference has put us on a whole new historical track. Endless possibilities this time. Should be kind of fun. No resets necessary, I guess. Not this time. Just go back, pick up living, see how it all comes out. You ready?"

Mavra Chang sighed. "I still haven't seen much to like on that little dirt ball, but I'm open to persuasion. All right, Nathan. I think I like you better as a human, anyway; you're a lot less like some pontificating god. I almost wish sometime you'd make a mistake. Not a *big* mistake, mind, but *some* mistake. Just enough to take a little of the wind out of those sails."

Nathan Brazil chuckled. "Let's go home, Mavra."

"*Computer: open Well transfer type forty-one to native mode. Reset Watchers to prior human form but create new identities this timeline and insert subjects . . . now!*"

Just one little detail . . .

While Nathan had remade his old, now mortal body into the image of Terry, he'd forgotten that he was still inside the *real* Terry's body. The Well had simply taken this rather than the old form as the default, since all shapes, forms, races, and creatures were all the same to it, and Brazil's own instructions for insertion had been to revert them to their "prior human form."

And so Nathan Brazil had rematerialized back on Earth not as his eternal old self but rather as a dead ringer for Terry Sanchez, stretch marks and all. And he'd be stuck as a she, and looking *precisely* that way, until they had to travel back to the Well World once more and could get inside.

Although startled, Mavra was more than pleased to see her wish granted so quickly. It wasn't necessarily permanent, of course; all Brazil had to do was go back into the Well and change things. That, however, was easier said than done; once in Watcher mode, travel to the Well World was at the convenience not of the Watchers but of the Well. It had taken thousands of years for it to need either of them the last time. Who could know how long it might take again?

In the meantime, although she was sorry Nathan couldn't experience the more negative side of being female in ancient times as she had, Brazil would sure as hell have a *very* different life for *quite* a while, and into a future that was not as certain as before.

It almost made Brazil bearable this time. Mavra thought they might stay together for a while, maybe a *very* long while, this time, now that Nathan would have a taste of *her* side of life. In the meantime, Brazil was already struggling to adapt, but given enough time, *she* would get used to it. She'd already played the role to perfection, after all. And, she'd noted, there was a bright side. When they came through again at last, nobody would be looking for a big-breasted brown woman whose documents said she was Danielle Brazza of West Palm Beach, Florida, USA, just as Mavra Chang was now from a city called San Francisco that she'd never really heard of in a country she'd yet to visit. Next time should be a piece of cake.

And she had a *very, very* long time to practice . . .

A DEAD WORLD
IN THE CONSTELLATION ANDROMEDA

The Kraang had realized the trap the moment he'd stepped into it, but by then it was too late.

He went out regularly and just stared at the Well Gate, which opened and closed with monotonous regularity whenever he approached, as if inviting him to come on in.

It wasn't awful here; the internal planetary computer was rusty, but it still worked, at least on the limited basis that the Kraang needed for his requirements.

But it was a dead, silent world, offering only regrets and memories.

Somehow I'll do it! the Kraang swore. *I will survive here as long as I must! As long as the universe survives, I will be here, building my hatred, plotting my revenge! One day, one day, I will find the way out! One day, someone will come, or something will occur, to liberate me again! Then, my old nemesis,* then *we will see who is the better!*

But only the darkness, and the memories, and the aching loneliness heard his cries or felt his rage.

He was God! Absolute ruler!

God of loneliness!

God of the dark.

ABOUT THE AUTHOR

Jack L. Chalker was born in Baltimore, Maryland, on December 17, 1944. He began reading at an early age and naturally gravitated to what are still his twin loves: science fiction and history. While still in high school, Chalker began writing for the amateur science-fiction press and in 1960 launched the Hugo-nominated amateur magazine *Mirage*. A year later he founded The Mirage Press, which grew into a major specialty publishing company for nonfiction and reference books about science fiction and fantasy. During this time, he developed correspondence and friendships with many leading SF and fantasy authors and editors, many of whom wrote for this magazine and his press. He is an internationally recognized expert on H.P. Lovecraft and on the specialty press in SF and fantasy.

After graduating with twin majors in history and English from Towson State College in 1966, Chalker taught high school history and geography in the Baltimore city public schools with time out to serve with the 135th Air Commando Group, Maryland Air National Guard, during the Vietnam era and, as a sideline, sound engineered some of the period's outdoor rock concerts. He received a graduate degree in the esoteric field of the History of Ideas from John Hopkins University in 1969.

His first novel, *A Jungle of Stars*, was published in 1976, and two years later, with the major popular success of his novel *Midnight at the Well of Souls*, he quit teaching to become a full-time professional novelist. That same year, he married Eva C. Whitley on a ferryboat in the middle of the Susquehanna River and moved to rural western Maryland. Their first son, David, was born in 1981.

Chalker is an active conversationalist, a traveler who has been through all fifty states and in dozens of foreign countries, and a member of numerous local and national organizations ranging from the Sierra Club to The American film Institute, the MAryland Academy of Sciences, and the Washington Science Fiction Association, to name a few. He retains his interest in consumer electronics, has his own satellite dish, and frequently reviews computer hardware and software for national magazines. For five years, until the magazine's demise, he had a regular column on science fantasy publishing in *Fantasy Review* and continues to write a column on computers for *S-100 Journal*. He is a three-term past treasurer of the Science Fiction and Fantasy Writiers of America, a noted speaker on science fiction at numerous colleges and universities as well as a past lecturer at the Smithsonian and the National Institutes of Health, and a well-known auctioneer of science fiction and fantasy art, having sold over five million dollars' worth to date.

Chalker has received many writing awards, including the Hamilton-Brackett Memorial Award for his "Well World" books, the Gold Medal of the prestigious *West Coast Review of Books for Spirits of Flux and Anchor*, the Dedalus Award, and the E.E. Smith Skylark Award for his career writings. He is also a passionate lover of steamboats and particularly ferryboats and has ridden over three hundred ferries in the U.S. and elsewhere.

He lives with his wife, Eva, sons David and Steven, a Pekingese named Mavra Chang, and Stonewall J. Pussycat, the world's dumbest cat, in the Catoctin Mountain region of western Maryland, near Camp David. A short story collection with autobiographical commentary, *Dance Band on the Titanic*, was published by Del Rey Books in 1988.